TALES OF THE CAUCASUS
THE BALL OF SNOW AND SULTANETTA

The Romances of Alexandre Dumas.

NEW SERIES.

TALES OF THE CAUCASUS:

THE BALL OF SNOW,

AND

SULTANETTA.

ALEXANDRE DUMAS.

BOSTON:
LITTLE, BROWN, AND COMPANY.
1906.

INTRODUCTORY NOTE.

FROM fresh fields and pastures new, Dumas gathered the material of the two romances of this volume. The scenes and characters of " The Ball of Snow " are as vividly Oriental as those of his French novels are French, and yet they possess a keen, next-door-neighborly savor, such as could be developed only by passing through the alembic of his brain. The precision with which Dumas lays his finger on the kindred touches of nature is his greatest charm. That East is West is no paradox to him.

In " Sultanetta " Dumas evidently struggled against assimilating the story of the Russian novelist whose romance he admits, under a somewhat specious plea, that he " re-wrote." His pen rebelled against another's tactics, and oftener than not became a free lance.

In giving these two tales of the Caucasus to the readers of English only, the translator enjoys the delights of an approving conscience, properly tempered, however, by the cold douche administered to all translators, — " *i traditori traduttori*."

ALMA BLAKEMAN JONES

SIERRA MADRE, CALIFORNIA.

THE UNIVERSITY PRESS, CAMBRIDGE, MASS., U. S. A.

LIST OF CHARACTERS.

—————

THE BALL OF SNOW.

Period, 1830.

HADJI FESTAHLI, a holy Mussulman.
KASSIME, his niece.
KITCHINA, friend to Kassime.
ISKANDER BEG, a young Tartar in love with Kassime.
YUSSEF, his friend.
HUSSEIN ⎫
FERZALI ⎭ inhabitants of Derbend.
DJAFFAR, a goldsmith.
MULLAH SÉDEK, friend of Hadji Festahli.
MONZARAM BEG, chief of police at Derbend.
MULLAH NOUR, a brigand.
GOULCHADE, his wife.

SULTANETTA.

Period, 1819-1828.

ACKMETH, Khan of Avarie.
SULTANETTA, his daughter.
AMMALAT BEG, in love with Sultanetta.
SOPHYR ALI, his foster brother.

LIST OF CHARACTERS.

FATMA, an old Tartar woman, nurse of Ammalat Beg.
DJEMBOULAT, a Kabardian prince.
COLONEL VERKOVSKY,
GENERAL YERMOLOF,   } Russian officers.
CAPTAIN BETOVITCH,
COLONEL KOTZAREV,
HADJI SOLEIMAN, a pious Turk.
NEPHTALI, a young Circassian.
ALIKPER, a blacksmith.

CONTENTS.

THE BALL OF SNOW.

LIST OF ILLUSTRATIONS

TALES OF THE CAUCASUS

THE BALL OF SNOW

SULTANETTA

THE BALL OF SNOW.

I.

FORTY DEGREES IN THE SHADE.[1]

THE sad, sonorous voice of the muëzzin was heard as a dirge for the brilliant May day that was just sweeping into eternity.

"Allah! it is hot weather for Derbend! Go up on the roof, Kassime, and see how the sun is setting behind the mountain. Is the west red? Are there clouds in the sky?"

"No, uncle; the west is as blue as the eyes of Kitchina; the sun is setting in all its glory; it looks like a flaming rose upon the breast of evening, and the last ray that falls upon the earth has not to pierce the slightest fog."

Night has unfurled her starry fan; the shadows have fallen.

"Go up on the roof, Kassime," bade the same voice, "and see if the dew is not dripping from the rim of the moon. Is she not lurking in a misty halo, like a pearl in its brilliant shell?"

---

[1] 1° Réaumur is equivalent to 2¼° Fahrenheit.—TR.

1

"No, uncle; the moon is floating in an azure ocean; she is pouring her burning beams into the sea. The roofs are as dry as the steppes of the Mogan, and the scorpions are playing about gayly."

"Ah," said the old man, with a sigh, "it means that to-morrow will be as warm as to-day. The best thing to do, Kassime, is to go to bed."

And the old man falls asleep, dreaming of his silver; and his niece falls asleep dreaming of what a young girl of sixteen always dreams, whatever her nationality may be, — of love; and the town falls asleep dreaming that it was Alexander the Great who had built the Caucasian Wall and forged the iron gates of Derbend.

And so, toward midnight, everything slept.

The only sounds to be heard, in the general stillness, were the warnings of the sentinels to each other, "*Slourhay!*" (watch!) and the moaning of the Caspian sea, as it advanced to press its humid lips upon the burning sands of the shore.

One could have fancied the souls of the dead to be communing with eternity, and this conception would have been the more striking, since nothing so resembles a vast cemetery as the city of Derbend.

Long before day the surface of the sea seemed ablaze. The swallows, awake before the muëzzin, were singing upon the mosque.

True, they did not much precede him. The sounds of his footsteps put them to flight. He advanced upon the minaret, bowing his head upon his hand, and crying out in measured tones that lent his words the effect, if not the form, of a chant, —

"Awake ye, arise, Mussulmans; prayer is better than sleep!"

One voice answered his; it said, —

"Go up on the roof, Kassime, and see if a mist is not descending from the mountains of Lesghistan. Tell me, is not the sea obscured?"

"No, uncle; the mountains seem covered with pure gold; the sea shines like a mirror; the flag above the fortress of Nazinkalo hangs in folds along its staff like a veil about a young girl's form. The sea is still; not the slightest puff of wind lifts an atom of dust from the highway; all is calm on the earth, all serene in the sky."

The face of the old man became gloomy, and, after performing his ablutions, he went up on the roof to pray.

He unfolded the prayer-rug that he carried under his arm and knelt upon it, and, when he had finished his prayer by rote, he began to pray from the heart.

"*Bismillahir rahmanir rahim!*" he cried, looking sadly about him.

Which means, —

"May my voice resound to the glory of the holy and merciful God!"

Then he proceeded to say in Tartar what we shall say in French, at the risk of divesting the prayer of Kassime's uncle of the picturesque character imparted to it by the language of Turkestan.

"O clouds of spring-time, children of our world, why do ye linger on the rocky heights? why hide ye in caves, like Lesghian brigands. Ye like to rove about the mountains, and sleep upon the snowy peaks of granite. Be it so; but could ye not find yourselves better amusement than pumping all the humidity from our plains, only to turn it upon forests that are impenetrable to man and permit to descend into our valleys naught but cataracts of flint that look like the dried bones of your victims, ye capricious children of the air!

See how our unhappy earth opens a thousand mouths!
She is parched with thirst; she implores a little rain.
See how the wheat-blades shrink; how they break when
a butterfly imprudently lights upon them; how they
lift their heads, hoping to inhale a little freshness, and
are met by the sun's rays, which lap them like flame.
The wells are dry; the flowers hold no perfume; the
leaves on the trees shrivel and fall; the grass dries up;
the madder is lost, the crickets grow hoarse, the death-
rattle of the cicada is heard, the buffaloes fight for a
streamlet of mud; the children dispute over a few drops
of water. O God! O God! what is to become of us?
Drouth is the mother of famine; famine is the mother
of pestilence; pestilence is the twin of robbery! O
cool wind of the mountains, waft hither on your wings
the blessing of Allah! Ye clouds, life-giving bosoms,
pour the milk of heaven down upon the land! Whirl
into storms, if ye will, but refresh the earth! Strike
down the wicked with your thunderbolts, if ye deem it
best, but spare the innocent! Gray clouds, wings of
the angels, bring us moisture; come, hasten, fly! Speed
ye, and ye shall have welcome."

But the old Tartar prays in vain, the clouds are invisible. It is sultry, it is stifling, and the inhabitants
of Derbend are quite prepared to seek for coolness in
their ovens.

And note well that this was the month of May, just
when St. Petersburg hears a loud crashing at the north-
east as the ice of the Ladoga breaks up and threatens
to sweep away the bridges of the Neva; when a man
catches cold while crossing the Place d'Isaac; when he
gets inflammation of the chest by turning the corner of
the Winter Palace; when people shout at each other,
from Smolnyi to the English embankment, —

"You are going out? Don't forget your cloaks!"

At St. Petersburg they were thinking of the spring, which was, perhaps, approaching; at Derbend they took thought of the harvesting, which was almost at hand.

For five weeks, not a drop of rain had fallen in South Daghestan, and it would have been forty degrees in the shade if there had been any shade in Derbend. As a fact, it was fifty-two degrees in the sun.

A drouth in the Orient is a terrible thing. It scorches the fields and deprives every living creature of nourishment, — the birds of the air, the beasts of the field, the dwellers in cities. In a country where the transportation of grain is always difficult, often impossible, drouth is invariably the forerunner of famine. An Asiatic lives from day to day, forgetful of yesterday, unmindful of to-morrow. He lives thus because ease and *far niente* are his dearest enjoyments; but when there is no Joseph to interpret the parable of the seven lean kine, when misfortune falls suddenly upon his shoulders in the hideous guise of famine, when to-morrow becomes to-day, he begins to complain that he is not granted the means of living. Instead of seeking them, he waxes wroth, and, when he should act, his cowardice augments the evil, as his incredulity has abridged it.

You can now judge of the trouble they were in at Derbend, a city wholly Tartar, and, consequently, wholly Asiatic, when this desert heat began to destroy the prospects of both merchants and husbandmen.

To tell the truth, at that time Daghestan had many reasons for anxiety; the fanatical Kasi Mullah, the adoptive father of Schamyl, was at the height of his fame; the inhabitants of Daghestan had revolted, and more bullets had been sown in their fields than wheat; fire had destroyed the houses, whose ashes the sun kept

hot; and the mountaineers, instead of harvesting, rode
under the standard of Kasi Mullah or hid themselves in
caves and forests to escape the Russians, or, rather, to
fall upon their backs when they were least on guard.

The result was not difficult to foretell, — it was
famine. The sowing not having been done, the harvest
was wanting.   Anything that the war had spared —
silver plate, rich arms, beautiful carpets — was sold for
a mere trifle at the bazaar.   The most beautiful necklace
of pearls in Derbend could have been bought with a
sack of flour.

The man possessed of neither plate, nor arms, nor
tapestries, nor pearls, began upon his flocks, eating such
as had been left him by friend and foe, or Russian and
mountaineer.   The poor began to come down from the
mountains and beg for alms in the city, while waiting
until they could take without asking.

At last, vessels loaded with flour arrived from Astrakhan.   Through pity or fear, the rich helped the poor;
the people were quieted for a time.

The new harvest could yet right matters.

The fête of the Khatil had come, and it had been
celebrated by the inhabitants of Derbend.

The Khatil is a religious festival in memory of the
fate of Shah Hussein, the first caliph, a martyr of the
sect of Ali.   They made merry while it lasted, with
the childish gayety of the Orientals.

Thanks to this fête, the only diversion of the people
during the entire year, they had gradually forgotten the
crops and the heat, or, rather, they had forgotten nothing; no, they had in all simplicity thanked Heaven that
the rain had not interfered with their pleasures.   But,
when the fête was over, when they found themselves
face to face with the reality, when they awoke with

parched mouths, when they saw their fields baked by the sun, they lost their heads.

It was interesting then to note the wagging of red beards and black, to mark the rattling of beads as they slipped through the fingers.

Every face was long, and only repinings were heard.

It was really no laughing matter to lose a crop, and have to pay two roubles a measure for flour without knowing what must be paid for it later.

The poor trembled for their lives, the rich for their purses. Stomachs and pockets crept close together at the mere thought of it.

Then it was that the Mussulmans began to pray in the mosque.

The rain came not.

They prayed in the fields, thinking that in the open air they stood two chances to one, — the one of being seen, the other of being heard.

Not a drop of water fell.

What was to be done?

They fell back on their magi.

First, the boys spread their handkerchiefs in the middle of the streets and collected the coins that were thrown into them. Purchasing wax tapers and rose-water, and fastening tree branches to the body of the most beautiful boy, they decked him with flowers and covered him with ribbons, and then followed him in a procession through the streets, chanting verses to Goudoul, the god of rain.

The hymn ended with a strophe of thanksgiving. They did not doubt that Goudoul would answer the prayers of his worshippers.

Thus, for three days, the young boys shouted at the tops of their voices this thanksgiving, which we translate, without any pretension of rendering otherwise than very feebly the Arabic poem: —

> "Goudoul, Goudoul, O god of rain,
> The drouth has fled from mount and plain;
> Thy voice from heaven the rain doth send.
> Then go, fair maid, unto the rill!
> And high thy jar with water fill,
> Till thou beneath its weight doth bend."

And all the youths of Derbend danced around the beribboned and garlanded Tartar, so sure of rain that, as we see, they were sending the young girls in advance to the fountain.

And, in truth, clouds gathered in the sky; the sun sulked like a miser obliged to surrender the treasure that had been intrusted to him. The city took on the dreary look that dull weather imparts.

But the darker the sky became, the greater was the people's joy.

A few drops of rain fell.

They cried out with fervor, —

"Sekour Allah!"

But their joy was short-lived; the wind blew up from Persia as hot as if it had come from a furnace, and drove away the very last remnant of a cloud, which betook itself to St. Petersburg to fall as snow. The sun glared worse than ever; the grass crumbled under the heat; the flowers bent their heads, and the faithful began to doubt, not Mahomet's might, but Goudoul's.

Another day dawned; the sun pursued his blazing path, then he sank behind the mountain, like a weary traveller in the burning sands of the desert.

On that night and the next morning the two conversations which opened this chapter took place between Kassime and her uncle.

The old Tartar had then addressed to the clouds the prayer that we have attempted to translate. But, in spite of his fervent prayer, that day, like the preceding one, passed without a drop of rain.

And on that day the commander of Derbend announced that the thermometer had registered forty-two degrees in the shade and fifty-two degrees in the sun.

II.

A HOLY MUSSULMAN.

Ah! when you go to Derbend, traveller, from whatever country you hail, — whether you come from the south, the north, the east or the west, — go, I entreat you, to see the principal mosque.

Otherwise, as the Catholics say, you will have been to Rome without seeing the pope.

What would you have to relate about Derbend, I ask, if you had not seen the great mosque?

While, if you have seen it, it is a very different matter.

"The great mosque," you say, snapping your snuffbox, or flicking the ashes from your cigar, if you are only a smoker, "the mosque," you say, "was formerly a Christian church — "

Proceed boldly, I assume all responsibility.

" It was a church, a Christian church, rather, because its face is turned to the east, while the Mussulman mosques of the northern Orient should veer southerly, in nautical phrase, in order to look toward the two holy cities, — Mecca, where the prophet was born; Medina, where he was buried."

This gives you at the outset a somewhat learned air which sits well. Proceed.

" Upon entering, you discover a great court shaded by magnificent plane-trees, with a well in the centre.

Three doors, always open, symbolically and practically, summon the Mussulmans to prayer.

" A verse from the Koran inscribed over the principal door attracts the attention. Enter: but first put off the shoes from your feet; put away earthly thoughts from your mind. Into the house of Allah bring not the clay of the street, nor of the mind. Fall upon your knees and lift up your prayer. Reckon not your rents, but your sins. *La illah il Allah! Mohammed rassoul Allah!* — that is to say: There is no God but God, and Mahomet is his prophet."

Here you cough and make a pause; that was quite worth the trouble. You have an air of knowing Turk.

You resume : —

" Mussulmans are long at their prayers, remaining on their knees or prostrate on the prayer-rug, as they pass from adoration to ecstasy, and nothing, especially in this last state, can then distract their attention."

Memory then reverts to the past, and you exclaim, —

" Where are you, Christian builders of this temple? are you now remembered anywhere but in heaven? You are forgotten, even in the history of Derbend, and the words of the Koran echo to-day where formerly sounded the hymns of the prophet king."

And now that you have given your account, now that you have acquired the right to be a corresponding member of the section of inscriptions and *belles-lettres* of the French Academy, the most learned, as you know, of all academies, I again take up the thread of my history; for this, pray take note, is history.

I resume then, the thread of my history.

Among Mussulmans of all countries, and particularly among the Mussulmans of Daghestan, the court of the mosque is the usual place of meeting. There the mer-

chants gather to talk over their commercial interests, and
the Tartar chiefs, their political issues. The first have
but one aim, — to get the better of their customers; the
second, but one hope, — to throw off the yoke of their
master. The former have vowed to Allah to be honest;
the latter have sworn to the emperor to be faithful.
But, in Asia, oddly enough, — and this will astonish
our public officers, our judges and senators, — the oath
is regarded as a simple formality, of no consequence and
not binding.

Does this, perchance, mean that the Asiatics, whom
we believe to be behind us in the matter of civilization,
are, on the contrary, in advance?

This would be very humiliating, and, in such case,
we must hasten to overtake them.

You must know that at this period of frightful heat,
which we have tried to depict, the court of the mosque
— the only place where there were any trees, consequently any shade, consequently only forty degrees of
heat — was full of people. Effendis with white beards,
muftis with red, were talking in the centre of circles
more or less wide, according as they were more or less
eloquent; but the learning of these and the dignity of
those did not cause the sky to sweat the least drop of
moisture, and the beards of all lengths and of all colors
were powerless even to invent an equivalent. They
talked much, they argued still more; but at last discourse and discussion ended this way: —

"*Nedgeleikh?* (What shall we do now?)"

Shoulders went up to the ears, eyebrows to the
papaks; many voices in many keys united in one
cry, —

"*Amani! amani!* (Spare us! spare us!)"

Finally, a prince began to speak.

He was not only a prince, but a saint, — a combination which was formerly seen in Russia and France, but which is to be met with to-day only in the Orient.

It is true that his saintship, like his principality, came to him by inheritance; he was related in the sixty-second degree to Mahomet, and, as we know, all relatives of Mahomet, of whatsoever degree, are saints.

His eloquence grew heated in the smoke of his kabam, and golden speech emanated from the fumes of the Turkish tobacco.

"'*Amani! amani!*' you cry to Allah; and think you that, for this one word, Allah will be so simple as to pardon you and put faith in your repentance without other proof? No! kiss not the Koran with lips still smeared with the fat of pork; no, you do not deceive God with your flatteries and plaintive tones. He is not a Russian governor; he has known you this long while. Your hearts are covered with more stains than there are sins in the book in which the angel Djebrael records the faults of men! Do not think to cleanse your hearts from one day to the next by prayer and fasting. God beholds your image in the sunlight of day and the starlight of night; he knows every thought of your mind, every impulse of your heart; he knows how you go to the pharmacies, and, on a pretext of buying balsam, manage to get brandy under a false label. But God is not to be deceived by such means. The word of Mahomet is decisive: 'He who in this world has drunk the juice of the vine, in the other shall not drink the wine of gladness.' No! you will have no rain for your crops, because you have drained the source of the rains of heaven by exhausting the patience of the Lord! Allah is great, and you are yourselves the cause of your misery."

The orator ceased speaking, raised his eyes toward
the heavens, grasped his beard with his hand: and, in
this attitude, he was not unlike Jupiter about to hurl
from his mighty hand a sheaf of thunderbolts.

And, sooth to say, a very eminent scholar was Mir
Hadji Festahli Ismaïl Ogli. From the beginning of his
speech it was as if one were listening to a brooklet's
murmuring or a nightingale's singing. Every word
produced upon the by-standers the effect of a melting
pastel, and there was not, in all Daghestan, a single
effendi who understood the half of what he was saying.
The interpreter of the commander of Derbend himself,
Mirza Aly, who had swallowed, digested, and thrown
up criticisms upon all the poets of Farzistan, after having talked with him for more than two hours, ended by
saying, —

" I can make nothing of it."

This, in Tartar, corresponds to the Russian saying,
which, I think, is also a little French: " I throw my
tongue to the dogs."

This time our orator had taken the trouble to make
himself clear, so that he had been understood by everybody, as was expedient in a conjuncture of such importance; hence his discourse had produced the greatest
effect. They gathered around him with mingled respect
and awe, and these words were heard murmured on all
sides: " He is right, he speaks the truth;" and each
man, like a bee, regaled him with the honey of praise.

Thereupon, addressing himself anew to his auditors,
with the confidence gained from his first success, he
said, —

" Listen, brethren; we are all guilty in the eyes of
Allah, and I stand quite the first; our faults have
mounted to the third heaven, but, happily, there are

seven of them, and four remain to us in which to seek
for God's mercy. He punishes the innocent with the
guilty; yet, sometimes, for a single good man, he saves
a whole people. Well, I am going to make you a proposition. Whether you will accept it or not, I do not
know, but here it is: This is not the first time that
Daghestan has prayed for water; well, our fathers and
grandfathers, who were wiser than we, were accustomed,
under such circumstances, to chose from among the
young Mussulmans a youth' pure in mind and body, and
send him, with the prayers and blessings of all, up to
the summit of the mountain nearest to Allah, — that
is, to the top of Schach Dagh. There he must pray
fervently, as one who prays for a whole people; he must
take some unsullied snow from the mountain, make a
ball of the size of his head, enclose it in a vase, and
then, without permitting it to touch the earth, he must
bring it to Derbend. Finally, at Derbend he must
turn the melted snow into the sea. God is great. The
snow-water from Schach Dagh will scarcely have mingled
with the waters of the Caspian sea before the clouds
are heaped above the mingled waters, and the down-
pouring rain refreshes the parched earth."

"It is true! it is true!" cried every voice.

"I have heard my father tell about it," said one.

"And I my grandfather," said another.

"And I have seen it," said, as he advanced, an old
man with a white' beard whose extremity alone was
tinged with red.

They turned and listened to him.

"It was my brother," continued the old man, "that
went to get the ball of snow; the miracle was performed;
the waters of the Caspian sea became as fresh as milk;
the raindrops were as large as' silver roubles; never,

in the memory of man, had there been so fine a harvest as that year's."

The old man was silent.

Then there was but one cry.

They must choose a messenger, must pick him out that very instant, must send him to Schach Dagh without losing a moment.

"To Schach Dagh! to Schach Dagh!" they shouted.

As by a train of gunpowder, the words reached the town, and all Derbend cried with one voice, like an echo of the mosque,—

"To Schach Dagh! to Schach Dagh!"

The solution of the great puzzle was therefore discovered; they knew then at last a sure way to bring rain. Everybody danced with delight and screamed for joy.

The rich especially appeared enchanted that a means had been found that would not cost a kopeck.

There is no one like a rich man for appreciating economical measures.

The young men said proudly,—

"They will choose from among us; upon one of us depends the fate of Daghestan."

But where was this young man to be found, pure of body and mind? In any nation it would be difficult; but among the Asiatics!—

While reflecting upon this question, the inhabitants of Derbend were much embarrassed, and the effervescence of their first exultation subsided.

Where, indeed, was this innocent young man to be found who knew as yet neither the savor of wine nor the sweetness of a kiss?

They began to consider the matter seriously, to point out this one, then that one; but the one was too young, the other too experienced. The first had as yet no moustache; that of the second was too long. It was a dreadful affair to manage successfully.

What we have just said is not entirely to the credit of the inhabitants of Derbend; but, I repeat, this is history that I am writing: truth, then, before everything.

If this were a romance! Ah! *purdieu!* my hero would already be found.

"We must take Sopharkouli," said some; "he is as shy as a young girl."

So shy that, afraid of no one knows what, he had been seen, three days before, to leap, at peep o' day, from his fair neighbor's terrace into the street, enter hastily his own house, and lock his door with a double turn.

"Or Mourad Annet; he leads a life as quiet and solitary as a lily."

But it was affirmed that a month before, upon returning home with a bottle of balsam in each hand, after a visit to the pharmacy, the immaculate lily had sung songs that would have made the devils themselves clap their hands to their ears.

There still remained Mohammed Rassoul; surely no one could speak evil of him. However, they might think it. He had in his house a charming Lesghienne whom he had bought from her father; he had paid only twenty-nine roubles, and had since refused a hundred for her. He was a man after all; a sword of steel sometimes rusts.

They sought in vain; too much was said of this one; that one said too much of himself.

Melancholy began to possess the inhabitants of Derbend, and under such circumstances there is but a step from melancholy to despair.

2

"And Iskander Beg?" said a voice in the crowd.

"Iskander Beg, surely! Excellent! Iskander Beg! Perfect! How did we forget Iskander Beg? It is incredible! incomprehensible! As well overlook a rose in a bouquet, a pomegranate in a dish of fruit! Allah! Allah! The heat has shrivelled up our wits."

"Well," said a voice. "Allah be praised! we have found our man! Call Iskander Beg!"

"Iskander Beg! Iskander Beg, hallo! Iskander Beg, hallo!"

"Now indeed are we saved," was declared on all sides. "This dear Iskander Beg! this excellent Iskander Beg! this noble Iskander Beg! Why, he scarcely eats! he never drinks! *He* is not hand-in-glove with unbelievers. No one remembers having ever met him in a garden. Who has ever seen him look at a woman? Have you?"

"No."

"Or you?"

"Nor I, either. He lives apart like the moon."

"Well, then, let us run to Iskander Beg's house!" cried several voices.

"But people don't go to Iskander Beg's like that."

"Why?"

"Because he is so dignified that a man does not know how to approach him; so haughty that one speaks only when spoken to; so sparing of speech that one would say every word cost him a rouble. Who ever saw him laugh, hey?"

"Not I."

"Nor I."

"Nor I. We must think twice about it before going to his house."

"There is but one man that might venture to run the risk," said a voice.

And every one answered, —

"That man is Mir Hadji Festahli Ismaël Ogli."

It was indeed very proper that the one who had given the advice should finish what he had begun.

"Go, Hadji Festahli, go," cried the by-standers, "and entreat Iskander in the name of us all! Get his consent; you will have no difficulty, you are so eloquent!"

Hadji Festahli was not eager for the honor; but, in the end, he agreed to undertake the commission. They gave him two begs as escort, — the fat Hussein and the lean Ferzali.

The deputation set out.

"Ah!" said the crowd, "that is well."

"I am as tranquil now," said one, "as if Iskander had accepted."

"If Festahli has a mind, he is sure to succeed," said another.

"He could coax half a beard away from a poor man."

"He is cleverer than the devil."

"A very respectable man!"

"He is a genius!"

"He could make a serpent dance on its tail."

"And what eloquence! when he speaks, they are not mere words that fall from his mouth — "

"They are flowers!"

"The ears have not even time to gather them in."

"He could so cheat you that he could get judgment against you for having been taken in by him."

"But we could not have sent him for the ball of snow."

"He is not chaste enough for that."

"Nor sober enough."

"Nor brave enough."

"Nor quite —"

Permit us to break off from the eulogies of Mir Hadji Festahli. We are not of those who, after bathing a man's eyes with rose-water, — as the Tartars say, — give him, while he is drying them, a scorpion instead of a cherry to eat, or an aconite blossom in place of a jasmine to smell.

III.

ISKANDER BEG.

THE respectable Hadji Festahli proceeded slowly as he climbed the ladder of streets that leads to the higher part of the city, in which stood the house of Iskander Beg. From time to time he had to pass through streets so narrow that his two honorable companions, Hussein and Ferzali, who walked beside him along the streets where they could go three abreast, were then obliged to fall back and walk behind him in single file, — a humiliation from which they made haste to escape as soon as the street became wide enough for three abreast. Occasionally one or the other would attempt to engage the hadji in conversation; but so great was his preoccupation, he did not hear them, did not answer; and he was even so absent-minded that he failed to observe that in spitting to right and left, he sometimes spat upon the black beard of Hussein, sometimes upon the red beard of Ferzali.

His inattention continued so long that his two companions began to be angry.

"This is a singular man!" said Hussein; "he is spoken to, and, instead of replying, he spits."

"May it fall into his throat!" cried Ferzali, wiping his beard. "The proverb says truly, Hussein: 'If the master is at home, it is sufficient to speak his name, and the door will be opened to you; but if he is not there, you will get nothing, even by breaking in.'

Useless to speak any more to Mir Hadji Festahli; his mind is elsewhere, the house is empty."

Ferzali à *la barbe rose*, as they called him in Derbend, because, instead of employing the two substances in use among the Tartars for coloring the beard, — substances, the first of which begins by tinting the beard red, and the second finishes by dyeing it black, — Ferzali, who used only the first, and who, consequently, kept his beard the color of the first streak of dawn as it appears on the verge of the horizon — Ferzali was deceived. The house was not empty; it was, on the contrary, so full of its own occupants, and their strife was creating such an uproar, that, not being able to understand even the voice of his own mind, Hadji Festahli could not understand other people's voices.

This was what his thoughts were urging: " Have a care, Festahli! every step that you take toward the dwelling of Iskander Beg brings you nearer to danger. Remember how seriously you have offended him. Beware, Hadji Festahli, beware!"

What, then, had passed between Hadji Festahli and Iskander Beg?

We are about to relate it.

Iskander was born at Derbend, when the city was already occupied by the Russians, — this occupation dates from 1795; but his father had been the intimate friend of the last khan, who had been driven from his provinces by Catherine's army. In 1826, he died of chagrin because the Persians, whom he was expecting at Derbend, had been routed at Kouba, to which point they had advanced; but, when dying, he had charged his son, then fifteen years of age, never to serve the Russians, and never to make friends with the inhabitants of Derbend, who had repelled the Persians.

. He was dead; but his convictions, his habits, his opinions, all survived in his son, whose ideas, thoughts, and desires were all opposed to the desires, thoughts, and ideas of the inhabitants of Derbend. A handful of rice, a glass of water, a little light, much air, were all of which the young Iskander Beg had need.

In the spring, when the entire world was awakening to the breath of love and poetry, he would saddle his good Karabach horse, swing from his shoulder the fine gun from Hadji Moustaff, the most celebrated gunsmith in Daghestan, and, with his bold yellow falcon perched upon his thumb, he would hunt the pheasant over mountain and valley until he was ready to drop with fatigue, if you grant there can be fatigue in the pursuit of a passion. Then he would dismount from his horse, which he allowed to wander at will, lie down in the shade of some great tree beside a stream, and sleep tranquilly to its gentle sound. Whether its sweet harmony caused him to dream, whether his dreams were prosaic, whether he was poet or philosopher, rhymer or reasoner, I know not. This I do know, — he lived tingling with the thrill of life. What more would you have?

In winter, when the snow, driven by the wind, beat against his windows, he loved to listen to the howling of the storm whirling over his chimney; stretched upon his rug, his eyes would follow the play of the embers upon his hearth, or the curling smoke from his pipe.

Did he see the figure of the devil in the embers? Did he see angels' wings in the smoke from his pipe? He said so, himself. The fact is, he dwelt in a nameless realm, and in this realm, of which he was king, he rummaged boxes of .emeralds, pearls, and diamonds; he carried off women beside whom the houris, green, yellow,

and blue, promised by Mahomet to the faithful, were
but Kalmucks or Samoyedes; he cast himself into unheard of perils; he fought gnomes, giants, enchanters,
and fell asleep amidst the creatures of his fancy, and
awoke in the morning, the ideal so confused with the
real that he did not know whether he had been awake
or dreaming.

And sometimes he would summon his Lesghian noukar
and have him sing. The Lesghian sang of the freedom
of his brothers upon their mountains, their courage in
combat and the chase; and then the Asiatic heart of
Iskander would begin to swell. He would take his
dagger and feel its point; he would sharpen the blade
of his shaska, and mutter, —

"Shall I, then, never fight?"

His wish was not long in being realized; Kası
Mullah attacked Derbend. It was a fine opportunity
for brave men to test their mettle.

Iskander Beg did not overlook it.

He sallied forth with the Tartars, mounted on his
fine Karabach charger, which knew neither rocks nor
abysses; and he was always at the front. To join him,
yes, that might be possible; but to pass him, never.
He did not run, he flew like the eagle, despatching
death far and near, first with his gun, then, the discharged gun swung from his shoulder, with kandjiar on
high, hurling himself with savage shouts upon the
enemy.

One day there had been an engagement near Kouba,
and having dislodged the Russians from a vineyard, the
Tartars began, notwithstanding their success, to riot,
according to the Asiatic custom, with two heads lopped
off and fastened to a standard taken from the enemy.
The Russian troops had already re-entered the town,

but a young Russian officer and a few Tartars, among whom we find Iskander Beg, had halted near the fountain. Bullets and balls were whistling around them; the Russian officer was at the time drinking of the pure, limpid water. Lifting his head, he saw before him Iskander Beg in simple close tunic of white satin; his rolled-up sleeves revealed hands and arms reddened with blood to the elbow.

He was leaning upon his gun, his lips curled in scorn, his eyes flashing through tears, blazing with wrath.

"What is the matter, Iskander?" demanded the Russian. "It strikes me that you have acquitted yourself well of your share of the work, and have nothing to regret."

"Hearts of hares!" he muttered. "They march regularly enough when advancing, but in retreat, they are wild goats."

"Well, after all," said the young Russian, "the day seems to be ours."

"Of course it is ours; but we have left poor Ishmael over there."

"Ishmael?" demanded the officer. "Isn't that the handsome lad that came to me at the beginning of the fight and begged me to give him some cartridges?"

"Yes; he was the only one I loved in all Derbend; an angelic soul. He is lost!"

And he wiped away a single tear that trembled upon his eyelid and could not decide to fall.

"Is he captured?" inquired the Russian.

"He is dead!" answered Iskander. "Braver than a man, he had all the imprudence of a child. He wanted to pick a bunch of grapes, and he cleared the space separating him from the vines. He lost his head by it. Before my eyes, the Lesghians cut his throat. I could not help him; there were ten men to deal with. I killed three of them, that was all I could do. Just now they are retreating; they are insulting his body, the wretches! Come," cried he, turning to three or four Tartars who stood listening, " who of you still has some love, fidelity, and courage in his soul? Let him return with me to rescue the body of a comrade."

" I will go with you myself," announced the Russian officer.

" Let us go," said two of the Tartars also.

And they four rushed upon the band of Lesghians, who, not expecting this sudden attack, and believing that these four men were followed by a much greater number, retreated before them; and they advanced to the boy's body, took it up, and bore it back to the town.

At her gate, the mother was waiting. She threw herself upon the decapitated body with heart-rending shrieks and tears.

Iskander gazed at her, his eyebrows drawn together; and now it was not a single tear that trembled alone upon his eyelid, — there were streams of them coursing down his cheeks like waters from a fountain.

A mother's despair melted this lion's heart.

" How unfortunate that you are not a Russian! " said the officer, extending his hand.

" How fortunate that you are not a Tartar! " replied Iskander, grasping the hand.

One thing is well known: the moustache, which is an indication of approaching maturity, is likewise the herald of love.

Iskander had not escaped the universal law. Every hair of his moustache had sprouted upon his lip at the very instant that a desire had sprung up in his heart,

—desires vague as yet, inexplicable to himself, but,
like orange boughs, bearing on the same branch both
fruit and flowers. Why do women like the moustache
so much? Because, the symbol of love, it springs from
the same source, and crisps in the warmth of desire.
What seeks the youth with head erect, humid eye, smiling face, and ruby lip under the budding moustache?
Neither honors nor fortune, — only a kiss.

A virgin moustache is a bridge thrown across two
loving mouths; a moustache —

Let us leave the moustaches here, they are carrying
us too far; then, too, why, with gray moustache, talk
of black or blonde?

Besides, moustaches, of whatever color, lead me from
my subject.

I return, then.

In the month of the preceding April, Iskander had,
according to his custom, set out for the chase. The
day was beautiful; it was a true spring holiday; it was
warm without heat, fresh without humidity. Iskander
plunged into the midst of an ocean of verdure and
flowers. He had now, for several hours, been going
from gorge to gorge, from mountain to mountain; he
wanted something, he knew not what. For the first
time the air seemed difficult to breathe, for the first
time, his heart beat without cause; his unquiet breast
fluttered like a woman's veil.

And, speaking of veils, let us note a fact.

When Iskander formerly passed through the streets
of Derbend, he would never have cast a look toward a
woman, had she been unveiled to her girdle; while, on
the contrary, from the very day on which he was able
to twist the ends of his little black moustache between
his fingers, every nose-tip, every lip, every brown eye

or blue that he could catch a glimpse of through a peep-hole in a veil, turned him hot and cold at once.   It is a positive fact that he had never studied anatomy; well, in spite of his ignorance, he could picture to himself a woman from the toe of her slipper to the top of her veil, not only without error but even without oversight, merely from catching sight of a little silk-stockinged foot in a velvet slipper under a kanaos trouser embroidered with gold or silver.

I will not tell you whether, on this occasion, his hunt was successful; I will say only that the hunter was very distrait, — so distrait that, instead of seeking the lonely haunts where pheasant and partridge are wont to hide, he turned his horse toward two or three hamlets where he had absolutely no business.

But the day was fine, and, whether standing at their gates, or sitting on the house-tops, he hoped to see one of those pretty little contemporaneous animals that he had reconstructed with as much precision as the learned Cuvier had reconstructed a mastodon, an ichthyosaurus, a pterodactyl, or any other antediluvian monster.

Unfortunately, he had to be content with the specimens already known.   Women were at their gates, women were on the terraces; but the Mohammedan women, who sometimes put aside their veils for unbelievers, never lift them for their compatriots.   The result was that, the desires of Iskander Beg, not finding a face upon which to fix themselves, were scattered to the winds.

The young man became sad, drew a profound sigh, threw the bridle on his horse's neck, and left him master to go what way he would.

This is what travellers and lovers ought always to do when they have an intelligent horse.

The horse knew a delightful road leading home; on this road, under some tall plane-trees, was a spring forming a pool, at which he was in the habit of slaking his thirst: he took this route.

Iskander Beg paid no attention as to what path his horse was taking.

Little it mattered to him; he was riding in a dream.

And along with him, on both sides of the road, stalked all sorts of phantoms; these were women, all veiled it is true, but their veils were so carelessly worn that not one of them prevented his seeing what should have been unseen.

Suddenly Iskander reined in his horse; his vision seemed turned into reality.

At the edge of the spring was hidden a girl of fifteen or sixteen years, more beautiful than he had ever dreamed a woman could be. With the pure water she was cooling her beautiful face, which the April sun had tinted like a rose; then she gazed at herself in the shimmering mirror, smiled, and took so much pleasure in seeing herself smile, that she saw nothing else, listening the while to the birds that sang above her head, and hearing only their songs, which seemed to say: " Gaze into the fountain, beautiful child! Never was flower so fresh as thou mirrored there before; never will flower so fresh as thou be mirrored after thee! "

They doubtless said it to her in verse; but I am obliged to tell it in prose, not knowing the rules of poetry in bird language.

· And they were right, the feathered flatterers; it was hard to imagine flower fresher, purer, more beautiful than this one which appeared to have sprung up from the edge of the pool in which it was reflected.

But it was one of those human blossoms that Granville

knows so well how to paint, — with black locks, eyes
like stars, teeth like pearls, cheeks like peaches; the
whole enveloped, not by one of those thick, ill-advised
veils that conceal what they cover, but by a gauze so
fine, so silky, so transparent, that it seemed woven from
the filmy beams which Summer shakes from her distaff
when Autumn comes.   .

Then if the imprudent eye descended in a straight
line from her face, that was indeed another matter.
After a neck, which might have served as a model for
the Tower of Ivory of Scripture, came —

Undoubtedly what came after and was half hidden by
. a chemise of white *maufe,* embroidered with blue, and
an *arkabouke* of cherry satin, was very beautiful, since
poor Iskander could not repress an exclamation of
delight.

The cry had no sooner escaped him than Iskander
wished that he had been born dumb; he had driven
himself out of Paradise.

The girl had heard the exclamation; she turned
around and uttered a cry on her part; over her transparent veil she threw a thick one, and ran, or, rather,
flew away, twice gasping the name of Iskander Beg.

He, stricken dumb when it was too late, motionless
when perhaps he would have run, his arms extended,
as if to stay the reality which, in fleeing, again melted
into a vision, stood breathless with staring eyes, like
Apollo watching the flight of Daphne.

But Apollo very quickly darted forth' upon the track
of the beautiful nymph, while Iskander Beg did not
budge so long as he was able to catch a glimpse through
the thicket of a hand's breadth of that white veil.

And when it was lost to view he became much agitated, for he felt then as if life, a moment suspended,

was returning in waves upon him, rudely and noisily
invading his heart.

"Allah!" murmured he, "what will they say of her
.and of me if any one has seen us? — How beautiful she
is! — She will be scolded by her parents. — What lovely
black eyes! — They will think that we had planned a
rendezvous! — What lips! — She knows my name; twice
as she ran she cried: 'Iskander! Iskander!'"

And he again sank into his revery, if a state can be
called a revery in which the blood is boiling, while
harps are ringing in one's ears, and when all the stars
of heaven are seen in broad daylight.

Most certainly would night have surprised Iskander
on the borders of the pool, into whose waters his heart
'seemed to have fallen, had not the horse, feeling his
bridle, tightened for an instant, gently relax, continued
on his way without consulting his rider.

Iskander reached home madly in love.

We are sorry indeed not to have found either time or
space in this chapter to tell why Iskander bore malice
to Mir Hadji Festahli; but we promise our readers,
positively, to tell them in the following chapter.

IV.

IN WHICH ISKANDER LEARNS THE NAME OF HER WHO KNOWS HIS.

AND yet Iskander recalled his father's words. His father had been wont to say: " The loveliest rose lasts but a day, the smallest thorn endures a lifetime. Caress women, but do not love them if you would not become their slave. Love is sweet only in song; but in reality its beginning is fear; its middle, sin; and its end, repentance."

And to these three sentiments he added a fourth, their fitting complement: " Look not upon the wives of other men, and listen not to your own."

Let us hasten to add, to Iskander's credit, that he forgot all these precepts in less than five minutes.

The young Tartar loved and was afraid. The first part of his father's premonition, " The beginning of love is fear," was then fulfilled in him.

Eight days before, poor Iskander had slept so tranquilly, the night had seemed so short and refreshing.

Now he tossed about upon his mattress; he bit his pillow; his silk coverlet stifled him.

But who was *she?*

At this question, which he had put to himself for the tenth time, Iskander leaped from his bed to his feet.

She! what a villanous word!

Love tolerates no pronouns, and especially love in Daghestan.

Until he knew her true name, Iskander would give her a fictitious one.

"I must know the name of my — Leila," said he, thrusting his kandjiar into his girdle; "I shall die, perhaps, but I will know her name."

A moment later he was in the street.

Probably the devil left one of his serpents at Derbend: to some he takes the form of ambition, — how many celebrated men have disputed the possession of Derbend! to others he goes in the guise of love, — how many young people have lost their wits at Derbend!

The latter serpent, decidedly, had bitten Iskander Beg.

He wandered up and down the streets, looked through every gate, scanned every wall and every veil.

It was all in vain.

Whom could he ask for her name? Who would point out her house?

His heart's eagerness urged him forward.

"Go!" it bade him.

Where? He did not know.

He joined the crowd; the crowd conducted him to the market-place.

If he had wished to learn the price of meat, he was in a fair way; but the name of his beloved? No!

He approached an Armenian. The Armenians know everybody, dealing in everything.

This one was selling fish.

"Buy a fine *chamaia*, Iskander Beg," said the Armenian.

The young man turned away in disgust.

At last he approached the shop of a goldsmith, a skilful enameller.

"God save you!" said he to the Tartar.

3

"May Allah grant you happiness!" responded the goldsmith, without raising his eyes from a turquoise that he was mounting in a ring.

On the counter behind which the goldsmith was working stood a copper sebilla, filled with different objects more or less precious.

Iskander Beg uttered a cry.

He had just recognized an earring which he was certain of having seen, the day before, swinging in the ear of his unknown.

His heart gave a leap; it seemed to him that he had just learned the first letter of her name.

It was as if he saw her pretty little hand with the pink nails beckoning to him.

He dared not speak a word. He hesitated to put a question; he did not know what to say; his voice trembled, his thoughts were in a tumult.

Suddenly a light flashed across his brain.

He had hit upon a truly military ruse, — one of those that capture cities.

He emptied the cup into his hand, as if to look at the jewels. The goldsmith, who had recognized him, allowed him to do so.

He adroitly withdrew the earring from the heap of jewels, slipped it into his pocket, and suddenly ejaculated, —

"There! I have dropped an earring!"

And he replaced the other jewels in the cup.

"What earring?" demanded the merchant.

"The one with little bells on it."

"*Par Allah!* pick it up quickly, Iskander; I would not have that lost for five hundred roubles."

"Oh! it is not lost," said Iskander.

Then, after a pause, he said, —

"It is very strange, though, that I do not see it anywhere."

"One loses sight of a thing as it falls," said the merchant, laying down the ring upon which he was working; and rising, he looked under his bench as he raised his spectacles.

Iskander stepped about feigning to search.

"I do not find it," said he.

Then, a moment later, he added, —

"It is certainly lost."

This time the goldsmith took his spectacles from his forehead and laid them on his table.

"Allah!" he exclaimed, "what have you done, Iskander Beg?"

"I have lost an earring, that is all."

"But you don't know what will happen to me. That old rascal of a Hadji Festahli is capable of bringing suit against me. An earring of Baku enamel!"

"On my soul, you are laughing at me, Djaffar. Do you expect me to believe that a man as serious as Hadji Festahli, a descendant of Mahomet, a saint, wears earrings?"

"And who says that he wears earrings?"

"He has neither wife nor daughter, that I know of at least."

"He is too stingy for that, the old miser! But it is as much as ten years now since his brother Shafy fled into Persia, leaving him his wife and daughter. The little girl was only six years old then, she is sixteen now."

"It must be she! it must be she!" murmured Iskander under his breath.

Then he asked aloud, —

"What is she called — this niece?"

"Kassime," replied the goldsmith.

"Kassime, Kassime," repeated Iskander to himself.

And the name seemed to him far prettier than Leila, which he discarded as one throws away a lemon from which he has squeezed all the juice.

"And since her father's departure," he added aloud, " I presume that the little one has grown."

"You know our country, Iskander: the child of one year looks as though it were two; a girl of five appears to be ten. Our young girls are like the grape-cuttings which are scarcely planted before the grapes are ripe; I have never seen her, but her uncle says that she is the prettiest girl in Derbend."

Iskander Beg tossed the earring into the goldsmith's hand and darted off like an arrow. He knew all that he wished to know,—the name and dwelling of his lady fair.

He ran straight to the house of Hadji Festahli. He did not hope to see Kassime, but perhaps he should hear her voice; then, who knows? she might be going out with her mother, perhaps, and, whether he saw her or not, she would see him. She would certainly suspect that he was not there to get a glimpse of her uncle.

But, as usual, old Hadji Festahli's house was shut up; Iskander foresaw one drawback, — it was, in all Derbend, the most difficult house to enter.

He heard, not Kassime's voice, but a dog's bark, and it was redoubled every time that he drew near the gate. Finally, the gate opened.

But an abominable old hag emerged, broom in hand.

She was some old witch, doubtless, going to her vigil.

She did not even have the trouble of shutting the gate behind her; it closed quite of itself, one would have thought had he not heard a hand push the bolts.

Iskander had resolved to remain there until evening, until the next morning, until Kassime came out. But his presence could not fail to be remarked, and his presence would announce openly to Hadji Festahli: "I love your niece; hide her more carefully than ever."

He returned home, and threw himself down upon a rug.

There, as he was no longer afraid of being seen or even heard, he threshed about, he roared, he bellowed.

Iskander loved 'after the manner of lions.

A good Mussulman, a true believer, has no conception of what we call perfect love; Iskander was purely enraged, he wanted Kassime that very moment, without delay, instantly.

He was one of the readers that skip the preface of a book and proceed immediately to the first chapter.

Terrible people for authors and uncles!

But Iskander very soon reached the conclusion that he might vainly roll on his rug all day long, roar a whole week, howl for a month, and it would not bring him a hair's breadth nearer to Kassime.

He must bestir himself, then.

Finally, by dint of saying over to himself: "Kassime's uncle," he was reminded that, if he himself had no uncle, he had an aunt.

An aunt! Why were aunts made, if it were not to take charge of their nephew's love affairs?"

That is all aunts are good for.

You do not know of an aunt who ever served any other purpose; neither do I.

He went out and purchased some silk stuff for a dress; then he ran to his aunt's house.

The aunt took the dress, listened to the whole story of her nephew's love affair, and as an aunt, however old

she may be, remembers the days when she was young,
Iskander's aunt, sending a sigh after her own lost youth,
promised him to do all in her power to bring about an
interview.

"Come to my house to-morrow, at noon, my child,"
she said; "I will send for Kassime, under pretext of
darkening her eyes with kohl. I will hide you behind
this curtain, you rascal! But be discreet. Do not
move, do not breathe, and, above all, beware of whispering a word to any one of what I am doing for you."

As one can well understand, Iskander returned home
in high spirits.

He went to bed at sunset, hoping to sleep, and that
the time would pass swiftly while he slept.

Sleep had been good once upon a time.

He fell asleep at one o'clock, and awoke at two.

By seven in the morning he was at his aunt's house,
insisting that it was almost noon.

At every sound made at the gate he ran and hid
behind the curtain.

Then he would resume his position beside his aunt,
shaking his head and saying, —

"She will not come."

Whereupon, falling into a rage, and stamping his
foot, he would exclaim, —

"Ah! if she does not come I will set fire to her
uncle's house; she will have to come out so as not to
be burned; then I will seize her, I will put her on my
Karabach and run away with her."

And each time his aunt would soothe him, saying, —

"That could not have been she; it is only nine o'clock
— it is only ten — it is only eleven."

But at noon the aunt exclaimed, —

"Ah! there she comes this time."

Iskander, like his aunt, had heard the heels of little Turkish slippers pattering on the paved court, and he had sprung behind his curtain.

It was indeed she, with her friend Kitchina, — blue-eyed Kitchina, as they called her.

The maidens took off their slippers at the threshold of the door and came in, seating themselves beside the old aunt.

The two veils fell to the floor. The curtain was agitated; happily, neither of the girls looked that way.

No; they were watching the old aunt, who was stirring with a small ivory stick the kohl at the bottom of a little silver jar.

Kassime knelt before the good woman, who first pencilled her eyebrows, then the under-lids; but when Kassime, for the latter operation, raised her beautiful eyes, Iskander felt as if his heart were pierced by a bullet.

The old woman herself was struck with their wonderful beauty, and in her admiration for the girl, she said, embracing her, —

"How soon, my pretty Kassime, shall I be painting you in the bath amid the songs of your friends? You have such beautiful eyes that I could wish them each morning to awake tearless and to be sealed every night by a kiss."

Kassime sighed, and affectionately kissed the old woman.

Iskander heard the sigh and felt the warmth of the kiss.

"My uncle Festahli says that I am too young," answered Kassime, sadly.

"And what says your heart?" demanded the old lady.

Instead of replying, Kassime took down the tambourine hanging on the wall, and sang: —

> " Fair dawn, oh, why did I so early feel
>   The dewy coolness of thy wings ?
> Fair youth, oh, why this eve did thine eyes steal
>   Into my heart their fiery stings ?

> " Oh, why, though I have seen in cloudless sky
>   Enthroned the god-like shining star, —
> Oh, why, though I have seen from storm-cloud high
>   A serpent fire o'erleap heaven's bar, —

> " Oh, why, since I 've forgotten dreaded woes
>   And longed-for weal, sad earth, gay skies —
> So much forgotten, sun and fire, dawn's rose —
>   Oh, why forget I not thine eyes ? "

While singing the last verse of the song which she
was improvising, Kassime blushed to her shoulders;
then, laughing like a child, she dropped her tambourine
and threw herself into her friend's arms; and then the
two silly young things both began to laugh.

Why were they laughing, and what was there so
laughable in all that ?

But Iskander's aunt understood very well, and, for
the sake of her nephew's happiness, she determined to
bring out the secret of the enigma immediately.

" O my sweet rose," she said, playing with Kassime's
rings, " if my nephew could have heard the song you
have just sung, he would have staved in the wall to see
the singer, and after seeing her, he would have carried
her off as a lion does a kid."

And just then a jar filled with jasmin water fell from
the chest that stood near the curtain and broke into a
thousand pieces.

The old woman faced about; the two young people turned pale.

"Why did it fall?" asked Kassime in trembling tones.

"That devil of a black cat!" exclaimed the old lady; "there was never another like it!"

Kassime was reassured.

"Oh, I detest black cats!" said she. "It is said that they sometimes lend their skin to the devil, and that is why we can see their eyes glare in the dark."

Then turning to her friend, she said,—

"Come, Kitchina, mamma allowed me but an hour, and there is the mullah's call."

Kassime rather coldly embraced the old woman, who saw that the reserve was assumed.

"Nonsense!" said the aunt, accompanying her to the door, "it is useless for you to be angry, Kassime. I should like to see you with flowers upon your head; your happiness is as dear to me as a link of gold, and with a link of gold, I know a young man who would like to bind his soul to yours. But be at ease, my dear child, only Allah, he, and I know the secret."

Kassime opened her great eyes, whose size was doubled with amazement, but she was just then at the threshold of the street-door; her friend, who was behind, pushed her gently, the door was shut, and, for all explanation, she heard the key creaking in the lock.

Iskander Beg fairly stifled his aunt in his arms when she returned from Kassime. The good woman scolded him well because he had not been able to keep still at his post of observation.

"Oh!" she exclaimed, "when that dreadful jar fell I nearly died from fright! Wicked child! it would have been the death of me if Kassime had guessed who made it fall."

"Is it my fault, aunt?" cried Iskander; "and could
I keep quiet when my heart threatened to burst at sight
of the roses that overspread Kassime's cheeks after you
had spoken of me? I longed to gather them with my
lips. What could you expect? Who sows must reap!"

"Not when he sows in another's garden."

"Then buy me this garden, aunt; do not let me
expire like a nightingale on the thorns of a rose-bush.
Kassime must be my wife; ask her uncle for her, then,
without delay, and rest assured that I shall be as grateful as I am loving. Succeed in your embassy, dear aunt,
and I promise you the most beautiful pair of buffaloes
in Daghestan."

On the morrow Iskander Beg received the answer of
Mir Hadji Festahli.

Alas! it was very far from being what he had hoped.

Here it is, for that matter; the reader can judge how
much of hope it left to poor Iskander.

"Tell your Iskander, for me," Festahli had replied
to the aunt, "that I have not forgotten his father. His
father was a brute. One day, before everybody, he
called me, — I will not repeat what he called me; I
could take no revenge, because it was just at the time
when the Russians were interfering with our customs;
but I have not forgotten the offence. I have not burned
his coffin. It is proper for the son to pay his father's
debt, and I am no dog to fawn on the hand that has
beaten me. But, to tell the truth, had there been no
feud between us, Iskander should not have had my
niece in any case. A great honor to be the uncle of
this beg! There are seventy begs in Derbend just like
him; I will give him their names whenever he likes.
Why talk to me of a dowry? Yes, faith, by ruining
himself, he could pay for my niece; but after that

how would he provide for her? Has he any relatives
to help him in case of need? How many raven's-eggs
does he get from the rent of his huts? How many
bundles of nettles has he reaped in his fields? He is
destitute, utterly destitute, your beggar of a nephew.
Tell him no,—a hundred times no. I will not have
such a good-for-nothing as he is in my family. A head
and a purse so empty that with only a breath both
head and purse would fly away. Good-evening, old
woman!"

With the knowledge that you already possess of
Iskander Beg's disposition, you can imagine his rage
when his aunt brought him this answer, word for word.

At last, his wrath cooled; and he had sworn to be
terribly revenged upon Mir Hadji Festahli.

He was a Tartar.

This explains why Hadji Festahli was so preoccupied
while climbing the streets which led to the dwelling of
Iskander Beg; why, in his preoccupation, he spat upon
the black beard of Hussein and the red beard of Ferzuli,
and why, at last, arrived at Iskander Beg's door, instead
of knocking impatiently, he knocked very gently.

V.

A BARGAIN.

ISKANDER was neither rich nor married: his door, therefore, was quickly opened, not half way, but wide open;
for he had no fear that in coming to see him people
would see either his wife or his strong-box.

Hence Iskander received his visitors, not on the
threshold, as do Mussulmans who are fathers of a family,
but in his innermost room. There was nothing in his
house to tempt the pilferer of either hearts or money.

" Welcome! " he cried from the other side of the door
to the arrivals, even before knowing who they were.

And the door was opened.

Iskander Beg himself had come to let them in, as his
noukar was grooming his horse. He stood amazed at beholding Mir Hadji Festahli and his associates in the
street.

The blood rushed to his head, and his first impulse was
to feel for his dagger.

But, thanks to a violent effort, curiosity overcame the
anger within him.

He respectfully placed his hand upon his heart, bowed
to his visitors, and invited them to enter.

They seated themselves upon the rugs, stroked their
beards with oriental gravity, regulated the folds of their
garments, and the conversation opened with common-
places.

Finally, after five minutes lost in trivialities, Mir Hadji Festahli broached the question.

He spoke of the misfortunes which threatened Daghestan in general and the town of Derbend in particular, if such a drouth should continue eight days longer.

At every pause he turned to his companions, as if to ask their support; but it was now their turn to be silent, and if they spat not upon his beard, it was certainly not the desire that was lacking.

Iskander, on his part, appeared very little moved at the pathetic picture that Mir Hadji Festahli drew of the hardships of the city and province; but from the flush on his face it could be seen that a fire was smouldering in his bosom.

Finally, Hadji Festahli rounded up his discourse with this threefold lamentation : —

" Woe ! woe ! woe to Derbend ! "

"Probably ! " answered Iskander.

" Certainly ! " added Hussein.

" Absolutely ! " whimpered Ferzali.

After which ensued a moment of silence.

During this pause Iskander looked from one to another of his visitors with questioning glance; but they were dumb.

Iskander began to be impatient.

"You have not come, brethren," said he, "that we might wipe away our perspiration and shed our tears together, and I presume that, on your part, or on the part of those that sent you, — for you impress me as being ambassadors to my august presence, — you have something to say to me of more importance than what you have communicated."

" Our brother is possessed of great penetration," returned Hadji Festahli, inclining his head.

And then, with an abundance of oriental circumlocution on the honor to Iskander of being the object of such a choice, he recounted what the inhabitants of Derbend were expecting from his devo Iness.

But at that, Iskander's bio. 'agan to cloud threateningly.

"Strange choice!" he cried with emphasis. "Until now the inhabitants of Derbend, for whom, however, I have fought tolerably well, — though it is true that I fought on my own behalf rather than theirs, — not only have not spoken to me, but they have hardly saluted me. And here they offer me a commission which I was not soliciting and of which I am unworthy. It is true that there are many precipices on the heights of Schach Dagh; true, too, that in the gorges of Schach Dagh are the haunts of the brigand Mullah Nour, that there are ten chances to one of my rolling over a precipice, and twenty to one of my being killed by Mullah Nour; but little it matters to them, — I can be of use to them in this, and they have turned to me. And why, pray, should I, who love warmth and sunshine, ask Allah for clouds and rain? On the contrary, I am delighted that my house is dry, my stable wholesome, and that there is neither fog in the air nor mud in the street. Besides, the sun hatches my raven's-eggs, and my nettles grow well without rain. You scoffed because I have no grain to reap! Why, having no grain, should I disturb myself about yours? You have maligned my father, you have robbed him, you have persecuted him, you have scorned me, and now, you wish me to risk my life for your sake, and to pray God to have mercy upon you! But I mistake, — doubtless it is for some new affront that you come to me, and, that nothing may be wanting to the insult, the task of making me such a proposition has been confided to

this holy man, the respectable Hadji Festahli. They do
not load the camel when he is on his feet, but when he
kneels; and I, pray observe, am on my feet."

And Iskander stood as haughty as a king, as terrible
as a god.

"Now," said he, "we have a little matter to settle,
Hadji Festahli and I. We will absent ourselves a few
moments; excuse us, worthy lords!"

And he beckoned Hadji Festahli to follow him into
an adjoining room.

Thereupon the face of the holy Mussulman became as
long and sombre as a night in autumn. He arose smiling; but, as every one knows, there are two kinds of
smiles; one puts out the lips as if to kiss, the other shows
the teeth as if to bite.

They passed together into the next room.

What black-bearded Hussein and red-bearded Ferzali
were talking about meanwhile, we are unable to tell our
readers, because we were listening at the keyhole of the
room to which Hadji Festahli and Iskander had retired.

The two enemies returned in a short time with radiant
faces; they looked like the two diamond-set medals of
the Lion and the Sun, hung side by side on the breast of
a Persian Minister.

Iskander then turned to his other guests and said:—

"At first I had certain motives, best known to myself,
for not conforming to the desires of the people of Derbend; but the honorable Hadji Festahli, whom God preserve, has given me such excellent reasons for complying
that I am now ready to go and bring the snow from the
summit of Schach Dagh, at the risk of plunging over precipices and getting my moustache singed by Mullah
Nour. Allah is all-powerful, and if an earnest, fervent
prayer can touch his heart, I venture to prophesy that it

will soften, and that the very clouds will weep so many tears that the earth's thirst will be quenched not only for this year, but for a year to come. I set out this evening. Pray, — I will act."

Then he added : —

" Time is precious, I will not detain you."

The ambassadors thanked Iskander ; their feet glided into their slippers and the visitors were gone.

Iskander was left alone ; it was what he wanted.

" Well," cried he, joyfully, when he was sure that no one could hear him, " he is a little better than I took him to be, that old knave of a Hadji Festahli. He could have killed me because my father, one day, before everybody, had called him a son of — no matter what ! and now, like a true patriarch, he sacrifices his resentment for the public good, and gives me his niece in exchange for a little snow. Excellent man, that ! "

Hussein and Ferzali, as they went away, were saying : —

" That Iskander is not a man, but an angel. He was furious against Derbend, enraged against Festahli ; but when we had spoken of the wailing and suffering of the poor, he could refuse us no longer."

And as for the people, overjoyed that Iskander had given his consent, they began to dance and sing.

Festahli — laughed in his sleeve.

" A promise, a promise ! " murmured he. " What is a promise, especially when no witnesses are by ? He cannot hold me to it ; I should have died of shame if I had gone before the people with Iskander's refusal. And besides, I added, ' If your journey ends happily.' Now, Iskander has not returned, the paths of Schach Dagh are very steep, and Mullah Nour is very brave. We shall see ! We shall see ! "

A very holy man was Mir Hadji Festahli Ismaël Ogli !
He was a direct descendant of the prophet.

Iskander kissed his good Karabach from very joy,
saying :—

"They are fools, on my word of honor, to suppose that
I am doing all this for the sake of their wheat. Ah! for
Kassime, for my beloved, for my adored Kassime, I
would climb not only Schach Dagh, but the moon besides! Ibrahim! Give my horse some oats. Oats!"

VI.

A DISSERTATION ON THE NOSE.

HAVE you ever considered, dear reader, what an admirable organ is the nose ?

The nose, yes, the nose !

And how useful is the nose to every creature that lifts, as Ovid says, his face to heaven ?

Ah, well, strange to say, — ingratitude unparalleled ! — not a poet has yet thought of addressing an ode to the nose !

It has remained for me, who am not a poet, or who, at least, claim only to rank after our great poets, to conceive such an idea.

Truly, the nose is unfortunate.

Men have invented so many things for the eyes !

They have made them songs, compliments, kaleidoscopes, pictures, scenery, spectacles.

And for the ears :

Earrings, first of all, *Robert the Devil, William Tell, Fra Diavolo,* Stradivarius violins, Érard pianos, Sax trumpets.

And for the mouth :

Carême, The Plain Cook, The Gastronomist's Calendar, The Gourmand's Dictionary. They have made it soups of every kind, from the Russian *batwigns* to the French cabbage-soup ; they have garnished its dishes with the reputations of the greatest men, from cutlets à *la Soubise* to puddings à *la Richelieu;* they have compared its lips to coral, its teeth to pearls, its breath to benzoin; they have set before it peacocks in their plumes, snipes undrawn; finally, for the future they promise it larks roasted whole.

What has been invented for the nose?

Attar of roses, and snuff.

Ah! that is not well, O philanthropists, my masters! O poets, my confrères!

And yet with what fidelity this member —

"It is not a member!" cry the savants.

Pardon, messieurs, I take it back: this appendage — Ah! And yet, as I was saying, with what fidelity has this appendage served you!

The eyes go to sleep, the mouth closes, the ears are deaf.

The nose, alone, is always on duty.

It guards your repose, contributes to your health. All other parts of your body, the feet, the hands, are stupid. The hands let themselves be caught in the act, like the fools they are; the feet stumble and let the body fall, like the clumsy creatures that they are.

And, in the latter case, who suffers for it, generally? The feet commit the fault, and the nose takes the punishment.

How often do you hear it said, —

Monsieur So-and-so has broken his nose!

There have been a great many broken noses since the creation of the world.

Can any one cite a single nose whose fault it was?

No. Everything assaults the poor nose.

Well, it endures all with angelic patience. True, it sometimes has the hardihood to snore. But where and when did you ever hear it complain?

We forget that nature created it an admirable instrument for increasing or decreasing the volume of the
voice. We say nothing of the service it renders us in
acting as a medium between our souls and the souls of
flowers. Let us repress its utility and regard it only from
its æsthetic side, that of beauty.

A cedar of Lebanon, it tramples underfoot the hyssop
of the moustache; a central column, it provides a support
for the double arch of the eyebrows. On its capital
perches the eagle of thought. It is enwreathed with
smiles. With what intrepidity did the nose of Ajax con-
front the storm when he said, "I will escape in spite of
the gods!" With what courage did the nose of the
great Condé — who would never have been great except
for his nose — with what courage did the nose of the
great Condé enter before all others, before the great
Condé himself, the entrenchments of the Spaniards at
Lens and Rocroy, where their conqueror had been so
bold, or, rather, so rash as to flourish his bâton of command? With what assurance was thrust before the public Dugazon's nose, which knew forty-two ways of
wriggling, and each funnier than the last!

No, I do not believe that the nose should be condemned to the obscurity into which man's ingratitude has
hitherto forced it.

Perhaps, also, it is because the noses of the Occident
are so small, that they have submitted to this injustice.

But the deuce is to pay if there are none but Occi-
dental noses!

There are the Oriental noses, which are very handsome
noses.

Do you question the superiority of these noses over
your own, gentlemen of Paris, of Vienna, of Saint
Petersburg?

In that case, Viennese, take the Danube; Parisians,
the steamer; Peterbourgeois, the *perecladdoï*, and say
these simple words : —

"To Georgia!"

Ah! but I forewarn you of a deep humiliation; should
you bring to Georgia one of the largest noses in Europe,
— Hyacinthe's nose or Schiller's, — at the gate of Tiflis
they would gaze at you with astonishment and exclaim :

"This gentleman has lost his nose on the way, — what
a pity!"

At the first street in the town, — what am I saying!
at the first house in the faubourg, you would be convinced
that all other noses, Greek, Roman, German, French,
Spanish, Neopolitan even, should bury themselves in
the bowels of the earth with chagrin at sight of the
Georgian noses.

Ah! blessed God! Those beautiful Georgian noses!
robust noses! magnificent noses!

To begin with, there are all shapes.

Round, fat, long, large.

There is every kind.

White, pink, red, violet.

Some are set with rubies, others with pearls; I saw one
that was set with turquoises.

You have only to squeeze them between two fingers,
and a pint, at the very least, of Kakhetia wine will flow.

In Georgia, Vakhtang IV. abolished the fathom, the
metre, the archine; he retained but the nose.

Goods are measured off by the nose.

They say : "I bought seventeen noses of termalama
for a dressing-gown, seven noses of kanaos for a pair of
trousers, a nose and a half of satin for a cravat."

And, let us add, the Georgian dames find this measure
more convenient than the European measures.

But, in the matter of noses, Daghestan is not to be sneezed at.

Thus, for instance, in the centre of the face of a Derbend beg, Hadji Yussef, — God give strength to his shoulders! arose a certain protuberance for which his compatriots are still hunting a suitable name, although some call it a trumpet, some a rudder, others a handle!

In its shade three men could sleep.

One can understand how such a nose would be greatly respected at Derbend during a hot spell of fifty-two degrees in the sun, since on the other side of this nose, that is to say in the shade, it was but forty degrees.

We need not be greatly surprised, then, that Yussef had been assigned to Iskander as a guide.

But let us confess the whole truth : it was not entirely on account of his nose that he had been appointed.

As indicated by the title Hadji, prefixed to Yussef's name, Yussef had made the pilgrimage to Mecca.

In order to get there, he had traversed Persia, Asia Minor, Palestine, the Desert, a part of Arabia Petræa, and a portion of the Red Sea.

And, on his return, wonderful tales did Yussef tell of his travels, of dangers encountered, of bandits slain, of wild beasts whose jaws he had broken like a Samson!

Whenever he appeared at the bazaar of Derbend, people stepped aside, saying, —

"Make way for the lion of the steppe!"

"He is a remarkable man!" assented the most pointed moustaches and the longest beards, as Yussef Beg turned their heads with the current of his plausible speech. It was said that in going over the summit of a mountain in Persia, his papak had caught on the horn of the moon, the mountain was so high; that for a long time, his sole nourishment had been derived from omelettes of eagles' eggs; and that he had passed nights in caverns where, when he sneezed, the echo itself had responded, "God bless you!"

It is true that he spoke without reflection for the greater part of the time; but when he did speak, his words supplied food for reflection to others. What beasts had he not seen! What men had he not met! He had seen animals having two heads and a single foot, he had met men who had no heads and who thought with their stomachs.

All these tales were really a little old; doubtless that was why no one had thought of sending him for the ball of snow; but when by common consent this commission had fallen to Iskander, Yussef mounted his Persian steed, put his Andrev poniard, his Kouba pistol and Vladikafkaz schaska in his girdle, and rode proudly through the streets of Derbend, proclaiming, —

"If you like, I will accompany poor Iskander; for how do you imagine poor Iskander can get along without me?"

The people answered, —

"Ah, very well; accompany Iskander."

Then he went home to reinforce his defensive armor with a breastplate of copper links, his offensive armor with a Nouka gun. Yellow boots with high heels completed his costume; last of all, he suspended whip and sabre from his saddle.

He could hardly stir in the midst of his arsenal.

He was ready long before Iskander, and awaited him at the city gates, declaiming : —

"Well! will he never come? If they had selected me I should have been off two hours ago."

About six o'clock in the afternoon, Iskander issued from his court on his Karabach horse, wearing the cos tume and arms with which all were familiar.

Iskander traversed the city slowly, — not that he had
the least intention in the world of exhibiting himself, but
because the streets leading from his house to the gates
of Derbend were thronged with people.

At last, he succeeded in joining Yussef Beg, gave him
his hand, saluted for a last time the inhabitants of Derbend and set off at a gallop.

Yussef followed on a Khorassan charger. For some
time horses and riders could be distinguished, then only
the dust, then nothing at all.

Horses and riders had disappeared.

Arrived at a vast cemetery, Iskander Beg slackened his
Karabach's pace.

Night began to fall.

But Iskander heeded neither night nor cemetery; he
was dreaming of his darling Kassine.

Yussef kept glancing to right and left with a certain
degree of uneasiness, and he profited by Iskander's slack-
ening speed to approach him.

Iskander was plunged in thought.

Ah! if you have ever been youthful in soul, if you
have ever loved with all your heart, and if, youthful and
loving, you have been going far away from the place
where lives your dear one, you will then understand
what feelings were uppermost in the breast of Iskander
Beg. It is folly, doubtless, to imagine that in breathing
the same atmosphere we have the same dreams; that in
gazing ten times at a window, although it be shut, we
bring away ten memories; but this folly is solacing.
Fancy is always more picturesque than fact: fancy is
poetry; it flies, light as bird or angel, and never are its
white wings sullied with either mud or dust from the
highway.

Fact, on the contrary, is prose: it plunges into details;

while clinging round the bride's fair neck it fails to note
the delicacy of her skin, but asks itself if the pearls of her
necklace are real or false, if she makes love to her husband, pets her dog, or gives money to the servants.

Ma foi! long live poetry!

Iskander was making very nearly the same reflections
as ourselves, — but he at least was making them at twenty-
five, which necessarily imparted to them both the colors
of the rose and the perfume of May-bloom, — when he
felt himself touched on the elbow by Yussef Beg.

"Well," he asked, emerging from his revery, "what is
it, Yussef?"

"Merely that, as we have not seen fit to stay in the
city with the living, I see no reason why we should remain in a cemetery with the dead. How I would burn
their graves, did not every stone appear to be rising, and
were not that she-devil of a gallows stretching out her
lean black hand toward us!"

"She is longing for you, Hadji Yussef; she fears that
you may escape her," laughed Iskander.

"I spit on the beard of him that put her there," said
Hadji Yussef. "Allah protect me! but whenever I pass
this place, good Mussulman as I believe myself to be, pure
of heart as I think I am, it always seems to me as if she
were about to clutch me by the throat; and avow the truth,
Iskander, confess that if we were not under Russian rule
we should not remain very long in the city, foot in the
stirrup and gun on the shoulder. Down with the
troops! Ah! but I should like to settle those troops, —
I would hack them into bits no larger than millet-seed!"

"Really, my dear Yussef, I did not know you were so
brave at night. At the time of Kasi Mullah's attack, I
saw how you fought in the day-time, or rather I did not
see you; were you not in Derbend?"

"Ah, now! my dear Iskander, you are always making fun of me! Did I not indeed in your own presence cut off the head of that Lesghian, who was so enraged against me that his head, after it had fallen to the earth, bit my foot so cruelly that I suffer from it to this very day every time the weather changes? What! seriously, did you not see that?"

"Allah denied me that pleasure."

"Besides, are those Lesghians men? Is it worth while to pit one's head against their balls? If I kill a Lesghian, it matters little; but, if a Lesghian kills me, Allah will find it difficult to fill my place. So, after I had killed that one, I thought it quite enough of hand-to-hand combat. I went into the citadel every day: I appropriated a cannon; yes, I constituted myself its artillery-man, I aimed it and I gave the gunner the order, 'Fire!' and then I saw some dancing in the group at which I had pointed my gun. Ah! Allah! I had great sport. I have never boasted of it, but I can say this to you as a friend; I am sure that I was the principal cause, in view of the damage that I did, of Kasi Mullah's raising the siege; and when you reflect that I have never received a single cross, not even that of Saint George — Eh! do you not hear something?" added the valiant Beg, shrinking against Iskander.

"What the devil could you hear in this place, except the whistling wind and howling jackals?"

"Cursed brutes! I could kill their fathers, mothers, and grandparents. What wake are they keeping now, I want to know."

"Perhaps they expect to feast to-morrow night on our carcasses. You know, really, Yussef, that the one that captures your nose will be in luck."

"Come, come, no sinful jesting, Iskander! Ill word

brings ill work. This is the very hour for brigands.
When night comes, the devils walk the highways.
Iskander, what if we should meet Mullah Nour?"

"Who is Mullah Nour?" said Iskander, as if he had
never heard the name that his fellow-traveller had just
pronounced.

"Not so loud, Iskander! not so loud, I beg of you in
the names of Hussein and Ali, or I swear I will not stay
with you. This cursed Mullah Nour has ears in every
tree; just when you are not thinking of him — crash! he
falls on your head like a thunderbolt."

"And then?"

"How 'and then'?"

"I ask, what happens afterwards?"

"Afterwards you are caught. He likes to laugh and
joke, but, you understand, with a brigand's pleasantry.
If he knows you to be miserly he will first take all that
you have in your pockets, without counting the ransom
that he will put on your head. From another, if he is
poor, he will take nothing; he will even give."

"What! he will give?"

"Yes, there have been such instances. Fine fellows
who are in love and who have not twenty-five roubles to
buy them a wife, — well, he gives them the money.
From some he will take in gold the weight of the shot in
his cartridges; of others still, he will demand as many
roubles as he can hold on the blade of his sword. 'What
would you have?' says he; 'I am myself a poor merchant,
and every trade has its risks, especially mine.'"

"But," laughed Iskander, "those whom he stops must
carry pipes instead of guns. Or is Mullah Nour made of
iron?"

"Of iron! Say rather of steel, my friend. Balls
flatten against him as against granite. Allah is great!"

"After what you tell me, Yussef, I am inclined to think that Mullah Nour is the devil in person. He must be the devil instead of a man, to be able to stop whole caravans."

"Ah! one can see, poor boy, that you have never heard anything but the crowing of your own cock! And who, pray, says that Mullah Nour has no comrades? Why, on the contrary, he is surrounded by a parcel of knaves who think it better to eat bread raised by others than to be at the pains of raising their own. Comrades! By Allah! he is not wanting for comrades. Why, I myself, for instance, have often thought of it. If I had no relatives, no inheritance to expect, brave and adventurous — But what is the matter now, Iskander? Where are you going at that gait? They say that night is the devil's day, and I am beginning to believe it, for this night is as black as hell. But answer me, Iskander; what are you thinking about?"

"I am thinking that you are a bad soldier, Hadji Yussef."

"I, a bad soldier? Aren't you ashamed to say such a thing to me? It is to be regretted that you were not present when I settled a band of brigands near Damascus. I can say without boasting that after I had saved them the whole caravan of pilgrims was at my feet, and with good reason, too. I killed so many that my gun waxed red-hot and went off of itself. As for my sword, it was in pretty shape; it had teeth like a comb. I left seven dead on the field of battle and took two alive."

"What did you do with them?"

"I burned them the next morning; they were in the way."

"That was savage, Yussef."

"What can you expect? I am as I am."

"And you can tell me such tales without blushing? Your musket had more conscience than you; it turned red, at any rate."

"You do not believe me? Ask Sapharkouli; he was there."

"How unfortunate that Sapharkouli died eight days ago!"

"True. As if he could not have waited, the fool! Well, well! but, according to you, I must be a poltroon. *Par Allah!* Set me face to face with a dozen brigands, and you shall see how I will settle them. Come, where are they? Point your finger at them, — but not at night. Oh! I don't like to fight at night. I want the sun to shine on my valor; and then, I have a habit of taking aim with my right eye."

"I cannot recover from my surprise, Yussef. A dozen brigands, and you will consider them your affair?"

"I will make a breakfast of them."

"Let day come, then, and may we meet a dozen brigands, — a round dozen. I promise to leave them to you, Yussef. I will not touch one, not even with the hilt of my dagger."

"My dear, never wish to see the devil, lest he immediately appear. Now, as brigands are devils, and as we are here on their ground, it is best not to invoke them. For that matter, it gets darker and darker. Satan must have made off with the moon. Cursed night! how it drags! Ah! help! help!"

"What ails you?"

"A brigand has caught me, Iskander! Let me go, demon!"

"Stand aside, and I will fire."

"Stand aside, stand aside! that is very easily said. I believe he has claws. He has got me as a hawk holds its prey. Who are you? What do you want? Come, friend, let us make terms."

Iskander approached Yussef.

"I suspected as much," said he. "Fear has big eyes; your brigand is a thorn bush. Oh, my dear Yussef, you ought to have ridden an ass to the fountain for water, instead of coming with me to get snow on the top of Schach Dagh."

"A bush? I swear that it was certainly a Lesghian or Tchetchen; but he saw me put my hand on my poniard, and he loosed his grip."

"He saw you put your hand on your poniard in such darkness as this, when you yourself say the devil has run away with the moon?"

"Those knaves are like cats; it is well known that they can see in the dark. Oh! my dear Iskander, what is that in front of us?"

"It is the river. What! with a nose like yours, can you not scent water? See, my horse knows more than you."

"Do you mean to cross the river to-night?"

"Certainly."

"Iskander, you are undertaking a very imprudent thing. Better wait till to-morrow, Iskander. It is no trifling matter to cross the river at this hour, and the Karatcha, too!"

Iskander was already in the middle of the stream.

Yet Yussef preferred to follow his companion rather than to stay behind; he plunged into the black river,[1] and, after exclaiming at the coldness of the water, after shrieking that he was being dragged down by the feet, after calling Allah to witness that he was a lost man, Yussef finally reached the opposite bank.

---

[1] Karatcha means black river.

The comrades resumed their journey and crossed successively the Alcha and the Velvet.

At daybreak they had reached the banks of the Samour.

The Samour flowed swiftly; they saw enormous boulders roll with the waves, and uprooted trees were following its current, floating on the surface like so many wisps of straw on a brooklet.

This time Iskander yielded to Yussef's advice, and halted.

The riders dismounted to give their horses time to rest, they themselves lying down upon their bourkas.

But Yussef was not the man to go to sleep without relating some of his daring deeds.

Iskander listened this time, neither interrupting him nor laughing at him.   He was falling asleep.

The one told of what had never taken place.

The other dreamed of what was to come.

At last, finding himself without support in the conversation, Yussef decided to go to sleep.

Iskander had been asleep a long time.

VII.

MULLAH NOUR.

It is delightful to be awakened by the sun's first ray, as it peeps through a silk curtain, and lifts the black covering of night from the face of the wife sleeping near you, as fresh as the dewdrop on the leaf. But it is more delightful still, after a short sleep, to open the eyes under a cloudless sky and find yourself face to face with the smiling countenance of Nature. The *fiancée* is always more beautiful than the wife; and what is Nature, if not the eternal *fiancée* of man?

Iskander slowly raised his eyelids, still weighted with dreams, and admired the splendid picture of the morning. All around him undulated the forest, rich with its Southern verdure; above his head glittered and smoked the snowy peak of Schach Dagh. At his feet rolled the noisy Samour, sometimes leaping in cascades, sometimes winding its waves into great coils, like a serpent writhing amidst the rocks.

On the banks of the channel where the river roared, the nightingale sang.

Iskander enjoyed a brief moment of enchantment; but just as the bird was renewing an interrupted song, a terrible snore from Yussef roused him to reality.

The sleeper's nose projected from his bourka, whose surface it overshot by two or three inches.

Iskander shook Yussef by the nose and awoke him.

"Hallo! Who goes there?" demanded Yussef, speedily opening his eyes. "Ah! it is you. May the devil fly away with you!" was his greeting to Iskander on recognizing him. "Is a man to be rung by the nose as a Russian official rings a bell to summon his aids? Know, Iskander, that when Allah favors a man by giving him such a nose, it is that he may command respect and admiration from others. I admire and respect my nose; share my sentiments in this regard, or we shall have a falling out."

"My dear Yussef, excuse me; but when I am in haste I seize a man by the first part of him that comes to hand. The first—I will even say the only part of you that I saw, the rest being hidden under your bourka—happened to be your nose, and I took hold of it."

"Iskander, my friend, some day we shall quarrel, and that day, I foresee, will be a sorry one for you. What the deuce was the matter? Out with it!"

"I was vexed at that confounded nightingale, whose singing interfered with my listening to your snore. Why, my dear Yussef, you snore so musically that, compared with the melodies that you play naturally in your sleep, the Georgian djourna's performance is like a penny trumpet's."

"Ah, yes, appease me now. But may you all your life feed only on the odor of roses, and have all their thorns in the soles of your boots, if ever—"

Iskander interrupted him.

"Do you not hear something, Yussef?" he asked.

Yussef listened uneasily.

"No, nothing," said he, after a pause; "nothing but the voice of the mullah at Seyfouri."

"Well, what says the voice, Yussef? 'Wake ye, faithful Mussulmans; prayer is better than sleep.' We

5

have a journey to make, Yussef; let us pray and be
setting forth."

Yussef yielded to the invitation, although with grum-
bling. It seemed to him that Iskander had yielded
ground in the discussion, — an event happening with
them so rarely that he would gladly have profited by
his comrade's frame of mind.

Having performed their ablutions and their prayers,
our travellers made ready to ford the river.

The water was not unusually high; yet it is admitted
by those who are acquainted with mountain torrents,
and especially with the Samour, that the fording of a
river is always more perilous than a battle.

Everything depends, in such a case, upon your horse;
if he makes a misstep, you are lost. But habit renders
travellers indifferent to these dangers, although, every
year, more than one is left at the ford forever.

Our two begs, thanks to their skill, to their acquaint-
ance with this sort of exercise, and especially to the
excellence of their horses, reached the opposite bank of
the Samour safe and sound.

Yussef, who had been as mute as a tench during the
whole time of their crossing, began to scold again the
very instant that he touched the farther bank.

"May the devil take this river!" said he; "I will
heave a pig at it! And to think that it is so dry during
the autumn and winter that a frog crossing it could not
manage to wash his feet!"

"Where shall we stop in Seyfouri?" inquired
Iskander, without heeding the tirades of his comrade,
who, the danger past, had already forgotten it. "I do
not know a living soul there; yet there our horses must
breakfast, and so must we."

"I will burn their beards with a wisp of straw, — the

blackguards!" responded Yussef. "It is very clear
that, without an order from the governor, not one of
them will offer us a drop of water, or even a radish, if
they see us drop down with hunger and thirst."

"The people of Seyfouri are neither better nor worse
than those of Derbend; but when it comes to that, we
are all Tartars."

"Here we are! we shall see. Perhaps with a little
money we can get something from them. As we ride
along, look well on your side into the courts; I will
keep watch on mine. Perhaps we shall come across a
grey-beard; the grey-beards are better than the red
ones. The grey-beard is a starost, while the red-beard
is a rich man. The red-beard almost always has money
and a pretty wife, — two reasons for shutting his doors
in the faces of two handsome fellows like us. And here
is just the man I was looking for. Hey! friend," continued Yussef, addressing a grey-beard, "can we rest an
hour at your house, and have a bite to eat?"

"Are you on government service?" demanded the
man, a tall, dark-hued Tartar.

"No, my friend, no."

"Have you an order from the governor?"

"We have money, nothing more."

"That is sufficient to obtain a welcome in my house;
I receive many lords from Khorassan, and, thanks be to
Allah, never have horse or horseman had reason to com-
plain of Agraïne."

The gates were thrown open; the travellers entered
the court, dismounted, unsaddled their horses, and gave
them oats.

Let us say, in passing, that the people of Daghestan
are remarkably neat, and usually have two-story houses
of brick white-washed with lime.

Agraïne's house was one of these. He invited his guests to ascend to the first floor.

Yussef required no urging, and led the way for Iskander.

At the door of the first room, Agraïne took their arms and set them against the wall, as a sign that, being in his house it was now his duty to provide for their safety.

This custom is so widespread that our two travellers opposed no resistance.

Within this room they saw nothing but a pair of woman's trousers.

Nothing so irritates an Asiatic, and, in general, a Mussulman, whoever he may be, as a question about his wife.

Hadji Yussef was dying to question his host about those trousers; but Agraïne was the owner of one of those faces that check raillery on the lips of the jester.

"Have you not a pinch of pilaff to offer us, my friend?" he asked the Tartar.

"The prophet himself never ate the like of that my wife used to prepare," answered Agraïne. "Allah! my guests wore out their fingers with licking them, it was so rich."

"What the deuce is he talking about?" demanded Iskander Beg of his companion.

"I don't know, but it seems to me that, speaking as he does of the past, the idiot thinks to regale us only with his wife's trousers."

"Why not?" said Iskander; "they are greasy enough for that!"

Then, to the Tartar, —

"Tell us, now, friend, is there any chance of our having a dish of soup and a bit of chislik? Here is bread and cheese, it is true; but the bread is very moist and the cheese very dry."

" Soup? And where should I get soup?" answered Agraïne. " Chislik? And where should I get chislik? Khan Muel has eaten my sheep to the very last. Ah! my wife, my beautiful young Oumi, used to prepare such delicious chislik!"

And the Tartar smacked his lips.

" And where is she, your young and beautiful Oumi?" asked Yussef.

" She is dead and buried," replied the Tartar, " and I buried my last fifty roubles with her; I have nothing left of her but her trousers, over which I weep."

And, in fact, the Tartar took up the trousers, which he pressed to his lips, and fell to weeping.

" A precious souvenir," remarked Yussef. " She must have been a charming woman, your lovely young Oumi. Give us each a glass of milk and we will weep with you."

" Milk? Oh! you should have seen my dear Oumi milking the cows with fingers whiter than the milk itself. But no more Oumi, no more cows; and no more cows, no more milk! and now — "

" Now you are beginning to weary us, my dear fellow, with your young and lovely Oumi. Fifty kopecks if you bring us each a glass of milk; if not, take yourself off."

And he thrust him out of the room.

" I will sell your mother for two onions, you villanous beast!" continued Yussef, returning to his seat near Iskander, and trying his teeth on the cheese. " All the cocks of the village are crowing in my stomach, and this scoundrel tries to entertain us with the trousers of his beautiful young Oumi. — Good! there he is now

meddling with our guns and gossiping with the passers-
by. — What do you mean by whispering to that vicious
Lesghian, like a Schummak Bayadere, you wretched
knave, instead of bringing us something to eat? So
help me, Allah! but I am hungry enough to devour
the fish that caused the universal flood by flopping from
the Ganges into the sea. Come, bring us something,
quickly!"

"Immediately," replied the Tartar.

And, indeed, he returned a few minutes later holding
in each hand a bowl of milk.

Our travellers dipped their bread into the milk, while
their host resumed his weeping where he had left off,
again contemplating his wife's trousers.

Having ended their frugal repast, Yussef threw down
sixty kopecks on the trousers of the beautiful young
Oumi, and, leaping to their saddles and taking the
mountain road, they had very soon left the village of
Seyfouri behind.

"Look back now," bade Yussef, always on the alert,
to Iskander. "The very Lesghian that the soft-hearted
Agraïne was talking to is keeping us in sight and watching where we go."

In fact, behind the two travellers, on a slight rise of
ground, they could descry the interlocutor of the Tartar
landlord.

But when the Lesghian discovered that he was himself
an object of interest to the travellers, he disappeared.

"Well, what of it?" demanded Iskander.

"I distrust these beggarly Lesghians, — that is
what!"

"According to you, every shepherd is a robber."

"As if shepherds were honest men in this country!
The mountaineers murder travellers and pillage cara-

vans, and the shepherds feed the mountaineers and receive
their booty. Mullah Nour's entire troop, entire gang,
rather, what is it? Made up of mountaineers. And
who feeds Mullah Nour and his gang? The shepherds."

" Well, what then? Are not Mullah Nour and his
mountaineers made of flesh and blood as we are? The
devil take me if you do not make me wish to meet this
bandit of yours, were it only out of curiosity, and to .
see whether, as you have said, his skin is proof against
a ball."

" Well, well, here we are back on the old subject.
You are either a dog or a pagan, however, to express
such a wish. Does it seem, then, such a burden to
carry your soul around in your body and a head on your
shoulders? May the devil seize my nose if I would
not rather meet a lion than this Mullah Nour. Why
—why do you halt?"

" If you had not been in such a panic, you would not
have lost your way. Look, pray, where you have
brought us. The devil could not pass here without a
lantern!"

And, indeed, the two found themselves upon a steep
mountain, forming, so to speak, the first round of the
ladder up Schach Dagh. Their way was becoming so
perilous, that our travellers were obliged to dismount
and lay hold of their horses' tails.

At length they reached a plateau, and, as usual,
Yussef, who had maintained silence in the presence of
danger, began as soon as the danger was over to curse
and swear.

" May the devil's tail hack this mountain into mince-
meat!". said he; " may all the wild boars of Daghestan
root holes into it! may an earthquake upset it, and may
thunderbolts grind it to powder, —curse it!"

"The fault is yours, and you lay the blame on the mountain," said Iskander, shrugging his shoulders. "What was it that you told me? 'I know the way as well as I know my mother's pockets; I will conduct you through the defiles of Schach Dagh as easily as I could make the rounds of the bazaar. I have played at hucklebones on every rock, and at pitch-penny in every cranny.' Did you or did you not say all that?"

"Certainly I said it. Did I not, three years ago, make the ascent of Schach Dagh's topmost peak? However, three years ago it was not so steep as now."

And, indeed, at the point where our travellers had now arrived, Schach Dagh rose before them, a sheer wall surmounted by white battlements; and the white battlements were snow.

The two men comprehended the impossibility of scaling the peak from that side.

They resolved to attempt the task from the east side. Yet it was easier to resolve than to execute. All was wild and lonely on those steep and rocky declivities; the eagles' cries alone broke the solemn stillness which seemed like that of the dead.

Iskander Beg turned toward Yussef and looked at him as if to say: "Well?"

"May a thousand million curses fall on the head of this miserable Schach Dagh! Ah! this is the way he receives his visitors, the ill-mannered pig! He pulls his bashlik over his ears, shuts himself within his walls, and hauls up his ladder after him. Where shall we go now? Over the mountain or under the mountain? I' faith, ask advice of whom you will, Iskander; as for me, I shall take counsel of my bottle."

And Yussef drew from his pocket a full flask of brandy.

"What a hardened sinner you are, you wretch!" exclaimed Iskander to his comrade. "Have you not enough folly of your own without adding that of wine?"

"This is not wine, it is brandy."

"Wine or brandy, it is all one."

"Not at all; observe the distinction: Mahomet has forbidden wine, but not brandy."

"I am aware of that; it was not invented in Mahomet's time: he could not forbid what did not exist."

"That is where you are wrong, Iskander. As a prophet, Mahomet knew very well that brandy would be invented later, or, if he did not know it, — why, he was a false prophet."

"No blasphemy, Yussef!" remonstrated Iskander, frowning; "let us seek, rather, our way."

"Our way? It is here," said Yussef, slapping his flask.

He approached the bottle to his lips, blissfully closed his eyes, and tossed off five or six swallows of the liquor whose orthodoxy was contested.

"Yussef, Yussef," said Iskander, "I can myself foretell one thing: with such a guide, you will more speedily attain hell than heaven."

"Well, what did I tell you, Iskander?" returned Yussef. "Before I had given that fraternal kiss to my flask, I could not see a single path; now, *brrruh!* I see a dozen of them."

"That may be, Hadji Yussef; I shall not follow your paths, however," said Iskander. "Take the right, take the left, take whichever you will; I shall attempt to climb straight ahead. If either of us finds a good way, he can return here and call the other, or wait for him. I shall take half an hour and give you as long for the quest. *Au revoir!*"

Hadji Yussef, animated by the five or six swallows
of brandy that he had taken, deigned no reply to
Iskander. He set out bravely to seek a path.

Iskander, therefore, leading his horse by the bridle,
began to ascend straight ahead, as he had said.

The day was drawing near its close.

VIII.

HOW YUSSEF REACHED THE SUMMIT OF THE MOUNTAIN SOONER THAN HE WISHED.

DIRECTLY above the spot where the two travellers separated, near the border-line of clouds and snow, arose an enormous rock.   On its flattened top men and horses found refuge.

Sixteen Tartars and one Lesghian were lying around a fire; as many horses as there were men were eating grass that had been mowed with poniards.

A few steps away, lying on a rug, was a man of about forty years, distinguished by the beauty of his countenance and its serenity of expression.

He was dressed very simply; yet — and this was indicative, not of wealth, but of the customs of a warlike life — gold and silver gleamed from his gunstock and from the sheath and blade of his kandjiar.

He was smoking a chibouk, and fondly regarding a sleeping youth, whose head was resting on his knees. At times he sighed, shaking his head, and again he would sigh heavily, casting an anxious glance around.

It was Mullah Nour, the scourge of Daghestan; the brigand, Mullah Nour, and his band.

Suddenly, a thousand feet below, he caught sight of Yussef, who, still seeking a path by which to scale the heights of Schach Dagh, was cautiously advancing amid the rocks.

Mullah Nour, resting on his elbow, watched the
traveller's movements a little while; then he smiled,
and bending down to the youth's ear, he said, —

"Awake, Goulchade."

Goulchade, in Tartar speech, means *the rose.*

The youth opened his eyes, smiling also.

"Goulchade," said Mullah Nour, "would you like
me to bow down to the earth before you?"

"I should like it very well," said the young man,
"and it would be a strange sight to see you at my feet."

"Softly, softly, Goulchade! Before the bee's honey
is the sting. Look down there."

The young man lowered his gaze in the direction
indicated by Mullah Nour.

"Do you see that traveller riding along?"

"Of course I see him."

"I know his name and his courage. He is as fearless as a leopard; he is the best shot in Derbend. Go
down, disarm him, and bring him to me. If you do
that, I will be your slave the whole evening, and before
all your comrades will I do you homage. Come, do
you consent?"

"Gladly," returned Goulchade.

And the young man leaped upon a wiry little mountain horse and set off by a narrow trail, which seemed
rather a line traced with a crayon than a road channelled
in the rock.

The stones could still be heard rolling from under his
horse's hoofs, when the rider himself was no longer
visible.

Mullah Nour's entire band peered over the rock,
curious to see what would happen.

The chief was more intent than all the rest.

Perhaps he regretted that he had exposed the youth

to this danger; for, when Goulchade was but a few paces from Yussef, his chibouk fell from his hands, and anxiety was portrayed on his countenance.

Hadji Yussef had no idea of what was happening, or rather, of what was about to happen. Stimulated by the few swallows of brandy that he had taken, he was endeavoring to keep his courage up by talking aloud, and was putting on as bold a front as Shinderhannes or Jean Shogar.

"Oh! ho!" he was saying. "No, it is not for nothing that my gun bears the inscription: '*Beware! I breathe flame.*' I will burn the beard of the first bandit that dares to cross my path. Besides, I have nothing to fear; my breastplate is proof against bullets. But where are these brigands now? They are hiding, the cowards! Doubtless they can see me. Allah! for my part, I detest cowards!"

And suddenly, having reached a turn in the path, as the last syllable came thundering from his mouth, he heard a gruff voice cry out, —

"Halt! and dismount!"

And as he lifted his head in great dismay, he perceived, ten feet distant, the muzzle of a gun pointed at his breast.

"Come, come, down from your horse, and speedily!" was ordered a second time, in a tone that seemed gruffer than the first. "Make no attempt to put your hand to your gun or schaska! If you try to fly, I shall fire. The gun first!"

"Not only my gun, but my soul, master bandit," replied Yussef, quaking. "I am a good fellow, incapable of harming any one whatever. Don't kill me, and I will be your slave. I will take care of your horse and brush your clothes."

"Your gun! your gun!" repeated the voice.

"There it is," said Yussef, laying it down upon a rock with trembling hand.

"Your other arms, now,—schaska! kandjiar! pistol!"

"Here it is," faltered the unhappy Yussef at each item of the command, simultaneously casting on the ground the weapon designated by the bandit.

"Now turn your pockets."

Yussef flung all his money down beside the arms, imploring the bandit's mercy while executing his orders.

"I will cut off your tongue and throw it to the dogs if you do not hold your peace," said Goulchade. "Be silent, or I will silence you forever!"

"Excuse me, master bandit; I will not speak another word, if that is your desire."

"Silence, I tell you!"

"I hear and obey."

But not until Goulchade had pointed a pistol at Yussef did he cease to talk.

Goulchade bound his hands, took up his arms, and made him walk in the direction of the plateau where Mullah Nour and his comrades were awaiting the end of the comedy.

After a quarter of an hour's climbing, Yussef stood before the chief of the brigands.

His comrades formed a circle round him; all maintained an ominous silence.

Goulchade laid Yussef's weapons at the feet of Mullah Nour.

Then Mullah Nour saluted Goulchade three times, bowing down to the ground, and the third time, he kissed the youth's forehead.

Then turning to Yussef, he demanded,—

"Do you know who disarmed you, Yussef?"

Yussef's whole frame shook at the sound of that voice.

"The bravest of the brave, the mightiest of the mighty! How could I prevail against him, before whom a lion would become a hare, and Goliath be as a child but eight days old?"

The bandits burst into laughter.

"Behold, then, the bravest of the brave, the mightiest of the mighty," said Mullah Nour, as he lifted the white papak from Goulchade's head.

And the long black locks fell down upon the shoulders of a girl, who became as pink as the flower whose name she bore.

Mullah Nour held open his arms to her, and she threw herself on the brigand's breast.

"Yussef," said Mullah Nour, "I have the honor to present my wife."

A wild burst of laughter greeted the ears of the unhappy prisoner.

He turned purple with shame, and yet, recovering himself, he said, —

"Do me a favor, master; do not sell me in the mountains. I can pay you a noble ransom."

Mullah Nour's eyebrows drew together as black as two thunder-clouds.

"Do you know to whom you are offering a ransom, skin of a hare?" he cried to Yussef. "Think you, wretch, that I am a Derbend butcher that I should sell spoiled meat for fresh? Do you suppose that I would demand gold for you when you are not worth an ounce of lead? Why should I sell you in the mountains? Tailless dog that you are, what are you good for? Not even to root the earth with your nose. You will tell me that you can, as well as any nurse or old governess, tell tales of ogres and giants to the little ones; but, for that, you must dress like a woman, and, instead of amusing the poor innocents, you would frighten them. Well, Yussef, you see that I know you; you see that I am not a flatterer. Now, do you in turn tell me what you think of me. I am Mullah Nour."

Upon hearing that terrible name, Hadji Yussef fell on his face to the earth, as if he had been struck by a thunderbolt.

"Allah!" said he, "you wish me to say what I think of you, how I regard you, — I who would be proud to perform my ablutions with the dust [1] of your feet? May Hussein and Ali preserve me!"

"Listen, Yussef," said Mullah Nour, "and bear this in mind: I have an abhorrence of giving the same command twice. I have asked you once what you think of me; I ask you a second time, but know that it is the last. I am listening."

"What do I think of you? May the devil crack my head like a nut, if I think anything of which you could complain. I, think ill of you? I, a cipher! I, a mere atom of dust!"

"Yussef," said Mullah Nour, stamping his foot, "I tell you that I have never repeated the same order thrice."

"Be not angry! be not angry, mighty Mullah Nour! Consume me not with the fire of your wrath. Your wish has transformed the ideas of my brain into pearls, but these pearls are mere glass in comparison with your endowments. What do I think of you, illustrious Mullah Nour? Well, since you insist, I will tell you.

[1] When water is not to be had, Mussulmans may perform their ablutions with dust or sand.

I think that your mind is a gun adorned with silver and gold; its charge is wisdom; it never misses fire and always hits the mark; I think that your heart is a flask of attar of roses, diffusing the perfume of your virtues on all around you; I think that your hand dispenses good broadcast, as the husbandman scatters grain; I deem your tongue a branch bearing flowers of justice and fruits of mercy. Even now I hear you say: 'Go home, my good Yussef, and remember Mullah Nour as long as you live.' Well, am I right, mighty man?"

"It were nothing to say that you are a great orator. But you are a false seer, and, to prove that you have lied, here is my·decision: Because you, a beg, allowed yourself to be disarmed, bound, and taken prisoner by a woman — "

"Is not Death herself a woman also," interrupted Yussef, "and more terrible than the most terrible of men?"

"Let me finish, Yussef; I shall not be long. Since whoever is afraid of death is unworthy of life, you shall die."

Yussef gave a groan.

"To-morrow will be the last morning of your life, and if you say a single word, if you put forth a single plea, if you utter one complaint," added Mullah Nour, putting his hand to his poniard, " you will not even see to-morrow. Come, let him be more securely bound, let him be taken to the cave, and leave him there alone. There he can talk at will and as much as he pleases."

Mullah Nour gave the signal, and poor Yussef was picked up and carried off like a sack of meal.

"He will die of terror before to-morrow," said Goul-chade to her lover. "Do not frighten him so, my beloved."

6

"Nonsense!" laughed Mullah Nour, "this will be a
lesson for him; he will learn, the craven, that fear
saves no one. The coward dies a hundred deaths;
the brave man only one, and even then he goes to
meet it."

Then, turning again to the bandits, he said, —

"My children, I am leaving you for an hour; if anything should happen to me, — if, by chance, I do not
return, — well, Goulchade could lead you. She has
proved to-day that she is worthy to command men. Ill
betide him who does not obey her! Adieu, Goulchade,"
he added, straining the young woman to his heart and
kissing her brow; "and I bid you adieu and embrace
you because I anticipate an encounter somewhat more
serious than yours. For a long time I have wished to
measure my skill with Iskander Beg's, and, thanks to
my noukar, I know where to find him. If I do not
return before night, follow my trail in the mountains
and endeavor to recover my body, that I may not be
eaten by jackals, like a dead horse. If you hear shots
and voices, let no one stir. If Iskander kills me, let
no one avenge my death. Let the man that kills Mullah
Nour be sacred to you, for he will be a brave man. I
go in pursuit; adieu."

He slung his gun across his back and departed.

IX.

THE PRECIPICE.

MEANWHILE Iskander Beg had found a path that wound around the mountain.

On his right dropped a precipice; on his left arose walls furrowed at intervals as by thunderbolts.

But there was no return for the dauntless traveller; he needs must always advance. The way was too narrow for a horse to turn, and he went forward.

At last he came to an overhanging rock, under whose arch he must pass.

Beneath its vault the road was missing, but a block of ice, dislodged from the mountain, constituted a frail, transparent bridge.

Below this bridge, at the bottom of the abyss, thundered a torrent.

The young man halted; for an instant he paled, and the perspiration dampened his brow; but a thought of Kassime restored his self-possession.

Then his practised eye observed a horse's tracks on the ice; he pressed his own forward, urging him on with knees and voice. By crossing swiftly, the strain would be less.

Behind, he could hear the broken ice crashing into the gorge.

At last he began to breathe more freely, perceiving at the farther end of the tunnel the light's increasing brightness from the reflection of the snow.

But suddenly, enframed in the opening, appeared a horseman whom the optical effect rendered of gigantic proportions.

"Halt, and throw down your arms, or you're a dead man!" cried the horseman to Iskander; "I am Mullah Nour."

In his first surprise at the unlooked for apparition, Iskander had reined in his horse; but, upon hearing the name of Mullah Nour, one danger made him forget the other.

He spurred on his horse, and, detaching the gun from his shoulder, he said, —

"You are Mullah Nour? Well, out of my way, Mullah Nour! You see very well that there is not room here for two."

"Let God decide, then, who shall pass," said the brigand, aiming his pistol at the breast of Iskander, who was not more than ten paces distant. "Shoot first."

"Shoot yourself. I am not hiding behind my horse, am I?"

They stood thus for some seconds face to face, each with his weapon raised, and waiting for the other to fire.

Then the one lowered his pistol, the other his gun.

"Well, you are brave, Iskander," said Mullah Nour, "and no one deprives a brave man of his arms. Give me your horse, and go where you will."

"Take my arms first, and then you shall take my horse; but as long as I have a load for my gun, as long as the soul remains in my body, the hand of dishonor shall not touch my horse's bridle."

Mullah Nour smiled.

"I do not need your gun, nor your horse," said he; "I merely wish you to do my will. Not for the sake of miserable plunder has Mullah Nour made himself a chief of brigands, but because he is accustomed to command. Then ill befall him that obeys not his command. I have many times heard you spoken of; often has your courage been extolled to me, and now I see for myself that you are brave, Iskander. But I did not cross your path for nothing. We do not part until our swords have crossed. That is my last word. Salute me; say, offering your hand, ' Let us be friends,' and the way is yours."

" Stay, this is my answer," said Iskander, carrying his gun to his shoulder and pulling the trigger.

But no discharge followed; doubtless a drop of water fallen from the arch had dampened the priming.

Enraged, Iskander swung back the gun, drew the pistol from his belt, and fired.

The ball flattened against the silver cartridge-boxes that ornamented Mullah Nour's tcherkesse.

The latter did not move; he folded his arms and replied by a mocking laugh to Iskander's rage.

" Oh, that shall not save you, brigand! " cried Iskander.

And, with schaska uplifted, he bore down upon Mullah Nour.

Mullah Nour's sword flashed from its sheath with the swiftness of lightning.

Iskander's blade whistled above the brigand's head, and the stroke descended like the wrath of God.

Then, with a rending crash, the icy bridge broke beneath the feet of the two combatants. Iskander's horse had upreared just as his master's sword was descending upon the head of Mullah Nour; but the brigand was not touched.

He had fallen into the chasm.

Iskander Beg, thrown over backward, had seized hold of a projecting rock; he clung to it with double tenacity upon feeling that his horse was for some cause sinking from under him. The ice-bridge had become an inclined plane, and the horse was slipping down its steep descent.

The animal made a supreme effort, gathered his whole strength into his hams, and, impelled by their steely springs, he cleared the yawning space and landed on the other side of the gulf, streaming with sweat, and quivering with terror.

Fortunately, Iskander had disengaged his feet from the stirrups. Encumbered by the rider's weight, the horse could not have cleared the abyss. Behind him, under him, the ice-bridge was crashing with a frightful sound. The gulf roared, as with the greed of a tiger devouring its prey; then a deathlike silence succeeded.

Iskander hung from the arch.

Below him, uncovered by the rupture of the bed of ice, a rock jutted upward, presenting a surface of two or three feet. All around it floated space.

Iskander felt his arms grow numb, his sinews snap.

He knew that he could not long sustain himself in that position; if his hold loosened, he was lost in spite of himself.

He calculated the distance with the cool eye of a mountaineer, straightened his arms to diminish this distance by their entire length, and let himself drop vertically upon the rock.

He stood on this granite pedestal like a bronze statue of Volition.

He was saved, at least for the time being; but to avoid dizziness, he was obliged to close his eyes for an instant.

He was not long in opening them again to note his surroundings and seek an issue.

This rocky excrescence, if it may be so called, was sloping on the outer side, slippery, crumbling in places, and yet practicable to the foot of a mountaineer.

Clinging with hands and feet, Iskander succeeded in achieving a semi-circle around the immense column.

He then found that he was on the farther side of the ravine.

To go back by the way that he had just come was impossible. It would have been like climbing a wall.

There remained, then, but the one recourse of descending to the foot of the precipice and then following the torrent until he should find a practicable path.

But Iskander Beg was tormented by one idea, — to learn what had become of Mullah Nour.

A brave man, after all, was Mullah Nour, out-and-out brigand that he was. If he were merely hurt, he must receive assistance; if dead, his body must be saved from the teeth of wild beasts.

For any one other than Iskander or a mountaineer born on the side of a precipice, such a descent would have been impossible.

Iskander undertook it.

The road, or rather the path, by which he had come with his horse, was cut off, as we have said, by a deep gorge spanned by the ice-bridge, which had broken from under the horses' feet. He gained the steep side of the gash-like cleft and made its descent, aided by the projections of its rugged surface.

It took more than an hour to advance a quarter of a verst.

At last he reached the bottom; then only did he dare to look above his head.

Mullah Nour, falling from a height of five hundred feet perhaps, had crashed through several bridges of ice, superposed one above another, and had ended by plunging into a vast bed of snow, from which the torrent gushed as from a glacier.

This snow, without possessing the firmness of rock or ice, could yet sustain a man's weight.

Iskander ventured upon it, at the risk of being engulfed. Only a pale, wan light penetrated the cleft. It was gloomy and cold.

He soon saw, by the line through the broken bridges above his head, that he must be nearing the spot where Mullah Nour had fallen.

The fall of horse and rider had indented an immense funnel in the snow.

Iskander carefully lowered himself into it and found resistance under his feet.

He had come upon the horse, whose neck was broken.

He searched for the man and found an arm. He drew the arm toward him, making the horse his vantage ground, and succeeded in drawing the body out of the snow in which it was buried.

Mullah Nour was like one dead, — his eyes were closed, he did not breathe.

However, no limb was broken; no serious wound was apparent. In accordance with the laws of gravity, the animal's fall had preceded the man's, clearing a path for him. The horse had saved the rider.

Iskander succeeded in loading the body upon his shoulders, in getting out of the snow-funnel, and gaining the bottom of the valley.

He rubbed Mullah Nour's face with his rough cloak; he slapped the palms of his hands and threw ice-cold water into his face.

Mullah Nour remained unconscious.

"Just wait," muttered Iskander; "if you are not dead, I know how to waken you."

He sat down, placed Mullah Nour's head upon one of his knees, loaded his pistol and fired beside his ear.

The report echoed like a clap of thunder.

Mullah Nour opened his eyes and moved a hand toward his kandjiar.

"Ah! I was sure of it!" murmured Iskander.

Mullah Nour's hand was unable to execute its design, and fell back at his side.

His eyes stared vacantly; his mouth essayed to articulate some sound, but his tongue would not obey.

At last he breathed a sigh; thought, returning to his brain, lighted up his eyes with the fire of intelligence. His gaze fixed itself upon Iskander; he recognized him, understood that to him he owed his life. With an effort he whispered, —

"Iskander Beg!"

"Ah!" said the latter, "this is very lucky. Yes, Iskander Beg, who is not willing that you shall die — do you understand? — because you are a brave man; because jackals and foxes are common, but lions are rare."

A tear sprang to the brigand's stern eye; he pressed Iskander's hand.

"After God," said he, "I owe you my life; to you, then, as to God, is due my eternal gratitude. It is not for my life that I thank you, but for your having endangered yours to save mine. Men have insulted, scorned, betrayed me; I owe them ill-will; I have paid them in hatred. Nature has endowed me with many wicked instincts; men have attributed to me more than nature gave; but neither my friends nor my

enemies can accuse Mullah Nour of being an ingrate.
Listen, Iskander," added the bandit, raising himself a
little, "misfortune follows every one; possibly it may
some day overtake you. My heart and hand are at your
service, Iskander, — a heart and hand that fear nothing
in the world. I would sell and cut off my head to save
you. For the rest, you shall judge me by my deeds.
Let us see now how much I am hurt."

The bandit tried to rise, and after a few attempts, he
found himself upon his feet. He felt of his arms, first
one and then the other; then his thighs, then his legs;
took a few steps, unsteadily, it is true, but still a few
steps.

"My head," said he, "is still a little light, but nothing is the matter with the rest of me, by my faith!
Come, let us go! Allah has preserved me! it would
seem that I am still necessary to his designs on
earth."

"And now," asked Iskander, "how do we get out of
here?"

"You are putting me to it," said Mullah Nour; "but
I am forced to say what is so hard for men to admit, —
I do not know."

"Yet we cannot die of hunger here," said Iskander.

"Before dying of hunger, we would first eat my horse,
then yours; for, as I was falling, although I could not
see much, I saw him ready to follow me."

"No, fortunately," said Iskander, with a feeling of
real joy, "my poor Karabach was saved. And hark!
by Allah! he is neighing!"

Both turned in the direction of the neighing, and
they saw the horse coming toward them, following the
bed of the stream.

"On my faith," said Mullah Nour, "you were asking

how we should get out of here; your horse is answering
us. He must be the devil if we cannot go up the way
he came down."

Overjoyed, Iskander went to meet his horse. The
latter, in turn, ran to his master as rapidly as the difficult road permitted.

When horse and master were side by side, the man
put his arms around the animal's neck and kissed him
as he would have kissed a friend. The horse whinnied
with delight; the man wept for joy.

" There," said Mullah Nour, who had looked on with
a smile, " now that the meeting is over, if you will ask
your horse the way, nothing need detain us here any
longer, it seems to me."

Iskander sent his horse ahead of them, as if he had
been a dog, and doubtless the animal understood the
service that was demanded of his intelligence, for he
took the very route by which he had come.

After nearly a demi-verst, he stopped, scented the
ground, cast a glance overhead, and, without hesitation,
began to ascend the mountain.

On looking carefully, they discerned a narrow path,
scarcely perceptible, worn by the wild goats when descending to drink at the torrent.

The horse went first.

" Follow my horse and lay hold of his tail, — I will
not say in case your head grows giddy, but in case your
legs fail."

But Mullah Nour shook his head.

"I am at home," he said; "the mountain is my
domain. It is for me to do the honors of my house;
go first."

Iskander followed his horse. At the end of half an
hour's almost impossible climbing, they found them-

selves upon the path which the bandit had taken in order to intercept Iskander.

Of course this path led to the platform where Mullah Nour had left Goulchade and her companions.

The sun was just setting. Goulchade and the brigand's comrades, not seeing him return within the time that he had fixed, were on the point of starting out to search for him.

Goulchade threw her arms about her lover's neck; his comrades gathered round.

But Mullah Nour put Goulchade aside, waved back his comrades, and made way for Iskander to enter within the circle of joyous faces, which overclouded at sight of him.

" This is my elder brother," said he to his fellows. " From this time forth you owe him three things which you have sworn to me, — love, respect, and obedience. Wherever he shall meet one of you, he may command you as I myself. Whoever shall render him a service, however small, becomes my creditor, and shall have the right to exact his price with usury. To the one who does him a great service, I shall be beholden forever; but if one of you shall harm a hair of his head, that one shall never be safe from my vengeance, even at the bottom of the sea, or within the tomb; I swear it, — and may the devil claw out my tongue with his nails if I do not keep my oath! Now let us sup."

A rug was spread and a scanty meal was served. The anxiety felt by the bandits concerning the absence of their chief had caused them to think little about supper.

Goulchade, according to the custom of the Tartar women, did not eat with her lover. She stood shyly back, leaning against a rock.

Iskander noted her tearful sadness; he asked that she should have a place on the rug.

"It is just," said Mullah Nour; "this day Goulchade has been a man, and not a woman."

The supper ended, Iskander, moved by the beauty of the summer night, touched by the brotherly attentions lavished on him by Mullah Nour, could not retain the secret that filled his heart. He told his love for Kassime.

"Oh!" he exclaimed, "if some time I could take wings like a bird, I would bring Kassime up to this height! I would show her all that makes me sad and ashamed to gaze upon alone, so beautiful it is! I should rejoice in her admiration, and when she would say, 'It is magnificent!' I should press her to my heart, answering, 'It is beautiful, but you are more beautiful; you are better than anything in the world! I love you more than the mountain, more than the valley, more than the streams, more than the whole of Nature!' See, Mullah Nour, how the earth, softly lighted by the moon, sleeps in the midst of Nature's myriad smiles. Well, I believe it to be sweeter still for man to fall asleep under the kisses of the woman he loves. You are very fortunate, Mullah Nour; you are as free as the wind. The eagle lends you his wings to fly among the highest peaks. You have a fearless consort; that does not surprise me, but I envy you."

Mullah Nour sadly shook his head as he listened to the young man speaking thus upon life's threshold.

"To every man his fate," he replied; "but mark me, Iskander, envy not mine, and especially follow not my example. It is dangerous to live among men, but it is sad to live without them. Their friendship is like the opium that intoxicates and puts to sleep; but, believe me, it is bitter to live with their hatred. It is not my own will, it is fate that has thrust me outside of their circle, Iskander. A stream of blood separates us, and it is no longer in my power to overleap it. That liberty is a gift from heaven, the most precious of all, I know well; but the outlaw has no liberty, — he has but independence. True, I am lord of the mountain; true, I am king of the plain; but my empire is peopled only with wild beasts. There was a time when I hated men, when I scorned them; to-day, my soul is sick of scorning and hating. I am feared, men tremble at my name; the mother uses it to still her crying babe; but the terror one inspires is but a plaything, of which, like all others, he quickly tires. Undoubtedly, there is a joy in humiliating men, in mocking at all they boast, in exposing their baseness by opening their whited sepulchres. It yields one a moment's pride; he feels himself more criminal, yet less contemptible than others. That feeling gladdens for an hour and saddens for a month. Man is wicked; but, after all, man is man's brother. Look about us, Iskander. How vast are the mountains! how green the forests! how rich the lands of Daghestan! yet there is not a cave in the mountain, not a tree in the forest, not a house in the plain where I can rest my head and tell myself, ' Here you can sleep tranquilly, Mullah Nour; here an enemy's ball will not find you in your sleep; here you will not be bound like a wild beast.' Your cities are peopled and often gorged with inhabitants; yet, rich or poor, every man has his place, his own roof to shield him from the rain, to shelter him from the cold. As for me, my bourka alone is my roof, my shelter, my cover. The town will not grant me even a bit of earth in which to lay my bones. Sorrow is like the wife of the kahn; she knows

how to tread on velvet carpets, but she must also know,
like the goat, how to leap from rock to rock. Sorrow
is my shadow, and, as you see, my shadow follows me
even here."

"You have suffered much, Mullah Nour?" Iskander
asked, deeply interested.

"Do not remind me of it, friend. When you pass
the gorge into whose depths I fell, and from which you
rescued me, do not ask whether it was lightning or
frost that ploughed the chasm in the granite, but pass
over quickly; the bridge is frail and may give way
beneath you. Flowers are planted in gardens, but the
dead are not buried there. No, I will not cast a gloom
over the morning with the storms of noon-tide. The
past is past; it cannot be changed, even by the will of
Allah. Good-night, Iskander. And God grant that
no one may dream what I have suffered in reality. I
will show you to-morrow the shortest way to reach
Schach Dagh. Good-night!"

And he lay down, wrapped in his bourka; the others
had been asleep for an hour.

Iskander waited long for sleep to come; he thought
much of the day's events and Mullah Nour's solemn
words.

Then, once asleep, he was troubled with the most
fearful dreams. Sometimes it seemed as if a ball were
piercing his heart, sometimes as if he were falling into
a bottomless abyss.

Our dreams are but memories of the way we have
come, — the confusion and excitement of past events.

There is but one dreamless sleep, — the deep sleep,
death.

X.

THE sun, tinting the mountain-tops, awoke Mullah
Nour and his men. All first prostrated themselves in
prayer, then they set about polishing their arms, curry-
ing their horses, and preparing breakfast.

"Your travelling companion spent a bad night,"
announced Mullah Nour to his guest, with a laugh.

"What! Yussef?" inquired the latter.

"Yussef in person."

"You know where he is, then?"

"I have an idea."

"I begged you twice yesterday to have him searched
for, but you gave me no answer."

"Because I knew where to find him."

"And where is he?"

"Fifty paces from here."

"What do you intend to do with him?"

"Nothing at all. I give him to you; you may do
what you like with him. Eh! my lads," continued
Mullah Nour, addressing his men, "carry our prisoner
something to eat, and say that Mullah Nour does not
wish to starve him to death."

Then he told Iskander how Goulchade had stopped
Yussef, forced him to surrender his arms, and brought
him back with her as a prisoner.

When breakfast was over, Mullah Nour took Iskander by the hand and held him to his heart, and cheek to cheek.

"You are at home here," said he; "I shall always greet you with joy, I shall always love you with gratitude. Now I have pointed out a route by which you can ascend Schach Dagh, and the one by which you are to descend; make haste to serve your fellow countrymen. I myself am going in the opposite direction and for another purpose. Adieu! remember Mullah Nour; if you are in need of a friend, summon him, and the avalanche will not more swiftly reach the mountain's foot than he will reach you."

And, like a flight of wild pigeons, the chief and all his band whirled out of sight.

Iskander then went to the cave.

Yussef was lying down with his hands tied, his eyes bandaged.

The young beg could not resist the desire to experiment on the courage of his companion.

"Get up, and prepare to die!" said he, roughly, disguising his voice.

Yussef trembled in every limb; but, thanks to a strenuous effort, he managed to get upon his knees.

He was deathly pale; his nose seemed to have lost that firm base by whose help it ordinarily formed an acute angle with his mouth, an obtuse angle with his chin, and drooped inert over his lips. He raised his hands to heaven and implored pardon between his groans.

"O Angel Azraël," he cried, "spare my head, it is not ripe for death! Where and how have I offended you?"

"It is not my will, it is Mullah Nour's. He said:

7

' Yussef fought like a tiger; now that Yussef knows my
retreat, there is no more safety for me in the mountain.
Besides, the blood of my comrades spilled by him at
the siege of Derbend cries aloud for vengeance, and it
must be taken.' "

"I!" cried Yussef, "I! I fought in the siege of Derbend? What abominable calumniator says that? Shame
befall the tomb of his fathers and of his grandfathers,
even to the tenth generation! No, no! I am not the
man to fight against my compatriots, not I.   When
trumpet or drum called to the rampart, for my part I
descended at once to the bazaar; and when it was my
turn to march, I took refuge in the mosque and slept
there honestly and conscientiously, to the glory of the
prophet.   True, one day I fired three shots; but it is
an established fact that the enemy was five versts away.
As for my sabre, try yourself to draw it, and if you can
get the blade out of its sheath, you may strike off my
head with it.   Not once, since the days of my father,
has it ever been out.   And why should I have fought
against Kasi Mullah, against a brave, a holy man, a
prophet? Had he not cut off the heads of all who drank
and smoked, I should be to-day one of his most ardent
fanatics."

"That may be; but there is a religious side to Mullah
Nour's wrath against you; he knows that you are a
partisan of Ali, and he has sworn to slay all who believe
in Ali."

"A partisan of Ali, I? Why, I would pluck him
by the beard, this Ali and his twelve caliphs! What
is more, if I had lived in Egypt in the time of the
Fatimites, I should not have rested until I had dragged
them from the throne.   I am a Sunnite, pray understand, a Sunnite, heart and soul! Who is he, this Ali?

An atom of dust, — I give a puff and it flies away; a grain of sand, — I crush it under foot as I walk."

"But, above all, look you, the thing Mullah Nour will never forgive you is your friendship for Iskander, his mortal enemy."

"My friendship!" cried Yussef.

"Was it not a proof of friendliness, then, your accompanying him to Schach Dagh?"

"Of friendliness, no doubt, directed especially toward my own pleasure."

"Well, the affair has ended rather worse for him than for you, and his head has fallen before yours."

"His head has fallen?" echoed Yussef. "Ah, well, it was no great loss, that. His head was not of much account. But instead of bearing me ill-will, Mullah Nour ought to thank me, since it was I who brought him Iskander, who delivered him up, bound hand and foot. Iskander my friend? A precious friend he is now! but when he was alive, I would have exchanged him for a piece of gingerbread. Iskander my friend! one of the greatest rakes in Derbend, who ate ham with the Russian officers? He my friend? I would burn his mother's beard."

"Wretch that you are! Leave the dead in peace. If fear had not turned your head, you would reflect that his mother couldn't have a beard."

"No beard? Why, I tell you, myself, that she used to shave. Allah! the number of razors that she broke! Iskander's friend? I? — why, would I have been such a fool as to make a friend of a man whose father was a brigand, whose mother was a lunatic, and whose uncle made boots?"

"I am tired of hearing you perjure yourself, renegade! liar! tongue of a dog! Bend your neck, the sword is raised!"

Iskander made his schaska whistle around Yussef's head; but instead of touching him with its blade, with his usual skill he lifted on its point the handkerchief that bandaged his eyes.

Yussef, terror-stricken, looked at his pretended executioner and recognized . skander.

He uttered a cry and sat stupefied.

" Well, and what do you see, you wild boar stuffed with folly ? Come, tell me again that my father was a brigand, my mother was a lunatic, and my uncle made boots ! "

Yussef, instead of seeking pardon and looking confused, burst out laughing, and threw himself upon Iskander's neck.

." Ah ! then I have managed to put you in a rage. There was no lack of skill on my part. It took a long time, but I succeeded at last. Ha ! ha ! snare a nightingale, and catch a crow ! Why, do you think that, with the very first word, I did not recognize your voice, — your voice, the voice of my best friend ? Why, I should know it amidst the crying of jackals, the miauling of cats, and the barking of dogs ! "

" Very well; you knew me ? "

" Do you doubt it ? " .

" No; you scoffed at me. "

" Just for a laugh, a joke, — for nothing else; you understand, surely ? "

" But how about your surrendering to Mullah Nour's wife ? How about your letting her disarm you ? "

" Do you not recall having seen at the house of the commandant of Derbend an engraving which represents a very beautiful woman indeed, unlacing the breastplate of a beg called Mars ? Underneath, it says in. Russian : *Mars disarmed by Venus.* That is the reason why I allowed myself to be disarmed, my dear friend. Why, to such a beautiful creature I would have given up everything, Iskander, from my bourka to my heart. I would like to know what you would have done, you rogue, on meeting her face to face. Such a nose! such eyes! and a mouth no bigger than the hole in a pearl bead! And her figure, too! A connoisseur like you would have noticed her figure. I longed to rob her of her belt to make me a ring."

"And so it was for love that you let yourself be bound, and that is why you followed her at the end of a rope?"

"I would have followed her at the end of a hair."

"Perhaps; yet one thing is very certain, — you will not talk in Derbend, and especially in my presence, of your devotion to Goulchade."

"Goulchade? Her name is Goulchade? What a charming name! But you are the one that is making me prate; that is the reason why I have not asked how you chance to be here."

Iskander briefly related what had passed between him and Mullah Nour. When he reached the point of the brigand's fall over the precipice, Yussef interrupted him.

"Then he must be dead?" said he.

"No."

"What! not dead?"

Iskander told how he had saved Mullah Nour and returned him to his men.

"Then he is there, this dear Mullah Nour?" demanded Yussef.

"No, he has gone away."

"Where?"

"On an expedition."

" You are very sure of it ? "

" I have seen the dust flying after his last horseman."

" And he fell from a height of five hundred feet, say you, and the devil did not break his neck ? and he did not shatter his arms and legs into a thousand pieces ? I shall spit on the gun of that brigand yet. Ah! if he had come to bar my way himself, instead of sending his wife, I should have taught him how to write the word *brave*. But he did not dare, the coward ! "

" Come, come, be silent, you braggart ! Why, if you had met Mullah Nour in person, you would have left off lying and boasting, for you would have been frightened to death. "

" Frightened ! I ? Learn, my dear Iskander, that there is but one man in the whole world that can make me afraid, and he is the man I see in the mirror when I look at myself. "

This time Iskander could not contain himself. The gasconade was so strong, even for a Tartar, that he burst out laughing.

" Come," said he, " enough of this. You have just taught me something new about yourself, and yet I thought I knew you very well. To horse ! and away, brave Yussef ! "

" You know the road ? "

" Yes; Mullah Nour pointed it out to me."

" Well, go ahead and I will follow you, and he shall fare ill that attacks us in the rear."

Iskander took the path which the bandit had shown him.

Watching them from below, one would certainly not have thought that human beings would venture on such a road.

When they had reached the snow line, Iskander gave

his horse to Yussef to hold, and he alone, jar in hand, began to scale the highest peak.

For the first time, this virginal snow was receiving the imprint of a human foot.

Iskander prostrated himself upon the peak where, hitherto, only the angels had prayed.

When he lifted his head and gazed about, he looked upon a land of marvellous beauty.

Before him ran down the whole chain of mountains which extend from the Caspian Sea to the Avari; his sight penetrated the depth of the valleys, where he saw rivers as shining and slender as silken threads.

All was calm and silent. Iskander was too far distant to be able to distinguish either men or animals; too high up to hear a sound.

He might have remained a long time admiring the splendid spectacle, had not the atmosphere, totally free at this height from all terrestrial vapors, been too rare for human lungs.

The young beg's every artery began to throb, as if the blood, not being sufficiently compressed by the air, were ready to issue from the pores.

He then bethought him to acquit himself of his mission, and in his profound faith that everything was possible to the God between whom and himself nothing seemed to intervene, he formed a ball of snow, placed it in his vase, and began to descend, holding the vessel high above his head, in order that, in accordance with the decree, it should not be sullied by contact with the earth.

The descent was as difficult as the ascent, in a very different way; but throughout the entire expedition, a higher power had seemed to watch over Iskander.

At the end of almost an hour he found himself beside Yussef.

Yussef questioned him, but Iskander shook his head.

Yussef tried to engage him in jest, but Iskander gravely pointed to the sky.

He was descending to the plain, full of the sublimity of those tall summits.

"Umph!" said Yussef, "you must have taken a bite of the sun up there; you seem afraid of dropping a morsel if you open your mouth."

But Yussef spoke in vain; he did not succeed in extracting a single word from Iskander.

He finally became silent in turn.

In spite of all their haste, our travellers did not arrive at Derbend until far into the night, and long after the gates had been shut.

Iskander's heart beat as if it would rend his breast; fear, doubt, hope, challenged each other with every throb. He hung the jar on a branch of a tree, and moodily regarded, sometimes the black wall, which separated him from what he held dearest on earth, sometimes the heavens, which seemed to be frowning at him. He appeared to be asking all Nature: "Must I fear? May I hope?"

Ere long he saw with joy that clouds were gathering in the sky and stealing over the brilliant face of the moon.

Overjoyed, he plucked the sleeping Yussef by the arm and exclaimed, —

"Look, Yussef! look at these clouds scudding across the heavens, hurrying like a flock of sheep!"

"A flock of sheep!" muttered Yussef. "Pick out the tenderest, and take the ramrod from my gun to make chislik out of him. I am literally dying of hunger."

"Listen to the animal," said Iskander; "he never thinks of anything but his stomach. The sheep that I

am talking about are in the clouds, Yussef; it is going
to rain, my friend."

"Ah!" murmured Yussef, "if that meant larks, I
would get under the spout, with my mouth wide open,
too!"

"Well, sleep then, brute, for there is a proverb that
says: 'Who sleeps, dines.'"

"Good-night, Iskander!" said Yussef, yawning.

And he went to sleep on his bourka. As for Iskander,
he did not close his eyes during the night, nor did he
cease scanning the heavens, which became more and
more overcast.

At daybreak the gates of Derbend were opened, and
in a brief space of time it was known throughout the
town that Iskander had arrived with the snow from
Schach Dagh.

After a short prayer, the mullahs, accompanied by
the people, led the way to the sea.

Iskander modestly bore the vessel containing the
melted snow; but Yussef, the centre of an immense
crowd, narrated with great gusto the events of their journey. Only, in Yussef's story, Iskander wholly disappeared. As for himself, Yussef, he had gone so near to
heaven as to hear the snoring of the seven sleepers and
the voices of the houris. He had suffered horribly from
the cold; but, fortunately, he had got warmed up in a
fight with two bears and a serpent of frightful dimen-
sions. He had wished to bring home the serpent's
skin, and had flayed it for that purpose; but his horse
was so terribly afraid of it that he was obliged to
abandon it on the way. However, he knew exactly
where it lay, and, on the morrow, he would send the
muëzzin to fetch it.

But, however interesting Yussef's tales might be, he

had not a single auditor when the time came for Iskander
to turn the water from his jar into the sea.

Since early morning a high wind had been blowing;
but the wind brought no rain,— not one drop of water
fell.

When, after a long prayer by the mullah, Iskander
was ready to empty his jar into the Caspian, he turned
to Festahli, who was walking in the front rank, and
said, —

" Remember your promise."

" Remember the conditions," Festahli in turn replied.
" Your fate lies not with the snow, but with the rain.
If you are dear to Allah, you are very dear to me."

Iskander elevated the jar above his head, and in the
sight of all he poured the snow-water from Schach Dagh
into the sea.

Immediately, as if by magic, a great tempest arose;
clouds, which seemed charged with rain, blackened
the sky; thunder was heard rumbling in the distance;
the leaves, violently agitated by the wind, shook off the
dust which covered them. Young Tartar girls peeped
brightly from the veils which the wind tried to snatch
from their heads. The hands of all were outstretched
to feel the first drops of the rain so impatiently awaited.
At last a flash rent the dome of clouds amassed above
Derbend, and it seemed as if all the windows of heaven
had opened at once in another deluge.

A torrent of rain poured from the clouds and flooded
the land of Daghestan.

This time no one dreamed of fleeing, no one thought
even of opening his umbrella.

Not joy, but delirium, possessed the people.

Papaks flew up into the air and fell back into the
water; prayers and shrieks of delight joined in flight to

heaven.   They hugged each other, they congratulated
each other, they gazed at the water which was descending like a giant waterfall, or rather, like a hundred
waterfalls, from Tartar city to Russian city, and leaping
from the citadel into the sea.

Iskander alone felt more joy within himself than all
the other inhabitants of Derbend put together.

For him, a wife was coming down from heaven with
the rain.

XI.

TWO HOLY MEN.

YOUTH — what is it without love? Love — what is
it without youth?

The fire burns readily in pure air, and what air is
purer than the breath of spring?

True, the walls of Mussulmans' courts are high, and
the locks of their gates are strong; but the wind blows
over the walls and through the key-holes.

The hearts of beautiful women are well protected, —
they are kept behind the padlocks of a thousand prejudices; but love is like the wind, — it easily finds a
passage.

Kassime was already in love without the courage to
confess it. Iskander Beg had the most of her thoughts
by day and the most of her dreams by. night; while
embroidering in advance with gold, as every young
Tartar girl does, the pistol-case for the *fiancé* whom
she did not know, Kassime kept saying to herself, —

" Oh! if this might be Iskander's! "

Judge, then, of her joy when her uncle came officially
to announce that she was the promised bride of this
handsome young man!

She became redder than a cherry, and her heart began
to beat like a wild dove's.

And so her dearest and most secret wishes were to be
realized.

From that moment, her nameless hopes were called
Iskander; from that moment she could receive with
pride the congratulations of her companions, and, in her .
conversations with them, she, too, could speak of her
future husband.

As for Iskander, he did not feel the earth under his
feet, and to console himself for not being allowed to
see his promised bride, he thought of her incessantly.

" She will work here on this rug; she will drink out
of this cup; she will refresh her rosy cheeks with the
water from this silver ewer; she will sleep under this
satin coverlet."

Into those countries of the Caucasus that follow the
religion of Ali, there frequently come priests and
mullahs from Persia to expound the Koran and recount
the miracles of their imáms.

This, as a rule, takes place in the month of May.

Beginning with the first day of this month, the
Shiites celebrate the death of Hussein, Ali's son, who,
after the death of his father, rebelled against Yazíd,
son of Moawyah, with the intention of seizing the
caliphate; but engaging in battle with Obaid Allah,
Yazíd's general, he was killed in the combat. The
Shiites celebrate the anniversary of this event with great
splendor. The fête takes place at night, by the light of .
numberless torches; and this time, coming from Tabbas
to direct the fête, Mullah Sédek had remained in Derbend throughout the entire month of May.

Mullah Sédek was a man of forty years, affecting
extreme dignity, for which reason he walked as slowly as
a man of seventy,—in a word, for twenty paces round
him he exhaled the odor of sanctity and attar of rose.

And yet, while Sédek's eyes were raised to heaven,
he never quite lost sight of earth. He had few friends;

but as soon as a man came to him with money in his hand, that man found a welcome. He had reaped a rich harvest of presents at Derbend, but it was his desire to carry away something else besides money and jewels. He thought of marrying, and after having secured information as to the best matches in the city, he made overtures to Hadji Festahli, with respect to his niece, whom he knew to be richly endowed.

He began his overtures by flattering Hadji Festahli, and as vanity was the weakness of Kassime's uncle, Sédek had, in a short time, come to be his most intimate friend.

"Ah," said Sédek, "the end of the world is not far distant now. Houtte, the fish on whose back the universe rests, is weary of bearing, along with the weight of men, the otherwise heavy burden of their sins. The Mussulmans are corrupt: they worship money; they wear decorations in their button-holes and ribbons of many colors on their swords. Truly, I know not what would have become of Derbend when she was threatened by the Lord, if you had not been there to act with your virtues as a counterpoise to the crimes of the people. You are a pure man, a respectable man, a holy man, a true Shiite; you are in league with neither the Armenians nor the Russians. The only thing I will not and cannot believe is that you are marrying your niece to this wretched Iskander, who is as poor as a dervish's dog. When I heard that report I said to myself: 'It is not possible! A man like Hadji Festahli would not cast the pearl of the prophet into the mud; he will not give his brother's daughter to the first-comer.' No, I am sure it is either a lie or a jest."

"And yet, it is the truth," admitted Festahli, quite embarrassed.

And he told Sédek the whole story; how Iskander had made his conditions, and how he himself had been obliged to consent to this marriage.

"I can say with truth," he added, "that there are in Derbend no eligible young men with fortunes; the rich men, as if by a curse, are all old."

Mullah Sédek stroked his beard and said: "All is from Allah! all shall return to Allah! Are there no true worshippers of Hussein in the land of Iran? The sun rises and sets twice each day in the great king's empire, and there is where you should choose a husband for your niece. O holy prophet, if you would mate the moon with one of the most glorious stars of heaven, I will send you my nephew, Mir Heroulah Tebris. He is intelligent and handsome; he is so rich that he does not know the number of his pearls and diamonds, and yet he is as shy and modest as a girl. When he passes through the bazaar, every one bows, and it is who shall provide him with fruits, with cakes, with raisins. There is no danger of a single visitor's presenting himself at his house without a present. If ever your niece becomes his wife, you can rest assured that she will have the first place in the baths of Tabbas."

This proposition was all the more pleasing to Festahli as it must destroy the hopes of Iskander, whom he could not endure.

However, he had scruples against thus breaking a sacred promise.

He therefore told Sédek that if such a transaction could be brought about, he would be rendered the proudest and happiest man in the world; but it was to be feared that Kassime's mother might not approve. Then, too, the commandant of Derbend would certainly not permit a native of his own town, and consequently a

Russian, to wed a Persian. And, besides, what would the people of Derbend say ?

" *What will people say?* " has some weight in Paris or at Saint Petersburg; but on the shores of the Caspian Sea, in the Orient, it is an afterthought of one who has forgotten his first.

" ' What will they say ? ' " replied Sédek, banteringly. " Why, they will say that you are a man of judgment! To commit faults is pardonable, — to repair them, praise-worthy ; and, to be frank, what has this Iskander done that is so wonderful ? Do you really believe that his snow brought the rain ? Let me manage the thing, and I will show you how this affair can be arranged. In the meantime, give out that your sister is dangerously ill, and that, in fear of death, she has sworn to marry her daughter to none but a descendant of the prophet, to an imám. Your sister never leaves her room; in her room, even, she is as dumb as a fish : do not consult her. Have you not read in the sacred books how Job beat his wife when she counselled him to make friends with the devil ? Besides, is Kassime's mother your wife ? What is she to you ? A sister; that is all. Then spit upon her caprices."

" And the commandant ? " said Festahli, smiling.

" What can the commandant do ? And then, cannot the commandant be tricked ? What hinders your getting a passport to go to see your relatives in Persia ? "

Festahli consented, or rather; he had already consented long before.

The next day they sent back to Iskander the *kalmi*, or wedding-present, which he had already given to his betrothed.

The young man, not being able to tear his hair, very nearly tore off his ears. For a long time he could not

believe in this insult.   But the bag, with the money it
contained, was certainly there, under his very eyes.
The old aunt could make nothing of it, and she pitied
him with all her soul.

Iskander was overwhelmed.

He reviewed in his mind every means of avenging
himself on Festahli without breaking the Russian laws.
Ah! if there had been a khan at Derbend instead of a
colonel!   One thrust of a dagger, all would have been
said, and Kassime would be his own.

But he must not think of such a measure, expeditious
though it was.

Iskander became moody, and spoke no more than a
dead man.   He did not see Hadji Yussef, who had been
standing in front of him a long time.

Apart from his cowardice and lying, Hadji Yussef
was truly an excellent man.   He was really moved by
his friend's grief; he would have wept, had he known
how.

" Why, what is the matter, my dear Iskander?" he
asked.

" What is the matter yourself? what do you want of
me?" demanded Iskander, frowning.

" I came to tell you that three vessels loaded with
grain have arrived, and the people are well pleased.   It
is good news, Iskander."

" If you had come to tell me that three vessels loaded
with poison had arrived, the news would be better
still."

" Oh! oh! it is cloudy weather, is it?   Come, tell
me what vexes you."

" Why should I tell you?   As if you did not know
already.   As if all Derbend did not know, for that
matter."

8

"Is it true that Kassime's mother refuses you for a son-in-law?"

"Her mother?"

Iskander burst into a laugh that made Yussef shiver.

"Her mother? No; it is that wretch, Festahli," said he; "but I will kill him!"

"It is easily seen that you have eaten bread on the mountains, my poor Iskander. It is not difficult to kill a man and run away; but, to the end of life, all thought of returning to one's native town must be given up. For my part, I advise you to content yourself with a good drubbing; afterwards, you can tranquilly retire to Baku. If you absolutely wish to take a wife, well, you can get married there for three months; it will cost you twenty-five roubles. It is a magnificent invention, especially for travellers, that sort of marriage. I have tried it. I was married one day, just as I am, for six weeks only. I lacked the patience to serve out my time; I ran away at the end of a month. When asleep, I was in constant fear lest my wife should bite off my nose, she was so crabbed and spiteful. Try it, and I will wager that on your return you will bring me a present by way of thanks."

Iskander continued pensive and silent.

"My dear heart, my handsome lily, my proud palm, Iskander," resumed Hadji Yussef, "do you not hear me? are your ears full of water? A bride! i' faith, a little matter that, a bride! Take a handful of roubles, go and show them in the Derbend market, crying, 'A bride! a bride!' and brides will flock around you like chickens."

Iskander still maintained silence.

"But what is there about it, then, to grieve you so, Iskander. The devil! that Kassime of yours is no star.

In the first place, one of her eyes is larger than the other, and then she is so black that she will ruin you in the one item of Spanish white. I can even add that she is slightly hump-backed. Don't contradict me, I know her, I have seen her."

Iskander heard this time; he seized Yussef by the throat.

"You have seen her! Where have you seen her? how did you see her? when? in what place did you dare raise your basilisk eyes to her? Why don't you answer me, wretch?"

"How can I answer you? you are choking me! Oh! in Allah's name, let me go! Can't you see that I am joking? You know very well that I keep my eyes in my pockets, and my pockets have no holes, thank God! And when could I have seen her, why should I have looked at her? Do I not know that she is the promised bride of my best friend? Never marry, Iskander; you are really too jealous for a man that is on good terms with the Russians. You would be obliged to stand guard all night, and to spy all day upon those who came to visit you. For that matter, I cannot see how they manage, these devils of Russians; they are not in the city ten days before they have already made friends with every one of our beauties. You know Mullah Kasim? — bless God; but he is jealous, that fellow; well, he bought himself a charming wife. As he had paid dearly enough for her, he determined to keep her to himself. His wife had but one friend in the world, — a woman could not have less. Three times a week the friend came to Mullah Kasim's house; he himself conducted her to his wife and stood guard at the gate, lest the two women should come upon the balcony and look down into the street. Do you know who that friend was? It was a young Russian ensign who had as yet no beard."

Iskander clutched Yussef's arm, but not in anger this time.

"A man dressed as a woman?" said he. "Yes, that might really be possible indeed. Thanks for your story, Yussef; it is very amusing."

"That is right. Well, now that you are in a better humor, I will leave you. I have a heap of business. This evening I represent the French ambassador at Yazíd's court. I must try on my tight trousers; I am afraid I shall not be able to get into them. May the devil make himself a jacket of a Russian's skin for having thought of inventing these damned pantaloons! Now, if I meet a cock, he may as well stand still, — I shall get his tail for a plume. You will see, Iskander, how haughty I shall be when I appear on the scene. Every soldier greets me with: ' We hope you are in good health, your Highness.' Adieu! I have no time to lose if I wish to be admitted."

And Yussef departed, throwing the sleeves of his tchouka back over his shoulders, that he might walk the faster.

Iskander sat alone, pensive, but smiling in his revery. The anecdote related by Yussef had given rise, in the midst of his garrulity, to an idea which was nothing less than to take advantage of the fête which they were then celebrating, — a kind of Mussulman carnival, — to disguise himself as a woman and approach Kassime.

Let us say forthwith that nothing adapts itself to such a disguise more readily than the Tartar costume, with its wide trousers, arkalouke, and immense veil.

After he had decided upon this step, Iskander ceased to despair.

"Ah, I shall see her," said he, " and she shall be mine! Then, Festahli, you shall know what it means to awaken a tiger. Kassime, Kassime, expect Iskander, even if the road between us were paved with daggers ! "

And, on the instant, Iskander set off for the bazaar, and purchased a woman's complete costume, pretending that it was a present for his *fiancée*.

Returning home, he despatched his noukar, whose indiscretion he feared, to the meadow with the horses; then, as soon as the noukar was gone, he shaved off all his beard, which, for the matter of that was· barely beginning to grow; he stained his eyelids, painted his brows, put on some rouge and donned the trousers, arkalouke and veil; he practised the gait of the Tartar women in his new costume, retaining his bechemette so that he might be in masculine attire in case of necessity for attack or defence.

He awaited the evening impatiently; but the day, like a rich uncle, could not make up its mind to die.

At last, the gong beat for prayer, and the theatre was lighted.

Then Iskander placed on his cheeks two indispensable little spangles of gold, slipped his kandjiar into his girdle on one side and his pistol on the other, enveloped himself from head to foot in an immense white veil, and set out, carrying a little lantern in his hand.

At the end of a quarter of an hour, Kassime issued forth with two friends; all three were on their way to see the religious drama which was being enacted at Derbend in honor of the death of Hussein, and which very much resembles the Mysteries which the Brothers of the Passion used to perform in France during the Middle Ages.

Both streets and public squares were full of people

afoot and on horses; for it is remarkable that at out-of-
door performances in the Orient, no matter how crowded
the spectators may be, at least a third of them is on
horseback. This third circulates about, goes and comes
without concerning itself as to the feet it crushes or the
shoulders it injures. It is the pedestrian's business to
get out of the way and take care of himself. His only
due is the Circassian warning, "*Kabarda! karbarda!*"
uttered from time to time, and equivalent to our own
"look out, there!"

The house-tops, the only points inaccessible to the
horsemen, were covered with women enveloped in long
veils of every color.

The play had not yet begun. Upon the stage fitted
up for the presentation of "Yazíd," the name of the
tragedy, Mullah Sédek, between two other Mussulmans,
was reading the prologue, and, at the pathetic places,
he interrupted himself to cry to the spectators, "Weep
and wail, O ye people!" The people responded to the
apostrophe with groans and lamentations.

Utterly reckless, Iskander, who had followed Kassime,
climbed after her up the small staircase which led them
to the roof of a house which was already covered by a
throng of Moslem women irradiated by numerous torches.

The women embraced as they met and recognized each
other, laughing and talking with ceaseless babble.

All were richly dressed, and adorned with gold and
silver necklaces, and each exhibited to the others, as
rival to rival rather than as friend to friend, the finery
which she was wearing for the first time.

One who has had no experience of the Asiatic woman
does not know, and never will know, the half of an
Asiatic man, should he live with him many years. In
the presence of unbelievers, the followers of the prophet

eternally wear a mask, and, outside of the harem, the
Oriental man never shows to his own brother either the
bottom of his heart or the depths of his purse. All
nations have the same ruling passion, — that of vaunt-
ing their own customs. The Mussulmans are addicted
to this more than any other people. If their word is
to be accepted, you can regard them every one as saints.
According to them, husbands and wives in the performance of their duties walk between the lines of the Koran
and never step aside either to right or left. Only within
his home does the Mussulman show himself as he is;
it is because he has to render no account of his conduct to either wife or children. The wife, contrariwise,
is quite free in her husband's absence. No sooner has
she seen the heels of his slippers, than she becomes unrecognizable. Speechless and humble before him, she
becomes garrulous, boastful, shameless even before her
female companions, with whom she is always sincere,
as jealousy exists among the women of the Orient only
in matters of costliness of apparel and value of gems.

Hence arises a double life entirely foreign to that of
Europe, whose nature this book will be at least one of
the first to signalize and impress, — a life less accessible
even to men than to. women, because man constantly
reveals himself to woman, woman to man, never.

Now, suppose that in some way, — what way? that is
not my affair, — suppose that in some way you are in
the company of a Moslem woman; suppose that you
have penetrated to the bath and listened to her prattle
with a friend; that you have entered the harem and
seen her romp — it is the only word that presents itself
to my pen — romp, I say, with her companions; clearly,
you will learn more yourself than a Mussulman would
ever tell you, more than he himself will know.

Judge, then, of Iskander's astonishment when he
found himself surrounded by feminine indiscretions.
Lost in a flock of young women, pretty and talkative,
— he who had never spoken to a woman who had not
passed·her sixtieth year, — his eyes devoured them; he
was eager to hear every word that they were saying.

"Ah, my dear, what a pretty coiffure you have! My
stingy old husband has been to Snizily, and he brought
me back some embroidered trousers. I am wrong to
call him stingy, for he is not so with me; he refuses
me nothing that I ask of him. It is true that he is
very exacting, and that, for my part, I do just as he
wishes."

"Do you know, Fatima," said another, "that my old
ape of a husband has taken a second wife at Baku? I
began to weep and reproach him. Guess what he
answered me! 'Can I go without rice?' Oh! I shall
have my revenge. He takes a second wife, the old
rascal, and is in no condition to observe Saturday with
me. Not he, my dear, no. It is incredible, is it not?
But that is the way. By the by, do you know that a
ukase has been issued in Russia ordering the women to
wear trousers? I have myself seen ladies in Derbend
with white trousers all embroidered and open-worked.
— It was high time! They were scandalous to behold
when the wind blew."

"Oh! how good that soap is you gave me, my dear
Sheker!" said a third; "and how grateful I am to you
for it! Fancy, since using that, my skin has become
like satin."

"Ah, well, yes, she is dead," a fourth was saying;
"he killed her, so much the worse for her. When she
fell in love with some one else, she ought to have known
how to keep it to herself. As soon as her husband left

the house, she went visiting, with a lantern, too. Faith! he killed her in short order."

"Ah, my dear," said a fifth, "how my children worry me! I never saw children grow so fast! To look at them, one would think I was an old woman; and they have sore heads, besides. You understand; I have never had a pimple myself; it comes from their father."

"Ah! your little children may trouble you with their heads, but mine trouble me with their hearts. Mégely torments me beyond measure; he will give me no peace until I buy him a wife."

"Ah well, buy one for the boy; he is tall and old enough to have a wife. I saw him pass just yesterday."

"You are a silly one, you are! You talk as if a wife called for two kopecks. A wife costs something. Where shall I get the money, pray?"

"Ah!" cried a sixth, "what a shame! and you say, my dear, that she is with an Armenian? Are there no more Mussulmans or Russians, then?"

"How kind my husband is! if you but knew," said a seventh; "and he is so handsome! he might be taken for the prophet himself, and although large—"

Iskander listened so intently that he almost forgot why he was there. But the cries, "They are beginning! they are beginning!" put an end to all chattering.

Each turned to the stage and gave her attention to the play. Yazíd, in red caftan and green turban, was seated on his throne. Below him, at his left, standing on the fourth step of his throne, was the European ambassador, represented by Yussef in a fantastic costume, whose conspicuous features consisted of a three-cornered hat surmounted by an immense plume, an enormous sword, and spurs six inches long.

Yazíd's suite, composed of white-turbaned super-
numeraries, formed a semi-circle about his throne.

But not Yazíd's self upon his throne, not the magnificent white-turbaned suite, produced an effect to be
compared with that of Yussef, with a hat that would not
keep its balance on his shaven pate, a sword he knew
not where to put, and spurs that tore the trousers of the
noblest and gravest lords of Yazíd's court.

But what especially excited great hilarity among the
men, and the liveliest discussion among the women, was
that gigantic nose and that colossal plume.

" Oh, look, sister," said a little girl of rank, " look
at that creature beside Yazíd! What kind of beast does
he represent ? "

"That is a lion, you silly child," responded the
sister. " Did you not know that the abominable tyrant,
Yazíd, that brute among caliphs, always had a lion near
him ? If any one incurred his displeasure, he was
thrown to the lion, who ate him up. Come, listen,
there is Yazíd saying to Hussein, ' Adopt my religion
or you shall die ! ' Hussein sneezes, which signifies,
' I will not. ' "

" That 's not a lion," pursued the insistent little one;
" lions have n't beaks; it 's a bird."

" A bird with a tail on his head ! Have you ever
seen birds with tails on their heads ? "

" Yes; it 's a top-knot."

" It 's a mane."

" The child is right," said a third, entering upon the
discussion. " Can you not see that it is a parrot ? This
parrot was interpreting secretary at Yazíd's court. Do
you not see how the caliph caresses him ? "

" Then why does he shout like the devil ? "

" Oh, do keep still, now, parrots of nieces that you

are!" said a good Tartar dame weighing one hundred and fifty kilogrammes, and occupying the space of four ordinary people, with whom listening for herself was like listening for a whole society.

The dispute became general at this juncture. Some continued to maintain that it was a lion, others contended that it was a bird; but Yussef ought to have felt highly flattered that the general opinion held him to be some sort of an animal.

He, little suspecting the flutter which he heard to be occasioned by his own nose and feathers, was discoursing meanwhile with the tyrant.

"My king," he was saying, "the ruler of France, having heard of your conquests, sends me to offer you his friendship."

Yazíd answered: "Let your king cease to eat pork, let him forbid his allies to eat it, and let him order them to become Mussulmans."

"But if his friends refuse?" replied the ambassador.

"Then let him introduce my system."

"Let us see your system," demanded the ambassador.

"Bring me my system," said Yazíd.

An executioner entered, naked sword in hand.

Yussef shook his head.

"What do you mean by that?" demanded Yazíd.

"I mean, great prince, that your system would not succeed in Europe."

"Why not?"

"Because it would be impossible to cut off a European's head as you would an Arab's."

"Impossible?" said Yazíd. "You shall see whether it is impossible."

And, turning to his guards and the executioner, he commanded, —

"Take the European ambassador and cut off his head, that he may see that my system is adapted to every country."

Guards and executioner advanced towards Yussef; but he had so recently taken part in a similar drama with Mullah Nour, that fact and fancy became confused in mind and sight; when he saw the guards about to lay hands on him, he wanted to run away; when he saw the executioner raise his sword, he emitted piercing shrieks. He was arrested when about to leap from the stage into the street, and brought back amid the frantic applause of the multitude, who had never seen terror simulated with such fidelity.

He was still heard calling Iskander to his rescue long after he had gone behind the scenes.

But Iskander had quite another affair on hand.

Iskander had at last got next to Kassime. He could scarcely breathe for joy; his heart was burning; he felt the warmth of Kassime's cheeks; he inhaled the perfume of her breath.

What could you expect? He was in love; he was twenty years old; he loved for the first time.

But he could contain himself no longer when, in shifting her position to be more at her ease, Kassime leaned her hand on his knee.

"Kassime," he whispered in her ear, "I must speak with you."

And he gently pressed her hand.

The young girl's heart and head were full of Iskander; she was hoping to see him at this fête, at which all Derbend was present. She had not come for Yazíd's sake; no caliph's executioner was occupying her mind.

Her eyes had searched for Iskander on all sides, but he was nowhere to be seen.

Imagine, then, her amazement, fancy her joy when she heard in her ear that well-known, that beloved voice !

She had not the strength to resist.

Iskander rose; she followed him. He led her to the darkest corner of the roof.

Those around were so occupied with Yazíd that there was nothing to fear.

Yet Iskander understood that he had no time to lose.

"Kassime," said he, "do you know how I love you? do you know how I worship you? You see what I have risked for the sake of seeing you for one moment, for the sake of saying a few words to you. Then consider what I am capable of doing if you say, 'Iskander, I love you not.' Yes, or no, Kassime? yes, or no?"

Iskander's eyes flashed lightnings through his veil; his left hand pressed Kassime's waist, his right rested on his pistol. The poor child trembled as she looked about her.

"Iskander," said she, "I ask of you but two things, —do not kill me, do not disgrace me! I would gladly clasp you in my arms as closely as your sword belt; but you know my uncle."

Then, urged on in spite of herself, after a moment's hesitation, she added, —

"Iskander, I love you!"

And, like steel to the magnet, her lips were drawn to those of the young man.

"And now," said she, "let me go."

"So be it; but on one condition, my darling, —that we meet here to-morrow night."

Kassime answered nothing; but the word *to-morrow* was so clearly revealed in the look which she gave her

' friend at parting, that Iskander took the rendezvous for granted.

I cannot tell you how Kassime passed the night; but Iskander's sleep was very sweet.

There are some sins after which we sleep better than after the best of good works.

XII.

ACCUSED AND ACQUITTED.

Two days after the fête, there was a large meeting in the fortress of Narin Kale, near the commandant's house.

Armed noukars held their masters' horses by the bridle; there were people in the courts, about the fountain, on the stairs; the salon was full of visitors, and these visitors were the leading people of the town. At the entrance door the commandant's interpreter was eagerly rehearsing something extraordinary, no doubt, for he was listened to and questioned. Elsewhere, they spoke in low tones. The old men shrugged their shoulders; in short, it was easy to see that something strange and out of the common was taking place, or had already taken place.

"Yes," said the interpreter, "this is exactly how the thing was done. The brigands made a hole in the wall and entered the room of Soliman Beg. He awoke, but only when one of the robbers was in the act of taking down the arms that hung above his head. Soliman then drew a pistol from under his pillow and fired, but the ball hit no one. Meanwhile, two or three other bandits were binding his wife in a neighboring room. Hearing the shot, they rushed out and came to the aid of the two who were in Soliman's room. The darkness interfered with the effectiveness of his shots, yet Soliman wounded two or three of the bandits; however, he him-

self fell dead under four or five dagger-thrusts. The
· shooting, and the cries of Soliman and his wife, awoke
the neighbors; but while they were dressing, lighting
their lanterns, and rushing to Soliman's house, the
robbers had broken into his coffers and emptied them,
and they were gone without having been seen, and,
consequently, without a single one's having been
identified."

"So not one of the knaves has been arrested?" demanded a new-comer.

"No; and yet it is believed that an accomplice is
caught."

"An accomplice?"

"Yes; he had been stationed as a watch; he had a
rope around him, for the purpose no doubt of aiding his
comrades in scaling the wall. He carried a pistol and
a dagger in his belt; but it must be admitted that, as a
beg, he had a right to carry arms."

"What! a beg? But it is impossible that a beg
should be an accomplice of thieves!" cried several
voices at once.

"And why is it impossible?" replied a mirza, casting around him the scoffing glance so much affected by
Tartar youths.

"Yes; but this one is really a beg belonging to one
of the best families in Derbend, and you will indeed be
astonished when I tell you his name. It is Iskander
Ben Kalfasi Ogli. Wait, at this very moment the
commandant is reading the report of the chief of police,
and you will presently see Iskander; an order has been
given to bring him here."

In fact, the news astonished everybody. Iskander
was greatly pitied. How could a young man whose
conduct was so irreproachable, who had been chosen to

bring the snow from Schach Dagh, be the accomplice of
such bandits?

The commandant's entrance put a stop to all discussion, and a profound silence was established. He was
one of those men who thoroughly understand the Asiatic
character. He was discriminately affable, the better to
make his affability appreciated, severe without the rude-
ness that envenoms justice, even when she is just.

He entered the salon in full uniform.

All the by-standers saluted him, placing their hands
over their hearts and letting them fall to the knee.

The commandant bowed to all, and spoke briefly on
current matters. Some he gently chided for inefficient
service; others he thanked for having performed their
duties conscientiously; he pressed the hands of some of
the Derbend freeholders, — there are freeholders everywhere, — and invited two of them to dine with him the
next day.

Then, addressing himself to all, he said, —

"Gentlemen begs, I suppose you all know what took
place last night. I have every reason to think it an
enterprise of our friends the mountaineers, and not the
deed of residents of Derbend. I entreat you all to do
your utmost to capture the thieves and bring them before
me. Well," he added, turning to the mirza, "has the
mullah questioned Iskander? In that case, what has
the beg to say?"

"Iskander naturally replies that he is as innocent
as a new-born babe of this whole affair. He says that
he carried the rope to get outside of the city for a walk,
and climb back again whenever he pleased, because, he
asserts, the air of the city is stifling. As to his arms,
he gave no other explanation than this: 'As a beg, I
have a right to carry them.'"

9

"A singular walk, that," said the commandant, "with a rope around the loins! and yet I must say the whole of Iskander's past conduct is a protest against the crime of which he is accused. I wish to see and question him myself; bring him in."

Iskander Beg entered, his papak on his head, according to the Asiatic custom; he bowed respectfully to the commandant, haughtily to the people, and waited in the place assigned to him.

The commandant regarded him coldly. At the thought of being an object of suspicion, the young beg could not help blushing; but his eye was steady and clear.

"I little suspected, Iskander," said the commandant, "that I should ever see you brought before me as a criminal."

"It is not crime, but fate, that brings me here," replied Iskander.

"Do you know the consequences of the crime of which you are accused?"

"Only here have I learned of my supposed crime. I acknowledge my imprudence; appearances are against me, I am aware; but guilty? God knows I am not!"

"Unfortunately, Iskander," returned the commandant, "men must be governed by appearances, and until your innocence is proved, you are in the hands of justice. However, if there is any one here who will answer for you, I will consent to your going at liberty."

Iskander cast a questioning glance around; but no one offered to become his surety.

"What!" said the commandant, "not one?"

"At your pleasure, commandant," replied the bystanders, bowing.

"Well, I will answer for him myself, and be his bondsman," said Hadji Yussef, coming forward.

The commandant smiled; the lookers-on laughed aloud; but the commandant frowned, and the faces grew long.

"Truly, I am astonished, gentlemen," said the commandant, "that you, who so readily give bail for the greatest rascals to be found in our city, for wretches . who have twenty times fled to the mountains after you have gone on their bonds, should hesitate to do as much for a young man whom, eight days ago, you recognized as the purest and most upright among you. His good reputation will not save him from chastisement; on the contrary, if he is guilty, he shall be severely punished. But until he is convicted, he is your compeer, and his exemplary life should be respected. Go home, Iskander; if you had not found security, I should have served you myself."

The commandant saluted the assembly and set off for the mosque.

The young beg went home, his eyes dimmed with tears of gratitude.

The morning sun gilded the porch of the mosque of Derbend. The old men were warming themselves in its vivifying rays as they talked of bygone days; two or three beggars had halted at the entrance of the court.

A few steps farther on, a wayfarer was sleeping under his bourka; not far from the traveller sat Mullah Sédek on his rug.

The holy man was ready to leave Derbend the next morning, and was reckoning up from memory all the small profits by which his journey had enriched him. While mentally recalling the trifling items, he was

eating a sort of pastry which he dipped into a dish of
garlic and milk.   From time to time he plunged his
reed pen into a wooden ink-bottle, and wrote a few
words on a little scrap of paper that he had beside him.
It was curious to note with what appetite the holy man
ate his breakfast, and with what pleasure he footed up
his accounts.

He was so deeply engrossed in this twofold enjoyment that he did not see a poor Lesghian before him
begging for alms.   The wretch was asking for a kopeck
in such pitiful accents that it was truly a crime to deny
him.

Mullah Sédek finally heard the sort of litany that the
poor devil was chanting; he raised his eyes, but almost
as quickly lowered them again to his accounts.

"For three days I have had nothing to eat, master," the Lesghian was saying, as he held out his
hand.

"Ten, twenty-five, fifty, one hundred," counted
Mullah Sédek.

"A kopeck will save my life and open the gates of
Paradise to you."

"One hundred, five hundred, one thousand," continued Mullah Sédek.

"You are a mullah," persisted the Lesghian; "recall
what the Koran says: 'The first duty of a Mussulman
is charity.'"

Mullah Sédek lost his patience.

"Go to the devil!" he angrily exclaimed.   "Was
it for wretches like you that Allah invented charity?
You have sticks in the town and herbs in the fields.
When you are strong enough, you rob; otherwise, you
ask alms, and they are no sooner given than you
laugh at the fool that gave.   You will get nothing

from me; I am a poor traveller, too, and all that I had has been taken away by your brigand of a Mullah Nour."

. The wayfarer lying under his bourka, who had not said a word until then, quietly raised himself, and stroking his beard with his hand, he politely demanded of Mullah Sédek, —

"Has Mullah Nour been so cruel as to leave you absolutely without money, — a holy man like you? Yet I have heard it said that Mullah Nour is a conscientious man, and that he rarely takes more than two roubles from one traveller."

"Two roubles! that rapacious Mullah Nour! Trust yourself in his hands and you will be very lucky if he does not pick out your two eyes. Would that he might be struck down by the destroying angel, and boil throughout all eternity in the gold that he took from me, even if I had to melt the gold myself. Did he not take even my aba of camel's-hair?"

"That is true," said the old men. "Mullah Sédek came to us without an aba and with only his mantle; we have done our best to reclothe him. Curses on this Mullah Nour!"

The wayfarer with the bourka arose smiling, and drawing a piece of gold from his pocket he held it out to the Lesghian, saying, —

"Curse Mullah Nour as these honest men have just done, and this *tchervoniès* is yours."

The Lesghian at first extended his hand; but almost instantly withdrew it, shaking his head, and replied, —

"No, Mullah Nour has helped my brother in misfortune, — he gave him a hundred roubles; on ten occasions he has aided my compatriots. I do not know his

face, but I know his heart. Keep your gold, I will
not curse Mullah Nour. I sell neither my benedictions
nor my maledictions."

The wayfarer regarded the beggar with astonishment,
and Mullah Sédek with scorn.

Then, drawing out four other gold pieces, which he
added to the first, he gave them all five to the poor
Lesghian. ·

Thereupon, resting one hand on Mullah Sédek's
shoulder, and pointing with the other above his head,
he said, —

"In heaven there is a God of truth, and on earth are
some good men."

After which, picking up his bourka, he threw it over
his shoulder, mounted his horse, which had been tied
to the mosque wall, and slowly descended to the
bazaar.

Then, having crossed the bazaar, always at a walk,
he entered the street in which was to be found the house
of the chief of police.

This official was at his door, surrounded by several
persons to whom he was doling out justice; he was
already old, but so black did he keep his beard that
he was himself deluded as to his age, and fancied that
he was at least ten years younger than he was. His
tchourka was trimmed with lace, no more nor less than
that of a man of fashion, and, as a much livelier
reminder of his youth, he still had four wives and three
mistresses, and drank several bottles of wine every
evening. In short, had he not worn spectacles, had he
not been as wrinkled as an old apple, had he not had a
paunch like a pumpkin, one might have believed, after
what he himself had said, in the youth of this most
worthy man.

That day his Excellency was in a bad humor; he was in a rage with everybody, and quarrelled even with the passers-by.

It was in this state of mind that he saw a traveller dismount from his horse and approach him.

"*Salaam Aleikoum,* Mouzaram Beg!" was the wayfarer's greeting.

The chief of police shook as if he had been stung by a scorpion, and laid his hand on his pistol.

But the traveller bent down to his ear and said, —

"Mouzaram Beg, if I were to give you a bit of advice, it would be that you do not meddle with old friends. I have come, too, for your own good; I can do you a service, only, let us go within. I can tell you something for which all Derbend will thank me. But if you make a doubtful sign, you know my pistol carries a ball, and that that ball goes, too, just where I wish it to go, as surely as if, instead of placing it with the eye, I were to place it with my finger. At the first move, then, I fire. I appear to be alone, but do not trust to that. A dozen of my brave men keep me in sight, and at my first summons they will be here. Come, lead the way, Mouzaram Beg."

The chief of police made no protest and went in first.

What took place then? The interview was without witnesses; no one can tell.

We know only that a quarter of an hour after entering, the unknown came out, calmly mounted his horse, threw a silver rouble to the noukar who had held the bridle, and left the city.

But two days later it was told how the celebrated brigand Mullah Nour had had the audacity to enter the city; how, thanks to his active surveillance, the chief

of police had been warned of his presence, and had sent
after him a dozen noukars, to whom Mullah Nour was
glad to show his horse's heels.

Ill-bred people said much worse; but one never has
to believe what ill-bred people say.

During this time poor Iskander was moping within
the four walls of his house. He had but to say one
word to establish his innocence; but he would a hundred times have preferred to die rather than dishonor
Kossime.

To await trial is purgatory for every native of Asia.
An Asiatic can better sustain an undeserved punishment
than a merited trial if the latter is delayed.

"Ah!" he cried in his impatience, "eternal chains,
the snows of Siberia, everything rather than the suspicion of the Russians, who force me to love them, and
the mockery of my compatriots, whom I detest. I am
ready to die by the sword, but to die by the rope is to
die twice."

And, bound by his parole, he began to roar and rage
like a caged tiger, to rend the sleeves of his tchourka
and weep like a child.

In the evening, at an hour when all the streets in the
city were empty, when the houses were enlivened by
the sound of voices and the flashing of lights, when the
married Mussulman was enjoying repose of soul beside
his wife, — even beside the four wives allotted him by
the prophet, — and when, on the other hand, the celibate
was moping at his hearth, Iskander, sitting by his own
with his head thrust between his two hands, heard one
of his window-panes crash under a blow from some
object, and that object fell into his room.

It was a pebble, to which was attached a small note.

He unfolded it, and read, —

"Mullah Nour to Iskander, greeting! Better to be a captive and innocent, than a free man and guilty, believe me.

" I know all; I will declare everything in order to prove your innocence.

" The rest lies with Allah!

" Patience and hope; your deliverance shall not be long in coming."

The next morning, Iskander was summoned before the commandant; but he had not had time to arrive before every one was already congratulating him upon the happy turn in his affairs.

The robbers were captured; they had got together to divide the booty at Baktiara, where they had been surrounded and made prisoners.

Two were Lesghians, two were men of that city.

In the house of one of the latter was a double wall in which the plunder had been secreted.

Iskander Beg was quite innocent.

Then Iskander, deeply touched by the kindly regard bestowed on him by the commandant, in turn sought a private interview. He confessed all, — his love for Kassime, Festahli's broken promise.

The commandant listened, half smiling, half sad.

" Iskander," said he, " you see yourself into what your imprudence has led you. Festahli did wrong, doubtless; but one is not avenged of a wrong by doing wrong. Thieves of gold are not the only thieves; an upright man does nothing underhandedly. Secrecy and night are the cloaks of ravishers and brigands. Your future happiness occupies your heart; I shall do what I can to make it expand from your heart into your life. Adieu, Iskander. In the name of those who love you, remain what you are, and what you nearly ceased to be, — an honest man!"

And he pressed his hand affectionately, again wishing
him happiness.

Iskander was proclaimed innocent, Iskander was free;
his enjoyment of the twofold happiness lasted but a
moment.   It was such grief for the young man to
believe that he must renounce his Kassime.

The kiss that he had snatched from her lips thrilled
him yet to the depths of his heart. He recalled minutely
every detail of his last meeting with his beloved; his
soul seemed ready to fly at the thought of that sweet
voice whose echo it had become.

"No," said he, "Mullah Nour has written nonsense,
and as for what the commandant told me, it is easily
seen that he is not in love.   I am ready to purchase
Kassime even with a crime, and I am sure that in spite
of the crime I should be happy with her, — happy, even
if I should be forced to carry her to the mountain, with
her consent or without it.   I will take her away, if
only for an hour; I will steep my heart in heavenly
delights."

Poor Kassime was sorrowful also.   In her solitude
she was learning with tears to count the hours of
separation.

"I fastened a rose on my breast," sighed she, "and
it whispered, 'I am the Spring;' a nightingale sang
me his song of love, and I called it joy; Iskander looked
into my eyes and gave me a kiss, and with that kiss I
knew love.   But where art thou, lovely rose? where
art thou, sweet nightingale? where art thou, Iskander?
They are gone where my happiness has flown."

XIII.

THE MILLER.

KNOW you the Tengua?

It is sometimes a brooklet, sometimes a torrent, sometimes a stream, and at times a river.

For a quarter of a verst it runs cramped within a narrow gorge, into which it plunges with abhorrence, and through which it madly courses.

The storms of many centuries have not washed the blackened traces of lightning from the walls of the gorge where the Tengua thunders.

Entire masses of rock, precipitated from the mountain's height to the bottom of the gorge, form the bed over which it leaps and foams with maddening uproar.

The neighborhood of this chasm is wild and gloomy; its entrance is formidable.

The right bank of the torrent casts the shadow of its rocks far over the valley.

The left bank lowers into the water a narrow path which first traverses a little wood.

Ill luck to the horseman who, without guide, engages in a struggle with this liquid hell, especially at seasons of thaw or melting snow.

Ill luck to him if he encounter brigands in this pass, which seems expressly planned for an ambuscade. De·fence and flight are impossible here.

At this spot Mullah Nour, the bandit from the book of whose life we are taking a page, — this very Mullah

Nour with a dozen of his fellows stopped three regiments which were returning with the enormous spoils of General Pankratief's expedition.

When they were just on the point of descending into the river, he appeared before them mounted and completely armed, threw his bourka on the ground and said, —

"I salute you, comrades! Allah has granted you victory and spoils. Honor be to you! but it would only be like the good Christians you are to let me share your happiness. I exact nothing, — I entreat; be generous, and let each give me what he will. Think now, brothers, you are returning rich, carrying presents to your relatives. As for me, I am poor, I have no home; and for an hour's repose under others' roofs, I pay a handful of gold. Yet, know you, brothers, men have, like cowards, stripped me of everything. Happily, Allah has preserved my courage; more than that, he has given me these gloomy ravines and these naked rocks which you yourselves scorn. Of these rocks and ravines I am king, and no one shall pass through my territories without my permission. You are in great numbers, you are brave; but if you mean to pass by force, it will cost you much blood, and of time much more, for you will cross only when I and my brave men have fallen. Every stone will fight for me, and as for myself, I will shed here the last drop of my blood; I will burn here my last grain of powder. Choose; you have much to lose, and I nothing. Men call me Nour, *The Light*, but my life, I swear, is gloomier than the darkness."

A murmur rose from the ranks of the troopers; some frowned, others were wrathful.

"Let us trample Mullah Nour under our horses'

feet," said they, "and go on. You see how many we are, how many you are. On! let us charge the bandits!"

But no one ventured first into the roaring stream, whose ford was covered by the guns of a dozen brigands.

Rashness made way for reflection, and the three regiments yielded to Mullah Nour's demands.

"We shall give you what we like, and nothing more."

And so saying, each cavalier threw a little money down on the bandit's bourka.

"But understand that, by force, you could not have taken a nail from our horses' shoes."

And they passed one by one in single file before Mullah Nour.

Mullah Nour smilingly bowed to them.

"Allah!" said he, after this adventure which had brought him three or four thousand roubles, "it is no feat to shear the wool from the sheep of Daghestan, when I have shaved the hair from the wolves of the Karabach. I do not know why these people of Daghestan should complain about their crops; I take no pains to sow, plough, or cultivate; I stand on the highway and pray, and my prayer brings me an ample harvest. Only know how to set about it, and you can extract an abassi, not from every carriage, but from every gun-barrel."

But early in the summer of the year in which the events that we are relating took place, no one had seen Mullah Nour, no one had heard Mullah Nour spoken of as on the banks of the Tengua. Where was he, then?

In the government of Shekin perhaps; perhaps in Persia, where he might indeed have been forced to take refuge; and perhaps he was dead.

Nobody knew anything about him, — not even Mullah Sédek, who pretended to have been robbed by him on his way from Persia to Derbend.

He had left Kouban early in the morning, this worthy, this respectable Mullah Sédek, and, toward noon, he had reached the spot where the Tengua, freed from the confines of the gorge, goes on its way. Insatiate as the desert sand, he was unwilling to take a guide, whose trouble he must have paid for by a few paltry pieces of the coin that he had gathered by the bushel at Derbend.

The June sun was terribly warm, and our wayfaring mullah was in the act of transferring his gun from the right shoulder to the left.

When he caught sight of a little wood in the distance, he was delighted; but when he saw the river close at hand, he was in despair.

"May the devil take me!" murmured he; "had I known what this river was like, I would not have attempted to cross it without a guide, although its bed were silver and gold instead of rocks. In fact, I was crazy not to have hired one."

And he gazed about him in terror; the spot was deserted and solitary.

However, after careful search, he discovered, tied to a tree in the wood, a horse all saddled and bridled; and under this same tree was a simple Tartar, armed only with his kandjiar, a weapon that no Tartar ever goes without.

Mullah Sédek approached step by step and looked attentively.

The flour whitening the Tartar's coat and beard indicated that he was a miller. The miller was eating his breakfast.

Our holy man, who had felt his heart beat for an instant, became reassured.

"Hi! friend!" cried he to the unknown, "it seems to me that you belong hereabouts, do you not?"

"To be sure I belong here," replied the miller with his mouth full.

"In that case, you ought to know all the fords of this river?"

"Oh! I certainly think I ought to know the fords of the Tengua; she runs only with my permission. Such as you see her, this river is my servant."

"You will do me a great service, my good man, and Allah will bless you, if you will conduct me to the other side of the gorge."

"Wait until night," tranquilly returned the miller. "Between now and night the river will fall, my horse will be rested, and I, too, shall be refreshed. It will not take us more than a quarter of an hour then to ford the torrent; but just now it is dangerous."

"In the name of Allah! In the names of Ali and Hussein! In the name of my prayers! I am a mullah; lead me across without delay, now, instantly!"

"Oh!" said the miller, "neither prayers nor blessings will bring that to pass. Never, at such high water, will I try to ford the Tengua!"

"Have some feeling, my friend; Allah will reward you, you may be sure, if you do anything for a mullah."

"Mullah as much as you like, but I would not risk getting drowned to guide the prophet himself."

"Do not despise me; I am not so poor as you think, perhaps, and if you render me this service, it shall not be for nothing."

The miller smiled.

"Well, let us see, what would you give me?" he
said, scratching his beard.

"I will give you two abassis; I hope that is
reasonable."

"Good! two abassis? With two abassis I should
not even have the means of getting my horse shod. No,
I will not take you across for two roubles even; because
a new head is not to be bought with two roubles, and a
man would plainly be risking his head in that frightful
ford."

They bargained a long time; at last Mullah Sédek
ended by promising the sum exacted by the miller.

On giving up his horse's bridle to the guide, Mullah
Sédek surrendered at discretion and trusted himself
entirely to the other's experience. The holy man
nearly died of fright when he began to ford the river
and penetrated the entrance of the gorge. But when,
through the opposite gap, he again caught sight of the
valley covered with grass, with sunlight and flowers,
his courage revived, and supposing there was nothing
more to fear, he addressed his guide, —

"Come, will you get on a little faster, you rascal?"

But our brave mullah had found his courage a little
too soon. The last part of the ford was the deepest and
most dangerous.

The guide halted just at that part, and turning his
horse, he said, —

"Well, Sédek, ten steps more and you are on the
bank. Now let us settle our accounts. You know
that I have well earned your gold-piece, eh?"

"A gold-piece! Have you no conscience, friend?
No, you are joking, surely. I might as well have
built me a silver bridge to cross on. Go on, now, good

fellow, and on the other side I will give you two abassis and you can be off."

"Good! we shall come to better terms, I fancy."

"Undoubtedly, undoubtedly. Necessity — you hold a knife to my throat, and I must certainly cross over. Where do you expect a poor traveller to get so much money? Alas! I have already been robbed. Come, come, take me to the other side, brother; and once there, you can go about your business, and I will go about mine."

"Not so," said the miller, shaking his head; "I told you, and I repeat that I will not leave this spot without having settled my account with you, and our account does not date from to-day. You have no conscience, Mullah Sédek, but you doubtless have a memory. To excite sympathy and obtain money at Derbend, you invented the story that Mullah Nour had stopped you, stripped you, and taken everything. Tell me, where did that happen?"

"I have never said such a thing!" cried Mullah Sédek; "may Allah condemn me if I said that!"

"Recall the court of the mosque, Sédek; remember what you said to the Lesghian, what you told the wayfarer who slept on his bourka. And now look me in the face, as I am looking at you, and perhaps we shall recognize each other."

Mullah Sédek scanned the face of his guide; under the flour which covered it he was at first unrecognizable, but the flour had disappeared; gradually the whitened beard had become black; under the frowning brows glittered two black eyes. However, seeing that he had no weapon but his kandjiar, Mullah Sédek seized his gun; but before he could cock it, the kandjiar's point was at his breast.

"If you twitch so much as a hair of your moustache," said the counterfeit miller, "I warn you that, like Jonah, you shall go to preach to the fishes against drinking either wine or brandy. Come, now, away with your gun, away with your sword! Your business is to cheat people in the shops and in the pulpit; to lie in the morning, to lie in the evening, to lie at all times; but fighting is the business of brave men, — not yours, therefore. Do not move, I say, you son of a dog! In this place, there is no need for me to waste even one charge of powder on you, and that is why I carry no fire-arms; I have only to drop your horse's bridle, and in five minutes you are a corpse."

At these words Mullah Sédek turned as white as wax. He clutched his horse's mane, conscious that he was growing dizzy, and about to slip from his saddle. But, without for an instant losing sight of the wicked kandjiar that glittered against his breast like a flashing light, he cried, —

"Mercy! I am a mullah!"

"I am myself a mullah," responded the guide, "and even more than a mullah, — I am Mullah Nour."

Mullah Sédek gave a shriek and cowered to his horse's mane, clasping both hands about his own neck, as if he already felt the steel's sharp edge upon its nape.

Mullah Nour began to laugh at Sédek's terror; then raising him up at last, he said, —

"Your story to the people of Derbend maligned me; you made everybody believe that I had robbed you of your last kopeck, of your last shirt even, — I, who give the poor man the bit of bread that he begs in vain at the rich man's door, — I who never take more than one piece of gold from the merchants themselves, and that not for myself, but for my comrades, — comrades who would kill and plunder without shame and without remorse, did I not restrain them. And more than that, —you are the robber, for you meant to rob your guide by refusing him what you had promised; lastly, you are an assassin, for when I demanded what was legitimately my due you would have assassinated me."

"Have pity on me, pardon me, good Mullah Nour!" said Sédek.

"Have you ever pitied the lot of the poor man whom you saw dying of hunger? Would you have felt any remorse if you had killed me? No; for you are a miserable wretch. You coin every letter of the Koran into money, and in your own interests and for your own profit you sow dissension in families. I recognized you; I knew what sort of a man you were, and I did not touch you when you passed along here on your way to Derbend. You did not see me; you did not meet me; you did not know me; yet you insulted me. Well, now you will not be lying when you say that I have robbed you. Mullah Sédek, give me your money!"

Mullah Sédek sent up shriek after shriek, he shed great tears; but he was entrapped, he had to submit. One after another, he cast his poor roubles into the sack held out to him by Mullah Nour, squeezing each coin before letting it go, as if a coating of silver might cling to his hands.

Finally, he reached the last piece.

"That is all," said he.

"You would swear to a lie on the edge of the grave!" cried Mullah Nour. "Look here, Sédek, unless you wish to become more intimately acquainted with my poniard, count better. You still have money; you have gold in the inside pocket of your tchouska. I

know how much, and I can tell you, — fifteen hundred
roubles. Is n't that it ? "

Great was the lamentation of Sédek, but he was
forced to yield up his very last piece of gold.

Mullah Nour had spoken the truth, he knew the
amount.

Mullah Nour then conducted Sédek to the much.
desired bank, and made him there dismount from his
horse.

Mullah Sédek believed himself at quits with the
bandit, but he was deceived.

"Now, that is not all," said the latter; "you have
hindered the marriage of Iskander Beg, and you must
mend what you have marred. You have a bottle of ink
in your girdle; write to Hadji Festahli that you have
received on the way a letter from your brother, in which
he tells you that his son does not wish to marry, and
has gone on a pilgrimage to Mecca; or say that he is
dead, if you like. The deuce! you ought not to be put
to it for a lie! Only, arrange it so that Iskander can
wed his promised bride. Otherwise, I shall see to
marrying you to the houris, Mullah Sédek!"

"Never!" cried Mullah Sédek, "never! No, no,
no, I will not do it! You have taken all I had; be
content with what you have robbed me of."

" Ah! is it so?" said Mullah Nour.

He clapped his hands three times, and, at the third,
a dozen bandits appeared, as if they had issued from the
rocks.   .

"The worthy Mullah Sédek wishes to write," said
Mullah Nour; " second him, my friends, in the laudable
intention."

In a twinkling, Mullah Sédek, if such was indeed
his desire, had nothing left to wish for. One bandit

detached his ink-bottle, another dipped his pen in the ink, a third handed him paper, and last of all, a fourth, bracing his hands against his knees, and lowering his shoulders, offered his back for a desk.

Three times Mullah Sédek began to write, but, whether from errors or unwillingness, three times he broke off.

" Well ? " demanded Mullah Nour, his voice but the more threatening for appearing to be perfectly calm.

" The ink is bad, and my head is so bothered that I can think of no words. "

" Then write with your blood and think with your papak, " said Mullah Nour, with an emphasizing flash of the terrible kandjiar; " but write very quickly ! If not, I will put such a point between your two eyebrows that the devil alone can tell which letter of the alphabet you resemble. "

Mullah Sédek saw that his hesitation had gone its length, and he finally made up his mind to write.

" Set your seal now, " said Mullah Nour, when the letter was finished.

Mullah Sédek obeyed.

" There ! now give it to me, " demanded Mullah Nour; " I will see to posting it. "

He took the letter, read it, assured himself that it was what he desired, thrust it into his pocket, and then, tossing to Mullah Sédek all that had been taken from him, he said, —

" There is your gold and silver, Sédek; take it back, not a kopeck is missing. And now which of us two is miser or thief ? Answer. However, it is not a gift, but a payment. You have blackened my name at Derbend, you must regild it at Schumaka, and that in open mosque. Go, then, and know that if you do not

carry out my orders, my ball will find you, however
well hidden you may be. I have convinced you that I
know everything; I will prove to you that I can do
everything."

Mullah Sédek pledged himself to all that the bandit
exacted, took possession of his money very joyfully,
restored it to his pockets, after first assuring himself
that his pockets contained no holes, and, remounting
his horse, he set off at full gallop.

Two days later, Mullah Sédek scandalized the people
of Schumaka by a discourse in which he eulogized
Mullah Nour, comparing him to a lion that bore the
heart of a dove in his breast.

XIV.

CONCLUSION.

PROBABLY the letter written to Festahli by his friend, Mullah Sódek, left the former not a ray of hope for the union on which he had counted; for, one evening after the letter had reached his address, music and songs were heard in the streets of Derbend.

Kassime was being escorted to the home of her betrothed husband, Iskander.

All Derbend followed her; shouts and acclamations rent the air on every side, and from every house-top innumerable guns discharged their fires, like brilliant rockets.

The whole town seemed ablaze, rejoicing in Iskander's happiness.

Iskander Beg, on hearing the noise and music, had twenty times drawn near to his door, and every time custom forbade his opening it.

Finally, at the twenty-first time, when the procession was almost at his threshold, as he half-opened his door and shyly put out his head, a horseman extended his hand, saying, —

"Iskander, may Allah grant you all the happiness that I wish you!"

And the same instant he wheeled his horse away, that he might not be caught in the midst of the crowd.

But, just as the horse turned, he found himself face to face with Yussef, who, naturally, was the best man at Iskander's wedding.

Yussef Beg recognized the horseman, and could not restrain an exclamation of terror.

"Mullah Nour!" he cried.

That name, as one can well understand, threw the fête into great confusion.

The cry "Mullah Nour! Mullah Nour!" re-echoed on all sides.

"This way! that way! catch him! hold him fast!" howled the ten thousand voices together.

But Mullah Nour shot away like a flash of lightning.

All the young men who were on horseback in the bride's train dashed off in pursuit of the bandit.

Mullah Nour flew through the streets of Derbend, and all they saw of him in the dark was the shower of sparks from his horse's hoofs. .

But as the city gates were closed Mullah Nour could not get out.

By the glare of shots fired at him along his course, they saw that he was headed toward the sea.

He would there find himself caught between the ramparts and the water.

One instant the bandit paused; the sea was high. They saw the leaping waves and tossing foam; they heard their roar.

"He is caught! he is ours! Death to Mullah Nour!" shouted his pursuers.

But Mullah Nour's whip whistled like the wind, flashed like the lightning, and from the rock where he had an instant paused, at one leap his horse plunged into the sea.

His pursuers drew rein as the waters of the Caspian Sea washed their horses' flanks.

They strained their eyes, screening them with their hands, in an effort to pierce the gloom.

"He is lost! drowned! dead!" they shouted at last.

A formidable peal of laughter answered their shouts, and a hurrah sent up from a dozen throats was heard in the direction of a little island uprising about a quarter of a verst from Derbend, which announced to the disappointed pursuers that not only had Mullah Nour escaped, but that he was even surrounded by his comrades.

In Iskander's house the doors are closely shut. All is very quiet within; a faint whispering can scarcely be heard.

Gayety seeks the crowd; happiness loves silence and solitude.

SULTANETTA.

PREFACE.

ONE word as to the way in which the story I am about to relate fell into my hands.

I was at Derbend, the city of the Iron Gates, at the residence of the commander of the fortress. During breakfast the conversation turned on the novelist Marlinsky, who was no other than the Bestuchef that was condemned to the Siberian mines for the conspiracy of 1825, and whose brother was hanged at the citadel of St. Petersburg together with Pestel, Mouravief, Kalkovsky, and Ryleief.

Exempted from labor in the mines in 1827, Bestuchef had been sent as a soldier to the army of the Caucasus. Brave, and casting himself with desperation into every danger, he soon won the rank of ensign, and with this rank he lived a year in the fortress of Derbend.

You will read in my "Voyage au Caucase" what new catastrophe gave him a distaste for life, and how, in an encounter with the Lesghians, he met at their hands a death as voluntary as suicide.

Among the numerous papers left in his room at the time of his death, was found a manuscript. This manuscript has since been read by different persons, and among others by the commandant's daughter, who mentioned it

to.me as a novel of great interest. Upon her recommendation I had it translated, and finding, not only much
of interest, as she had done, but also a very remarkable
local coloring in the little romance, I determined to pub-
lish it.

I took it, consequently, from the hands of my translator; I rewrote it to render it comprehensible to French
readers, and such as it is, without changing anything, I
am publishing it, convinced that it will impress others in
the same way that it has impressed me.

It is, moreover, a curious picture of war as carried on
between the Russians, those representatives of the civilization of the North, and the wild, fierce tribes of the
Caucasus.

ALEX. DUMAS.

SULTANETTA.

I.

" Be slow to offend and quick to avenge." [1]

IT was Friday.

Near Bouinaky, a large village of northern Daghestan, the Tartar youth had assembled for a horse-race, supplemented by every feat of hardihood and courage that could be annexed to this sort of fête.

Let us give some idea of the magnificent landscape in which the scene is enacted.

Bouinaky ascends the two spurs of a lofty mountain and commands the surrounding country. To the left of the road leading from Derbend to Tarky is outlined the crest of the Caucasus, covered with forests; on the right is the shore, against which the waters of the Caspian Sea beat with ceaseless murmur, or, rather, with ceaseless lamentation.

The day was fading.

The villagers, allured by the crispness of the air much more than by interest in a spectacle too often repeated to be novel, had left their huts, descended their mountain slopes and ranged themselves in rows on both sides of the road.

[1] Inscription engraved on the poniards of Daghestan.

As for the men, they stood in groups or squatted in Turkish fashion. Old men were smoking Persian tobacco in their Tchetchen pipes. The sound of hilarity prevailed over all, and mingling with the incessant uproar was heard from time to time the clashing of a horse's hoofs against the flints of the road, and the cry of "*Katch! katch!*" ("Clear the way! clear the way!") uttered by the riders making ready for the race.

Nature is radiant in Daghestan during the month of May; thousands of roses cover the granite with the ruddy tint of dawn, and the air is redolent of their perfume; the nightingales, deep in the green twilights of the groves, are perpetually singing. Bounding over the rocks are flocks of sportive sheep, embellished with orange-colored spots which the shepherds, full of whimsical fancies with regard to them, make with henna, the same material that their masters employ in staining the nails of the hands and feet. Buffaloes, plunged in the marshes in voluptuous enjoyment, gaze at the passer-by with great profound eyes which would seem menacing were they not pensive. The steppes are covered with heather of many hues. Every wave of the Caspian glistens like the scaly coat of a giant fish. With every breath, in short, quickening the senses and gladdening the heart, is inhaled something of that seductiveness of air, of sky, of atmosphere, which inspired in the Greeks the instinctive divination that the world was born here, that the Caucasus was its cradle.

Such is the impression that native or foreigner would have received on nearing the village of Bouinaky that jocund Friday, the birthday of the events we are about to chronicle.

The sun was gilding the sombre walls of the flat-roofed houses, whose shadows gathered the greater depth and strength the farther he withdrew. At a distance could be heard the doleful creaking of the *arabas*[1] of which a long line was distinguishable among the Tartar rocks that stood like ghosts in a graveyard, and in the lead of their noisy procession galloped a horseman raising a cloud of dust upon the road.

The snowy crest of the mountains, and the calm sea opposite, invested the scene with a vast magnificence.

One felt that Nature was alive with the keenest, most ardent spirit.

" It is he! it is he! he is coming! there he is!" cried the throng at sight of this dust and the horseman it screened from view, but whose identity they already guessed.

At these cries there was great commotion among the crowd.

Horsemen who had been standing about until then with their bridles over their arms, talking with acquaintances, leaped upon their horses; those who had been galloping right and left at random and according to their whim drew together, and all hastened away to meet this horseman and his suite.

It was Ammalat Beg, nephew of the Chamkal[2] Tarkovsky.

He wore a black tchouska of Persian make, trimmed with the exquisite galoons whose secret only Caucasian manufacturers possess; the sleeves, half hanging, were caught up by the ends to the shoulder. His arkalouke of tarmalama was confined to the figure by a Turkish scarf;

---

[1] The *arabas* are carts whose wheels, never being greased, on account of their proprietors' repugnance to pork, at every revolution emit a groan that can be compared to nothing but that of the Spanish *norias*.

[2] A Tartar title equivalent to the Russian *kness*, prince.

his red trousers were lost in yellow boots, with high heels; his gun, poniard, and pistols were mounted in silver embossed with gold; his sword-hilt was adorned with precious stones. Added to this, the heir of Chamkal Tarkovsky was twenty-four years old, handsome, well made, and of an open countenance; add, too, that long ringlets of black hair fell from his papak on his neck, that a little black moustache which seemed traced by a pencil adorned his lips, that his eyes glowed with haughty kindliness, that he was mounted on a black charger always ready to run, that he was seated on a light, silver-embroidered, Circassian saddle, that his feet rested in black Khorassan stirrups of steel embossed with gold, that twenty noukars in embroidered tchouskas galloped at his side on splendid horses, and you will realize the impression created by the arrival of the young prince in the midst of a people upon whom wealth, grace, beauty, the external endowments, in short, which Oriental skies lavish upon its elect, have such supreme influence and for whom they have such irresistible attraction.

The men stood up and saluted him, bowing with hands upon hearts.

Murmurs of delight, of awe, and especially of admiration, rose from among the women.

Reaching the centre of the crowd, Ammalat Beg stopped.

The old men, leaning on their staffs, and the leading citizens of Bouinaky gathered round him, hoping the young beg would speak to them; but the young beg did not even look their way.

Instead, he raised his hand for the race to begin.

Without other orders, a score of riders then dashed off at a gallop, each striving to outdistance his neighbor.

Then they all seized their djerids, or javelins, and hurled them at each other at full speed.

The most skilful ones picked them up again without setting foot to earth, while swinging down and under their horses' stomachs.

Others, less skilled, trying to imitate them, rolled in the dust amid shouts of laughter from the by-standers.

The shooting began.

Thus far during the race Ammalat Beg had held aloof; but his noukars had one after another allowed themselves to be drawn away and were mingling with the competitors.

Only two remained with the prince.

But, with the excitement of the races, the echoing shots, and the pungent smell of powder-smoke filling the air, the young chamkal's icy indifference seemed to thaw. He began to shout at the combatants, rising in his stirrups to urge them on, and, when his favorite noukar's ball missed the papak that he had thrown into the air in front of him, he could no longer restrain himself, but seized his gun and dashed at full gallop into the midst of the marksmen.

"Make way for Ammalat Beg!" was heard on all sides.

And they moved aside as quickly as if the warning had been: "Way for the waterspout! Way for the hurricane!"

Along a verst's distance ten poles had been erected, a papak crowning each.

Ammalat Beg set his horse at a gallop, rode past them from first to last, his gun held high above his head; then when he had passed the last, he turned again, and rising in his stirrups, fired without a halt.

The papak fell.

Then, still galloping, he reloaded his gun, retraced his course, returning the same way that he had come, dropped the second papak in like manner, and·so on to the last of the ten.

This display of skill, ten times repeated, elicited universal applause.

Ammalat Beg did not pause; once aroused, his pride demanded a complete triumph. He tossed away his gun, took his pistol, whirled in his saddle so as to ride backward, and, as the horse threw up his hind feet in the gallop, he fired and unshod the right foot; then, reloading, he did the same with the left foot.

There were shouts of admiration.

Next, picking up his gun, he ordered one of his noukars to gallop ahead of him.

The two set off, swift as thought.

In mid-career, the noukar threw a silver rouble high into the air.

Amalat Beg brought his gun to his shoulder, but at that instant his horse stumbled and rolled over, ploughing the dust of the road with his head.

A single cry was heard; it had issued simultaneously from all throats.

But the skilled horseman remained standing in the stirrups, no more disconcerted than if nothing had happened, and, just as his two feet were touching the earth, he fired.

The rouble, driven by the ball, fell far outside of the assemblage of people.

The crowd, intoxicated with delight, burst into frantic hurrahs.

But Ammalat Beg, calm, and to all appearance, unmoved, quickly disengaged his feet from the stirrups, aided his horse to rise, and threw the rein to one of his noukars to have him instantly shod.

The racing and shooting continued.

Just then the foster-brother of Ammalat Beg, Sophyr Ali, the son of a poor beg of Bouinaky, approached.

He was a handsome youth, simple-hearted and happy; he had been raised and had grown to manhood by the side of Ammalat. The same intimacy existed between them as between two brothers.

He jumped down from his horse, bowed, and said, —

" The noukar Mohammed is tiring out your old horse Antrim, trying to make him leap a ravine over fifteen feet wide."

" And does n't Antrim take it ? " cried Ammalat, frowning with annoyance. " Bring him to me at once."

He went to meet the horse, made a sign for the noukar to dismount, vaulted into the saddle, and directed Antrim straight to the ditch to make him look at it.

Then, retracing his steps, he started from the field at full gallop towards the ravine.

The nearer he approached, the harder he pressed with his knees and drew on the bridle.

But, not having confidence in his strength, Antrim swerved to the right with a sudden dash.

Ammalat Beg rode back into the field and again he set off at full speed.

This time, stimulated by the whip, Antrim rose to his hind feet as if about to make the leap.

But instead of taking the ditch, he turned on his hind feet as on a pivot, and refused it a second time.

Ammalat Beg was furious.

In vain did Sophyr Ali beg him not to urge the poor beast that had so honorably spent his powers in races and battles; Ammalat paid no heed, and, drawing his schaska from its sheath, he forced him to make a third attempt, rousing him this time not only with the whip but with the blade of his sword.

But it was of no avail; as twice before, the horse stopped at the edge of the ditch.

But this time Ammalat Beg gave poor Antrim such a blow between the ears with his schaska, that the horse dropped like a felled ox.

Ammalat Beg had killed him at one stroke.

"That is a faithful servant's reward!" remarked Sophyr Ali, with a sigh, looking sadly at the dead animal.

"No, it is punishment for disobedience," angrily retorted Ammalat Beg.

Sophyr Ali was silent.

The horsemen continued riding.

Suddenly there was a sound of beating drums, and, rising gradually from behind the mountains, the glittering points of Russian bayonets could be seen.

It was a company of Kousinsk's regiment on their return from escorting a wheat-train to Derbend.

The captain commanding this company marched with another officer a little in advance of the troop.

Thinking it time for his men to rest, the captain ordered a halt.

They stacked their arms, left a sentinel in charge, and stretched themselves on the grass.

The arrival of a detachment of Russians was no novelty to the people of Bouinaky in 1819; but such a sight is not a very agreeable one, even to-day, to the men of Daghestan. Their religion causes them to regard the Russians as their undying enemies, and if they sometimes smile upon them, it is to conceal their real feelings behind the smile; and the real feelings are of hatred, implacable and deadly.

A murmur passed through the crowd as the Russians halted on their race-course. The women regained their

houses, not however without a glance at the new-comers
through the openings of their veils; the men, on the contrary, eyed them askance, gathering in groups and speaking in low tones.

But the older men, more prudent, approached the captain and asked after his health.

"I myself am very well," said he; "but my horse has
cast a shoe, so that he limps. Fortunately, here is a
good Tartar," he continued, pointing to the smith that was
shoeing Ammalat's horse, "who will remedy the matter."

Then, approaching him, he said, —

"Eh! friend, when you have finished putting a new
sole on the horse you are working at, you shall do as
much for mine."

The smith, whose face was doubly blackened by sun
and soot, turned a glowering look upon the captain,
twisted his moustache, crushed his papak down to his
ears, but made no reply; and when he had done with
Ammalat Beg's horse, he tranquilly replaced his instru-
ments in his sack.

"Ah! see here! did you understand me?" demanded
the captain.

"Perfectly," retorted the smith.

"What did I say, then?"

"That your horse had cast a shoe."

"Well, since you understand, set yourself to work."

"To-day is Friday, it is a holiday; no one works on
holidays."

"Listen," said the captain, "I will pay whatever you
ask; but understand one thing, — if you will not do it of
your own accord, you shall be made to do it."

"Before all other commands I must obey Allah's, who
forbids me to work on Friday. I already sin too much
on ordinary days, but I will think twice on a day like

this ! I am not anxious to buy my own coal to burn me in hell."

"Then what were you doing just now?" insisted the captain, beginning in turn to knit his brows. "Were you not at work? It strikes me that a horse is a horse, especially mine; he is a pure blooded Mussulman. Look, don't you recognize him for a Karabach?"

"A horse is a horse, it is true, and there is no difference between them when they are of good blood; but it is not so with men. The horse that I have just shod is Ammalat Beg's and Ammalat Beg is my chief."

"Which is saying that if you had not obeyed him, he would have cut off your two ears, you knave! and because you do not grant me the right to do as much, you will not work for me. Very well, my man! I'll not cut off your ears, because the thing is forbidden to us Christians; but you can be sure of getting two hundred lashes on your back if you don't obey me. Do you hear?"

"I hear."

"Well?"

"Well, as I am a good Mussulman, my second answer shall be the same as my first: to-day is Friday, and Mussulmans do not work on Fridays."

"You think so?"

"I am sure of it."

"Since you worked for your Tartar chief's pleasure, you shall work for a Russian officer's necessity. I say necessity, because if my horse is not shod I cannot continue my journey. — Here, soldiers!"

Already a large group had collected round the two disputants; but it became suddenly greater and more crowded at this point in the quarrel, and voices from among the Tartars were heard: —

"No, that must not be; it cannot be permitted. This
is Friday; no one works on Fridays."

At the same time many of the blacksmith's friends
began to cram their papaks down over their eyes and
grasp the hilts of their poniards, crowding upon the captain and shouting to the smith, —

"Don't you shoe the Russian's horse, Alikper, don't
you touch his beast; what you do for Ammalat Beg, a
good Mussulman, you need not do for a dog of a
Muscovite."

The captain was brave; besides, he knew the
Asiatics.

"Clear out, you rabble!" he cried, drawing a pistol
from its holster; "or, if you stay, hold your tongues!
for, as sure as that you will all be damned, the first one
who says a word will get his lips sealed with lead."

This threat, backed by the bayonets of numerous
soldiers, had its effect. The cowards disappeared, the
courageous stood their ground, though without saying
another word.

As for Master Alikper, seeing that matters looked
serious for him, he cast about for some way of escape,
and perceiving none, he muttered a few words in Turk
which evidently framed an excuse to the Prophet, rolled
up his sleeves, opened his sack, extracted his hammer
and chisel, and proceeded to obey.

It should be added that Ammalat Beg knew nothing of
what was passing. As soon as he saw the Russians, not
desiring a disagreeable encounter with them, he addressed
a few words to an old woman, his nurse, who had
watched him with maternal affection throughout all
the feats of skill which he had just executed, and
leaping upon his horse he took the road to his own house

which, like an eagle's eyrie, overhung the village of Bouinaky.

But, although one of the important characters in our story was just departing in one direction, another character, also important to a certain degree, was at the same moment approaching from the opposite one.

II.

THIS was a cavalier low of stature but strongly built. He seemed to belong to the easily recognized tribe of the Avares: he wore a helmet and breastplate of chain armor, carried a small shield in his left hand, and a straight-bladed schaska hung from his side.

The only thing lacking in the new arrival's costume, a costume which is to-day exactly the same as was that of the Crusaders, was the cross of red cloth worn on the right breast by those mountaineers who had remained faithful to the Christain religion.

The others, becoming converts to the Moslem religion, from either necessity or conviction, retain the same costume but without the sign of our redemption.

This horseman was accompanied by five noukars,[1] thoroughly equipped like himself.

From the dusty covering of the riders and the foaming flanks of their horses, it was easy to surmise that they had made a long and rapid journey.

As the head horseman, whom we have accorded particular mention, was leisurely passing the Russian soldiers, to whom he seemed insolently indifferent, he passed their guns so closely as to graze one of the stands of arms and knock it down.

But without appearing to remark the incident, he continued on his way, while his noukars carelessly allowed their horses to trample the overturned guns.

[1] Noukars are squires or equerries to be found in the suite of every noble Tartar.

The sentinel, who from a distance had warned the horseman, " Keep off !" — an injunction which it is seen had produced no great effect, — sprang to his horse's bridle, while the soldiers, considering themselves insulted by the contemptuous behavior of the Mussulmans, began to mutter threateningly among themselves.

"Who are you?" cried the sentinel, seizing, as we have said, the bridle of the chief of this little band.

"You are new to the country, if you have not recognized Ackmeth, khan of Avarie," composedly responded the horseman, snatching his horse's bridle from the sentinel's hand. "It seems to me, however, that a year ago, near Backli, I made a deep impression on the Russians."

Then, as he had spoken in Tartar, turning to one of his noukars, he added, —

"Tell these dogs in their own language what I have just done them the honor to say."

The noukar repeated in Russian, word for word, what Ackmeth Khan had just said in Tartar.

"It is Ackmeth Khan! it is Ackmeth Khan!" repeated the soldiers in chorus. "Seize him! Don't let him escape, now that we have him! We must be avenged for the Backli affair!"

"Back, wretches!" yelled Ackmeth Khan, fetching the sentinel's hand a blow with his whip. "Have you forgotten that I am to-day a Russian general?"

And this time he spoke in such pure Muscovite that the soldiers lost not a word of it.

"A Russian traitor, you mean!" cried several of the soldiers. "Let us take him to the captain, or to Derbend, to Colonel Verkovsky."

"Only to hell would I go with such an escort," sneered Ackmeth Khan.

At the same time he made his horse rear to his hind feet, swayed him to the right, then to the left, and at last, striking his hind-quarters a violent blow with his whip, he leaped him over the sentinel, who was overthrown by the shock.

The noukars set their horses at a gallop and followed their khan, who rode about a hundred paces at full speed and then allowed his horse to resume his ordinary gait, all the while indifferently trifling with his bridle.

Then only was his attention attracted by the crowd of Tartars gathered about the farrier, who had begun to shoe the captain's horse; for, just as the captain had failed to see what was taking place behind his back, so had Ackmeth Khan been in ignorance of what was going on ahead of him.

"Is there any disturbance here?" inquired the khan, pulling up his horse. "What is the trouble? what is the dispute about?"

"Ah! the khan!" cried the Tartars.

And they bowed respectfully.

Ackmeth Khan repeated his question.

They related the affair of the captain and the farrier.

"And you stand looking on, as unmoved and stupid as buffaloes, while your brother is being outraged, your customs are set at naught, and your religion is trampled under foot!" cried Ackmeth Khan; "and you mumble like so many old women, instead of taking your revenge! Why don't you weep?"

Then three times in tones of deepest scorn he exclaimed, —

"Cowards! cowards! cowards!"

"And what can we do?" returned several voices. "The Russians have muskets and bayonets."

"And you, have you no guns and poniards? Shame!

shame to the Mussulmans! The sword of Daghestan to
cower under the Muscovite whip!"

Eyes flashed.

Ackmeth continued:—

"Ah! you fear muskets and bayonets, but you do not
fear dishonor. Between hell and Siberia, you choose
hell. Did your ancestors behave in that way? Did
your fathers think as you do? They did not count the
enemy, but whatever their number, they rushed upon
them shouting, 'Allah!' and if they fell, they at least
fell with glory. Are the Russians, perchance, of better
mettle than you? Have their guns never turned but
their muzzles upon you? A bull is to be taken by
the horns, wretches! A scorpion is seized by the tail,
cowards!"

And as before, he three times ejaculated,—

"Cowards! cowards! cowards!"

This time the insult struck the Tartars full in the breast.

"He is right!" they cried; "Ackmeth Khan is rigth!
We are too strong to take all that from the Russians.
Free the farrier! free Alikper!"

And, more menacing than ever, they began to crowd
upon the soldiers in whose centre the smith was shoeing
the captain's horse.

The revolt was growing.

Satisfied with having brought matters to this pass, and
not wishing to compromise himself in such a small affair,
Achmeth Khan left two of his noukars to egg on the
Tartars, and followed by the other three, he pursued up
the mountain the shortest route leading to the home of
Ammalat Beg.

The latter had already regained his house, and he was
lying upon a divan smoking his khalian.

On seeing Ackmeth Khan appear at his threshold, he
rose and went to meet him.

"May you conquer!" said Ackmeth Khan to Ammalat Beg.

This Circassian greeting was uttered with so much sig-
nificance that Ammalat Beg, after embracing Ackmeth
Khan, inquired, —

"Were you jesting or prophesying when you addressed
me just now, my dear guest?"

"That depends on you, and will be as you please. The
heir of Tarkovsky's principality has only to draw his
sword —"

"Never to sheath it again, khan!"

Then, shaking his head, he continued, —

"It would be a bad thing for me. It is much better
to be the quiet and undisputed lord of Bouinaky than to
be hiding in the mountains like an outlaw."

"Or like a lion, Ammalat. Lions, too, live in the
mountains to be free."

The young man sighed.

"It is much better to dream on without waking, Ackmeth, — I am asleep, do not wake me."

"It is the Russians who are administering the opium
that puts you to sleep; and, in your lethargy, another
culls the golden fruits of your garden."

"What can I do with the small force that I have?"

"Force lies in the soul, Ammalat. Do but dare, and
everything will give way before you."

Then, assuming a listening attitude, he added, —

"Hark! there's another voice besides mine calling on
you to arouse yourself; it is victory's!"

In fact, the sound of a lively fusillade reached the ears
of the two princes.

At that moment Sophyr Ali entered the room, his face
pale and agitated.

"Do you hear, chamkal?" said he. "Bouinaky is in

revolt.   A mob has surrounded the company of Russians
and the Tartars are firing on the soldiers."

" Ah ! the rascals ! " cried Ammalat Beg, springing for
his gun.   " How have they dared do such a thing without me ?   Run on, Sophyr Ali; command them in my
name to keep quiet, and kill the first who disobeys."

" I tried to quiet them," answered the young man;
" but they would not listen. Ackmeth Khan's noukars are
there urging them on, shouting, 'Kill the Russians !' "

" Did my noukars really shout that ?" asked Ackmeth
Khan, with a smile.

" They not only shouted that, but they set the example
by shooting first," said Sophyr Ali.

" In that case," remarked Ackmeth Khan, " they are
brave men, and they can take a hint when it is given to
them."

" What have you done, Ackmeth Khan ?" remonstrated
Ammalat Beg, sorrowfully.

" What you should have done long ago."

" How shall I face the Russians now ?"

" With ball and kandjiar. Fate is at work for you,
happy rebel. Come, out with our schaskas and let us
fall upon the Russians!"

" Here they are!" thundered the captain, bursting into
the room with two men, so rapidly had he climbed the
mountain slope which led to Ammalat's house.

Then, turning to his two men, he said, —

" Guard the doors, there, and see that no one goes out."
The soldiers obeyed.

Annoyed at this unexpected revolt in which he could
very easily be implicated, although he had not taken the
slightest hand in it, Ammalat advanced to the captain
and in a friendly tone, contrasting with the angry accents of the other, he inquired in Tartar speech, —

"Do you bring peace into my house, brother?"

"I do not know what I am bringing into your house,
Ammalat," said the captain; "but I do know the kind
of reception I am getting in your village; I am received
as an enemy, and your men have fired on the soldiers of
my—your—of our common emperor."

They have done wrong to fire on the Russians," inter-
posed Ackmeth Khan reclining indolently among the
cushions of the divan and drawing a whiff at the khalian
abandoned by Ammalat Beg; "they have not done well,
unless every shot has killed its man."

"See, there lies the cause of all the mischief,
Ammalat!" cried the captain angrily, pointing at
Ackmeth Khan. "But for him everything would be
quiet in Bouinaky. Really, you are a fine one,
Ammalat. You call yourself the friend of the Russians,
and receive their enemy as your guest! You conceal
him like an accomplice! Ammalat Beg, in the name
of the emperor, I demand that you deliver up this man
to me."

"Captain," replied Ammalat gently but firmly, "you
know that with us a guest is sacred. It would be criminal in me to deliver up my guest. Do not insist; have
some regard for our customs, and, if I must say it, for
my entreaty."

"And I say, Ammalat, duty before custom; hospitality
is sacred, but the oath is still more sacred. The oath
forbids our defrauding justice of even our own brother, if
that brother is a criminal."

"I would sooner betray my brother than my guest,
captain. Besides, it is not for you to dictate to me
what course I shall follow. If I sin, Allah and the
padishah will judge me. Let the Prophet guard the
khan on mountain or plain: once there, I have nothing

to say; but here, under my own roof, it is my duty to
defend him," and, added the young prince resolutely, " I
shall defend him."

" Then you countenance a traitor ? " the captain asked.

Ackmeth Khan had taken no part in the controversy;
he smoked his khalian as placidly as if some other person were in question; but at the word *traitor*, he bounded
rather than rose to his feet, and approaching the captain
he said, —

" You call me a traitor; say rather that I might have
been a traitor to those to whom I should be faithful.
The Russian padishah bestowed power on me, and I was
grateful to him as long as he did not demand the impossible. I was desired to admit the Russian troops into
Avarie, to permit them to build fortresses there. What
would you have called me then, had I betrayed the blood
and the liberties of those over whom Allah had set me as
father and chief? But, had I so wished, I could not
have succeeded; thousands of pouiards would have
pierced my heart; the rocks would have wrenched themselves from their places and fallen upon my head. I
held myself aloof from the friendship of the Russians,
but I was not yet their enemy. What reward had I for
my forbearance ? I was insulted by a letter from one of
your generals. He paid dearly for that insult at Backli.
For a few words, I spilled a river of blood, and that
river of blood separates you and me forever."

" And that blood cries for vengeance ! " yelled the infuriated captain; " vengeance which you shall not escape,
miscreant ! "

And he moved as if to seize Ackmeth Khan by the
throat.

But before his hand could touch the mountain chief-
tain, the latter's kandjiar was buried deep in his vitals.

Without uttering a syllable, without breathing a sigh, the captain fell dead on the carpet.

. Then, drawing his pistol from his belt with the same rapidity and snatching Ammalat Beg's from his, Ackmeth Khan, with two shots as swift as a flash, as deadly as lightning, laid at his feet the two Russians who were guarding the door.

Ammalat Beg saw him do it without having time to avert this threefold murder.

" You have ruined me, Ackmeth," said he, mournfully. " That man was a Russian and he was my guest."

" There are some offences that the roof does not cover, chamkal," said the khan; " but this is no time for argument: let us shut the doors, summon your men and march upon the enemy."

" An hour ago they were not my enemies," said Ammalat Beg, " and now how would you have me march against them? I have no powder, I have no balls, and my men are scattered."

" The Russians! the Russians!" cried Sophyr Ali, rushing in, and paling with horror at sight of the three bodies.

" Come with me, Ammalat," said the khan. " I was going into Tchetchina to arouse them over the border; what will come of it, God knows! But there is bread and water in the mountains, and powder and shot. That is all a mountaineer needs. What say you?"

" Let us be off, then," answered Ammalat, his decision made. " Nothing but flight is left for me. You are right, it is no time for recrimination and reproach. My horse and six noukars to go with me, Sophyr Ali, —"

" And I, and I, too?" said the young man, interrupting him with tears in his eyes. ·

" No. You, my dear Sophyr, must remain here to

watch that the house is not plundered.   Convey my salu-
tations to my wife and take her to her father's.   Do not
forget me.   Farewell! "

And, as Ackmeth Khan and Ammalat went out at one
door, the Russians came in at another.

III.

A SULTRY noon of spring hung over the Caucasus.

The muèzzins' voices were calling the people of Tchetchina to prayer, and their droning monotones, after having awakened for an instant an echo in the rocks, little by little died away on the still air.

The mullah, Hadji Soleiman, a pious Turk, sent into the mountains by the divan of Stamboul to strengthen the faith of the mountaineers and at the same time to incite them to revolt against the Russians, was reposing on the roof of the mosque, having performed his ablutions and prayers. Only a short time prior to this, he had been appointed mullah of the village of the Tchetchen-Igalis, and this, without doubt, was the reason why he so solemnly contemplated his beard, and so seriously watched the wreaths of smoke curling from his chibouk.

Moreover, from time to time his eye dwelt with satisfaction on the black mouths of two or three caves hollowed out of the rock just in front of him.

At his left rose the crests of the range separating Tchetchina from Avarie, and beyond them towered the snowy peaks of the Caucasus. The cottages scattered over the slopes descended in cascade-like groups half-way down the mountain-side, where they stopped, forming a fortress accessible only by narrow paths, and, created by nature, providing the mountaineers with an ark of safety for their liberties.

All was quiet within the village and on the neighboring mountains; not a soul was to be seen on highway or

hy-way. Flocks of sheep had sought the shade of the
ravines; buffaloes were huddled together in a narrow
muddy stream, and, embedded in its mire, only their
heads were exhibited above the water. The faint buzz-
ing of insects, the monotonous chirp of the cricket, were
the only signs of life that nature submitted amid the
mournful stillness of the mountains, and, lying under the
cupola, Hadji Soleiman was admiring, with the calm per-
taining only to a reposeful people, that inert splendor of
nature, so harmonious with the indolence of the Mussulman. He was all but closing his eyes, in whose wavering
sight the fire and light of the sun seemed to have been
extinguished, when, through that blurred vision, he
became conscious of two horsemen who were clambering
slowly up the mountain opposite the one with the hollow
caverns.

"Nephtali!" called the mullah, turning toward the
cottage nearest the mosque, and before whose door was a
saddled horse.

At this call, a handsome Circassian, his beard short
without being shaved, his head covered by a papak that
concealed half of his face, appeared in the street.

"I see two horsemen," continued the mullah; "and
they are skirting the village."

"They are Jews or Armenians," answered Nephtali.
"For economy's sake they have not been willing to hire
a guide, and they will break their necks on the path
which they have undertaken; none but wild goats and
Tchetchina's best riders follow that trail."

"No, brother Nephtali," said the mullah. "I have
made two trips to Mecca, and I know Jews and Armenians perfectly well. These horsemen are neither the one
nor the other. If they were Jews or Armenians, they
would be coming on commercial business, and would have

baggage; but, do you look, — your eyes are young and, consequently, keener than mine. I could once," continued the mullah, "at a verst's distance have counted the buttons on a Russian soldier's uniform, and the ball that I aimed at the infidel never missed its mark; but to-day, at the same distance, I can hardly tell a buffalo from a horse."

And he heaved a sigh.

While he was speaking, rather to himself than to his companion, the latter had quickly ascended to him, and was scanning the travellers, who continued to approach.

"The day is warm, and travel is fatiguing," said the mullah; "invite these two travellers to refresh themselves and rest their horses. Perhaps they have some news. The Koran tells us to welcome the wayfarers."

"Even before the Koran had penetrated our mountains," said Nephtali, "never did a traveller leave the village without resting in it and receiving refreshment; never did he say good-by without a blessing, or set out without a guide for the rest of his journey; yet I feel suspicious of these travellers. Why do they avoid friendly people? and, instead of going through the hamlet, why do they pass at one side at the risk of their lives?"

"At any rate, they seem to me to be compatriots," said Hadji Soleiman, shading his eyes with his hand to ward off the sun's rays. "They wear the Tchetchen garb; perhaps, again, these are the two brothers bound by an oath to avenge blood by blood."

"No, Soleiman," said the young man, shaking his head; "no, these men are none of ours. No mountaineer would come here expressly to boast of a fight with the Russians and to show their weapons. Neither are they

abrecks ;[1] the *abrecks,* were they passing through a village of their bitterest enemies, would not draw their
bachliks[2] over their faces.   The garb sometimes de-
ceives, hadji; who knows but what these are Russian
deserters? Not long ago a Cossack escaped from the
hamlet of Goumbet after killing the master of the house
where he lived, and stealing his horse and weapons.
The devil is very crafty, and often the strongest will
yield to temptation."

"There is no strength where the faith is weak, Nephtali; but stay, I see curls below the papak of the second
horseman."

"May I be ground to powder if it is not so!" exclaimed Nephtali.   "He is a Russian, or, worse still, a
Shiite Tartar.[3] Wait, wait, I will frizzle his curly locks
for him. I shall return in half an hour, Soleiman.   In
half an hour they shall either be our guests, or one of
us shall measure the height of the precipice."

Nephtali quickly descended the stairs, took his gun,
sprang to horse, and dashed off at full gallop over the
mountain, unmindful alike of rocks and ravines.   But
in the distance the stones could be seen flying like dust
behind this daring rider.

"*Allah akbar!*" said the hadji proudly, as he re-
lighted his extinguished chibook.

Nephtali soon overtook the two riders.   Their horses,
jaded, and covered with foam, were raining sweat upon
the narrow path along which they were toiling up the
mountain.   One rider wore the Tchepsour's coat of mail,

[1] The *abrecks* are mountaineers who have taken oath to court
peril, and who consequently use no precaution to avoid it.
[2] Hoods.
[3] Mussulmans are divided into two hostile sects, — Sunnites and
Shiites; Nephtali and Soleiman are Sunnites.

the other, the Circassian costume; only, at variance with this costume, a Persian sabre instead of a schaska was suspended from the rich girdle wound around his person.

Their faces could not be seen, their bachliks being drawn down; perhaps they desired protection from the sun, perhaps they did not desire to be recognized

Nephtali followed behind them along the narrow path on the verge of the precipice; but, the path becoming a little wider, he went ahead and barred the way.

"*Salaam aleikoum!*" said he, resting his loaded gun across the saddle.

The first of the two strangers raised his bachlik, but only enough to see without being seen.

"*Aleikoum salaam!*" he responded, detaching his gun and rising in the stirrups.

"God grant you safe conduct!" continued Nephtali, getting ready to slay, at the first hostile movement, the traveller for whom he asked God's protection.

"As for you," answered the unknown in the coat of mail, "God grant you enough intelligence to keep you from barricading a traveller's path another time. What do you want, *kounack?*"[1]

"To proffer rest and refreshment for yourselves, and a stable for your horses. There is ever room in my house for guests. The wayfarer's blessing multiplies the flocks. Cast not upon our village the reproach that any have passed without stopping."

"Thanks, brother. We have not come into the mountains to visit; we are in haste."

"Be warned!" replied Nephtali; "you ride to meet danger unless you take a guide."

"A guide?" repeated the traveller, with a laugh; "a guide in the Caucasus? Why, I know the mountain

[1] Brother, comrade.

much better than any of you; I have been where jaguars
have not, where serpents never crawl, where none but
eagles perch. Stand aside, comrade; your house is not
on my way, and I have no time to lose prating with
you."

"I will not yield an inch," answered the young man,
"until I know your name."

"Thank your stars, Nephtali, that I knew your father;
I have often ridden to battle by his side. But, out of
my path, or, in spite of the friendship I bear her, your
mother shall weep to-morrow at sight of shreds of her
son's flesh in the teeth of jackals and the beaks of eagles.
Unworthy son, you are coursing the highways, seeking
quarrels with travellers, while your father's bones are
bleaching on the Russian plain and the Cossack women
are selling his weapons! Nephtali, your father was
killed yesterday on the other side of the Terek. Now,
since you wish to know who I am, look at me."

"Sultan Ackmeth Khan!" exclaimed the young Tchetchen, doubly agitated by the tidings he had just received
and the severity of the traveller's regard.

"Yes, I am Ackmeth Khan," replied the prince; "but
bear in mind, Nephtali, that if you say to any one, 'I
have seen the khan of Avarie,' my vengeance shall pursue your descendants even to the last generation."

The young man stood respectfully aside, and the travellers passed him by.

Ackmeth Khan again relapsed into the silence from
which the young man's intrusion had aroused him. He
was plunged in sad reflections. The second traveller,
Ammalat Beg, — for it was he, — like the khan, was
pensive and silent. Their clothes bore traces of a recent
fight, their mustaches were powder-singed, and smears
of blood had dried on their faces. But Ackmeth Khan's

proud bearing seemed to challenge all nature; a scornful
smile played on his lips.

As for Ammalat Beg, his features wore a jaded look
of fatigue. He scarcely glanced about him; but from
time to time a sigh escaped his lips, wrested from him by
the pain of a wounded hand.

The gait of his horse, little used to the mountains,
fretted as much as it wearied him.

He was the first to break silence.

"Why did you refuse the invitation of that kind young
man?" he demanded of the khan of Avarie. "We could
have stopped an hour or two."

"You think and talk like a child, my dear Ammalat,"
returned the khan. "You are accustomed to governing
Tartars and ordering them about like slaves, and you
think the same course can be pursued with the mountaineers. The hand of fate lies heavy on us; we are
beaten and pursued; more than a hundred mountaineers,
your noukars and mine, have fallen by Russian balls.
Would you that we show the Tchetchens the vanquished
Ackmeth Khan, whom they are wont to look upon as
the star of victory? Shall I appear before them as
an outlaw? Shall I confess my own shame? To
accept a needed hospitality, to submit myself to reproaches for the deaths of husbands and sons drawn by
me into this engagement, is to lose their confidence. In
time, their tears will dry; then Ackmeth Khan will
reappear before them, the prophet of pillage and blood,
and I will then lead them again to battle on the Russian
frontiers. Were the desperate Tchetchens to catch sight
of me to-day, they would not recollect that Allah alone
dispenses and withholds victory. They might insult me
with some imprudent speech, and I have never forgiven
an insult; in that case, a petty personal vengeance might

thrust itself across my path on some day when I am setting out against the ranks of the Russians. Why should
I quarrel unnecessarily with a brave people? Why
should I myself prostrate the idol of glory upon which
they are accustomed to gaze with dazzled eyes? If I descend to the common ranks, every man will begin to
measure his shoulder by mine. As for you, you are in
need of a physician, and you will find none better than
mine. To-morrow we shall be at home; keep up your
courage till then."

Ammalat Beg carried his hand in graceful acknowl-
edgment to heart and brow; he recognized the force of
the khan's words, but he was weak from loss of blood.

Continuing to avoid the villages, they spent the night
among the Tartar rocks, eating a little rice and honey, —
provisions without which a mountaineer never under-
takes a journey, however short it may be. They crossed
the Koissu by the bridge near Scherté. They left behind them Andi, Boulins, and the ridge of the Salatahur.
Their way lay through forests and along precipices appalling to both sight and soul. At last they began to ascend
the range that separated them on the north from Khunsack, the capital of the khan. To reach the summit of
this ridge, the travellers were obliged to pursue diagonal
paths, continually doubling on their tracks, but at each
step gaining somewhat on the height. The khan's horse,
born to the mountains and accustomed to these arduous
trails, stepped cautiously; but Ammalat Beg's young and
spirited charger kept stumbling and falling at every
step. His master's favorite, and pampered by him, he
was unequal to such a forced march in the mountains.
Under a blazing sun, amidst fields of snow, he could
scarcely gasp, and with violent effort his dilated nostrils
appeared to breathe fire, while the foam tossed from
his bit.

"*Allah bereket!*"[1] cried Ammalat Beg, as they attained the culminating point of the mountain, whence his gaze embraced the whole of Avarie.

But, at the same instant, his horse sank under him; the blood gushed from the noble animal's mouth, and his last sigh burst the girth.

The khan assisted Ammalat Beg to free himself from his stirrups; but he saw with dismay that, in his fall, the young man's handkerchief had slipped from the wound, and the blood which they had with such difficulty stanched was flowing afresh.

But this time Ammalat was unconscious of his pain; he was weeping over his dead horse.

A drop is enough to overflow the full cup.

"Never again will you carry me like a feather in the wind, my brave charger," said he; "nor in a cloud of dust in the race while I hear the shouts of those left behind me, nor amidst cheering warriors through the fire and smoke of battles! With you, I had secured a horseman's renown; why am I condemned to survive my glory and you?"

He bowed his head between his knees and was silent, while the khan bandaged his wound. Finally, noticing the care which the khan was bestowing on him, he suddenly exclaimed, —

"Leave me, Ackmeth Khan, leave an unhappy man to his hard fate. The journey is not over, and I yield. If you remain with me, you will needlessly perish with me. Look at that eagle circling above us; he knows that he will soon take my heart in his claws, and, thank God! it is better to be entombed in the breast of a noble bird than trampled underfoot by the Christians. Farewell! Leave me!"

[1] God be praised!

"Are you not ashamed, Ammalat, thus to succumb
on stumbling against a straw? What is your wound?
What's a dead horse? In eight days there will be
no signs of your wound. We shall find a better horse.
Misfortune comes from Allah, but so does good fortune.
It is a sin to despair when one is young. Mount my
horse, I will lead him by the bridle, and before nightfall
we shall be at home. Come, every moment is precious;
come, time is dear."

"Time no longer exists for me, Ackmeth Khan,"
answered the young man; "I thank you again for your
fraternal friendship, but I will not abuse it. We have
still too far to go, and we cannot walk so far. Leave me
to my fate. On these heights, so near to heaven, I shall
die free and content. My father is dead; I am wedded
to a wife whom I do not love; my uncle and my father-
in-law are on their knees to the Russians. Exiled from
home, flying from battle, I ought not, nor do I wish, to
live."

"Your fever is speaking, not you, Ammalat; your
words are delirium. Are we not destined to survive our
parents? As for your wife, our holy religion gives you
the right to take three others. That you detest the
chamkal, I can understand; but you ought to love his
inheritance, which will some day make you a prince, and
independent! Besides, a dead man has no need of
wealth and power; a dead man takes no revenge, and it
is for you to avenge yourself on the Russians. Rouse
yourself, if only for that. We have been overcome; are
we the first to experience reverses? To-day the Russians conquer; to-morrow it will be our turn. Allah
grants happiness, but man wins his own renown. You
are wounded and weak; but I am sound and strong. You
are fainting with fatigue; while I am as fresh and active

as a man who has not yet crossed the threshold of his room, who has just put on his sandals and girded his loins. Mount my horse, Ammalat, and, as sure as that eagle is not there to feast on your heart, — look! he is flying away and disappearing in the distance, — we will make the Russians pay dearly for our defeat of yesterday."

The face of Ammalat Beg brightened.

"Well, yes," he said, "you are right. I will live for revenge, — for revenge, open or underhanded, but terrible, remorseless, deadly. Believe me, Ackmeth Khan, it is for the sake of revenge that I take up life again. From this moment I am yours, by the tomb of my father! I belong to you. Guide my steps, direct my blows, and, if ever I forget my oath, remind me of this moment, my dead horse, my bleeding hand, the eagle soaring above my head. If I fall asleep, I will waken and my poniard shall strike like the lightning."

Ackmeth Khan embraced the young man, took him in his arms like a child, and placed him in the saddle.

"And now," he said, "I recognize the pure blood of the emirs in you, — blood that riots in our veins like ignited saltpetre which, once fired, blasts mountains. Come with me, Ammalat Beg, and all that I have promised you Mahomet will make good."

And, while supporting the wounded man, Ackmeth Khan began to descend the mountain. Stones rolled from beneath their feet, more than once the horse fell; but at last, safe and sound, they reached the line where vegetation began.

Soon after, they entered a forest of many species of trees. The luxuriance of the forest and the oppressive stillness of the eternal twilight reigning under this green canopy impenetrable to the sun's rays, inspired man with respect for the savage freedom of nature.

At times the path threaded the forest trees, and again it was an escarpment on the edge of a cliff at whose foot glittered a brawling stream. Flame-throated pheasants sped from bush to bush. Everything exhaled that vivifying freshness of evening which is unknown to dwellers of the plain.

Our travellers had almost reached the village of Akhak, which is separated from Khunsack only by a small mountain, when they heard a shot.

They halted apprehensively.

But suddenly Ackmeth Khan announced, —

"They are my huntsmen; they are not expecting me at this hour, and especially in such a plight. I occasion Khunsack much joy and many tears."

Ackmeth Khan bowed his head and gave a sigh. His brow became clouded.

So quickly do sweet and bitter reflections succeed each other in an Asiatic's heart!

A second shot was heard, then a third. Then shot followed shot in quick succession.

"The Russians are at Khunsack!" cried Ammalat.

And he drew his sword, and dug his knees into his horse's sides, as if at a single leap he would clear the distance that intervened between him and them.

But the effort overpowered him; the sword slipped from his mutilated hand and fell to the earth.

As for him, he exerted his remaining strength to dismount from the horse.

"Ackmeth Khan," said he, "hasten to the aid of your people; your presence will avail more than the help of a hundred cavalrymen."

But Ackmeth Khan paid no attention; he was listening to the whistling balls as if he would distinguish those of the Russians from those of his own warriors.

" How came they down there ? " he cried. " Are they chamois-footed ? have they eagles' wings ? Farewell, Ammalat, I will go and die on the ruins of my own fortresses. "

But just then a ball fell at his feet.

He picked it up, and, smiling, said composedly, —

" Remount my horse, Ammalat. You will soon know what that means; the Russian bullets are lead, and this is copper. "

Then, looking at the ball, he said,—

" This blessed ally ! it has come from where the Russians cannot, — from the south. "

They proceeded to ascend the small hill that separated them from Khunsack.

Reaching the summit, they gazed down upon a veritable field of battle, beyond which rose the hamlet of Khunsack, overlooked by the two towers 'of the castle of Ackmeth Khan.

A hundred men, divided into two factions, were firing upon each other under cover of houses standing in front of great masses of rock or concealed behind them; while the women, unveiled, with babes in their arms and their hair flying, mingled with the combatants and urged them on.

Ammalat Beg regarded this spectacle with astonishment, and looked inquiringly at the Khan.

" That surprises you ! " he said, shrugging his shoulders; " it is common with us. Down in the plain, when a man has a grudge against another man, he gives him a knife-thrust, and all is over; in the mountain, one man's quarrel is every man's quarrel. The reason of all that uproar ? A trifle, very likely ; perhaps a cow has been stolen. With us it is no disgrace to steal; the disgrace is to let oneself be robbed, that is all. Admire the

courage of those women, Ammalat," pursued the khan
excitedly, inhaling the powder-smoke with dilated nostrils. "The balls whiz past their ears; death flaps her
wings above their heads, and they laugh at her. Oh,
those are the mothers and wives of brave men, and truly
it would be a pity were misfortune to overtake them! I
am just in time to stop this game."

And, taking his gun, he advanced to the highest part of
the ridge and discharged it into the air.

At that shot, coming from a direction whence it was
not expected, the combatants faced about in amazement.

Then, with his left hand, Ackmeth Khan put back his
bachlik.

There rose a great shout from both factions. The
combatants had recognized him.

"Keep your powder and balls for the Russians, men of
Khunsack," he cried; "not another shot. I will judge
your difference, and give justice to him that is right and
his deserts to him that is wrong."

But the khan's order was not needed for putting an
end to the conflict; their joy at seeing him again was so
great that all resentment seemed to be forgotten.

Men and women ran headlong toward him, crying, —
"Long live Ackmeth Khan!"

"That is well, that is well, my children!" responded
Ackmeth Khan. "I will descend to-morrow to the public square and speak to the old men; but I bring back a
wounded friend who is in need of prompt relief; do not
hinder me then, for such relief he will find only at my
house."

And, indeed, Ammalat Beg saw nothing of what was
passing except as through a mist; he had abandoned the
horse's bridle to maintain himself in the saddle.

In an instant they were shaping a litter from their

guns, all powder-blackened and hot from the fray. Friends and enemies joined together in spreading their bourkas across it. They laid the wounded man upon it; and Ackmeth Khan remounted his horse, as became a prince returning to his own stronghold.

Ammalat Beg was laid on the khan's softest rugs. He had fainted entirely away.

IV.

THE wounded man did not regain consciousness until the next day.

His ideas then returned to him like phantoms floating in mist.

He remembered nothing; he felt no pain.

This condition was agreeable rather than unpleasant. His torpor divested life of its sensibility and, consequently, of its bitterness.

He would have answered with equal indifference a summons to either life or death. He had neither the strength nor the desire to utter a word. Had his existence depended on a movement of the hand, he would not have taken the trouble to lift a finger.

This condition did not last long, however.

At noon, after the doctor's visit, when all the servants of the khan were at prayer, and he himself, according to his promise of the day before, had descended to the market-place, Ammalat Beg, left alone, thought he heard light and timid steps crossing the carpet of the room leading to his own.

· With an effort he essayed to turn his head; and he must have succeeded in so doing, for he fancied he saw, — he was too weak to distinguish between fact and fancy, — he fancied, we repeat, that he saw the portière of his room lifted, and a young girl with black eyes, in a yellow silk robe confined by a red arkalouke decorated with buttons of enamel, with long black hair falling upon her

shoulders, who very softly approached his bed, bending
over him with sweet and tender solicitude to look at his
wounded hand. Ammalat Beg, fanned by her breath,
brushed by her raiment, felt a thrill of fire course his
veins; then she poured the contents of a vial into a tiny
silver cup, passed her arm under his head, raised it,
and —

Ammalat felt nothing more, saw nothing more; his
weighted eyelids sank again; all his senses seemed blended
into a single one.

He listened.

He listened, and the rustling of the young girl's robe
seemed to him the rustling of angel's wings.

But, this angel was flying away —

All became quiet again; and when the eyes of the
wounded man reopened, he was alone, and it was impossible for him to invest his vision with any shadow of
substance. Fragmentary trains of thought, floating like
clouds in the immensity of space, were lost in feverish
dreams; and as soon as he could utter a word, he said to
himself, — .

"It was a dream."

He was deceived.

What he believed to be a creation of delirium was a
maid of sixteen, the daughter of Ackmeth Khan.

Among the mountaineers, even when Mussulmans,
young girls enjoy infinitely greater freedom among men
than do married women, although the Mohammedan law
prescribes exactly to the contrary.

Now, Ackmeth Khan's daughter enjoyed even greater
freedom than others, as it was only with her at his side
that her father could rest from his fatigue; only with her
did he unbend his brows in a smile. It meant salvation
to the culprit if the young princess were but present when

sentence was pronounced; the uplifted ax was arrested in
air.   To hor everything was granted, for her everything
was possible.   Ackmeth Khan knew not how to deny
her anything, and a suspicion had never entered his mind
that the pure child could do anything incompatible with
her duty or her rank.   Besides, who could inspire her
with the tender sentiments which might lead a young girl
to commit a fault?   Until now, her father had never received a guest who was his equal in birth; or rather, her
heart had never concerned itself as to the rank or age of
the guests who visited her father.   That fact of itself
had undoubtedly prolonged her girlhood, scarcely yet out
of its childhood; but, since the evening before, she had
been conscious of the beating of her own heart.   On the
day before, as she threw her arms about her father's neck,
she had seen lying at his feet a young man in a swoon,
almost dead.   Her first feeling had been of fear, and she
had turned her eyes away from the wounded man.   But
when her father had related why Ammalat came to be
his guest, she began to view the young man with looks of
melting pity; then, when the doctor had declared that
his appalling weakness was due merely to loss of blood
and not to the gravity of his wound, a tender anxiety
possessed the young girl.   Was the doctor not deceived?
Such a gaping, ghastly wound — was it not more dangerous than he thought?   She went to bed, full of this fear;
all night in her dreams she saw the handsome youth
covered with blood; more than once she opened her eyes
in the dark, thinking she heard him moan; and, for the
first time in her life, morning found her less fresh than
the dawn; for the first time, she employed a ruse to gain
a wish.   Her father was in the wounded man's room;
she chose this moment to bid her father good-morning.
But Ammalat's eyes were closed, and she could not see his

eyes. At noon she returned; Ammalat was alone, but
the dazed eyes of the young prince closed at sight of her.
The poor child was in despair. He must have such
beautiful eyes! Never, in all her girlhood, had she so
coveted a set of rich jewels. She would have given two
diamonds the size of her own eyes to open those eyes that
ought to beam with a fire very different, she thought,
from that of two diamonds.

Finally, in the evening she returned again.

In the evening for the first time she encountered the
invalid's wan but expressive clear eye; and, upon en-
countering it, the glance was not withdrawn. She knew
very well what those eyes were crying to her: "Do not
go away, star of my soul! Do you not perceive that you
are my only light, and that, departing, you will plunge
me into the darkness of night?"

She could not comprehend the change that was taking
place in herself; it was impossible for her to tell whether
she was still on earth or already in heaven. What she
was experiencing, she had never experienced before: the
blood surged to her heart so violently that she felt as if
she were being smothered; it receded from her heart so
quickly that she thought she was dying.

She had seen the eyes of the wounded man, and she
had discovered that they were the most beautiful eyes in
the world.

It remained for her to hear his voice.

But Ammalat Beg continued mute. Wholly absorbed
in the contemplation of her, it did not occur to him to
speak. What could be said that his eyes could not say
as well as his voice?

The young girl's wishes were born in quick succession.
With such fine eyes he must have a very sweet voice.
What a pity not to hear that voice!

Then an idea occurred to her: if the young man did
not speak, it was doubtless because he was too weak; if
he were too weak to talk, certainly the wound was
dangerous, more dangerous than the doctor had said.

Surely she could not go away filled with such dire un-
certainty; and so she determined to speak first. What
could be simpler? It was her duty to ask about his
health.

A man would have to be a Tartar, would have to re
gard it as insulting to address a woman, must never have
seen aught of one except a veil, and through this veil two
eyebrows and perhaps the eyes beneath them, in order to
conceive some idea of the thrill that sped through the
veins of the wounded man, when, already pierced by her
eyes, he received the girl's voice full in his heart.

And yet Sultanetta's words were very simple.

Her name was Sultanetta.

"How do you feel?" she asked.

"Oh! very well, very well," answered Ammalat Beg,
trying to rise on his elbow; "so well that I am ready to
die."

"Allah preserve you!" cried the girl, in dismay;
"you must live yet a long time. Would you not be sorry
to die?"

"To die in a happy hour is to die happy, Sultanetta;
and were I to live a hundred years, I should never have
a more fitting moment than this."

Sultanetta did not comprehend her guest's speech, but
she understood the expression of his eyes, the accent of
his voice. A flush tinged her cheek, and, with a sign
warning the young man to lie back, she escaped from the
room.

Among the mountaineers there are certainly skilful
surgeons, especially those who treat wounds. They have

secret remedies for closing wounds that are seemingly mysterious revelations of nature; but the most efficacious remedy acting on Ammalat Beg was the presence of the charming Sultanetta. At night he fell asleep with the fond hope that she would appear in his dream; in the morning he awoke to the certainty of seeing her in reality. His strength rapidly returned, and with his strength increased the feeling hitherto unknown which he had experienced at sight of Ackmeth Khan's daughter on that first day, and which was now so rooted in his heart as never again to leave it.

Ammalat Beg, as we have said, was married; but the marriage was arranged just as marriages in the Orient are arranged. Until the day of his wedding, he had never seen his betrothed; then, when he did see her, he found her ugly, and every sentiment akin to youth and love remained dormant in his heart. Following upon his marriage had come political wrangles with his uncle and his father-in-law. Tenderness, which among the Orientals appeals only to sensuality, was by degrees extinguished; so that his eyes on first beholding Sultanetta had no need to demand from his heart a sacrifice of the remains of an old love. The young man had been married, but his heart was virgin ground. Ardent by nature, independent from habit, Ammalat Beg abandoned himself completely to the sentiment by which he was possessed. To be with Sultanetta was his supreme happiness, and to look for her coming was his sole occupation when she was absent. He trembled on hearing her footsteps; he was shaken at the sound of her voice. Every tone filled his being with rapture. What he felt was like unto pain; but it was pain so sweet, an ill so full of recompense, that for want of this pain he doubted not he should die.

Doubtless these two young people, ignorant themselves
of what they were experiencing, gave this unfamiliar
sentiment the name of friendship; but, under no restraint,
they were constantly together. Khan Ackmeth took
frequent journeys in Avarie, and left his guest to his
daughter. He only perhaps was aware of their love;
but this love was the crown of his desires. A first marriage, as he had told Ammalat, was nothing to a Mussulman, who had the right to espouse four wives. Besides,
he knew the scant affection existing between the young
couple. To become the father-in-law of Ammalat Beg,
that is, of the heir of Chamkal Tarkovsky, of a man who
could be of such great assistance to him in his war with
the Russians, was more than a desire, it was an
ambition.

As for the two lovers, they made no calculations, we
came near saying that they had no wishes. They were
happy, asking nothing more, with no thought that this
happiness could end. The days passed without their
knowing how, in looking through the window at the
mountains, at the flocks of sheep on the heights, at the
rivers below. If Sultanetta was employed in embroidering
her father's saddle, Ammalat was reclining near her on
the cushions, telling her his youthful adventures, but
oftener without speaking a word, his eyes being fixed
upon hers. He thought not of the past, nor dreamed of
the future. He only felt that he was happy, and, without removing the cup from his lips, he drank drop by
drop the greatest felicity on earth for man, — to love and
be loved.

Thus the summer went by.

One morning, one of the khan's shepherds came down
in great fright.

At daybreak a tiger had come out of the forest, and,

creeping along like a cat towards the flock, had pounced on a sheep and carried it off.

The shepherd told it in the court, while all the noukars gathered around him in a circle.

"Well," said the khan, "does any one wish to kill the tiger? He may carry my finest and best gun. Let him kill the tiger, and the weapon is his."

One of the khan's noukars, an excellent shot, advanced, chose the weapon that pleased him best among all the khan's guns, and said,—

"I will go!"

The khan returned, related the incident to Sultanetta and Ammalat; but the young people were so engrossed by their love that neither of them appeared to hear what Ackmeth Khan had said.

The next day, they waited in vain for the noukar.

It was the shepherd's lad that came.

The boy told how, having arrived on the mountain towards evening, the noukar had discovered the tiger's path. The next morning before daylight he lay in ambush beside the trail that the animal had taken on leaving the forest to prowl for sheep.

But the tiger did not appear; yet he had been heard roaring in the forest about a verst away. Doubtless he had not devoured in one day the entire sheep, and had sufficient left for his morning meal.

Seeing that the tiger did not appear, the noukar had resolved to go in search of him. He had entered the forest. A quarter of an hour later, the boy had heard a report, then a roar; then all was silent.

He had waited an hour; but not seeing the man come out of the wood, he came to tell what had happened.

According to all probability, the man was dead.

They waited a day, two days, three days: the man had not been seen.

On the fourth day it was the tiger that put in an appearance, and he carried off a second sheep.

The little herder ran in terror to announce the ferocious brute's second attack.

This time it chanced that Sultanetta was sprinkling the flowers in her window, when the herder entered the court.

She heard all that the boy was saying.

She went back to Ammalat Beg and told him what she had just learned.

Ammalat Beg had not listened to a word of what Ackmeth Khan had said, but Sultanetta's words were too precious for a single one to be lost.

Ackmeth Khan entered just as Sultanetta was finishing her story.

"Well," he demanded, "what do you say to that, Ammalat?"

"That I have always desired to go on a tiger-hunt," returned the young man, "and that I am grateful to Allah for fulfilling my desire. I will try my luck against the tiger."

Sultanetta looked at Ammalat, pale but smiling; she understood, and, although filled with apprehension, she was proud.

Ackmeth Khan shook his head.

"A tiger is not the boar of Daghestan, Ammalat."

"Put me on the tiger's trail, and I will follow it as though it were a wild boar's."

"Tiger's tracks often lead to death," insisted Ackmeth Khan, who, having begun to be alarmed at his young friend's listlessness, with delight saw him emerge from his lethargy.

"Do you think my head will whirl on a slippery path, and that I cannot go where your noukar has been? If the heart of an Avare is as stout as mountain granite, the heart of a native of Daghestan is as hard as her steel."

Smiling, Ackmeth Khan extended a hand to him.

"And your heart's steel, brother, will break the tiger's teeth and the eagle's hooked beak. And when will you start?"

"Two hours before dawn."

"Very well," said Ackmeth Khan; "I will find you a guide."

"He is already found," said a voice behind the two men.

Ackmeth Khan, turning, recognized Nephtali.

"Ah! it is you?" he said.

"Yes, I heard that a tiger had eaten one of your sheep and killed a noukar, and I have come to say, My father's friend, I wish to prove that I am good for something else than waylaying travellers on the mountains to offer hospitality. I have come to slay the tiger."

"That may be," said Ammalat; "but you come too late."

"Why so?" said the young Tchetchen. "We shall be two on the trail and two in the fight. My father's son is entitled to walk beside a prince, were the prince Chamkal Tarkovsky's nephew. Ask Ackmeth Khan."

"I need no help to accomplish my undertaking," said the young man haughtily.

"There is no doubt that you need no one," said Ackmeth; "but you are wrong to refuse the companion who offers of his own free will to share your danger. I advise you to accept Nephtali's offer. Exchange vows like two brave abrecks, and may Allah watch over you!"

Ammalat's eyes turned toward Sultanetta. The young girl was regarding him with clasped hands. She knew

Nephtali to be one of the boldest and most skilful
hunters in the mountain, and she would not be sorry
that Ammalat should be accompanied by one of whose
courage she was sure.

" So be it! " said Ammalat.

And he extended his hand to the youth.

Among the Avares and Tchetchens, when two men
are engaging in a common danger together, it is their
custom to swear on the Koran not to abandon each
other.

If one of the two fails to keep his oath, he is thrown
over a precipice with his back to the abyss, as becomes a
coward and a traitor.

The two young men descended to the mosque, and
took the oath of abrecks. The mullah blessed their
weapons, and they set out upon the mountain road amidst
the cheers of the crowd.

" Both, or neither! " cried the khan after them.

" We will bring back the tiger's skin, or die," returned the hunters.

Ammalat did not say good-bye to Sultanetta; but, on
the highest tower of the khan's palace, the young girl
stood waving her handkerchief.

And the handkerchief fluttered until the two young
men had disappeared in the mountain.

It is unnecessary to observe that Ammalat Beg walked
behind, and was the last to lose sight of the village.

V.

THE next day passed.

They did not hope to have much news of the hunters for the first twenty-four hours.

Then came the following day, and the night.

On that evening the old men were worn out with gazing down the road.

They had seen nothing.

There was perhaps not a fireside in all Khunsack at which the expedition of the two abrecks was not being discussed; but of all hearts, the saddest and most anxious was Sultanetta's.

If a shout was heard in the court, if a step echoed from the stairway, her blood bounded madly through her veins, she was unable to breathe; she ran to the window, she inquired at the gate, and, deceived for the twentieth time, with bowed head and misty eyes she would resume her work, which for the first time seemed shockingly tedious. All her questions, without her tongue's framing Ammalat's name, had reference to Ammalat. She asked her father and brothers what kind of wounds the tiger inflicted, at what distance he could be seen, how long it would take him to reach the village from the place where he had been seen ; and after every question she would droop her head sadly and say to herself, —

" They are lost! "

The third day proved that they had not felt uneasiness without cause.

About two o'clock in the afternoon, a pale young man, his clothes torn, covered with clots of blood, and exhausted by hunger and fatigue, arrived at the outskirts of the village.

It was Nephtali. They pressed around him with curiosity, and eagerly questioned him.

This is what he had to tell: —

" On the same day that we left Khunsack, we discovered traces of the beast; but it was late, darkness was coming on; we might lose his trail, wander away, and expose ourselves to him without defence. We would reserve the attack for the morrow.

" I knew of a cave a hundred steps away; we entered that. A rock blocked up the entrance, and we slept tranquilly on our bourkas.

" The next morning at daybreak, we awoke; a roar that we heard in the mountain, told us that it was time to bestir ourselves.

" We examined the priming of our guns; we cleaned the barrels with our ramrods, assured ourselves that our kandjiars played freely in their sheaths, and set off.

" The farther we went in the forest, the narrower the path became, and the more significant were the traces of the tiger.

" Flecks of blood, broken bones, and shreds of flesh said plainly, ' This is the tiger's path.'

" On the way we found intact the two hands of a man: they were undoubtedly those of Ackmeth Khan's noukar.

" It is known that man-eating beasts which devour the entire body dare not touch the hands, which typify man's rule over nature.

" We advanced cautiously, step by step; evidently we were nearing the tiger's lair.

"Suddenly we came upon a glade white with bones. In the midst lay the tiger, and, having feasted, he was tossing a head, like a young kitten playing with a wooden ball.

"An ambitious desire took possession of me for which I deserve blame: it was to kill the tiger alone, without concerning myself about my companion. I took aim at the tiger and fired.

"Where did I hit him? I cannot tell. But through the smoke, before it could clear, I saw a tawny streak flash through the air, and at the same moment I felt as if Mount Elburz [1] were descending upon my head.

"I saw nothing more, heard nothing more, unless it were a cry and a shot.

"I had fainted.

"How long I was unconscious I do not know. When I again opened my eyes, it seemed, from the freshness in the air and the position of the sun, that the sun had been up for an hour or two.

"All around was quiet.

"I still had my gun in my hand.

"Ammalat's gun, broken into two pieces, was ten paces to the right of the spot where I had fallen.

"The stones were covered with blood; but whose blood? Ammalat's, or the tiger's?

"The bushes all about were torn up by their roots.

"It was evident that a terrible, maddening, deadly struggle had taken place.

"And yet I could find the body of neither man nor animal.

"I called Ammalat with all my strength, but no one answered.

"I wished to follow the tiger's trail, to find Ammalat

[1] One of the highest three of the mountains of the Caucasus.

14

alive, or to die on his body; but I was so weak that at
the end of a hundred steps I was forced to sit down.

"Suddenly a hope sprang up: perhaps he had killed the
tiger, and, believing me dead, had returned to Khunsack.

"I mustered all my strength again and took the road
back to the village.   You have not seen him?

"Brothers, I come like a crushed serpent; my head
is in your hands.   I have abandoned my kounack in
danger; do with me as you see fit.

"Whatever your verdict, I will not complain.   If you
think I have deserved death, I will die resignedly.

"If you leave me my life, I will live blessing you.

"Allah is my witness that I have done all that a man
could do — "

A murmur rose among the listeners.

Some excused Nephtali; others blamed him; all pitied
him.

The popular opinion was that Nephtali had fled, aban-
doning Ammalat; that he had invented the whole story
that he had just related; that, in short, he had betrayed
his kounack.

His wounds were but slight; how could the tiger's
blow have produced such a long, deep fainting-spell?

Then other suspicions began to creep out.

Nephtali had been almost raised in the house of Khan
Ackmeth, who was, as we know, his father's kounack.

He had ceased coming to the village, they said, because he was in love with the beautiful Sultanetta, and
was not of high enough birth, although all mountaineers
are equal, to wed the khan's daughter.

In the village there were rumors of a probable union
between Ammalat and Sultanetta.

Instigated by jealousy, might not Nephtali have left
Ammalat to die, or even have killed him?

When a wicked thought enters the head, it is like bad seed let fall on good ground; it sprouts more quickly and more vigorously than the other, takes up all the room, crowds out the other, and at last is alone.

But one cry rose above all others, one conviction prevailed over all the rest.

"Take him to Ackmeth Khan; Ackmeth Khan shall decide."

And with a great uproar the crowd directed itself towards the castle.

Sultanetta heard the clamor, she ran to the window, she saw the crowd: amid the crowd she searched for Ammalat Beg.

Then she recognized Nephtali, — Nephtali alone!

She too, poor child, who had never thought ill of her neighbor, was inspired by a wicked thought.

She ran to the flight of steps just as her father also arrived and Nephtali, conducted by the people, was entering the court.

He bowed before the khan.

"Speak," said Ackmeth.

Nephtali told the same story without altering a word of it.

Sultanetta listened, rigid, cold, motionless, silent as a statue.

"Coward!" Ackmeth Khan contented himself with saying. "By good luck, you are not an Avare, but a Tchetchen."

"By the bones of my father, whose death you announced, I have told the truth," answered Nephtali; "now dispose of me as you will."

"You took your oath," said Ackmeth Khan, "to return with your comrade or with the tiger's skin. You vowed to die, if you failed to keep your oath. You have not kept it, you must die."

"When?" asked Nephtali.

"I give you three days, during which a search shall be
made. If in those three days Ammalat is not found, or
some proof of your innocence is not forthcoming, you
shall die. — Hear, all of you," said Ackmeth Khan to
the crowd, "I grant him three days. During those three
days let no one rail at him, let no one insult him, let no
one touch a single hair of his head; but if he tries to escape, you may shoot him as you would a dog. — Son of
Mohammed Ali, I have judged you as your father would
have judged you."

And to his noukars, —

"Take him away," he added; "you shall answer for
him with your heads."

Then, bringing his papak down over his eyes, he said
to Sultanetta, —

"Come, let us go in. If we do not discover Ammalat
alive, he shall at least be avenged."

Nephtali was conducted to the prison within the
fortress.

That same day, thirty mountaineers set out armed as
for battle; they were going in search of Ammalat Beg.

It was a point of honor with Ackmeth Khan, if he did
not find Ammalat alive, to secure at least his bones and
give them burial.

Often do the Avares rush into the hottest of the affray
to rescue from the Russian's hands their slain friend or
chief, and then fall upon his corpse, preferring to die
with him rather than to abandon him.

Sultanetta had quitted her father's arm, and returned
to her own room. In appearance she seemed calm; she
did not complain, she did not weep.

Yet her mother spoke to her and she did not answer.
The sparks from her father's chibouk burnt holes in her

dress, but she gave no heed. The wind blew down from
the mountain, and to it she exposed her bared head.

The most antagonistic sentiments were struggling in
her heart and breaking it. But the heart was far from
the eyes : not a muscle in her face betrayed its suffering.

The pride of the daughter of the khan was struggling
with Sultanetta's love, and it would have been impossible
to tell whether pride or love would yield.

Thus she passed the remainder of the day.

At night, left alone, she was able to weep at her ease.

She opened the window, leaned her elbow upon it, and
kept her eyes fixed on the mountain.

It seemed to her as if at every instant she should hear
some sound announcing Ammalat's return, — her own
name issuing from the night in his dear voice, a song of
joy or a cry of pain.

She heard only the plaintive wailing of jackals, those
slaves of the tiger and lion, whom these sultans of mountain and desert use for toling their prey, and the distant,
ceaseless roar of the cascade which falls from the summit
of Gaudour d'Ach.

This sound recalled a walk that she had often taken
with Ammalat Beg.

It led to the ruins of a Christian monastery — the
Avares became Mohammedans less than two centuries
ago — situated two versts to the west of Khunsack.
The hand of time had respected the church, and man,
strange to say, had wrought no greater destruction than
time. It had remained intact, surrounded by the débris
of other structures; but the ivy had crept in at the broken
windows and spread its mantle of sober green over the
interior; the trees had pushed through crevices between
the stones, making the gaps wider and wider; a moss as
fine as the finest carpet spread itself over the flags, its

freshness being maintained by a spring which had made
an opening through the wall, and which ran clear as
liquid crystal down the whole length of the chapel, making it a delicious retreat on hot summer days.

Often had Sultanetta come with Ammalat, together
with Sakina, her attendant, to sit under the cool dome
and dream to the murmur of the brooklet; then, sometimes, a mountain goat, coming to slake his thirst, frightened at the sight of the two young people, would bound
away in flight.

"To-morrow," said she, "I will go without you to
the chapel, where so often I have gone with you, dear
Ammalat Beg."

And, tired of the jackals' wailing, which seemed to
her a bad omen, the young girl closed the window again
and cast herself upon her bed.

In the morning she called Sakina, and said, —

"We will take a walk along the banks of the Urens."

On the way, Sultanetta thought with sweet sadness of
that charming spot, so lovely, so fresh, so peaceful.

It seemed to her, on reaching the convent, that it
would be a profanation not to enter alone with her
remembrances.

She sent Sakina to gather some wild mulberries, telling her to return and look for her near the stream; then
she crossed the mossy threshold of the chapel.

The dim light of the church, the twittering of the
swallows which had nested there in the spring, the murmuring stream, all combined to dissolve in tears the
grief that oppressed her heart.

She sat down at the water's brink, and as through a
mist watched her tears falling into the water.

Suddenly she heard the sound of a step too firm to be
Sakina's. She lifted her head and shrieked with terror.

"She cast herself into his arms."

Before her stood a man covered with dirt and blood. A tiger's skin, the head of which enframed his face, fell from his shoulders to the ground.

Sultanetta's first cry had been a shriek of terror; the second was a cry of joy.

Through all the dust, mire, and blood by which he was stained, beneath the tiger's skin she recognized Ammalat Beg.

Then, forgetting everything else in the world, she sprang to her feet, and with a bound, filled with joy and love, she cast herself into his arms.

A cry escaped Ammalat also; his mouth, like a bee, lit upon the rosy lips of the young girl. They had no need of words.

This time, quite beside himself, the young man exclaimed,—

"And you love me then, Sultanetta?"

Abashed at her own boldness, blushing red under her lover's kiss, the girl withdrew her lips from Ammalat's, and gently repelled him.

Overcome with terror, and ready to let her slip from his arms, Ammalat Beg demanded,—

"Then you do not love me?"

"Allah save me!" said the innocent girl, drooping the eyelids, but not the eyes. "Love! what terrible word have you spoken?"

"It is the sweetest word in all the universe, Sultanetta! The sun is love! the Spring is love! the flowers are love!"

"Ammalat," said the young girl, "a year ago, a woman uttering frightful shrieks rushed out from her house without a veil, and, all bleeding, fell in the dust at my feet. A man was pursuing her with a poniard in his hand. I fled to the castle; but it seemed to me that the woman was following me. For a long time after, I would waken at night thinking that I heard her shrieks, and in the darkness I could see her again all bleeding and grovelling on the earth. When I asked why this unhappy woman had been killed, and what had been her crime that her murderer was not punished, they answered, 'She loved a young man.'"

"Oh! it was not because she loved him that she was killed, dear child."

"Why was it, then?"

"It was because she had betrayed the one she loved."

"Betrayed! what does that mean? I do not understand, Ammalat."

"Please God you may never understand!"

Then, mustering his heart's whole tenderness into his voice, —

"You love me, do you not, Sultanetta?"

"I think so," said the young girl.

"Well, do you think that you would ever feel for another what you feel for me?"

"Never!" cried Sultanetta, quickly.

"That, you see, would be betraying me — "

Sultanetta turned upon Ammalat the eyes of an Oriental woman, to which the poets find only the eye of the gazelle to compare.

"Oh!" exclaimed she, "if you but knew, Ammalat, what I have suffered during the four days in which I have not seen you! I did not know what absence meant. When my brothers or my father go away, I weep at saying good-bye. True, I said good-bye to you without weeping; but I have wept enough since, I am sure! Listen, Ammalat," continued the girl; "I have discovered one thing that I will tell you: I could not live without you."

"And I," said the young man, "not only cannot live without you, but I am ready to die for you, my darling, to sacrifice not only my life but my soul for you."

There was a sound of footsteps: Sakina was returning with her hands filled with wild mulberries.

She uttered a cry of fright at seeing the young man; but on recognizing him she exclaimed,—

"Oh, prince, then you are not dead!"

These words reminded Sultanetta that she was not the only one anxious about Ammalat, but that her father was impatiently awaiting news, and that there was a poor prisoner whose life depended on Ammalat's return.

On the way, the young beg gave Sultanetta an account of what had happened between himself and the tiger.

Of the first part of the adventure, Nephtali had told the exact truth.

This is what followed: —

Just as Nephtali had fallen under the tiger, Ammalat Beg fired a shot.

The ball from Ammalat's gun broke the creature's lower jaw.

At the same instant the tiger abandoned Nephtali and sprang upon Ammalat, who awaited him, pistol in hand, and then, dodging lightly to one side, fired close to his muzzle.

The bullet penetrated eye and brain.

Overpowered with pain, the animal began to leap in the air and roll on the earth. He acted as if blind and mad.

Ammalat threw down his pistol, took his gun by the barrel, approached the tiger, and dealt him a terrible blow on the head.

The gun flew into fragments.

The animal seemed to acknowledge himself to be van-

quished, and tried to run. One of his fore paws had
been shattered by Nephtali, one jaw was hanging, and an
eye was missing from its socket.

But, mutilated as he was, he made swifter progress
than Ammalat Beg.

Ammalat Beg set out to follow him, while reloading his
pistol. From time to time he found places where the
animal had stopped and struggled in torment. In such
places the blood-saturated earth was pawed, the grass
was plucked up, the bushes were in splinters.

From time to time he caught sight of the animal dragging himself along with difficulty, crawling rather than
walking. Then he would hasten his own pace; but, as
soon as the tiger felt himself to be pursued, he increased
his own efforts and gained on the hunter.

This sort of chase lasted all day without rest or
relaxation.

Night fell; Ammalat Beg was forced to stay during
the night, or he might have lost the animal's trail.

He had abandoned his bourka, his papak and tchouka,
everything that could impede his course: for clothing, he
had nothing left but his bechmet and trousers; for arms,
only his kandjiar and pistol.

In the morning he awoke chilled and famished.

As soon as the light would admit, he again took up
the tiger's trail.

It was not long before he found him.

But, this time, despairing of escape by flight, the tiger not
only awaited him, but he even came creeping towards him.

The ferocious brute could no longer stand, he could
not raise himself; his strength was exhausted from loss
of blood.

Ammalat Beg met him half-way. He halted at ten
paces from him.

One of the tiger's eyes was put out, but the other
glowed like a live coal. Ammalat Beg, whose pistol
never missed a rouble in air, placed a bullet in the
other eye as deftly as with his hand.

The animal leaped into the air, fell over on his back,
stretched out his three frightful paws in his last agony,
— the fourth being broken, — stiffened, yielded up his
breath in one roar, and was dead.

Ammalat Beg flung himself upon him; it was the famished man, this time, who seemed ready to devour the
tiger.

With his poniard he opened an artery in the neck, and
sucked the blood that flowed from it.

He then laid open the breast and ate a piece of the
heart yet warm. — The Arabs of Algeria on killing a
lion make their sons eat the still bleeding heart to render
them brave; the Greeks in like manner eat the hearts of
eagles. — He next skinned the animal with his kandjiar,
and threw the hide over his shoulders.

Not until then did he look about him; it was a drizzly
morning, a dense fog began to spread over the mountain; he was unable to distinguish objects ten paces
away.

He crouched down upon a rock and waited.

The day went by, and night came on; he heard the
whirring of the eagles as they regained their eyries amid
the clouds.

He built a fire with powder and dry leaves, by the aid
of his pistol.

A bit of the tiger's heart broiled over the coals fur-
nished his supper.

Then, spreading the animal's skin with the fur uppermost, he rolled up in it and went to sleep.

He was awakened in the morning by the first rays of

the sun; knowing that Khunsack lay to the east, he proceeded eastward.

Arriving at the outskirts of the wood, he beheld Khunsack bleaching on the rocks.

He was thirsty: the tiger had no more blood with which to quench his thirst. Ammalat Beg recalled the pure rill which ran through the chapel.

He descended by the shortest route, over rocks and cliffs, holding on by tufts of grass, the roots of trees, or jutting stones.

He at length reached the valley.

He ran to the chapel with the speed of a thirsting deer.

But on entering, he saw a woman, heard a cry, recognized Sultanetta.

He forgot everything, — hunger, thirst, fatigue; everything but his love.

" Glory to God, and thanks! "

As Ammalat Beg pronounced these, the last words of his story, he, together with the young maiden and her attendant, reached the outskirts of Khunsack.

The shout sent up by those who perceived them ran the whole length of the hamlet with the swiftness of a train of gunpowder.

Every dweller in Khunsack rushed out of his house, forming a procession after the two young people.

The cry of " Ammalat Beg! Ammalat Beg! " startled Ackmeth Khan in the depths of his harem.

He reached the head of the flight of steps in front of the castle just as the two young people had attained its foot.

In spite of the efforts that he made to remain grave and sedate, as every good Mussulman should in the face of grief or joy, he held out his arms to Ammalat Beg.

As if there were something for which she ought to be pardoned, Sultanetta sprang forward simultaneously with her lover to her father's breast, and he enveloped them both in the same embrace, welcomed them both with the same kiss.

"Dear father," said Sultanetta, "we have been unjust to Nephtali; everything happened as he said."

The khan gave an order for the prisoner to be released.

Then he had an ox and six sheep killed, in order that Ammalat's return might be an occasion of feasting throughout the entire village.

But when Ammalat had told Ackmeth Khan what he had already told Sultanetta, he sent for Nephtali.

"Nephtali," said he, "all justice is done you. If you will enter my household, you shall be made chief of my noukars."

"I thank you, Ackmeth Khan," was the young man's reply; "I am a Tchetchen, and not an Avare. I came to kill the tiger that was preying on your sheep; the tiger is dead, I have no more to do here. Farewell, Ackmeth Khan."

He approached Ammalat Beg, and held out his hand.

"Farewell, kounack; for life, for death!" said he.

Then, passing Sultanetta, he bowed low and said, —

"Shine forever, O morning star!"

And he departed with the gait of a king leaving the throne-room.

Ackmeth Khan waited until the door was again closed.

"And now, Ammalat Beg," said he, "be doubly welcome. After the tiger-hunt, that of the lion. Tomorrow we march against the Russians."

"Allah!" exclaimed Sultanetta sadly; "more expe-

ditions! more deaths!   When will blood cease to flow
on the mountain?"

"When the mountain streams shall descend into the
valley as milk, when sugar-cane shall grow at the summit of Elburz," rejoined Ackmeth Khan with a smile.

VI.

How grand is the Terek as it thunders through the Pass of Dariel! There, like a genie deriving his power from Heaven, he struggles with nature. In some places he flashes between rocky precipices glittering like a drawn sword which is piercing the granite wall; in others, dull and foaming, he struggles with enormous boulders along his course, overturning them as he goes and carrying them with him. On dark nights, when the belated horseman passes along the steep bank which controls it, he draws his bourka close about him. Not all the horrors to be conjured up by the most fantastic imagination can compare with the reality by which he is surrounded. The flood, swollen by the rains, rolls underneath his feet with a booming sound, and plunges from ledges of rock above his head, threatening each moment to crush him. A sudden flash rends the obscurity, and the terrified traveller sees only the gloomy cloud above him, and below him a hideous chasm. Everywhere are precipitous walls, before, behind, beside him; and, leaping from ledge to ledge, the maddened Terek is dashed into lustrous foam. For the moment, its swift waters, as troubled as the spirits of hell, writhe at the foot of a precipice with terrible din, and seem in the abyss like a throng of spectres driven by an archangel's sword. Great boulders follow the current of the stream with ominous crashing, and then it is that, blinded anew by a flying serpent of fire, he suddenly finds himself plunged into a

sea of darkness; then, in turn, the thunder rumbles, the
rocks vibrate with a sound as of a cascade of mountains
rolling over and over each other. Earth's echo is answering heaven's artillery, and again the flash, and again
night, then the thunderbolt, then once again the sound
of tumbling mountains. And, as if the whole chain of
the Caucasus, from Taman to Apsheron, were shaking
its granite shoulders, a shower of rattling stones comes
hurtling down, striking with a rebound. Your horse
stops dismayed, backs away, falls on his haunches, rears.
His mane, whipped by the wind, lashes your face; a
spirit moans in the air, as doleful as a lost soul. A
shiver passes through you, and perspiration stands in
beads on your face; your heart shrinks, and in spite of
you there rises to your lips the prayer that your mother
taught you when you were a child.

And yet, what charm, what softness the rosy-browed,
fair-footed Morning brings to the gorge where the Terek
roars! The clouds, chased by the wind, rise from the
earth and hover about the icy peaks; above them a
glow of light throws up the silhouette of the eastern
mountains; the rocks glisten, silvered over with raindrops; and the Terek, still dark, still raging, still foaming, bounds over the stones as if seeking a broad bed in
which to rest.

However, one thing is wanting in the Caucasus,— rivers
and lakes in which these giants of creation can mirror
themselves. The Terek, writhing in the depths of
gorges, looks like a stream, a torrent at the most; but,
below Vladikafkas, upon entering the valley, it spreads
the stones brought with it from the mountains and flows
broadly and at will, still swift but less boisterous, as if
resting and regaining breath, exhausted after its painful
toil. At last, having cleared the head of the Little

Kabardah, it turns eastward, like a pious Mussulman,
and, overflowing both banks, always at war with each
other, it hastens across the steppes past Kisliar to cast
itself into the Caspian Sea.

But, before reaching its long resting-place, it has
already paid its tribute, and, like a rugged workman,
has turned the great wheels of the mills. Along its
right bank between the woods and the mountains, are
scattered the Aoubs and Kabardians, whom we confound
by giving them the general name of Circassians, with
the Tchetchens below them and nearer the sea. These
Aoubs are conquered, but only on the outside; in reality
they are bands of outlaws, who derive profit from both
their friendliness with the Russians and their proceeds
from mountain brigandage; having free access to all
places, they forewarn their countrymen of the movements of the soldiers, of the numbers of their garrisons,
of the state of their fortresses; they conceal them in their
dwellings when on an expedition, share with them, or
buy, the booty when they return, furnish them salt and
Russian powder, and often assist in person on their
expeditions. The worst of it is that hostile mountaineers, wearing the same costume as those who have submitted, pass the Terek without hindrance, approach
travellers without being recognized, attack them if they
are the stronger, and if the weaker, pass them with a
bow, the hand on the heart.

It is the way of the vanquished.

And, as regards these last, we must say, their position
opposite to their terrible neighbors drives them almost in-
voluntarily into this duplicity. Knowing that, hindered
by the obstacle which the river presents to them, the Russians would not have time to come to their defence against
the mountaineers, they are forced to take their compa-

15

triots by the hand; but at the same time they pretend to
be friendly with the Russians, before whom they quail.
Every one of them in the morning is ready to become
the kounack of a Russian, and, in the evening, the guide
of a mountaineer.

As to the left bank of the Terek, it is covered with
rich stanitzas belonging to the Cossacks on the border.
Between these stanitzas lie rude villages. The Cossacks,
moreover, differ in no way from the mountaineers except
in their unshaven heads; but, aside from that, their
weapons, clothes, and ways are the same. It is a fine
thing to watch them in a bout with mountaineers. It is
not, properly speaking, a fight, but a tournament in
which each strives to show off superiority of strength and
courage. Two Cossacks will charge bravely on four
horsemen, and, with equal numbers, they will always
come off conquerors. All speak Tartar, all know the
mountaineers. Sometimes they are relatives, even, by
reason of the women whom they have kidnapped; but
in the field they are mortal enemies. Although the Cossacks are strictly forbidden to cross the Terek, yet the
bravest of them swim across, sometimes on pleasure,
sometimes on business. For their part, when night
comes, the mountaineers do the same; they crouch in
the grass, creep through the bushes, and suddenly stand
up in the traveller's path, taking him prisoner and setting a ransom on his head if he makes no resistance, but
killing him if he does.

It even happens that the most enterprising spend two
or three days in the vineyards near the village awaiting
an opportunity to do a stroke of business. That is why
the border Cossack never leaves his house unarmed, never
takes a step without his trusty poniard, nor goes into the
field without his gun. He ploughs, sows, cultivates, and

mows his piece of ground, always armed. That is why
the mountaineers avoid the stanitzas and usually prey
upon the rude villages, or boldly strike into the interior
of the provinces.

In this case a fight is inevitable, and the most daring
horsemen eagerly engage in it for the sake of fame, which
they value above everything, even above booty.

During the autumn of 1819, when the events we are
relating occurred, Kabardians and Tchetchens, taking
advantage of the absence of General Scrinokof, had mustered fifteen hundred men to plunder certain villages
lying on the other side of the Terek, to take prisoners
and carry off flocks.

Their chief was the Kabardian prince, Djemboulat.

Ammalat Beg, coming to him with a letter from Ackmeth Khan, had been very well received, and he would
have been made chief of a division, had there been any
such position or any regular troops among these bands.
His horse and his individual courage assign to each man
his place in the combat. At first, there is some question as to how to begin the affair, and how to engage
the enemy; but eventually there is neither command nor
obedience, and the fight is conducted at random to
the end.

After warning the neighboring princes who were to
take part in the expedition with him, Djemboulat appointed a place of meeting, and, at a given signal, was
heard through all the hamlets the cry, " *Guaray! guaray!* " that is, " To arms! to arms! " and in a few hours
Kabardian and Tchetchen riders were coming from all
directions.

Fearing treachery, no one except the chief knew where
the night would be spent, or where the river would be
crossed. Dividing themselves into small bands, the

mountaineers gained the subjugated hamlets and waited
there for night. The vanquished received their compatriots with every kind of joyful demonstration; but
the distrustful Djemboulat was not carried away by this
apparent loyalty. He placed sentinels on all sides, proclaiming to the inhabitants that whoever under any pretext tried to cross over the border would be run through
without mercy. Most of the horsemen lodged in the
houses of their relatives and friends; but Djemboulat
and Ammalat Beg camped in the field, lying before the
fire, as long as was necessary to rest their horses.

Djemboulat's mind was occupied with the Russians
and the fight in which he was about to engage; but Ammalat Beg was far from the battle-field; his thoughts
took eagle's wings, and flew beyond the mountains of
Avarie; and his heart, forced to remain far from the one
it loved, was full of sorrow. The sound of the mountain
balalaïka, accompanied by a monotonous chant, diverted
his sadness; he listened in spite of himself.

A Kabardian was singing this old song, —

> "Toward snowy Kasbek's towering peak,
>   Far from the wheat, far from the rye,
> As eagle birds their eyries seek,
>   The stormy clouds go wheeling by.

> "Who are these speeding cavaliers
>   Through fog and mist and white with frost?
> Ah! Allah, save! — our mountaineers,
>   Our heroes flee, the battle's lost.

> "The Russian hordes are at their heels,
>   Mount higher, braves, and faster, braves,
> The craggy steeps!   The laggard feels
>   Death's cohorts press with naked glaives.

"High up, and higher, Kasbek grows
A wooded slope whose leafage clads
A refuge from the foeman's blows.
Ha! higher! faster! courage, lads!

"False fate yields valor to the foe :
Their chargers pant, they toil in vain,
And naught can save, — oh, woe! oh, woe!
That mount should vanquished be by plain.

"But, hark! a pious mullah's prayer
From bended knees, — *Death, listening, hears,* —
Goes speeding through the lambent air,
And reaches Allah's heeding ears.

"To save his faithful, Allah bids
The wood obey Mahomet's call;
That fortress sure all danger rids.
To prophet praise! God's over all!"

"Yes, in other times it was so," said Djemboulat, with
a smile. "Our fathers believed in prayer, and God heard
them; but now, my friend, the finest refuge is courage,
the surest prayer, a schaska. Take heed, Ammalat," he
continued, caressing his mustache. "I do not hide from
you the fact that it will be a warm encounter. The colonel has mustered his command. But where is he?
How many men has he? That is something that I do
not know, something that none of us know."

"So much the better!" said Ammalat, composedly;
"the more Russians the better the mark."

"Yes, but the more difficulty there will be in getting
away with the booty."

"Little the booty matters to me. I wish vengeance
and seek glory."

"Glory is well when it lays golden eggs, Ammalat

It is a disgrace to show empty hands to one's wife.
Winter is approaching; in order to regale one's friends,
one must lay in his provisions at the expense of the
Russians. Choose your position beforehand, Ammalat:
march in the vanguard, or remain near me with the
abrecks."

"I go where there is danger; but what is the oath
among these abrecks?"

"Each has his own: here is one of the bravest. They
vow to expose themselves for a longer or shorter period
to every kind of peril, to grant no grace to enemies, to
pardon no offender, not even a friend, not even a brother;
to take whatever pleases them, especially when the thing
that pleases presents itself to view. This oath taken, the
man who has taken it can kill, pillage, plunder, without
being punished. He is fulfilling a vow. Abrecks of
this sort are bad friends, but good enemies."

"And," inquired Ammalat Beg, a dweller of the plain
to whom the customs of the mountaineer were for the
most part unknown, "what induces these horsemen to
take such oaths?"

"Some take them from excessive courage, others from
excessive poverty, others again because they are a prey
to some sorrow. There, for instance, — notice that
Kabardian rubbing up his gun rusted by the night-fog;
well, he became an abreck for five years because his mistress died of small-pox. During those five years you
might better have a tiger for a friend than him for a comrade. He has already been wounded three times, and
every wound, instead of curbing, spurs him on."

"Singular custom! And how does an abreck return to
his family after such a life?"

"Quite naturally; the past is past. The abreck for-
gets it, and the neighbors are wary of remembering it.

Freed from his oath, he becomes as gentle as a lamb.
But it is quite dark; the Terek is shrouded in fog: it is
time."

Djemboulat gave a whistle, and his whistle was instantly carried along the entire line of the camp. In less
than five minutes all were in the saddle. After deciding
upon the best place to cross the Terek, the little company
descended quietly to the river bank. Ammalat Beg
admired the stillness, not merely of the soldiers, but also
of the horses. Not one whinnied on the way. Each
in placing his feet seemed fearful of causing the stones to
roll and of thus warning the enemy. They soon reached
the river's edge. The water was low; a headland, half
sand, half stones, jutted out towards the opposite bank.
The whole company, by employing double the time,
could have crossed at that point almost dry-footed; but
half of the troops ascended the river to swim across and
hide the principal passage from the Cossacks. Those
who were sure of their horses leaped straight from the
bank into the stream. Others tied leathern bottles to
their horses; the swift current bore them away, but they
finally reached the bank and scaled it wherever they were
able. A dense fog had spread, apparently to conceal all
their movements.

It is essential for the reader to know that all along the
Terek — on the left bank of the river — there exists a
line called the border watch. Cossacks were stationed on
every hillock. As you pass during the day, you notice
on each rise of ground a tall post with a cask at its
extremity. This cask is full of straw, and ready to light
at the first cry of alarm. To this pole a saddled horse is
constantly tied, and near it, lying on the ground, is the
sentinel.

At night the watch is doubled.

But, in spite of all these precautions, the mountaineers, wrapped in their bourkas, enveloped in darkness and surrounded by fog, pass between the pickets like water through a sieve.

This time, also, it happened thus. The subjugated mountaineers, knowing the Cossack picket-posts marvellously well, were placed at the head of each band, and conducted it through the line.

At only a single point was there bloodshed.

Djemboulat himself struck the blow.

On reaching the opposite bank of the Terek, he ordered Ammalat Beg to climb the steep, get as near as possible to the picket, see how many men were stationed there, and strike his steel upon the flint as many times as there were men.

Ammalat Beg turned away and disappeared into the night.

Meanwhile Djemboulat wormed along like a snake up the slope of the mound.

The Cossack was dozing. He seemed conscious of a slight noise arising from the water-side, and gazed uneasily in the direction of the river.

Djemboulat was only three steps away from him: he was lying on his stomach behind a bush.

"The cursed ducks!" muttered the Cossack, who had come to the Terek from the banks of the Don, "they are in good spirits even at night; they flutter and frolic in the water like the elves of Kiev."

On the other hand, at this moment Ammalat Beg had attained a point from which he commanded the knoll.

There were two Cossacks: one was asleep wrapped in his bourka, the other was supposed to keep awake.

Ammalat Beg clicked the steel twice upon the flint.

The sound and the sparks drew the Cossack's attention.
"Oh! oh!" said he, "what is that? Wolves, perhaps;
their jaws snap, and their eyes glitter!"

And he faced about, the better to see.

Just then he thought he saw a man's figure through
the darkness.

He opened his mouth to cry, "To arms!" but the cry
was stayed on his lips, — Djemboulat's kandjiar was
plunged to the hilt in his breast.

He fell without a moan.

The other Cossack did not even wake, and passed
without knowing it from sleep unto death.

The post was wrenched out and thrown with its cask
into the river.

It was a breach through which the bulk of the troops
passed and overran the district.

The raid was complete and wholly successful. All
peasants attempting resistance were killed on the spot.
The rest hid themselves or fled. A large number of
prisoners were taken, both men and women.

The Kabardians entered the houses, took everything
they could find, and carried off all that was transportable;
but they did not burn villages, nor devastate fields, nor
spoil vineyards.

"Why touch God's gifts and man's labor?" said they.
"That would be the work of brigands instead of noble
mountaineers."

In an hour's time all was over for the inhabitants
within a radius of three leagues.

But all was not over for the plunderers.

The call to arms had echoed all along the border; a
shepherd had started the alarm.

He had been killed, but too late.

A great circle had been formed about the loose horses

ranging over the steppe, and those forming it collected the entire herd.

A Tchetchen horseman headed the band on an excellent horse, and darted off at a gallop.

Every horse whinnied, flung his tail, shook his mane to the wind, and set off in the train of the Tchetchen. He led the entire band to the Terek, passed between two pickets, and plunged into the stream on his horse.

All the rest of the horses followed in his wake.

They were seen to pass like shadows; the sound of their plunge into the water was heard, and that was all!

VII.

AT sunrise the fog lifted, uncovering a grand but dreadful spectacle.

A large troop of riders were returning to the mountain, dragging behind them their prisoners, some of whom were tied to the stirrups, some to the saddle, others to the horses' tails.

The hands of all were bound.

Tears and groans of despair were mingled with shouts of triumph.

Laden with spoils, hindered by the slow pace of the herds of cattle, the raiders were making their way to the Terek. The princes, nobles, and picked horsemen rode gayly along as escort, leading and flanking the cortege.

But, in the distance and from all directions, the border Cossacks began to appear, skulking behind trees and hiding behind bushes.

The Tchetchens sent out sharp-shooters, and the fighting began.

On all sides gunshots blazed and flashed.

The vanguard pushed on, driving the herds before, and forcing them to swim the river.

But clouds of dust were then seen rising behind them.

It was the storm.

Six hundred mountaineers, led by Djemboulat and Ammalat Beg, stopped their horses and faced about to give the others time to cross the river.

With no attempt at order they charged the Cossacks at full speed, yelling as they rode, though not a gun was taken from behind the back, not a sword gleamed in a horseman's hand.

The Tchetchens have a way of handling their weapons only at the last moment.

But at twenty paces from the Cossacks they brought their guns to their shoulders and fired; then they swung the guns behind their backs, and drew their schaskas

But, even while responding with a lively fusillade, the Cossacks drew rein, whirled, and fled.

Spurred on by their eagerness for a fight, the mountaineers started in pursuit. The fugitives led them on towards a wood.

In this wood the soldiers of the Forty-third Regiment were lying in ambush.

They formed a square, lowered their bayonets, and fired on the Tchetchens.

In vain did the latter leap down from their horses and endeavor to penetrate the forest in order to attack the Russians in flank and rear.

The artillery joined in with its boom.

Kotzarev, the dread of the Tchetchens, the man whose bravery was most noted among them, commanded the Russian troops.

From that time forward, there was no doubting the outcome. Three successive volleys of artillery dispersed the mountaineers, who retraced their course toward the river.

But on the bank of the Terek, raking the course of the stream, a masked battery had been stationed.

It opened fire.

The canister burst in the thickest of their flight.

At every shot several horses, struck dead, rolled over in the stream, dragging down their riders and drowning them.

It was fearful, then, to see the prisoners, bound to the horses, unable to help themselves, and exposed like their conquerors to the Russian fire.

The old Terek, reddened with blood, received all, friends and enemies, within its cold waves, tossing the bodies of men and animals and sweeping all, living and dead, toward the sea.

Waiting to the last, covering the retreat, and struggling like lions against the soldiers, Djemboulat and Ammalat Beg with a hundred horsemen guarded the crossing, charging the Russian infantry who came within reach, swooping down on the border Cossacks, returning to their comrades, and encouraging them by word and deed; and finally, they also, last of all, plunged into the Terek, and crossed.

Upon reaching the opposite bank, they leaped from their horses, and, guns in hand, stood ready to dispute the passage of the Russians, who, crowding on the bank, made a feint of clearing the river in turn.

But, meanwhile, two versts below the place where they were joining battle, a large body of Cossacks had crossed the Terek and taken up a position between river and mountain.

Their echoing shouts, joyous and triumphant, behind the Tchetchens, alone revealed their presence.

The destruction of the mountaineers was inevitable.

Ammalat Beg took in the situation at a glance.

"Well, Djemboulat," said he, "all is over, and our fate is decided. Do what you will yourself; as for me, the Russians shall not have me alive: it is better to die by the bullet than the rope!"

"And I," said Djemboulat,—"think you my hands are made for chains? Allah forbid! The Russians may have my body; my soul, never!"

Then, remounting his horse and standing in the stirrups, he cried,—

"Comrades, fate is against us, but our steel is left.
Let us sell our lives dearly to the unbelievers. The
conqueror is not he who wins the battlefield, but he who
wins glory; and glory belongs to him that prefers death
to captivity."

"We will die! we will die!" shouted the mountaineers in chorus.

"And let our good horses die with us, and when dead
serve us as a rampart," said Djemboulat.

And, leaping from his horse, he drew his sword and,
setting the example, stabbed him in the throat.

Every mountaineer did the same, while yelling defiance
at the Russians.

A great ring of dead horses encircled the Tchetchens.

Then each man crouched behind his horse with loaded
gun.

Seeing what a terrible defence the mountaineers were
prepared to make, the Cossacks paused, hesitating as to
whether they ought to attack men in such desperate
straits.

And then a voice rang out upon the silence; a
Tchetchen was chanting the death-song.

The voice was firm, vibrant, ringing; and the Russians
could hear the song from the first word to the last.

> "Glory be ours! Disgrace to the foe!
> Better to die than shame to know."

All the doomed men repeated in chorus,—

> "Glory be ours! Disgrace to the foe!
> Better to die than shame to know."

Then the solo voice continued,—

"Oh, weep, fair dames, on mountain-side,
  And to our hearts give sigh for sigh,
For, thinking of sweetheart and bride,
  Your mountaineers are now to die.
For this, the sleep that meets the brave
Is not the sleep that sweet life gave
  Mid songs of joy and lullaby.
No, 't is the dreary sleep that bids
The rock or clod that weights our lids,
  While tempests thunder in the sky.

"But, no; weep not, ye sweet brides, so.
  The houris green, your sister things,
Will come with eyes that catch the glow
  Of morning-stars through heaven that go,
And take us hence on white, white wings.

"Nay, mother, gaze not up the road,
  Put out the fire, then seek thy bed;
In vain thy heart its ill doth bode, —
  Dear mother, none wait for the dead.
Seek not thy neighbor of the plain,
And say, to lull thy bitter pain,
' My son will come to-morrow, and —'
Thy son is on the hill at rest:
His heart is broken in his breast,
His sword is broken in his hand.

Chorus.

"Glory be ours! disgrace to the foe!
  Better to die than shame to know.

"Weep not vain tears; though life be done,
  Oh, mother, I avenged have died:
Thy milk, while in my veins it run,
  To lion's blood had changed its tide.
And never in the hottest fight
Did thy son e'er in coward fright

Hear voice of fear in counsel deep.
He falls with hands nor clasped nor bound,
He falls at last on brave men's ground,
And here he sleeps his last long sleep.

" The rill that runs from mountain height
In spring, soon dries its waters pure;
The dawn that heralds morning's light
Wears robes all flowery-hued and bright, —
Her realm and rule an hour endure.
Oh, comrades, now we 'll make our prayer,
We go no farther on our way,
But like the brooklet, once so fair,
We cease, and fade like dawn of day.

" Yet we, at least, shall pass in wrath
And leave behind the tempest's path
Which stains the heavens with redness dire;
On flowers, on sands we 'll leave a trace
That time nor storm shall e'er efface,
The stains of blood and smoke and fire.

Chorus.

" Glory be ours! disgrace to the foe!
Better to die than shame to know."

Struck by the solemnity of the scene before their eyes,
Cossacks and soldiers listened respectfully to the death-
song of twelve hundred brave men.

At last the signal was given: a mighty huzza burst
from the Russian ranks.

The Tchetchens responded with a death-like silence.

But when the Russians were no more than twenty
paces from them, they rose; each sighted his man, and at
the order, " Fire!" given by Djemboulat and Ammalat
Beg, a wreath of flame enveloped the beleaguered men.

Then, breaking his gun, every man sent up a war-cry as he drew his schaska with the right hand, and his kandjiar with the left.

Three times did the Russians assail the bloody fortification, three times were they repulsed.

The fourth time, they gathered their forces for a final effort; during ten minutes longer, like a great serpent coiled in a circle, flashed the sabres and kandjiars counterfeiting its scales.

At last the gigantic reptile was broken into three or four pieces. The conflict became terrible. A hand-to-hand struggle ensued. Fountains of blood gushed forth amidst curses and death-shrieks.

The abrecks, that they might not become separated in the fray, bound themselves together with their girdles. None asked for mercy, none demanded quarter.

All fell under the Russian bayonets.

A small group was still on their feet and still fought on.

In the centre of this group, like two Titans, stood Djemboulat and Ammalat Beg.

For one instant the Russians recoiled before that hopeless defence, and made a pause.

" On ! " cried Djemboulat, leading his last onset. " On, Ammalat Beg! Death is liberty ! "

But Ammalat Beg was deaf to the last call of the Tchetchen chief. A blow on the head from the butt of a gun had stretched him senseless on the ground, covered with the dead and steeped in gore.

VIII.

COLONEL VERKOVSKY to his fiancée, Marie N., at
Smolensk: —

DERBEND, Oct. 7, 1819.

Two months! — It is a very brief period in the common course of life; but to me, the two months that have just rolled by, my darling Marie, are two centuries. Two centuries ago, then, instead of two months ago, I received your dear letter.

During that time the moon has revolved twice around the earth.

There is a past which I recall with pleasure; there is a future into which I plunge with hope; but, away from you, with no news of you, there is no present. The Cossack who brings the post appears; he holds a letter in his hand. I spring up, recognize your writing, break the seal, kiss the lines penned by your dear hand. I devour the thoughts dictated by your pure heart. I am happy, I have left the earth, I am in heaven! But scarcely have I closed your letter before ill-boding thoughts invade my mind. That is all well, doubtless, but all that is in the past, and is, perhaps, no longer, even now. Is she well, the one for whom I would give my life? Does she love me as well to-day as yesterday? Will the happy time ever come when we shall be reunited, never to part again; when there shall be for us neither separation nor distance; when the expressions of our love shall not become chilled in passing from heart to paper? Or, before

that time shall come, alas! will not the letters themselves
have grown cold? Will not the fire which burns on the
altar of her heart have gone out, dying little by little?
Pardon all these fears, my love; they are the growths
which flourish on the soil of absence. With my heart
near yours, I believe everything; away from you, on the
contrary, I doubt everything. You bid me take you into
my life, to tell you what I do, what takes place around
me in this little vortex of which I am the centre; what
I think, how I busy myself, even from hour to hour,
from minute to minute. It has forced me to endure
again all the pangs which I have just described, hard-
hearted being, who will that I shall not only suffer, but
analyze my sufferings, tear my wounds!

However, you command, I obey.

My life is the imprint of a chain on the sand. My
service, if not amusing, by its fatigue helps at least to
pass the time. I am thrown into a frightful climate
which no constitution can withstand, into the midst of a
fellowship which stifles my soul. I no longer find among
my associates the only one who could have understood
me, nor any one among the Asiatics with whom to share
a sentiment. Everything about me is so wild that I
bruise myself on everything I touch; so narrow that I
seem to breathe the air of a dungeon. Warmth could
more easily be drawn from an iceberg than a glow of
enjoyment from this accursed country.

I will give you a detailed account of my last week.
It is the most interesting and the liveliest of all that I
have spent in the City of the Iron Gates.

I recall having written you that we were returning,
with the Governor-General of the Caucasus, from the
expedition upon Akoutcha. We succeeded off-hand; Shah
Ali Khan fled into Persia. We burned a dozen villages

with the hay and corn; we flayed, spitted, and roasted the
enemy's sheep.   Finally, when the snow forced the inhabitants to come down from the cliffs, they surrendered
and gave hostages; after which, we returned to the fortress of Bounaïa.   There, our division was obliged to
break up for the winter, and my regiment has come back
to its quarters in Derbend.

The next day the general was compelled to leave us to
enter upon a second expedition on the border.   Consequently, there was a great throng of people anxious to
take leave of their well-beloved chief.   Alexis Petrovitch
left his tent and came to us.   Who does not know his
face, if not from life, at least from portraits?   I do not
know of such another in existence, another so expressive
as his.

A poet once wrote of him: —

> " Fly, Tchetchen, fly!   The man whose word
> In vain was never known to warn,
> Is roused; his rally-cry is heard,
> His order passed : 'We march the morn!'
> The whistling ball that carries death
> Takes but the heaving of his breath.
> His shout 's the cry the mighty saith,
> It is the thunder of the fight.
> He bends his brow with love or hate
> Of friends or foes, and names their fate ;
> And where he points, or soon or late,
> Death rushes on, nor stays his might."

And the poet has not said too much.

You should see his coolness in battle, his ease on his
reception day!   Sometimes he strews before the Asiatics
the garlands of his flowery speech, as full of imagery as
Persian poetry; sometimes he routs them, pursues, and
crushes them with a single word.   In vain do these

demons of deceit endeavor to hide their most secret plans
in the recesses of their hearts; his eye penetrates them,
and a week, a month, a year beforehand, he will tell
them what they intend to do. It is amusing to see how a
man of guilty conscience turns white and red under the
torture of his steady, piercing eye, and how readily the
same eye discerns merit wherever it is to be found, re-
wards it with a smile, and how, with a word that goes
straight to the heart, he repays courage and loyalty.

May God grant to every brave soldier the glory and
happiness of serving under such a leader!

It is curious to note his relations in his own house
with those who serve under him. It is a study for the
observer. Every man distinguished by courage, spirit,
or any talent whatever, has free entrance and full swing.
There is no more rank, no more etiquette. Each has a
right to say whatever enters his mind, to do as he
pleases. Alexis Petrovitch [1] talks and laughs with each
as a friend, advising and instructing him like a brother.

We were, then, in camp. It was last Tuesday, at tea-
time. His aide-de-camp had induced him to read Napo-
leon's campaign in Italy, that poem of the military art, as
he calls it. Surrounding him, we praised, criticised, and
discussed it. The great captain who, like Hannibal and
Charlemagne, had crossed the Alps, would have been
satisfied with the remarks and even with the criticisms of
one who had so long disputed with him the great redoubt
of Borodino. After tea, the reading finished, we engaged
in gymnastics, we ran races and leaped ropes and ditches;
we tested our strength in all sorts of exercises; the company was good, the view was magnificent. Our camp
was near Tarki, overlooked by the fortress of Bournaïa.

[1] The author has intended to portray the brave general, Yermolof, the senior and the model of Russian officers.

Behind the fortress the sun was setting. At the foot of the cliff was the chamkal's house, and farther away, on the steepest slope, lay the town. Beyond all, to the east spread the vast steppe, and beyond the steppe stretched the blue expanse of the Caspian Sea. Tartar begs, Tchetchen princes, Cossacks from every river in Russia, hostages from every mountain, and the officers of all our regiments, formed a most curious and picturesque scene in which uniforms, tchokas, and coats of mail were mingled. The singers, dancers, and musicians made a group apart, and the soldiers took their share in the fête a few hundred paces below, their shakoes jauntily perched over one ear.

The conversation turned on the quality of the different poniards of the Caucasus. Each vaunted his own as made by the best blade-smith. Captain Betovitch, who had a kandjiar purchased at Andrev and mounted at Kouba, laid a wager that he could pierce three roubles placed one on top of the other.

The bet was taken; three roubles were stacked up on a block, and, left-handed though he is, Betovitch pierced the three roubles.

Just then, a frightened buffalo dashed into the midst of the musicians, and to the great delight of the on-lookers, created utter confusion. They scattered in all directions, dodging and leaping out of his way, and enraging him by their screams as they endeavored to escape.

The furious animal aimed for the group where General Yermolof was standing. Some of the officers drew their swords, others their poniards, and placed themselves in front of the lieutenant-governor; but, brushing them all aside, he drew his schaska and stationed himself in the animal's path.

The buffalo doubtless thought that he had met a worthy adversary, and bounded towards him.

With the agility of a young man, the general lightly avoided the animal; but, in the very act of springing aside, his arm was uplifted, something was seen to flash like lightning, and, while the buffalo's head, detached from the shoulders by a single blow, fell at the general's feet and remained stuck in the earth by its horns, the body by its own impetus continued three or four paces in its course, and fell, gushing forth a torrent of blood.

A great cry of astonishment and admiration arose from the spectators.

All the officers gathered about the general, — some examining the animal's head, others its body.

"A terrible sword your Excellency has there," said Captain Betovitch.

"It is worthy of going with your poniard, captain," returned the general.

And he presented him the sword.

The captain hesitated to accept it.

"Take it, take it," said Yermolof; "it is yours."

And he gave him, as he would have given an ordinary sword, that schaska whose blade alone had cost three or four hundred roubles, and whose sheath was worth as much more merely for its weight in silver.

They were still talking about this prodigious feat when an officer of the border Cossacks was announced to the general, coming on behalf of Colonel Kotzarev.

The officer entered, and presented a report.

"Permit me, gentlemen?" said the general, as if he were among his equals.

And that is the admirable side of this man: he constantly raises you to his own level, without descending to yours.

You may suppose that the permission was granted.

He read the report, accompanying its reading with a slight undertone of approval.

Then he said aloud, —

"Gentlemen, I have good news: there is a cross of St. George for one of our brave officers."

We drew near with interest.

"Well, it seems that Kotzarev has exterminated a dozen or fifteen hundred mountaineers. The bandits had crossed the Terek and devastated a village; but Kotzarev has met and overpowered them, and he sends me five prisoners; these are all that remain of their band."

Then, turning to the Cossack officer, he said, —

"Bring me a few of those gentlemen; I 'll wager that some of my acquaintances are among the rogues."

They were brought before him; at sight of them his brows knit in a frown.

"Wretches!" said he, "this is the third time that you have been caught, and twice you have been released on an oath never to engage in your plundering again. What do you lack? Pastures?— you have them; flocks?— you have them; safety?— am I not here to secure it for you?— Take them away, and let them dangle from their own ropes. However, they themselves shall choose one of their number who shall be set at liberty after he has witnessed the execution, that he may carry an account of it to his comrades."

Four men were led away: a fifth remained.

He was a Tartar beg; not until then did we notice him; our whole attention had been absorbed by the others.

He was a young man of twenty-three, of marvellous beauty and with the figure of the Apollo Belvedere.

He was awaiting his turn in an attitude of supreme grace and regal pride.

As the general's eye rested upon him, he bowed and resumed his first attitude.

On his face could be read that perfect resignation to fate which is the virtue of the Mussulman.

The general's glance, charged with threatening wrath, fell upon him; but the prisoner's face underwent no change; he did not even lower his eyes.

"Ammalat Beg," the general at length said, after a moment's silence that had seemed a long time to those whose curiosity formed their sole interest in the proceedings, — "Ammalat Beg, do you remember that you are a Russian subject, that you live under the Russian laws?"

"I have not forgotten it," replied Ammalat Beg; "and if they had defended my rights, I should not to-day -be standing like a culprit before you."

"You are both unjust and ungrateful," returned the general. "You and your father have made war on the Russians. If a similar thing had happened during a reign of the fathers of the caliphs from whom you pretend to have descended, your family would not now be in existence. But our emperor is so good that instead of hanging you, he gives you a government. How have you repaid his kindness? By open revolt. But that is not your greatest offence, even: you received into your house an enemy of Russia; you allowed him to assassinate a Russian officer and two soldiers in your presence, and yet, if you had repented, I should have pardoned you, in consideration of your youth and your customs; but no, you fled into the mountains and, with Ackmeth Khan, you have attacked a Russian post. Over and above all that, you became one of Djembhoulat's chiefs,

and with him have just pillaged the lands of your former
friends. I need not say what fate awaits you, need I ? "

"No, for I know it," answered Ammalat, quietly;
"I shall be shot."

"No, a ball bestows too noble a death for me to let
you die by a ball!" answered the enraged Yermolof.
"No! a cart shall be set with its shaft in the air, to the
shaft a rope, and to the rope your neck."

"It is quite the same thing," replied Ammalat Beg,
"although not the shortest death. Yet," he continued,
"I have a favor to ask: since I am condemned beforehand, do not take the trouble to give me a trial. The
trial will not last long, I know, but it always causes
delay."

"Agreed," answered the general.

Then, turning to his aids, he said, —

"Remove him, and to-morrow let all be over."

He was led away.

The fate of this young man, so proud, so calm, so
resigned, touched all. Everybody pitied him, and the
more sincerely because they well knew it was impossible
to save him, — an example being necessary, and Yermolof's
decisions being irrevocable.

No one dared to plead for the unfortunate youth.

Each went his way.

I noticed that the general was gloomy as he returned
home. I, knowing his heart, told myself that perhaps he
was sorry that no one had opposed his decision.

I resolved to attempt it.

I went to head-quarters ten minutes after he had
returned.

He was alone, his elbow resting upon the table. On
the table lay the report which he was making to the
emperor.

Alexis Petrovitch has, as you know, a great friendship
for me; I am one of his intimates: he was not surprised,
therefore, at seeing me.

On the contrary, he seemed to have been expecting
me, for he said with a smile, —

"I think, André Ivanovitch, that you have a favor to
ask. Ordinarily you come here as if you were marching
to battle; but to-day one would suppose that you were
treading the air, like the Mignon of your favorite poet.
I will wager that you have come to ask pardon for
Ammalat?"

"In faith! you have guessed right, your Excellency,"
I answered.

"Sit down there and let us talk this matter over,"
said he.

Then, after a moment's silence, he continued, —

"I know that I am said to regard the lives of men as
so many playthings, and that the blood of these mountaineers is no more esteemed by me than the water that
flows from their mountains. The cruellest conquerors
hide their cruelty under a semblance of forbearance;
while I, on the contrary, have the false reputation of a
merciless man. My name ought to guard our frontiers
more surely than chains and fortresses. It is expedient
that all these Asiatics know my word to be as inexorable
as death. One can persuade the European, move 'him
by kindness, touch him by clemency; the Asiatic, never.
To pardon him is more than a weakness, it is a crime;
that is why I show them no mercy. I am cruel out of
humanity: the prospect of certain punishment alone can
guarantee the Russians against death, and prevent treason
among the Mussulmans. Among all these people who
appear to submit, there is not one who is not concealing
wrath, who is not plotting vengeance. My predecessors

have said and my successors will say: 'Every time that
the death-sentence is in question, I would like with all
my heart to pardon. I have the greatest desire to show
mercy; but, judge for yourself: can I do it?' Then
they shed some tears over the victim. That is all sham,
my dear fellow! The laws exist, they must be executed.
Lives are intrusted to me, and I must watch over them.
I never talk in that way, I never shed such crocodile
tears; but, every time that I sign a death-warrant, my
heart weeps tears of blood."

Alexis Petrovitch was moved. He rose, took several
turns about his tent, reseated himself, and continued,—

"Ah well, never has the necessity for punishment
seemed more cruel than it has seemed to-day. One that
has remained as long among the Asiatics as I ought not to
pay any more attention to a handsome face than to a
letter of recommendation. But, mark you, the face,
figure, voice, and bearing of this Ammalat Beg has made
a strong impression on me. I pity him."

"A good heart is worth more than intellect, general,"
said I, "and you are fortunately gifted: you have
both."

"The heart of a public man, my dear fellow, should
ground arms to his intellect. I know very well that I can
pardon Ammalat: it rests with me; but I know also that
I must punish him. Daghestan is filled with our enemies; Tarki, but half subdued, is ready to rise with the
first puff of wind from the mountains; we must cut short
all of that by a few executions, and show the Tartars
that all must bow down before the Russian laws, even
mercy. If I pardon Ammalat, there will be but one
cry: 'Yermolof fears the chamkal!'"

"Yes," I answered; "but since we are not to follow
the impulses of the heart, but to consider and reflect, do

you not think that the gratitude of Ammalat's family
would have great weight in the country?"

"The chamkal is an Asiatic like the rest, my dear
colonel," interrupted Yěrmolof, "and he will be enchanted if this claimant to the principality no longer
exists. No, in this entire affair, I am the least concerned in the world about his relatives."

Seeing this sort of hesitancy on the part of the governor-general, I pursued more bravely.

"Require me to perform triple service," said I; "give
me no leave this year, and grant me a pardon for this
young man. He is young, and Russia may find in him
a good and brave servant. I make myself responsible
for him."

Alexis Petrovitch shook his head.

"Listen," said he, "it is sad to relate, but it is a phil-
osophical observation of mine, and one that assails
neither God nor Providence: rarely have I done a good
deed of this kind that has turned out well, and, mind
you, they have not been common."

"Try it once more, general, and give us your word
that if it turns out badly, this shall be the last."

"Very well! you wish it, — I pardon him; although
I was only waiting for a petition like yours to excuse me
in my own eyes. I pardon him unconditionally. It is
not my custom, when I have yielded the main point, to
haggle over details. But remember one thing: you have
said that you will be responsible for him."

"Entirely. I will take him to my quarters, and be
personally answerable for him, general."

"Never trust him, and remember the old story of the
viper warmed in the bosom of the compassionate man.
Oh,. the Asiatics, the Asiatics! one day you will know
them, Verkovsky; God grant it may never be at your
own expense!"

I was so delighted that instead of replying to the general, or thanking him in the least, I ran to the tent where Ammalat Beg was held.

Three sentinels stood guard over him; a lighted lantern was hanging from the centre. I went in. He was so deep in his own thoughts that he failed to hear me.

I drew near enough almost to touch him; he was lying on his bourka, weeping.

That did not surprise me; it is not a cheerful prospect, to die at twenty-three.

The tears that I had just surprised gave me great pleasure: they showed the value of the pardon I brought.

"Ammalat," said I in Tartar, "Allah is great and the *serdar* is good: he grants you life."

The young man sprang to his feet; he tried to speak, but it was some time before he could utter a word, he was so overcome.

"Life! He grants me life!"

Then with a bitter smile,—

"I understand," he added; "for a man to die slowly in a gloomy prison, or, when he is accustomed to the Oriental sun, to be sent to languish amid the snows of the north, to be buried alive, separated from his relatives, his friends, his mistress; to be deprived of speech with others, and forbidden to complain to himself: that is called life; that is the pardon granted to the condemned. If that is the pardon I am granted, if that is the alternative I am given, say that I do not want such a pardon."

"You deceive yourself, Ammalat," I answered. "The pardon is entire, unconditional, without restrictions. You remain master of your estates, your actions, your will. Here is your sword; the general returns it to you, confident that you will henceforth draw it only on the side of the Russians. You shall live with me until the whole unhappy affair is forgotten, and you shall be my friend, my brother."

The idea was new to an Asiatic. He looked at me: two great tears rolled from his eyes.

"The Russians have vanquished me quite!" he cried. "Pardon me, colonel, for having thought so badly of you all. From this hour, I become a loyal subject of the Russian emperor, and my heart and sword are his. Oh, my sword! my sword!" he added looking affectionately at the blade; "let my tears wash away the Russian blood and the Tartar naphtha![1] When and how can I thank you for life and liberty?"

I am sure, dear Marie, that, for this affair, you will keep for me one of your sweetest kisses. Besides, in acting as I did, I had no thought but of you. "Marie will be pleased," I said to myself; "Marie will reward me." But when shall I claim my reward, my darling? Your mourning must still last nine months longer, and the general has refused my leave, reminding me that I renounced it myself when demanding Ammalat's life.

The fact is that my presence is necessary to the regiment. Barracks are being constructed for our winter-quarters, and if I leave the work will stop. Therefore, I remain: but my heart! my poor heart!

We have now been three days in Derbend; Ammalat is with me. He says nothing. He becomes more morose, and more barbarous day by day, but he interests me only the more. He speaks Russian well, but by rote. I am teaching him the alphabet; he progresses wonderfully. I hope to make a fine scholar of him.

[1] The Tartars give a blackish tint to the blades of their swords and poniards by dipping them in naphtha.

IX.

The thoughts of Ammalat Beg translated from the
Tartar:[1]—

Either I have been asleep heretofore, or to-day I am
dreaming. There is, then, a new realm called thought.
A beautiful, grand, magnificent world which has long
been as unknown to me as the Milky Way, which is
composed, I am told, of millions of stars. I seem to be
climbing up the mountain of science out of the night and
the fog; but day breaks, and the fog vanishes. With
every step my horizon becomes brighter and broader.
With every step I breathe more freely. I gaze at the
sun, it forces me to lower my eyes; but already the
clouds are under my feet. Cursed clouds! On earth
you hinder me from seeing heaven; in heaven you hinder
my sight of the earth.

Why is it that these simple questions, *why* and *how*,
never before presented themselves to my mind? The
entire universe, with all it contains of good and ill, is
reflected in my soul as in a sea or mirror; yet my soul
knows no more about it than the mirror. Indeed, I
remember many things; but what good does it do me?
The falcon does not know why the hood is placed over
his eyes; the horse does not understand why he is shod.
Neither do I understand why there are mountains here

[1] These fragments were found in the room occupied by Ammalat Beg at Colonel Verkovsky's quarters.

and steppes there; here eternal snows, there oceans of
burning sand. What need have we of tempests and
earthquakes? And as for you, man, the most curious of
the creatures issuing from the hand of the Creator, I had
never thought of following your mysterious course from
the cradle to the tomb. I confess that until now I have
regarded books and life in the same light, — books without
comprehending their import, life without comprehending
its aim. But Verkovsky has lifted the bandage from my
eyes, cleared the fog from my brain; he gives me the
opportunity of knowing and learning; with him I try my
newly fledged wings, like the young swallow with its
mother. Distance and height make me wonder still, but
they do not frighten me. The time will come when I shall
soar like the eagle through heaven's brilliant azure.

And yet, am I the happier since Verkovsky and his
lessons have taught me to think?

Formerly, a horse, a sword, a gun afforded me a child-
like joy, and now that I recognize the superiority of
mind over matter, I no longer desire the things that were
formerly my ambitions. Once I regarded myself seriously; once I thought myself a great man; now I am at
least convinced of one thing, that I am nothing. I saw
nothing back of my ancestors; all that had gone before
was veiled in obscurity. It was dense night, peopled
with heroes borrowed from tales and legends. The
Caucasus was my horizon; but, at least, I slept tranquilly through that night. I hoped one day to become
celebrated throughout Daghestan: I had chosen the
mountains for the pedestal of my statue, and, behold!
growing wiser, I learn from books that long before my
day history had peopled my chosen stage with nations
struggling for glory, with heroes whose names have re-
sounded to the echoes of Daghestan and the entire world,

17

and that I, forsooth, was ignorant of the very names of
these nations, was unaware that such heroes had been in
existence. What has become of those nations? What
became of those heroes lost in the night of Time, forgotten in the dust of ages? I thought that the earth
belonged to the Tartars, and lo! from a glance at a
simple geographical chart, I learn that they occupy a
very small portion of a very small world; that they are
poor barbarians compared with the European world; that
no one thinks of them, that no one knows anything of
them, that no one wishes to know anything of them.
No! all, all is an illusion! Kings, heroes, great men
are glittering illusions; that is all.

By Mahomet! it was well worth while to wear out
one's brain to arrive at such a truth!

What is the good of understanding the forces of nature
and the laws by which she is governed, when my own
powers are helpless to govern my soul? I can rule the
sea, and I cannot curb my own tears. I can divert the
thunderbolt from my roof, and I cannot keep sorrow out
of my soul. I was unhappy before, when I had but my
moods to torment my soul; and now, as if my moods
were not sufficient, here are difficulties preying upon me
as my falcons prey upon the poor birds that I begin to
pity, — a thing which I had never thought of doing before.
The sick man gains very little from learning his malady,
when on learning it he at the same time finds out that it is
incurable. My sufferings are doubled by analyzing them.

But no, I am unjust. Reading shortens the long
hours of separation that seem to me like winter nights;
and in gaining the ability to write my thoughts, to fix
the phantoms of my imagination on paper, I gain in
stoutness of heart.

Of heart or pride, I know not which.

Nay, of heart; for, some day, when I see Sultanetta
again, I will show her these pages in which her name
occurs more frequently than Allah's in the Koran.
"These are the memories of my heart," I will say;
"look: on such a day I thought of you like that; on
such a night I dreamed that dream of you. From these
lines you can count my tears; from these words, my
sighs." Perhaps we shall laugh together over these days
in which I have suffered so much; but can I think of
the past when beside you, my darling Sultanetta? No,
all will be blotted out before me and around me, and
naught of space will be illumined save the spot on which
falls the ray from your eyes. By that light my heart will
soften in my breast. To forget myself near you is sweeter
far than to make the whole world resound with my name.

You see plainly that it is not pride.

I read tales of love, portrayals of the passions of men
and women: in the first place, not one of these heroines
of romance is so beautiful in body, mind, or heart as my
Sultanetta, and, as for me, I bear no moral resemblance
to the men whose story I read. I envy their wit, their
science, their amiability, but not their love. Their
warmest love is sluggish and cold; it is like a ray of
moonlight shimmering on the ice. No, I cannot think
that men really love, whose love is manifested thus.

There is one thing, dear, which I must confess: in vain
I ask myself what friendship is. I cannot answer. I
have a friend in Verkovsky, a true, sincere, kind friend.
Well, he is my friend; I feel that I cannot respond as
he deserves, and I blame myself for it; but it is not in my
power to do otherwise. In my soul there is no room for
any but Sultanetta; in my heart, no feeling other than
love.

No, I will read no more; I understand nothing it says

to me. Decidedly, I am not made to climb the ladder of science. I catch my breath at the first round, I am lost in simple difficulties, I tangle the thread instead of unwinding it. I pull and break it. I have taken the colonel's encouragement for progress. But what hinders my progress? Alas! it is what makes my life's happiness and unhappiness, — love. In everything, everywhere, I see and hear Sultanetta, and often I see and hear nothing else. To forget her a single instant would seem a crime. I should as soon wish to still the beatings of my heart. Can I live without air? Sultanetta is my light, my air, my life, my soul!

My hand trembles, my heart beats. Were I to write with my blood, it would burn the paper. Sultanetta, do you know that you are killing me? Your image follows me everywhere. The remembrance of your beauty is more dangerous to me than your beauty itself. The thought that the treasure of love which I have held in my arms is forever lost to me drowns me in despair, goads me to madness. My mind is giving way, my heart is breaking. I remember every feature of your face, every change of your expression, every movement of your arm, every curve of your bust, and your foot, that seal of love, and your lips, like ripe pomegranate, and your shoulders, mine of marble! Oh! The memory alone of your voice shakes me to the soul, like the string of an instrument near breaking. And in the night time your kiss, the kiss from which I seem to drink the springs of life, falls again upon me like dew of fire. Oh! yet one kiss like that in the chapel, a single one, Sultanetta, and then, come death!

Colonel Verkovsky had, as we have seen, observed Ammalat's sadness, and, too, he had divined its cause.

Hoping to divert him, he organized a boar-hunt, a favorite pastime of the begs of Daghestan.

At the colonel's invitation, twenty begs arrived, attended by their noukars, each disposed to do his best.

December was beginning to cover the summits of the mountains of Daghestan with snow. The swelling Caspian, unnavigable during the winter, was storming the walls of the City of the Iron Gates. Through the fog whizzed the wings of bustards; all was gloomy and dull. The misting rain falling every evening seemed like the tears of the weather itself, lamenting finer days. Old Tartars, enveloped to their noses in pelisses and bourkas, were standing about the markets.

But such dull days are fine days for hunters.

The sun had barely risen from the other side of the sea, the mullahs had scarcely called to prayer, when the colonel and his guests, Ammalat included, gathered at the north gate of Derbend, after literally wading through the mud.

· The route they took is sorry enough to the eye; it is the one leading to Tarki; here and there lie a few fields of madder, then come vast Tartar cemeteries in which the graves are so crowded that they look like a forest of stakes; there are a few scattered vineyards; and beyond all lies the sea, which, at that season of the year, instead of holding a shining mirror to the sky, looked like a vast basin from which a constant fog arose. On both sides of the road enormous boulders, loosened from their bases by the violence of torrents, had rolled down and remained there in a litter, showing the unconcern of men for the cataclysms of Nature.

The huntsmen were at their posts.

On arriving, the colonel sounded three shrill, prolonged blasts from his silver-hooped hunting-horn, to which the huntsmen replied with a shout indicating that they were ready.

The hunters took their positions in line, some on horses, some on foot, and the battue began.

Boars were soon started, and the crackling of the first shots was heard.

The forests of Daghestan abound in these animals; and although the Tartars, considering them unclean, hold it a sin even to touch them, they are regarded as grand game for the chase. It is a good school of practice for both shooting and courage, as the speed of the wild boar is remarkably swift, and when wounded the mountain boar especially almost always turns upon the hunter.

The line of hunters comprising thirty shots extended over a very wide space. The boldest of the sportsmen, or those surest of their aim, chose the most isolated spots in order to share with none the glory of victory.

Colonel Verkovsky, relying on his own courage and skill, took one of these posts, deep in the forest and entirely isolated. Leaning against an oak-tree, in the centre of a sort of clearing which allowed the hunter, and likewise the boar, perfect freedom of movement, he awaited the event, which, in this country where the animal remains as wild as nature and man, is almost always a hand-to-hand struggle. Shots were heard to right and left; sometimes through copses and brushwood, the colonel could distinguish a boar passing like a flash. At last, he heard a great crackling of breaking bushes, and saw an enormous old boar heading straight for him.

The colonel fired, but the ball glanced from the animal's bony skull and wedge-shaped head. Yet, stunned for a moment by the violence of the shock, the boar stood trembling in every limb without moving backward or forward. The colonel, supposing him to be more injured than he was, left his cover and started toward him. Then the animal, not knowing before whence the blow had come, recognized his enemy, and with bristles erect and gnashing teeth he made for the colonel.

Verkovsky had a second shot; he waited.

At four paces, he pulled the trigger; only the priming smoked.

What then happened took place as swift as thought.

He experienced a violent shock that felled him to the earth; but, with the admirable coolness born of tried courage, he drew his kandjiar as he fell.

It was one of the best blades of Daghestan.

The boar spitted himself upon it, but the force of his onset wrenched the weapon from the colonel's hands.

The brute had received a terrible wound; yet, from the blood in his eye and his foaming mouth, the colonel could see that he was still full of fight.

Prostrate, disarmed, conscious from a pain in his thigh that he was already wounded, the colonel gave himself up for lost.

"Help, comrades!" he cried, without hoping to be heard.

Besides, should they hear, were they within a hundred paces, they could not reach him in time to help.

Suddenly the gallop of a horse was heard: a hunter was on the track of the boar which he seemed to be pursuing.

A shot echoed; the colonel heard a shrill whizzing, followed by the deadened sound of the ball striking a soft body.

At the same instant he felt as if a mountain had been lifted from his breast.

The boar was leaving him for a new enemy.

Verkovsky rose to his elbow; a mist was before his
eyes. Yet through the mist he saw a horseman who,
instead of fleeing from the boar or simply awaiting him,
jumped from his horse.

Man and beast rushed upon each other and rolled
together on the ground.

There was a brief space during which it would have
been impossible for a painter to have given any form to
this monstrous group.

Yet it seemed to the colonel that the man continued
to strike after the animal was already dead.

At length the infuriated slayer stood up, covered with
blood and froth and mire.

It was Ammalat Beg.

The boar's head lay beside the body, completely severed from it.

The colonel arose, and with open arms, although his
blood was issuing from two wounds, he ran gratefully
toward the young man.

"Don't thank me," said Ammalat Beg, spurning the
boar's head and stamping it with the iron heel of his
boot; "I am taking revenge. Ah! accursed! ah! unclean!" continued the youth, trampling the animal under
foot, as if it could still hear and feel. "It is not all for
killing my friend the beg of Tavannant. Instead of
turning round, you coward! instead of attacking me, who
killed your father and stabbed your mother, you continued your course to gore my benefactor, the man to whom
I owe my life. Ah! accursed! ah! unclean!"

"You owe me nothing now, Ammalat, and we are
quits," said the colonel; "and, accursed and unclean as he
is, I trust indeed that we shall be avenged by giving
him tit for tat. We will inflict the Tartar punishment
on him, Ammalat Beg, — retaliation. He has attacked us

with his teeth; we will eat him with ours. I hope that you will lay aside your prejudices in this instance, Ammalat, and eat your share of him."

"I would eat my share of a man, had he killed my friend," responded the savage hunter; "and the flesh of an animal with far greater excuse, were its flesh ten times forbidden!"

"And, to wash down this forbidden flesh, we will sprinkle him with forbidden liquor."

"Whatever you like, colonel; it is just as well to sprinkle my burning heart with wine as with holy water, since the holy water does it no good."

Then, pressing both hands upon his breast as if to still his heart, he gave a deep moan.

The hunt was ended, — that part of it at least.

They heard the notes of the recheat. The colonel sounded three blasts from his horn; a moment later, hunters and huntsmen were surrounding him.

In few words the colonel told what had happened; then, pointing to the boar with its head severed from the body, he said, turning to the young man, —

"It was a fine stroke, Ammalat, a brave stroke!"

"It is an Asiatic's revenge. An Asiatic's revenge is deadly!"

"Friend," said the colonel, "you have seen a Russian's revenge, a Christian's; let that be a lesson to you."

And both returned to the camp.

Ammalat Beg was distrait. Sometimes he gave no answer to Verkovsky's questions, sometimes he answered quite wide of the mark. He went along by his side, peering about in all directions as if he were expecting some one, and not even thinking to ask the colonel if his wounds were painful.

Supposing that Ammalat, like a fearless hunter, was
dreaming of the chase, and being in a hurry, moreover, to
return and submit his leg and thigh to the surgeon's care,
Verkovsky set off at a gallop and left Ammalat to his
reveries.

The young man allowed him to get beyond the hill,
and then, thinking himself to be alone, he rose in his
stirrups and looked in all directions.

Suddenly a horseman sprang up from the bottom of a
ravine, with clothes all torn by the thorny shrub grow
ing everywhere on the slopes of the Caucasus.

The rider made straight for Ammalat Beg.

One cry issued from both throats, —

" *Aleikoum salaam !* "

And both, leaping from their horses, threw themselves
into each other's arms.

" So you are here, Nephtali! " cried Ammalat Beg;
" you have seen her, you have spoken to her. Oh! I see
by your face that you bring good news."

He quickly took off his jacket, all embroidered with
gold, and presented it to Nephtali, saying, —

" Stay, accept this, herald of good tidings.[1] Is she
alive? is she well? does she love me still? "

" In the name of Mahomet, let me get my breath, "
said Nephtali. " You ask me so many questions, and I
in turn have so many things to say, that they crowd each
other like the women in the door of the mosque when
their slippers are lost."

" Well, tell everything in its place. You received my
letter? "

---

[1] It is a Tartar custom to make a present, almost always giving
a garment, to the bringer of good news. In this way I received
the nicham, for having announced to the bey of Tunis his cousin's
arrival at Marseilles. — A. D.

"You can see for yourself, since I am here. I received your letter, and by your desire betook myself to Khunsack. I went there so quietly and silently that I awoke not so much as a bird on my way. Ackmeth Khan is well; he is at home. He inquired anxiously about you, shook his head, and asked: 'Does n't he need a spindle for winding off the Derbend silk?' The khan's wife, who already looks upon you as her son-in-law," — Ammalat sighed and turned his eyes heavenward, — "sends you a thousand compliments and as many little pies. I bring you the compliments, but I have thrown away the little pies, which the gait of my horse had beaten into pulp."

"May the devil eat them! And — and Sultanetta?"

"Sultanetta, dear brother," said Nephtali, sighing in turn, "Sultanetta is as beautiful as the starry sky. Only, her sky, clouded over and gloomy at first, became azure when I spoke your name, when I said that I came from you. She nearly fell upon my neck; I emptied her out a whole sack of love from you. I swore that you were dying of love for her."

"And what did she answer?"

"Nothing. She fell to weeping."

"Dear heart! dear heart! and what message did she send me?"

"Ask rather what message she did not send and I shall have done sooner. She told me to say that since your going away she has not been happy even in a dream; that her heart lies buried under the snow which only your presence, like the sun in May, can melt. If I had waited for her to finish telling me all that I was to say, and to express all her wishes, we should not have met again, my dear Ammalat, till we were gray-headed; and yet she almost chased me away because she thought

I was not hurrying fast enough, and she wished you to know immediately of all her sufferings."

"Lovely being!" addressing himself to Sultanetta as if she could have heard him. "Oh, you will never know what happiness it is for me to be near you, what martyrdom not to see you!"

"Eh, by Allah! It seems as if I were listening to her, for she said exactly the same thing, Ammalat. 'Oh, let him only return,' she sobbed, 'were it but for one day, one hour, one moment!'"

"Oh, let me see her, let me see her, and die!"

"No, Ammalat, you must see her and live. Never does a man so desire to live as when gazing at her. A single look from her doubles the circulation."

"Did you tell her why I cannot carry out the dearest of all my wishes?"

"I told her so many things that if you could have heard them you would have taken me for the poet of the Shah of Persia. She wept her eyes out over them, poor child!"

"You need not have driven her to despair, Nephtali; perhaps what cannot be done now may be done later. To banish hope from a woman's heart is to banish love. A woman without hope does not love long."

"You are wasting your breath, Ammalat; on the contrary, hope, among lovers, is an endless ball of yarn. They hardly believe in estrangement when they see it. If they love you, they believe in everything, even in ghosts! Listen, Sultanetta is positive that were you even in the grave you would come out of it to see her."

"The grave and Derbend are the same thing to me, Nephtali; my body is at Derbend, my soul at Khunsack."

"And your mind, where is that, Ammalat? It is

running at large, it seems to me. Are you so badly off
with the colonel, for a man who six months ago was to
have been hanged? No. You are free, you are amused,
loved like a brother, treated like a betrothed. Sultanetta is beautiful, I know very well; but Verkovsky is
good, and you can well sacrifice to friendship a small
part of love."

"And what else am I doing, Nephtali? If you only
knew what it costs me! It seems to me that what I give
Verkovsky is a piece torn from my heart. Friendship
is a fine thing, but it does not take the place of love.
Nephtali."

Nephtali sighed.

"Have you spoken of Sultanetta to the colonel?" he
asked.

"I have never dared, although a hundred times I have
wished to speak; but the words stop at my lips. As
soon as I open my mouth the name of Sultanetta seems
to block the passage. He is so wise that I am afraid of
wearying him with my folly. He is so kind that I fear
to tire his patience. Imagine, Nephtali, he is in love
with a woman with whom he was raised. He was to
have married her; but, in 1814, during the war with
France, he was thought to have been killed. The woman,
who had already struggled for three years to keep her
heart for Verkovsky, believing that he was dead, yielded
at last, and married another man. In 1815 he returned.
His Marianne was married. What do you think I would
have done in his place? I would have buried my kandjiar in the perjurer's heart. I would have carried her off
to possess her, were it only for an hour. No; he knew
his rival to be an honorable man, as they say; he was cold-
blooded enough to remain his friend, and saw his former
promised bride without stabbing both of them."

"A rare man," said Nephtali; "he must be a true friend."

"Yes, but what a frozen lover! Forbearing as he was, the husband was jealous. What did Verkovsky do? He went into service in the Caucasus. Fortunately or unfortunately, the husband died. Ah! now he would saddle his horse, you would think, get on his back and start. No. The governor tells him that his presence is necessary here, and he remains — not for eight days, or a month, or three months, but for a year, a century, an eternity! As for his love, he feeds it with paper every eight days, when the post comes. No, you can see, Nephtali, such a man, however good he may be, would not understand my love. There is too great a difference between our ages and especially our ideas. All that chills my friendship and keeps me from being open."

"Strange man that you are!" said Nephtali, with a degree of sadness. "You do not love Verkovsky, although, of right, he deserves your love and respect more than any other."

"Who has told you that I do not love him?" cried Ammalat, with almost a shudder. "No, no, on the contrary, I must love him as my benefactor, as the man who saved my life. Oh! I love everybody since knowing Sultanetta. I would like to cover the earth with flowers, to make the universe one great garden."

"To love everybody is to love nobody, Ammalat."

"You are wrong, Nephtali. The universe might drink from my cup of love, and my cup would still be full," said Ammalat, smiling.

"That is what comes of seeing a beautiful girl without her veil, and never afterwards seeing anything but veils and eyebrows. Like a nightingale of the Valley of Aourmès, you need a cage to make you sing."

"What is the Valley of Aourmès like?" asked Ammalat Beg.

"In the spring it is the realm of roses; in autumn,
the realm of raisins," replied Nephtali.

And, as a body of belated hunters was advancing
toward them, the two friends turned their horses and
plunged into the depths of the wood.

X.

COLONEL VERKOVSKY to his fiancée: —

DERBEND, April, 1820.

Come, dear Marie, heart of my heart! come and admire with me a beautiful night in Daghestan.   Derbend, like dark-colored lava rock fallen from the crest of
the Caucasus, lies peacefully on a bed of flowers; the
wind wafts me the breath of the almond-trees; a nightingale is singing in the thicket behind the fortress.   All
things seem springing into life, all breathe of love.
Nature, blushing like a modest bride, hides in a misty
veil.   The ocean of mist works wonders with the Caspian.   Below, the sea heaves like an embossed cuirass
rising with the breath of a mighty breast.   Above, the
fog rolls in silvery billows lighted by the full moon which
is swinging in heaven like a golden lamp round which
gleam the stars, diamonds strewn on the azure.   Then
too, every moment, the moon's fickle beams change the
aspect — I will not say of the landscape: limitless fogs
and a boundless sea do not constitute a landscape — of
the horizon, which one might fancy to be the threshold
of the kingdom of phantoms, the empire of dreams.

You cannot imagine, dear love, the sad and, at the
same time, the sweet emotions inspired in me by the sight
and sound of the sea.   My thoughts at once dwell upon
the immortality of our souls, of the infinity of our love.
Love fills me and envelops me.   It is the only great and
immortal sentiment that man can have.   It is his ocean.

In the winter of sadness, its flame keeps me warm, its light is my guide through the night of doubt; I love then without weeping, and have faith in everything. You smile at my fancy, sister of my soul; you wonder at this melancholy strain. Ah! well, to whom should I tell my thoughts, if not to you? You know that I am a sort of lantern, and the flame burning in my heart outlines all my emotions on my face, and, as you will read me with your heart and not your mind, I am not disturbed. In any case, if any points in my letters seem obscure, your happy fiancé will explain them to you in the month of August next. I cannot think without delirium of the moment when I shall see you again; I count the hours that separate us, I count the versts between. Thus, in June you will visit the springs of the Caucasus, and then only a few icy peaks of the granite chain will be between us. How many years of my life would I give to hasten the happy hour of our meeting! Our souls have so long been affianced! Why then have they been separated until now?

Our Ammalat is always reticent with me. I do not blame him; I know how difficult it is, how impossible even, to change customs absorbed with the mother's milk and the air of one's native land. Persia's despotism has imbued the soul of the Caucasian Tartars with the basest passions, has filled their hearts with the most cowardly deceitfulness. Could it be otherwise in a government based upon the exchange of a great despotism for a petty one, in which even a just trial is a rare thing, in which power is nothing but the right to commit robbery without chastisement?

"Master, do with me what you will; but allow me to do as I will with my inferiors."

That is the whole sum of the Asiatic rule.

18

Hence it follows that every man, finding himself
between two enemies, the one who is oppressing him and
the one whom he is oppressing, is accustomed to conceal
his thoughts as he conceals his money. Hence every
man dissembles before the powerful to obtain power,
before the rich to obtain the price of persecution or de-
nunciation. Hence, in short, the Tartar of Daghestan
will not utter a word, will not take a step, will not give
a cucumber without the hope of a gift in return. Churl-
ish with whoever has neither power nor wealth, he
cringes before power and crawls before wealth. He will
lavish caresses on you, give you his children, his house,
or his soul, in order to keep his money; and if he
shows you any civility whatever, rest assured that the
civility covers some speculation. In business, a *denier*
will spoil a trade: it is hard to conceive the extent of
their love for gain. The Armenians have a viler, more
contemptible character than they; but the Tartars, I
think, are more treacherous and greedy. Now, it is
obvious that Ammalat, with such examples before him
from his infancy, has been influenced by them, although
in his nobility he has preserved a great scorn for all that
is base and unworthy; but nature conferred on him a
dissembling character as an indispensable weapon against
his enemies, open or secret. The ties of blood, so sacred
with us, do not exist among the Asiatics: the son with
them is the father's slave; brother is enemy to brother.
They place no confidence in their neighbor because their
religion has omitted to tell them to love their neighbor as
themselves. Jealousy, inspired by wife or mistress,
stifles all other sentiments. There is no friendship
among them. A child brought up by an enslaved
mother, ignorant of a father's caress, choked by the
Arabic alphabet, is secretive even with the children of his

own age. From his first tooth, he goes where he will;
at the first hint of a mustache, all doors, all hearts are
closed to him. Husbands regard him uneasily, and drive
him like a wild beast; and the first heart-throb, the first
impulse of his nature are already crimes in the eye of
Mohammedanism. He must let nothing of what passes
within him be seen by his nearest relative, by his best
friend. If he weeps, he must draw his bachlik over his
eyes, and weep in silence and alone.

I tell you all this, dear love, that you may not condemn Ammalat. These Asiatic customs are so at variance with ours that they need to be explained at every
turn. Thus, for nearly a year and a half of his stay with
me, I did not know the name of the woman he loves,
although he well understood that it was not from curiosity that I sought to learn the secrets of his heart.

At last, one day he told me all.

This is how it came about.

We were taking a ride, Ammalat and I, outside of the
town; we had followed the mountain road, and, advancing farther and higher, we discovered ourselves, without
having realized it, near the village of Kemmek, where
the famous wall passes which used to secure Persia
against invasions from the tribes that dwelt on the
northern steppes of the Caucasus. The chronicles of
Derbend have it that this wall was built by a certain
Isfendiar. Hence comes the tradition attributing the
work to Alexander the Great, who never came so far as
this. In all probability, it was Nushirvan who discovered it, had it rebuilt, and stationed sentinels upon it.

Since then, it has been repaired several times; finally,
for want of repairs, it has fallen into the state in which
we find it to-day. The wall is said to have extended
from the Caspian Sea to the Black Sea along the Cau-

casus, having iron gates at its terminus at Derbend, and
iron gates were at its centre at the Pass of Dariel.
Moreover, traces of it are seen in the mountains as far
as they can be followed. They are lost sight of only
over precipices and gorges. Yet, in spite of the searches
that have been instituted from the Black Sea to Min-
grelia, no trace of it is to be found. I looked with
interest at this old wall flanked by watch-towers, and I
was astonished at the greatness of the ancients, even in
their caprices,— caprices to which the Orientals of to-day
cannot attain. The wonders of Babylon, Lake Mœris,
the pyramids of the Pharaohs, the great wall of China,—
that wall carried through the wildest regions, over the
crests of the highest peaks, across the deepest gorges,—
testify to the giant will and boundless power of the
ancient kings. Neither time nor earthquakes have been
able to destroy the work of man, nor the feet of centuries
to stamp out the remains of this bold antiquity.

I confess that this sight inspired me with both solemn
thoughts and pride. I reviewed the work of Peter the
Great, that founder of a new empire. I pictured him
on the ruins of this Asiatic power, mapping Russia from
its midst with his powerful hand, and adding her to
Europe. How brilliant must have been the lightnings
of his eyes, flashed from the Caucasus! What thoughts
teemed in his brain! What inspiration swelled his
breast! The prodigious future of his country stretched
out before his vision, as boundless as the horizon. In
the great mirror of the Caspian he saw reflected the
future grandeur of Russia, planted by him, sprinkled
with the dew of blood. He aimed, not to achieve foolish
and brutal conquests, as these barbarians have done, but
to secure the happiness of human kind. Astrakhan,
Derbend, Baku, all are links of the chain by which he

wished to get round the Caucasus, thereby joining the commerce of India and Russia.

Oh, Idol of the North! you whom nature created to flatter man's vanity and cause him at the same time to despair of ever attaining your height, your giant shade rises before me, and the flood of years is dashed into spray at your feet!

Pensive and silent, I continued my way.

This Caucasian Wall extends in a northerly direction, and is built with square blocks of hewn stone, fitted in with stones that are narrower and consequently longer than wide. It is what the Greeks termed the Pelasgic structure. At many points the battlements still remain; but acorns have fallen into interstices and germinated, and the slow but irresistible levers of the roots have spread the stones, and gradually caused the falling of portions of the wall that had warmed in its bosom the oaken serpents. The eagles undisturbed make their nests in the towers formerly full of soldiers; and by the waysides, bleached by time, are found the bones of wild goats brought hither by the jackals.

At many points I lost every trace of the wall; then suddenly I would see it rising again from the grass and undergrowth.

Having proceeded thus for nearly three versts, we arrived at a gate, and passed from the north side to the south under an arch covered with herbs and roots.

We had hardly gone twenty paces when we came upon six armed mountaineers.

They were lying in the shade near their horses, which were browsing on the grass.

Then I saw what a mistake I had made in taking so long a ride outside of Derbend without an escort.

It was impossible to escape by flight on account of the

rocks and brush. On the other hand, it was rash for
two men to attack six. Nevertheless, I drew my pistol
from its holster; but Ammalat, taking in the situation,
decided at a glance, and, thrusting back my weapon into
its case, said in an undertone,—

"Don't touch your pistol, or we are lost; only,
don't take your eyes from me, and do what you see
me do."

The brigands had seen us; they rose quickly and
seized their guns.

One man only remained stretched on the grass.

Raising his head, he looked at us, and made a sign to
his companions.

Instantly we were surrounded, and a mountaineer
seized my horse by the bridle.

There was but one path in front of us, and the Lesghian
chief was lying in the middle of that.

"I beg that you will descend from your horses, my
dear guests," said he, smiling.

I hesitated. Ammalat made me a sign to remain on
my horse, but he sprang to the ground.

That appeared to satisfy the Lesghian chief.

Ammalat approached him.

"Good day, my dear fellow!" he said. "On my word,
I was not expecting to see you to-day; I thought the
devil had made you into chislik long ago."

"Not so fast, Ammalat Beg!" returned the bandit,
with a frown. "Before such a thing happens, I live in
hopes of giving the eagles a few carcasses of Russians and
of Tartars like yourself."

"How goes the sport?" demanded Ammalat, as tranquilly as if he had not heard.

"Badly. The Russians keep as close as cowards."

I started; but I encountered two glances fixed upon

me at the same time, — the hateful glance of the mountaineer and the gentle, serene gaze of Ammalat Beg.

"I have taken," continued the Lesghian, "only a few
flocks and a dozen cavalry horses, and really I was
deciding this very day that I must return empty-handed.
But Allah·is great, and he sends me a rich beg and a
Russian colonel."

On hearing these words, my heart seemed to stop
beating.

"Never sell your falcon when he is above the clouds,"
said Ammalat Beg, laughing, "but only when he has
returned to your hand."

The brigand took up his gun and looked steadily
at us.

"Ammalat," said he, "you are caught and well
caught: don't think to escape me, either you or your
companion. But," he added with a laugh, "perhaps you
count on defending yourself?"

"Nonsense, Chemardant! Do you think we are fools
enough to fight two to six? We like money very well;
but far above money we value our lives. We are caught;
we will pay, providing that you are not too exacting.
You know, indeed, that I am an orphan. Neither has
the colonel any parents."

"You have neither father nor mother; but you have
your father's inheritance."

"I have nothing, for I am the prisoner of the
Russians."

"If you are a prisoner, why not profit by the occasion
to escape? I will set you free myself."

"There is the only man who can set me free," said
Ammalat, pointing to me. "He has my word: until he
gives it back to me, I shall follow him wherever he is
pleased to lead me. A Mohammedan's word is as

invisible as a hair of a woman's head, but it is as strong as a chain of iron."

"If you have no money, we will be content with sheep; one word to Sophyr Ali, who stayed to guard your house, will settle the matter. But don't talk to me of the colonel's poverty: I know that there is not a soldier in his regiment that would not sell the last button of his uniform to ransom him. In any case, we shall see. Allah preserve me! I am not a Jew."

"Be reasonable, Chemardant," continued the young Tartar, "and we shall not think of either defence or flight."

"I believe you, and I would prefer to have the matter settled without powder or shot."

Then, with a bantering glance, he continued,—

"How fine you have become, Ammalat! What a horse! what a gun! Show me your poniard, now. It is of Kouba make!"

"No, it was made at Kisliar," replied Ammalat.

Then, drawing the weapon from its sheath, he said,—

"The scabbard is nothing to see, look at the blade. The blade is a miracle of workmanship. On the side you can see the name of the maker; read it for yourself: 'Ali Ousta Kasanisky.'"

Ammalat held up his kandjiar before the eyes of the bandit who was endeavoring to decipher the inscription engraved on the blade.

He shot me a glance that made me shudder.

Suddenly the kandjiar flashed like lightning, and disappeared to the hilt in the Lesghian's breast.

I had guessed as much. I seized the pistol in my holster, and aimed at the head of the mountaineer holding my horse.

Seeing two of their comrades fall, the other four took to their heels.

Ammalat tranquilly set to work to despoil the dead.

"My friend," said I, shaking my head, "I do not know whether I ought to commend you for what you have just done. A ruse is always a ruse,—that is to say, a narrow, mean trick, even against an enemy."

He looked up at me in astonishment.

"Really, colonel," he exclaimed, "you are a strange man! That bandit has injured the Russians terribly. Don't you know that he would have drained our blood drop by drop to get gold?"

"True, Ammalat," I answered; "but to lie, to call him your friend, to be talking with him in friendly fashion, and suddenly plunge your kandjiar into his heart! Could we not have begun as we ended?"

"No, colonel, no, we could not. If I had not approached the chief, if I had not addressed him as a friend, we should have been killed at the first movement that we made. I know the mountaineers very well. They are brave, but only in the presence of their chief. It was necessary therefore to begin with him. When he was dead, see how they ran!"

I again shook my head.

This Asiatic deceit, to which I owed my life, did not please me.

As for Ammalat, after taking the chief's weapons, he came to secure those of the Lesghian whom I had dropped with a shot from my pistol.

To my great amazement, the poor devil was not dead. On seeing him fall, I had turned my horse away from him.

He uttered a few words that sounded like a prayer.

Ammalat approached him, and his astonishment was greater than mine on recognizing the wounded man — the ball had pierced both cheeks — as a noukar of Ackmeth Khan's.

"How do you come to be with these Lesghian brigands?" demanded he.

"The devil tempted me," he answered; "Ackmeth Khan sent me to the village of Kemmek with a letter to Ibrahim, the physician, asking him to come to Khunsack without delay."

"You were sent for Ibrahim?" demanded Ammalat, quickly.

"Yes."

"Who, then, is ill at Khunsack?"

"The young Khaness Sultanetta."

"Ill?" cried Ammalat; "Sultanetta ill?"

"Here is the letter," said the noukar.

And, upon this, he handed Ammalat Beg a little roll of money with a paper.

Ammalat became as pale as death; tremblingly he unfolded the paper, and as he read, repeated in a scarcely audible voice,—

"'She eats nothing!—For three nights she has not slept! She is delirious; her life is in danger, save her!'

"My God! my God!" cried Ammalat, "and I was laughing, amusing myself, while the soul of my soul is on the point of leaving earth! Oh! may all the curses of Allah fall on my head, if only she may be cured! Dear, beautiful girl! oh! you are drooping, withering, O rose of Avarie! Death beckons you, saying, 'Come!' and, while calling on me to save you, you are forced to follow Death!—Colonel, colonel," he cried, seizing my hand, "in the name of your God, grant my sacred prayer, the only one I will ever make you. Let me see her once, once more, a last time."

"Whom do you wish to see, Ammalat?"

"Sultanetta, the soul of my soul, the apple of my eye, the light of my life; Sultanetta, the daughter of the khan of Avarie. She is ill, dying, dead perhaps. While I waste speech here, she is dying! and I have not received her last look, her last sigh. Oh! why do not the burning ruins of the sun fall upon my head? Why does not the earth open and swallow me up?"

And he fell upon my breast, suffocated by the tears which would not come, sobbing aloud, but unable to utter another word.

It was no time to reproach him with his long-continued reticence; but was it indeed right that I should let a prisoner return, even for one day, to the house of one of Russia's greatest enemies?

There are some situations in life before which all social proprieties, all political considerations efface themselves, and Ammalat was in such a strait.

Whatever might come of it, I resolved to grant his request.

I clasped him in my arms: our tears were mingled.

"Friend," said I, "go where your heart calls you; God grant that where you go you will carry health and peace of mind! *Bon voyage*, Ammalat!"

"Adieu, my benefactor!" he cried; "adieu forever, perhaps! If God takes Sultanetta from me, he will take my life at the same time. Farewell, and Allah keep you!"

And he set off at a gallop, descending the mountain with the swiftness of a rock bounding into the valley.

As for the wounded man, I put him in the saddle, and, leading my horse by the bridle, I brought him back to Derbend.

So then, it is true: he is in love.

Yes, I understand your remonstrance, darling Marie; but Khan Ackmeth is the enemy of the Russians. Pardoned by the emperor, he has betrayed us. There is no possible alliance between Ammalat and him except by Ammalat's betraying us in his turn, or by Ackmeth Khan's deciding to remain neutral.

We cannot believe one of these things, we cannot hope for the other.

What could I do? I have suffered so much from love myself, dear Marie! I have shed so many tears upon my pillow! I have so often desired the rest of the dead, the peace of the tomb, to still my poor heart, that I cannot resist such sufferings. Ought I not to pity a young man whom I tenderly love, for loving foolishly himself? Unfortunately, my pity is not a bridge that can conduct him to happiness. Had he not been loved, perhaps he would gradually have forgotten.

Certainly,—and I seem to hear your sweet voice making this observation, — certainly circumstances may alter for them, as they have altered for us. In this world, can unhappiness alone be everlasting?

I say nothing, but I suspect — I fear for them, and, who knows! perhaps for us.

We are too happy, my dearest Marie! the future smiles upon us, hope sings its sweetest songs. But the future! It is a calm sea to-day, a stormy one to-morrow! And hope is the siren. Yes, to be sure, everything is ready for our reunion; but are we reunited?

I do not know why, occasionally a fear stabs me to the heart like cold steel. I do not know why it seems to me that this separation, so near its close, will last forever.

Oh! all this affright, all these terrors, all this anguish will disappear, have no fear, my dear love, with the very moment when I shall press your hand against my lips, your heart against my heart.

Soon, soon, my darling!

XI.

ON the evening of that same day, Ammalat's horse fell under him, never to get up again.

He procured another, and continued his way without thought of food or drink. On the second day, he came in sight of Khunsack.

It was eleven o'clock in the morning. He had travelled twenty-four hours.

The farther he advanced, the stronger grew his fears.

Would he find his beloved Sultanetta alive or dead?

A chill passed through his frame as he saw the towers of the khan's palace.

He could see nothing, conjecture nothing.

" Which shall I find down there?" he asked himself,— " life or death?"

And he urged his horse with whip and knees.

A rider was preceding him, armed as for a fight; another was coming to meet that one along the road from Khunsack.

When they were within such distance as to be able to recognize each other, each pushed on at a gallop to meet the other.

Were they friends or foes?

In full career each drew his sword; on meeting, each lunged at the other.

Neither spoke a single word. Did not the sparks flying from their schaskas speak for them?

Ammalat Beg, whose way they barred, watched them in amazement.

But the combat was brief. The horseman who had come from the same direction as Ammalat Beg, fell backward upon his horse's crupper, and thence to the ground.

His head was laid open to the eyes.

The victor calmly wiped his sword, and, addressing Ammalat, said,—

" You are welcome, be my witness."

" I have witnessed the death of a man," replied Ammalat. " How can that help you ? "

" The man had injured me. It was not I who killed him, but God. Your presence helps me, in that no one can say that I murdered him by lying in wait, and afterwards murder me in the same fashion. It was in combat, was it not ? "

" Yes, certainly," answered Ammalat.

" And you will swear to it if need be ? "

" Since it is the truth."

" Thanks; that is all I desire of you. I do not ask your name, I know it. You are the nephew of Chamkal Tarkovsky."

" But why had you quarrelled ? " pursued Ammalat. " You were mortal enemies, then, to have fought so desperately ? "

" We were mortal enemies, as you say. We had caught twenty sheep between us: ten belonged to me, ten to him. He was not willing to let me have mine, and he killed them all, profiting nobody; then he slandered my wife. He would have done better, the miscreant, to curse the tomb of my father, and the name of my mother, than to attack the honor of my wife. I sprang upon him with my poniard, but we were separated. Then we agreed, wherever we might meet, to fight it out to the death. We have met: he is dead.

Allah has maintained the right.— You are going to
Khunsack, probably, to visit the khan?" queried the
horseman after a moment's silence.

"Yes," answered Ammalat, leaping his horse over the
dead man's body.

"The visit is untimely, Beg," admonished the other,
shaking his head.

Ammalat's blood surged to his heart. He nearly fell
from his horse.

"Has any misfortune overtaken the house of Khan
Ackmeth?" he demanded.

"His daughter Sultanetta was very ill."

"And — she is dead?" cried Ammalat, losing his
color.

"Perhaps so. An hour ago, when I passed the house,
every one was running about. On the stairs and through
the hall the women were weeping as if the Russians had
taken Khunsack. In any case, if you wish to see her
alive, make haste."

But Ammalat heard no more, he had set off at a run;
only the dust was to be seen rising from his horse's hoofs.
He cleared the hill still between him and the village,
tore through the streets, dashed into the court, leaped
from his horse, and, all breathless, bounded up the flight
of steps, and on to Sultanetta's chamber, brushing aside
everything and every one that he encountered on his way,
noukars and servants, and, almost senseless, fell on his
knees at Sultanetta's bedside.

Ammalat's unexpected arrival drew an exclamation
from all who were in the room.

At this exclamation Sultanetta, pale, dying, with life
already almost extinct, gave a start in the depths of her
delirium. Her cheeks burned with a deceptive tint. Like
the autumn leaf which reddens and falls, her eyes bright-

ened with the last glow of the departing soul. For several hours now, overcome by her weakness, she had been
motionless and speechless; but, amidst all the exclamations, she had recognized the voice of Ammalat.

Life, so near its flight, hesitated, like the trembling
flame of a candle steadying itself at the moment when
we think it is going out.

She rose on one arm; her eyes shone.

" Is it you ? " she murmured, extending her hands to
Ammalat.

" She speaks! she speaks! " cried Ammalat.

And every one stood open-mouthed and with breath
suspended.

" Allah be praised ! " she continued, " I die content, I
die happy."

This time, there rose a cry of despair; they thought
her dead.

A smile sealed her lips; her eyes were closed, she had
again lost consciousness.

In despair Ammalat took her in his arms; he listened
neither to the khan's questions nor to his wife's reproaches.

Force was employed to wrest him away and banish him
from the room. Crouching at the door, prostrating himself on the floor, sobbing, at times beseeching Allah to
save Sultanetta, at times blaming heaven and upbraiding
himself for the illness of his loved one, his grief, un-
tempered by Christian resignation, was terrible to witness; it was that of the tiger, with its threatening roar.

What should have killed the sick one, saved her.

What the science of the mountain physician could not
do, chance accomplished. A violent shock was needed
to set in motion the frozen current of life; she would
have died not so much from the malady as from the

exhaustion following it, like a lamp flickering out for
want of air, rather than from the violence of the wind.

At last youth gained the mastery. That violent
transport had awakened life in the depths of the dying
girl's heart, and, after a long, calm sleep, she awoke, in
possession of a part of her lost strength, and a freshness
of feeling which she had never hoped to experience again.

Her mother was leaning over her bed, waiting for a
sign of recognition. Ammalat was concealed by the
tapestry of the doorway; he had given his word not to
enter, and the khan was standing behind him for fear
that he would forget.

Sultanetta breathed a sigh, her eyes wandered vaguely
around; then her glance was arrested, became fixed, and
concentrated itself upon her mother.

She smiled before speaking.

"Oh, mother," she said, "it is you. If you knew
how light I feel! Am I poised on wings? How sweet
it is to sleep after long wakefulness, to rest after great
fatigue! How fair the day is! How brilliant the light!
How beautiful the sun! The very walls of the room
seem to be smiling on me. Oh, I have been very ill,
a long time ill, have I not?"

And with a sigh, while passing her hand over her
forehead still damp with perspiration, she continued,—

"Oh, I have suffered so much. Now, glory be to
Allah! I am only weak; but I feel that this exhaustion
will very quickly pass away. One would think that a
string of pearls was coursing my veins. Oh, how
strange it is! I see all that has happened as if through
a mist. I dreamed that I was plunged into an ice-cold
sea and yet was burning with thirst. Then, afar off
through the haze, I saw two stars. But they wavered,
grew darker and darker, and threatened to go out; I kept

19

sinking, drawn down more deeply by an irresistible
force. Suddenly a voice called my name, and I felt a
hand, stronger than the hand of death, raising me out of
that cold, gloomy abyss. Then, in a first ray of light, I
saw the face of Ammalat appear. At once the stars
became more brilliant, and a flash, like a serpent of fire,
struck me to the heart. Then I seemed to faint away,
for I remember nothing more."

Ammalat, with bursting heart, his cheeks bathed in
silent tears, and eyes and hands raised to heaven, was
listening; and as he listened, he murmured a heartfelt
prayer of thankfulness.

He started to rush headlong into the room when the
young girl spoke his name.

But Ackmeth Khan, as much moved as he, and weeping also, said in a whisper, —

" To-morrow, to-morrow."

The next day, indeed, Ammalat was permitted to see
the invalid.

Ackmeth Khan himself took him in, thus acquitting
himself of his promise.

" May all the world be as happy as I," said he.

Sultanetta had been forewarned; but her emotion was
none the less profound when her eyes met those of Ammalat, whom she loved so much and for whom she had so
long waited.

The lovers were unable to utter a single word; but
their eyes told each other all the sentiments of their
hearts. Each saw on the other's pale cheek the impress
of grief, the trace of tears. Undoubtedly the fresh
beauty of the woman one loves is full of charm; but
that sickly pallor which comes from separation is far
sweeter to the eyes of a lover. A heart of stone melts
away under a tearful glance that says without blame, —

"I am happy; I have suffered so much for you and through you."

These few words made the tears spring to Ammalat's eyes. Remembering that he was not alone, he made an effort at self-control, holding up his head; but his voice rebelled, and it was with great difficulty that he succeeded in saying,—

"It is, indeed, a long time since we have seen each other, Sultanetta!"

"And we came very near never seeing each other again, Ammalat," replied Sultanetta. "We were very nearly parted forever."

"Forever!" returned Ammalat, reproachfully. "You could think that, believe that, when there is a world in which beings meet who have loved each other in this one. Oh, had I lost the talisman of my happiness, with what scorn would I have flung away that rag they call life! Oh, I should not have struggled long, no. To have been vanquished would be to have rejoined you."

"Then why do I not die?" said Sultanetta, smiling. "You make out the other world to be so beautiful that it must be better than this, Ammalat, and I should like to go as soon as possible."

"Oh, no, no, Sultanetta; make no such impious wish. You must live a long time for happiness—"

He was about to add, "for love;" he stopped.

Gradually the roses of health budded on the young girl's cheeks. The breath of happiness caused them to bloom.

At the end of eight days things had resumed their ordinary course, and all went as before Ammalat's departure from Khunsack.

Khan Ackmeth made inquiries of Ammalat as to the number and position of the Russian troops.

The khauess questioned him about the fashions and jewels of the women; and as often as Ammalat told her that their women wore neither trousers nor veils, she invoked Allah's holy name.

Assured that health was returning to Sultanetta, Ammalat began to be gloomy. Often, in the midst of a cheerful, happy conversation, he would pause, his head would fall upon his breast, and his eyes fill with tears. Profound sighs seemed to rend his bosom. Sometimes he would spring from his place as if touched by an electric spark. His eyes shot angry flames, and, with a cold smile, he would caress the hilt of his kandjiar. Then, as if yielding to invisible bonds, he would groan, become pensive, and even Sultanetta could not win him from his revery.

Once, at such a time, the lovers being quite alone, Sultanetta, leaning upon his shoulder, said to him, —

" You are sad, my poor heart! you are tired of staying near me ! "

" Oh, don't cast such a reproach on one who loves you better than heaven," said Ammalat. " But I have already tried the hell of separation, and I cannot think of it without anguish. Oh, I would a hundred times rather die than leave you again, my beautiful Sultanetta."

" Leave me ! you speak of leaving me ! If you think of separation, it must be that you desire it."

" Oh, don't poison my wound with suspicion, Sultanetta. Until now you have known but one thing, — how to flourish like a rose, how to fly like a bird. Until now, twice happy child, your wish has been your only guide; but as for me, I am a man. Fate has welded about my neck a chain of steel, and the end of that chain is in the hands of a man, a friend, my benefactor. Duty and gratitude summon me to Derbend."

"A chain! a friend! a benefactor! duty! how many
words does it take to conceal your desire to leave me?
But, before selling your soul to friendship, had you not
given it to love? You had no right to pledge what no
longer belonged to you, Ammalat. Oh, forget your
Verkovsky, forget your Russian friend and your beautiful ladies of Derbend; forget war, forget glory. I hate
bloodshed since I saw your blood flow. What do you
lack in our mountains for a free and comfortable life?
No one will come here to look for you. My father has
many horses and plenty of money, while I — I have a
great deal of love. Surely, you are not going away!
surely, you will stay with me!"

"No, Sultanetta, I cannot, must not stay. To live
and die with you is my one prayer, my one desire; but
all that depends on your father. For having listened to
Ackmeth Khan I was about to die a death both cruel
and infamous. A Russian saved my life. Can I now
wed the daughter of the Russians' implacable foe? If
your father will let me make his peace with them, Sultanetta, I shall be the happiest of men."

"You know my father," answered Sultanetta, sadly.
"Day by day his hatred of the Russians increases, if it
were possible. He will sacrifice both of us to his hatred.
Besides, fate has decreed that the colonel should kill the
noukar whom he had sent for Ibrahim."

"Yes, Sultanetta, like you I regret the death of that
man. And yet it was owing to that circumstance that
I learned of what was happening here, that I saw
you again. If that man were alive, you would be
dead."

"Well, try your influence with my father."

"Do you think that it would be my first attempt!
Alas! Every time that I have spoken to Ackmeth Khan

of my hopes, 'Swear enmity to the Russians,' he has answered, 'and then I will listen to you.'"

"That means that we must renounce hope."

Clasping Sultanetta in his arms, the young man strained her to his heart.

"Why must we say good-bye to hope?" he asked; "are you, then, chained to Avarie?"

"I do not understand you," said the young girl, fixing upon him her limpid and questioning eyes.

"Love me more than all the world, Sultanetta, more than your father, more than your mother, more than your country, and then you will understand me. Sultanetta, I cannot live without you. If you love me, Sultanetta — "

"If I love you!" returned the young girl, proudly.

"Fly from here, Sultanetta; let us leave Khunsack."

"Fly!" repeated she. "Oh, my God! the daughter of the khan to fly like a fugitive, like a guilty thing, like a criminal! It is frightful, unheard of, impossible!"

"Do not tell me that, Sultanetta. If the sacrifice is great, my love is infinite. Order me to die, and I will die with the greatest contempt for life. Do you wish more than my life? Would you have my soul? I will cast it to the lowest depths of hell at a word from you. You are the khan's daughter; but my uncle wears the crown of a principality. And I, too, am a prince, and, I swear it, Sultanetta, worthy of you."

"But my father's revenge, — you forget that, unhappy man!"

"In the course of time, he will himself forget; on seeing how much I love you, and finding that you are happy, he will forgive. His heart is not of stone; our caresses will soften him, our tears melt him, and then, Sultanetta, fortune will cover us with its golden wings, and then we can proudly say, 'To ourselves we owe our happiness.'"

."My dear love," said Sultanetta, sadly shaking her head, "I have had small experience as yet; but do you know what my heart tells me? That one cannot be happy through ingratitude and deceit. Let us wait, since we cannot do otherwise without sacrificing the happiness of one of us, and we shall see what it will please Allah to send us."

"Allah inspired me with that thought; he will do nothing more for us. Have pity on me, Sultanetta; let us fly, if you do not wish the hour of marriage to sound above my tomb. I have given my word that I would return to Derbend, I must keep my word and keep it promptly. But to go without hope of seeing you again, with the agony of knowing that you will one day be the wife of another, is fearful, insupportable, impossible. If not out of love for me, Sultanetta, then let it be through your pity. Partake of my lot, do not hunt me from my Paradise, do not cause me to lose my reason. You do not know to what point of folly a defrauded passion can carry a heart like mine. I can forget all, trample all under foot, — the sanctity of the fireside, the hospitality of your parents; I can astonish bandits of most renowned fame by the bloody repute of my name. I can make the angels of heaven weep at the sight of my crimes. Sultanetta, save me from the curses of others, save me from your own scorn. Night has fallen, my horses are as swift as the wind; let us fly to kindly Russia, and wait there till the storm is past. For the last time, I implore you, on my knees, with clasped hands. Shame or glory, life or death, all rest on one word from you, — yes or no."

Restrained on the one hand by maidenly fear and her

respect for ancient usages, tempted on the other by the
love and fiery eloquence of her lover, Sultanetta drifted
uncertainly on that stormy sea whose every wave was a
passion; at last she rose, and, wiping away the tears
that shone upon her long lashes, with as much pride as
resolution, she replied,—

"Ammalat, do not tempt me; love's flame, all shining
as it is, does not blind me; I shall always know how to
distinguish between right and wrong and good and evil.
It is base, Ammalat, to abandon one's family, to repay
with ingratitude the long care and infinite tenderness of
parents who have reared us. Ah, judge now if I love
you, Ammalat! even while knowing the extent of my
sacrifice, even while measuring the extent of my crime,—
even so, Ammalat, I answer, Yes! and I say, My dear
love, I consent to fly with you, for I value you above all
the blessings and all the virtues in the world. I am
yours, Ammalat. But know this well: it was not your
speech that influenced me, but your heart. Allah willed
that I should meet and love you; let our hearts then be
bound together from this hour on, although the tie which
binds us be a withe of thorn! All is at an end, Ammalat; we no longer have but one destiny, one heart, one
life, one future. Let us go!"

If the azure curtains of the sky itself had fallen upon
Ammalat veiling him from the sun, he could not have
been happier than he was at the moment when that consent, so devoted, so complete, so tender, fell from the
lips of Sultanetta.

That same hour all was fixed upon for the flight of
the two lovers.

The next evening, Ammalat was to depart on a grand
hunt which would be supposed to last for three days; but
he would return on the same evening. The night was

favorable, as there was no moon. Sultanetta was to descend from her window by means of two scarfs knotted one to the other: Ammalat would receive her in his arms.

Horses would be awaiting them in the little chapel where Sultanetta and Ammalat had met after the tiger-hunt.

And then, woe to the enemy in the path who should try to bar their way!

A kiss sealed the compact, and they separated full of joy and fear.

The longed-for morrow came. Ammalat visited his horse, prepared his arms, and passed the entire day in consulting the sun.

One would have said that he, too, the star with golden rays, hesitated in his course, unwilling to leave that brilliant, warm sky and sink into the snows of the Caucasus.

Ammalat waited for the night as for his affianced.

Oh, how slowly moved that sun! how the heavenly traveller loitered along his luminous path, what a wide gulf still remained between hope and happiness!

Four o'clock in the afternoon sounded: it is the Mussulman's dinner hour. They were grouped around the rug; but Ackmeth Khan was very sad.

His eyes flashed under his knitted brows. Often they rested now on his daughter and now on his guest. Sometimes the lines of his face would contract into a derisive look. But that expression would soon be lost in the paleness of anger. His remarks were scoffing and brief, and all caused repentance to spring up in the heart of Sultanetta and fear in the mind of Ammalat.

Sultanetta's mother, as if she could have foreseen the threatened separation, was tenderer and more thoughtful than usual, and Sultanetta more than once came near bursting into tears and throwing herself into her mother's arms.

After dinner, Khan Ackmeth called Ammalat into the court. The horses were already saddled for the chase. Four noukars whom Ammalat had sent for were in waiting, mingling with the noukars of the khan.

"Let us try my new falcon," said the khan to Ammalat. "The evening is fine, it is not too warm, and we can still between now and night get a few pheasants or partridges."

Ammalat could not but comply; he nodded assent and sprang on his horse.

Ackmeth Khan and the young beg proceeded side by side, — Ammalat pensive, Khan Ackmeth silent. On the left and along a rocky steep, a mountaineer was climbing. His feet were equipped with iron crampoons by means of which he clung to the rocky crags, with the further aid of an iron claw at the extremity of his staff.

A hat full of wheat was fastened in front of him, at his belt.

A long Tartar musket was slung across his shoulders.

Khan Ackmeth halted and, pointing him out to Ammalat, said,—

"Look at that old man; at the risk of his life, he is hunting among the rocks for a little patch of earth in which to sow some grain. He harvests it with bleeding toil, and often it is only at the price of his blood that he defends his flock against men and wild beasts. His country is poverty-stricken. Ah, well, ask him, Ammalat, why he loves his country so much, why he does not change it for a richer land. He will answer: 'Here I am free; here I owe no man tribute; these snows guard my pride and my independence.' That independ-

ence the Russians would take from him, and you yourself,
Ammalat, have become the Russians' slave."

"Khan," answered the young man, lifting his head,
"you know very well that I have been overcome, not by
the power of the Russians, but by their good-will. I am
not their slave, I am their friend."

"Well, it is the greater shame to you, then; the
chankal's heir casts about for golden fetters! Ammalat
Beg lives at the expense of Colonel Verkovsky!"

"Don't say that, Khan Ackmeth. Verkovsky, before
giving me bread and salt, gave me life. He loves me,
I love him. Let that be said once for all, and let us say
no more about it."

"There is no such thing as a friendship with unbelievers. To fight when we meet, to exterminate them
when we can, these are the laws of the Koran and the
duty of a true follower of the Prophet."

"Khan, don't meddle with the bones of the Prophet;
you are no mullah to tell me my duty. I know what I
have to do as a man of honor, and I shall do it. I have
within me the sense of right and of wrong. Let us talk
of something else."

"This sense, Ammalat, should be in your heart rather
than on your lips."

Ammalat gave a sign of impatience.

But, taking no notice of this sign, which he had perfectly understood, Khan Ackmeth proceeded: —

"A last time, Ammalat, will you listen to the coun-
sels of a friend? Will you abandon the unbelievers and
stay with us?"

"I would have given my life for the happiness you
hold out to me, Khan Ackmeth," said the young man,
with a tone of conviction which there was no mistaking;

"but I have sworn to return to Derbend, and I shall keep my oath."

"That is your final decision?"

"It is final."

"Then, Ammalat, your oath must be the more quickly fulfilled. I have known you a long time, you know me also. We must not even attempt to deceive each other. I will not conceal from you that I had cherished the hope of calling you my son. I rejoiced that you loved Sultanetta. Your captivity weighed on my heart, your long absence was one of the sorrows of my life. At last you have returned to the house of the khan, and you have found everything as before your departure. But you have not brought us your heart again. It is sad; but what can be done? Ammalat, I would never accept a slave of the Russians for a son-in-law!"

"Ackmeth Khan!"

"Oh, let me conclude. Your unexpected arrival, your grief in Sultanetta's room, your exclamations, your sobs, your despair, exposed to all the world your love and our intentions. Throughout all Avarie you are known as my daughter's betrothed; but, now that the tie binding us is broken, we must cut short all these suppositions; for the sake of Sultanetta's peace of mind, for her reputation, you must leave us at once. Ammalat, we part still friends, but we shall meet only as kinsmen. May Allah in his goodness change your heart, and permit us to see you again as an inseparable friend. That is my dearest wish, my most earnest prayer; but until then, adieu!"

And, turning his horse face about, without adding a word Ackmeth Khan set off at full speed.

A thunderbolt, striking at Ammalat's feet and opening an abyss, could not have overcome him more than did these last words from Ackmeth Khan. Motionless, thunderstruck, he stood rooted to the spot, breathlessly watching horse and rider, who already seemed but a cloud of dust.

An hour later he was still on the same spot; but by that time night had fallen.

The night was dark.

XII.

IN order to arrest the revolt of Daghestan, Colonel
Verkovsky was with his regiment in the village of
Kjaffir Koumieck.

The tent of Ammalat Beg was pitched beside that of
the colonel.

Sophyr Ali, the young foster-brother of Ammalat, who
appeared in the beginning of this story, was lying within
the tent and drinking by the glassful that foaming wine
called the champagne of the Don.

Colonel Verkovsky had sent for the young man to
come from Tarki, hoping that the sight of him, together
with his friendship, would distract Ammalat Beg from
his melancholy.

In fact, Ammalat Beg was more than melancholy, he
was wrapped in gloom.

Haggard, pale, brooding, he kept within the seclusion
of his tent, lying on his cushions and smoking.

Three months previously, driven, like the first sinner,
from Paradise, he had come to rejoin the colonel and
was camping with his regiment.

In sight of the mountains whither his heart took wing
but where his feet were forbidden, he preyed upon himself; anger flared up in his soul, like a half-extinguished
light, at the first word. Rancor, like a slow sure poison,
spread more and more in his veins. Bitterness was on
his lips, hatred in his eyes.

"In faith," said Sophyr Ali, "wine is a good thing!
Since we are forbidden to drink it, it must be that Ma-

homet got hold of some bad wine. Really, these drops
are so sweet one can believe that an angel's tears fell
into the bottle. Take a glass and drink, Ammalat. Your
heart will rise on the wine as light as a cork. You know
what Hafiz, the Persian poet, says about it."

"I know that you bore me to death, Sophyr Ali.
Then let me hire you to spare me this nonsense, charge
it up to Saadi even, as well as Hafiz."

"Ammalat, Ammalat, you are very hard on your poor
Sophyr Ali. What would come of it if he were as hard
on you? ' Doesn't he listen patiently when you talk to
him of Sultanetta? Love makes you mad; with me it
is wine. But my madness has lucid intervals, the occasions when I am not drunk, while you have none; you
are ever in love. To the health of Sultanetta!"

"I have already told you that I forbid your uttering
her name, especially when you are drunk."

"Then here's to the health of the Russians!"

Ammalat shrugged his shoulders.

"Well!" said Sophyr Ali, who was getting more and
more tipsy, "you will be forbidding me to drink the
health of the Russians next!"

"What have the Russians done for you that you should
love them so much?"

"What have they done to you that you should hate
them?"

"They have done nothing to me, but I have observed
them close at hand. They are no better than we Tartars. They are covetous, back-biting, idle. How long
. a time have they been masters here, and in all the time
of their mastership what good have they done, what laws
have they introduced, what learning have they spread
abroad? Verkovsky has opened my eyes to the bad side
of my fellow-countrymen, and at the same time I have

seen the faults of his; and their defects are the more
unpardonable in them because they have grown up surrounded by good examples. But these good examples
they forget here for the sake of applying themselves
only to the unclean appetites of the body."

" Ammalat, Ammalat, I should hope that you would
except Verkovsky at least."

" Of course, he is the exception, he and a few others;
but, in your opinion, even, are there many of whom we
can say as much ? "

" Are not the angels of heaven to be counted too ? No,
no, look at it: Verkovsky is a marvel of goodness. You
will not even find a Tartar who speaks ill of him. Every
soldier would give his soul for him. — Abdul Amid, more
wine ! — To the health of Verkovsky, Ammalat ! "

" Just now I would not drink the health of Mahomet,
even."

" Why, if your heart were not as black as the eyes of
your Sultanetta, you would drink Verkovsky's health.
Ammalat, were this to reach the beard of the mufti of
Derbend, every imam and all the prophets would be up
in arms against you ! "

" Let me alone."

" It is not right, Ammalat. I would raise the devil
with my own blood for you, and you, you, — out upon
you! you refuse to take a drop of wine with me."

" No, Sophyr Ali, I will not take it, and I will not
take it, because I do not want it; and I do not want it, do
you hear? because my blood is already too hot as it is."

" A mere excuse, and a poor excuse at that! It is not
our first drink, is it? Not the first time our blood has
boiled? Wonderful stuff, Asiatic blood! Speak out, be
frank, you have a grudge against the colonel ? "

" Well, yes, I have."

" And can one know why?"

" Why?"

" Yes."

" For many reasons."

" But one?"

" For some time now he has been pouring poison into the honey of his friendship. Now, the poison that he has let fall drop by drop, drop by drop, has filled the cup; and behold the cup is running over. I hate friends that are too solicitous; they are good for advice, — that is, for what involves them in neither trouble nor risk."

" I see; he did not let you return to Avarie, and you cannot forgive him for refusing."

" If you had my heart in your breast, Sophyr Ali, you would understand the cruelty of such a refusal. Ackmeth Khan has softened, it seems: he asks to see me, and I cannot go to him. Oh! Sultanetta! Sultanetta!" cried the young man, wringing his hands in his anger.

" For my part, I say, put yourself in Verkovsky's place, and tell me frankly whether you would not have done as he is doing."

" No. From the beginning, I should have said: 'Ammalat, do not count on me; Ammalat, do not ask me to help you in anything.' I do not desire his help; only that he should not hinder me. No, he stands between me and the sun of my happiness. He does it out of friendship, he says; he asks me to let him direct my life, — he gives me poppy-juice to put me to sleep!"

" What matters the remedy, Ammalat, provided that it cures you?"

" And who asks him to cure me, pray? The divine malady of love, the only one of which one could wish to die, is my sole happiness, my only joy. If he takes that from me, my heart will follow."

20

When Ammalat finished speaking, night had already
fallen, and yet he could see that the presence of a stranger
at the door of his tent was rendering the darkness more
obscure.

" Who is there ? " demanded Ammalat.

" Is any one bringing my wine ? " said Sophyr Ali.
" My bottle is empty."

The shadow drew near without any response.

" Who is there ? " repeated Ammalat, laying his hand
on his kandjiar.

A name uttered in a tone so low that it was breathed
in his ear like a sigh, caused Ammalat Beg to tremble:

" Nephtali ! "

At the same time the shadow withdrew and left the
tent.

Ammalat Beg bounded to his feet, and followed the
form scarcely visible through the darkness.

Sophyr Ali followed Ammalat.

The night was gloomy, the fires were out, the line of
sentinels was at a distance.

Finally, the form halted.

" Is it really you, Nephtali ? " asked Ammalat.

" Speak low, Ammalat," answered the other; "I am
not a friend of the Russians myself."

" Ah ! " said Ammalat, " you too, you have come here
to reproach me ?   I should have thought you had a kinder
mission for your brother."

He extended his hand.

Nephtali took Ammalat's hand and pressed it con-
vulsively.

In the young mountaineer's friendship for Ammalat,
was something which the latter could not explain; one
would have said that the Tchetchen was constrained to
do violence to himself in order to love Ammalat.

"Speak," insisted Ammalat; "what news do you bring? How is Ackmeth Khan? Is Sultanetta well?"

"Ammalat," said Nephtali, "I am not sent to answer your questions, but to question you. Will you follow me?"

"Where?"

"Where I am charged to conduct you."

"What shall I do there?"

"You know from whom I come?"

"No."

"'The eagle loves the mountain.'"

Ammalat recognized Ackmeth Khan's favorite saying.

"You come from the khan?" said he.

"Will you follow me, Ammalat?"

"How far?"

"Four versts from here."

"Must we go on foot?"

"Are you at liberty to leave the camp on horseback?"

"Yes. But, that I may not arouse suspicion, I must notify the colonel."

"That is, you can go the length of your chain, but not leave it. Notify the colonel."

"Sophyr Ali, tell the colonel that we are going, for diversion, on a jaunt into the country. Get my gun and saddle my horse."

Sophyr Ali sighed; but, as his bottle was empty, it was the less difficult to obey. In a little while they heard the step of two horses.

It was Sophyr Ali riding one horse, and leading Ammalat's.

"Here," said he, "take your gun; I have renewed the priming. It is in good condition; you can rest easy."

"And why do you come?"

"Because the colonel asked me if I was going, and I

told him yes, and now if they saw you leaving without me it would look suspicious."

Ammalat comprehended the young man's motive: he had not meant to leave him alone in the dark with a stranger.

Nephtali was unknown to Sophyr Ali, although Sophyr Ali had heard his name.

"Can he come with us?" asked Ammalat of Nephtali.

"Yes, and no."

"Explain yourself."

"Yes, as far as to the entrance of the camp; no, to the rendezvous."

"Come," said Ammalat to Sophyr Ali.

And he sprang on his horse.

"And you?" demanded he of Nephtali.

"Don't worry about me, Ammalat; I came into camp without you, and I am very well able to leave it without you."

"Where shall I find you again?"

"It is not for you to find me; it is for me to find you."

And Nephtali was lost in the darkness, making no more noise than a ghost.

Ammalat and Sophyr Ali headed for the first sentinel, gave the password and went on.

Every evening, the password was communicated to Ammalat by Colonel Verkovsky. It was a delicate attention from the latter, although Ammalat well understood that he was only a prisoner on parole.

Twenty paces beyond the sentinel, Ammalat trembled in spite of himself. A third horseman was advancing beside them. He had arisen without any one's knowing whence he came. He might have issued from the ground.

"Ha!" ejaculated Sophyr Ali; "who goes there?"

"Silence!" said Nephtali.

"Silence!" repeated Ammalat Beg.

Sophyr Ali held his tongue, but not without muttering; the second bottle, abandoned just as it was about to be brought, stuck in his crop. At every step he grew angry, at the darkness, at the bushes, at the ditches. He coughed, spat, swore, in the hope of making one or the other of his companions say something; but it was useless: both remained dumb.

Finally, after a pause, his horse stumbled against a stone.

"The devil take our guide, who, for that matter, looks very much as if he had come in his own interests! Who knows where he is taking us? He is capable of leading us into some trap."

"There is no danger," answered Ammalat; "he is a messenger from a friend and is himself my friend."

"Oh! yes, that is quite possible; you have made many new friends since we took leave of each other, Ammalat. — May the new be as devoted to you as the old!"

They had left the main road and had plunged into a sort of undergrowth of those shrubs with the obstinate thorns, known to every traveller in the Caucasus.

"In the name of the king of Spirits," said Sophyr Ali to his guide, "tell us quickly whether you are in league with these bushes to get the galloon off my tchouska. Don't you know a better road? I am neither a snake nor a fox."

Nephtali halted.

"You are in luck," said he. "Your journey is ended; stay here and hold the horses."

"And Ammalat?" said Sophyr Ali.

"Ammalat goes with me."

"Where ? "

"To mind his own business, apparently."

"Ammalat," cried Sophyr Ali, "will you go without me into the mountain with this bandit ? "

"Which means," replied Ammalat, dismounting, " that you do not care to remain alone."

He tossed the bridle over the other's arm.

"As for that," said Sophyr Ali, "I would a hundred times rather be alone here than in the company of the knave that came for you."

"You will not be alone," said Ammalat Beg, smiling; "I leave you in delightful company, that of the wolves and jackals. There, do you hear them singing ? Listen ! "

"God trust that I shall not have to get your bones away from those songsters to-morrow morning," said Sophyr Ali.

They separated.

As he went away Ammalat heard Sophyr Ali loading his gun by way of precaution at all events.

Nephtali led Ammalat through the thicket as readily as if it had been broad daylight. One would have thought the young Tchetchen possessed the power, accorded by nature to certain animals, of seeing as well by night as by day.

After a demi-verst through bushes and over stones, the road began to descend; finally, after a very difficult passage the road became a little better, and they reached the entrance of a recess, in the depths of which a brushwood fire was burning.

Ackmeth Khan was reclining beside the fire, his gun across his knees.

At the noise made by the two young men, he raised himself upon his bourka.

By the quickness of the movement, it was easy to see that he waited impatiently.

Recognizing Ammalat, he stood up.

Ammalat cast himself upon his neck.

"I am glad to see you, Ammalat," said the khan, "and I am weak enough not to conceal the feeling from you. But I hasten to say that it is not for a simple interview that I have put you to this inconvenience. Be seated, Ammalat, and let us talk of a serious matter."

"For me, khan?"

"For both of us. I was your father's friend, and there was a time when I was yours."

"Is the time gone by, then?"

"No. It depended on you that it should last forever. You did not desire it; or rather, no; it was not you who did not desire it."

"Who, then?"

"That demon of a Verkovsky."

"Khan, you do not know him."

"You are the one who do not know him, but you very soon will, I hope. Meanwhile let us speak of Sultanetta."

Ammalat's heart gave a bound.

"You know that I desired to make her your wife, Ammalat; you refused the conditions on which I could give her to you. We will talk no more of that; I presume that you reflected as a man must do on serious occasions in life. But you will understand one thing: she cannot, and moreover must not, remain unmarried. It would be a dishonor to my house."

Ammalat felt the perspiration beading his forehead.

"Ammalat," continued Ackmeth Khan, "her hand has been demanded."

Ammalat felt his knees give way; the heart in his breast almost ceased to beat.

Finally his voice returned.

"And who is this bold wooer?" he demanded.

"The second son of Chamkal Abdul Moussaline. After
you he is certainly, of all the mountain princes, the most
worthy to become the husband of Sultanetta."

"After me?" said Ammalat. "But, by Mahomet,
it strikes me that you talk as if I were dead; has
my memory then quite died out of the hearts of my
friends?"

"No, Ammalat, your memory has not died out of my
heart, and just now I confessed to you yourself that I
was glad to see you; but be as frank as I am sincere; I
leave you to judge your own cause; what more do you
wish? What more do you exact? What must we do,
what can we do? You will not leave the Russians; I
myself cannot become their friend."

"Yes, it is possible. You have only to desire, only to
say the word, and all will be forgotten, all will be overlooked. I will wager my head upon it, and can answer
on the word of Verkovsky; it would be the best thing
for you, for the peace of the Avares, for Sultanetta's
happiness, for mine. Oh! I beg of you, I beseech you,
I implore you on my knees, on my knees! Ackmeth
Khan, be the friend of the Russians, and everything,
even your rank, will be restored to you."

"You answer for the lives of others, you who are not
even the master of your own liberty!"

"Who wants my life, who frets about my liberty,
when I spurn them myself?"

"Who wants your life, child that you are? Do you
think that the pillow under Chamkal Tarkovsky's head
does not turn of itself when he thinks of you as the heir
to his principality of Tarki, and that you are the friend
of the Russians?"

"I have never sought his friendship, I have never
feared him as an enemy."

"Fear not, but despise not, Ammalat. Do you know that an envoy has been sent to Yermolof to tell him to kill you for a traitor? Formerly, he would have killed you with a kiss, if it had been possible; but now that you have sent back his daughter, your father-in-law no longer hides his wrath, and he will use ball or poniard."

"Under Verkovsky's protection, no one can reach me, except an assassin. From assassins, Allah save me!"

"Listen, Ammalat, I will tell you a fable. A sheep, pursued by wolves, fled into a kitchen. He found shelter there, was well lodged, well fed; he loudly boasted of the care that was taken of him, and he had never been so happy.

"Three days later, he was roasted!

"Ammalat, that is your story.

"It is time that I open your eyes. The man whom you call the first among your friends has betrayed you first. You are surrounded by traitors, Ammalat. My principal desire in summoning you to an interview was to forewarn you. When Sultanetta's hand was asked, I was given to understand, on behalf of the chamkal, that through him I could become a friend of the Russians much more safely than through Ammalat, who was now an object of distrust even with those who are answerable for him. Besides, those who are answerable for you will very soon be rid of you. They will put you out of the way where you are no longer to be feared. I have suspected much, and have learned more than I suspected. To-day, I stopped a noukar of the chamkal's; he was sent to Verkovsky, under some pretext of which I know nothing, about which I am not concerned. What does trouble me is that the chamkal gives six thousand roubles to the one who will kill you. Verkovsky is not

concerned in that, of course; but, master of the chamkal,
he is not the master of his government. You are guilty
of treason. After swearing fealty to the Russians, you
have been taken in arms. They spare your life, perhaps;
but something, indeed, must be done with you. You are
to be sent to Siberia."

"I?" cried Ammalat.

"Listen, and see if I am not well informed. To-morrow the regiment returns to its quarters; to-morrow
a meeting, at which you and your fate will be discussed at great length, will be held in your own house at
Bouinaky. They will prepare denunciations against you
and get together a certain number of complaints. They
will poison you with your own bread, Ammalat, and
fasten an iron chain around your neck while promising
you mountains of gold."

If Ackmeth Khan desired to see Ammalat suffer, he
had that sorry pleasure during all the time that he was
talking. Every word, like a sharpened red-hot iron,
stabbed the young beg's heart; all his beliefs were
destroyed, if the half of what the khan said was true.
He repeatedly endeavored to interrupt him, to answer
him; each time the words died on his lips. The wild
beast that, tamed by Verkovsky, lay sleeping within
Ammalat, gradually became aroused by the words of
Ackmeth Khan; already it shook its chain, a little more
and the chain would break.

At last a torrent of threats and curses escaped from
the young man's mouth.

"Ah! if you are not lying," cried he, "ah! if you
are telling the truth, Ackmeth Khan, woe to them that
have abused my good faith and taken advantage of my
gratitude! Let me have proof of what you say, and
then revenge, revenge!"

"That is the first word worthy of you that has left your mouth, Ammalat," said Khan Ackmeth, not even attempting to conceal his joy at the wrath of the young prince. "You have bowed your head too long at the feet of the Russians. It is time for the eagle to spread his wings and fly above the clouds. You will have a better view of your enemies from up there. Give them vengeance for vengeance, death for death!"

"Oh! yes!" replied Ammalat; "death to the chamkal who bargains for my life! Death to Abdul Moussaline, who puts out his hand for my treasure!"

"Yes, death to them, by all means! but do not lose sight of another enemy whom you are omitting from your vengeance, and who threatens your destiny in quite another way from either of those whom you have just named."

A chill ran through Ammalat's veins.

"You mean Verkovsky?" said he, drawing back in spite of himself. "You are wrong, Khan Ackmeth; he cannot desire my death who saved me from death, — and such a death! an infamous death!"

"To give you over to an infamous life, Ammalat. And, for that matter, have you not saved his life too, — once from the attacks of a wild boar, again, from a Lesghian's poniard? Balance your accounts properly, Ammalat, and Verkovsky is the one in debt."

"No, no, Ackmeth Khan," said the young man, violently striking his breast with his hand; "no! a voice speaking louder than yours tells me that I am not at quits with Verkovsky; it is the voice of conscience."

Ackmeth Khan shrugged his shoulders.

"Conscience! conscience!" muttered he. "Come, Ammalat, I see clearly that without me you will not know how to set about anything, not even to marry Sultanetta. Then, listen: —

" Of the one who wishes to become my son-in-law, the first, the last, the only thing I ask, in exchange for which he will secure the hand of Sultanetta, is the life of Verkovsky. Verkovsky is the head of Daghestan. Let that head fall and the whole of Daghestan is decapitated. I have two thousand men ready to rise at a word from me. With them, I can descend like an avalanche upon Tarki; and supposing that you should be the one to merit Sultanetta's hand, it would make you not only the chamkal of Tarki, but of the whole of Daghestan as well. Your fate is in your own hands as it has never been in another man's. Choose: either a prison — eternal exile in Siberia, at least — or happiness with Sultanetta, power with me. After all, perhaps I have judged you ill and you have neither ambition nor love in your heart. And now, farewell! but remember that the first, the only time that we meet again, it will be as devoted kinsmen or as mortal enemies."

And Ackmeth Khan disappeared before Ammalat had time to think of detaining him.

He remained a long time motionless and silent, with his head drooped over his breast. Finally, he raised himself, looked about, and saw Nephtali waiting for him.

Without a word, the young Tchetchen led him to where Sophyr Ali was awaiting him with the two horses. Ammalat silently extended a hand to him in token of thanks, and left him without even pronouncing the name of Sultanetta.

Then, silent still, he mounted his horse, regained the camp, entered his tent, and flung himself upon his couch.

Then only did he turn and writhe with stifled cries and moans.

All the serpents of hell were let loose in his heart.

XIII.

"Son of a she-wolf, will you be still?" an old woman was saying to her grandson, awakened and crying before day. "Be still, or I will send you out in the street to sleep."

The old Tartar woman had been Ammalat's nurse. Her house was built near the beg's palace. It was a present from her foster-child.

We caught a glimpse of her in the first chapter of this story, watching the prowess of Ammalat Beg.

This house to which we are conducting our readers, one-storied and surmounted by a terrace like all Tartar houses, consisted of two rooms neatly arranged. The floor was carpeted. The corners were occupied by chests, bright with decorations of ironwork, on which were rolled up some feather beds with their blankets, symbols of competence in Tartar homes. On shelves suspended against the wall was an array of tin-plated pilaff-cups shining like silver. The old woman's face was stamped with the constant bad-humor which is the bitter fruit of a sad and solitary life, and, like the worthy representative of her compatriots that she was, she never ceased to scold and grumble at her grandson, at the top of her voice and from morning till night.

"Keep still, Kesse!" she cried again, "or I will hand you over to five hundred thousand devils! Don't you hear the noise they make on the roof, and how they are scratching on the window-panes to get at you?"

The night was dark, the rain was falling in torrents.
The storm beat on the terrace and against the windows,
and the wind swirling through the chimney sounded like
wailing sobs accompanying nature's tears.

The little boy stopped crying, and, opening his great
eyes with their black lashes, he listened fearfully to the
divers noises of the tempest.

But a noise more terrifying began to mingle with this
uproar, and in spite of the advanced hour of the night —
it was almost three o'clock in the morning — there was a
knocking at the door.

And then it was the old woman's turn to be frightened.

Her bosom friend, an old black dog, lifted his head
and plaintively howled.

The knocking was redoubled, and, in tones of distinguishable anger, an unknown voice cried, —

"Atch Kaninii ! Akhirine ! Akhirisi ! Will you ever
open the door ? "

" *Allah bismillah !* " exclaimed the old woman, first
looking at the ceiling, then kicking her dog, then trying
to calm the little boy, who had begun to cry again. "Who
is there? Who can be knocking at this hour ? What
well-meaning man would come on such a night and
knock at a poor old woman's door ? Are you the devil ?
Then go to neighbor Kachtkina's. It is time to show
her the road to hell. But if you are not the devil in
person, be off ! My son is not at home, if you happen
to have business with him. He is with Ammalat Beg.
As for me, the beg has retired me; and so you cannot be
coming from him. I owe him neither ducks, nor hens,
nor eggs; he has freed me from all rent. *Dame !* You
may be sure that I did not bring him up for nothing."

" You besom of hell, will you open the door for me ? "
cried the impatient voice; " if not, I will splinter your

door so that not a board shall be left to make you a coffin."

"You are welcome, you are welcome," said the old woman, hastening to the door and opening it with trembling hand.

The door swung on its hinges, and a man short of stature, but with a handsome yet gloomy countenance, appeared on the threshold.

He wore the Circassian costume. The water streamed from his bachlik and his white bourka. He threw the latter on the woman's bed without ceremony, and began to unfasten the bachlik which concealed his face. Fatma, in the meantime, lighted her candle and stood before the new-comer, trembling in every joint. The dog, taking his tail between his legs, thrust himself into a corner; and the little boy betook himself to the fireplace, which, never having a fire in it, was rather an ornament than a useful piece of architecture.

"Well, Fatma," said the new-comer, when he had finished taking off his bachlik, "you have grown proud, it seems; you do not recognize an old friend?"

Fatma regarded the stranger curiously, and an expression of relief overspread her face.

She recognized Ackmeth Khan, who, during this stormy night, had come from Kjaffir Koumieck to Bouinaky.

"May the sand blind my wicked eyes for not having known their old master!" said the crone, crossing her hands on her breast in token of submission and respect. "To tell the truth, khan, they are put out by the tears that I have shed for my country, — for poor Avarie. Forgive the unhappy Fatma, khan; she is old, and old age does not see much at night besides the grave that death is digging for it."

"Come, come, you are not so old as you make out,

Fatma. I remember, child, to have seen you as a young
girl at Khunsack."

" The strange country ages the stranger," responded
Fatma. " In our mountains, khan, I should still perhaps
be fruit worth culling; but here I am a wretched handful of snow flung from the mountain into the mud of
these streets. Sit here, khan; sit on this cushion, you
will be more comfortable. But how can I regale my
dear guest? Does the khan need anything? "

" The khan desires you to regale him with your good-
will, that is all."

" I am in your power, khan, you know it well. Command, then, give your orders; it is for your servant to
obey."

" Listen, Fatma, I have no time to waste in talk. In
few words, this is why I am here: Do me a service with
your tongue, and I will rejoice your teeth. I will
give you ten sheep if you do what I tell you, and I
will clothe you in silk from head to foot, slippers included."

" Ten sheep and a silken gown! Oh, my good chief!
oh, my dear khan! Never has such a guest entered my
house since I was captured by those cursed Tartars, and
was married here against my will. For a silken robe and
ten sheep, you can do what you will, you may even cut
off one of my ears."

" It is not necessary to cut off your ears, woman; no,
it is better that you should use them. This is what I
wish: Ammalat will visit you to-day with the colonel.
Do you know the colonel? "

" Allah! I should think so, — our mortal enemy."

" That he is! Chamkal Tarkovsky will be with them.
The colonel is Ammalat's friend. He is making him
drink wine and eat pig! "

"The child that sucked my milk?" cried the old mountain woman with horror.

"Yes. If we are not on guard, before three days Ammalat will be a Christian."

"Mahomet save him!" exclaimed the old woman, as she spat and threw up her hands.

"To save Ammalat from everlasting damnation, you see, woman, we must embroil him with his Verkovsky."

"Am I to take a hand in that, khan? As true as that I am your servant and Allah's, I will do it."

"Yes, pay attention."

"I am not losing a syllable, khan."

The old woman's eyes glittered with fanaticism.

"You are to throw yourself at his feet, to weep as if at the funeral of your own son. You will not need to borrow tears from your neighbors; you love Ammalat well enough to weep for the loss of his soul. You will tell him that you have overheard a conversation between the colonel and the chamkal; that the latter complained of Ammalat's having sent back his daughter; that he said he hated him because of his principality of Tarkovsky, in connection with which Ammalat believed himself to have some rights. You will say that the chamkal begged the colonel to permit him to take Ammalat's life."

"And I shall add that the colonel consented?"

"No, old woman," quickly returned the khan; "he would not believe you. Say, on the contrary, that the colonel was indignant and had answered — Listen now; understand me well."

"I am listening, and I shall understand; never fear."

"And say that the colonel answered: 'All that I can possibly do for you, chamkal — and that only on condition that you will faithfully serve the Russians — is to send him to Siberia.'"

21

" To Siberia ! "

" Come now, repeat what I have said."

The old woman had a good memory, and repeated it word for word. But, for the greater security, the khan required her to repeat it a second time.

"Now," pursued the khan, "embroider that as much as you like. You are celebrated for your tales. But don't get your mouth full of mud now, speak clearly, and add as proof of what you advance that the colonel means to take him to Georgievsk, to get him away from his family and his noukars, and then, to send him in chains to the devil."

Ackmeth added to this falsehood all sorts of details which Fatma stored in her mind, making the khan renew his promise of the ten sheep, and especially of the gown of silk.

The khan pledged himself, and to bind the bargain he gave her a gold piece, a thing so rare among the mountaineers that they make them into ornaments of dress.

" Allah ! " cried the old woman, clutching the piece of money in her hand. " May my salt turn to ashes, may I die of hunger, may — "

" Come," interrupted Ackmeth, "enough; don't feed the devil with your oaths; use words to some purpose. Ammalat has great faith in you, I know. Don't forget that his happiness is at stake; that in rescuing him from the Russians, you are extricating him from the hands of the devil. Once convinced that they intend to send him to Siberia, he will leave his new friends and marry my daughter. Then you will all come to live with me in Khunsack, in your old country, and you will end your life singing in the land where you began to sing. But beware ! if you betray us, or if you spoil the affair with your prating, I swear, for my part, I, who do not take

XIV.

COLONEL VERKOVSKY to his *fiancée:* —

August, 1822.
IN CAMP, NEAR THE VILLAGE OF KJAFFIR KOUMIBOK.

YES, Ammalat is in love, dear Marie. But how does
he love, the lunatic? Never, in my maddest youth, did
my love for you — the love that has been my life, moreover! — reach such a length. I myself was scorched
like paper ignited by the sun's rays; while he burns like
a ship struck by lightning and lost at sea.

Marie, do you remember when we once read — happy
time! — Shakspere's "Othello?" Well, "Othello" alone
can give you an idea of the tropical flame that leaps
through the veins of our Tartar. True, in Ammalat the
Tartar is grafted on the Persian.

Now that the ice is broken, he loves to talk long and
often of his Sultanetta. And I like to see him blaze up
as he talks of her. Sometimes he resembles a cataract
falling from the height of a rock, and again he is like
one of those naphtha springs of Baku. Like them, he
burns with an inextinguishable flame, his cheeks glow,
his eyes emit sparks. He is magnificent at such times.
I myself am so affected that I open my arms and take
him to my bosom, quite broken down by his excitement.
Very soon he becomes ashamed of himself. He dares
not look at me, releases my hand and goes away; and
he spends entire days, after one of these exhibitions,
silent and taciturn.

Since his return from Khunsack, he is gloomier than ever, and especially during these last few days.

He has begged me to let him go again to Khunsack to see his love just once more. But I have refused his request. I must guard his honor. With that violent passion, he might fail to keep his word some day, and I should lose the ideal that I have formed of this handsome, noble-hearted young man.

I have written all this to Yermolof. He has told me to take him with me to Georgievsk, where he himself will be. There, through Ammalat, he will form a treaty with Ackmeth Khan, which will be of the greatest utility to Russia, and which may achieve Ammalat's happiness by leading to his union with Sultanetta. I shall be very happy, dear Marie, on the day when I shall make this young man happy! And he, who can never feel by halves, what gratitude he will declare! Then, dear Marie, I will make him get on his knees before you, and I will say: "Adore her; if I had not loved Marie, you would not be the husband of Sultanetta."

Yesterday I received a letter from the lieutenant-governor. How kind he is! He has anticipated all my wishes. Everything is arranged, my love, and I am to join you at the springs. I have only to take my regiment to Derbend, and set off. I shall know neither fatigue by day, nor sleep by night before the hour when I shall rest in your arms. What eagle will lend me his wings for my journey? What giant will lend me his strength to support my happiness? In truth, my heart is so light that to prevent its flying away, I seize my breast with both hands. Could I but sleep until the moment of seeing you again, and until then live only in dreams in which you are present! And yet, my dear love, I awoke this morning as sad as death. I know not

what presentiment of evil assails my heart. I left my
tent and entered Ammalat's. He was still asleep; his
face was pale and haggard. In his heart some hate is
struggling with his love. He bears me ill-will for my
refusal; but what revenge I shall enjoy on the day when
I shall have secured his happiness, when I can say:
" Life, what is it? It is Sultanetta, now!"

To-day I shall say good-bye to my mountains of Daghestan for a long time. Who knows? perhaps forever.
It is curious, my dear love, when I catch myself gazing
at the mountains, sea and sky, by what sweet sadness
my heart is both oppressed and expanded.

O my dear soul! how happy I am that I can now say
with assurance: Till we meet again!

XV.

THE poison of the lie seared Ammalat's heart and spread through his veins.

His nurse Fatma had conscientiously earned her ten sheep, her silk gown, and her two pieces of gold.

She had on that very evening plied him at length with all the khan's conspiracy, Ammalat having come to Bouinaky with the colonel, and the colonel having had an interview with the chamkal.

He had tried at first to doubt; but how could he suspect Fatma, his good nurse, who loved him like a son, to be the accomplice of Ackmeth Khan!

The poisoned arrow had lodged deep in his heart. In his first transport of rage, he wished to kill both the colonel and the chamkal.

His veneration for the dues of hospitality withheld him.

He postponed his revenge till a later time, but as one puts his dagger into its sheath, only to draw it forth keen and deadly.

Thus the day went by; the regiment halted for two hours' rest.

During these two hours, this is what Ammalat wrote to Ackmeth Khan, hoping to relieve his heart by unburdening it on paper: —

"Midnight.

"Ackmeth Khan! Ackmeth Khan! why have you flashed this light into my eyes? Do you know that its flame has entered my breast? Oh! friendship forgotten! a brother betrayed! a brother murdered! what terrible extremes, and between them but a step, — or an abyss!

"I cannot sleep, I can think of nothing else. I am chained to this thought, like a prisoner to the wall of his dungeon. A sea of blood flows in upon me, and lightnings flash above the dark waves, instead of stars.

"My soul is like a rock to which the wild birds come by day to tear their prey, and the spirits of hell by night to plot murder. O Verkovsky! what have I done to you? Why efface from a mountaineer's heaven his most beautiful star, — liberty? Why? Because I have loved you too much, perhaps. I have sacrificed my love for you. You might have said simply, 'Ammalat, I need your life,' and I should have given it as simply as you had asked it. Like the son of Abraham, I should have lain down under the knife and died forgiving you.

"But to sell my liberty! To take me from Sultanetta! Oh, no, traitor!

"And he lives still!

"From time to time, like a dove flitting through the smoke of a fire, I see your beautiful face, my Sultanetta. Why, then, as once, does the sight not delight me? They would separate us, my darling, they would give you to another, and give me to the tomb. But it shall not be; I will come to you by a trail of blood. I will perform the frightful task imposed on me as the price of your possession and I shall possess you. Besides your friends, invite to our wedding the vultures and crows. Oh! I will set out a feast for all the guests. I will bestow a priceless kalim;[1] instead of a velvet cushion, I will place under the head of my bride the heart that I respected, that I loved almost as much as her own.

[1] Wedding-present.

"O innocent girl, you will be the cause of a horrible crime! Sweet creature, for you two friends will clutch each other's throats in an embrace of devilish rage. For you! for you! but is it indeed for you alone?

"I have twenty times heard Verkovsky say that it was cowardly to get rid of an enemy by a shot or a dagger-thrust.

"How strange these Europeans are! According to them, when an enemy has crushed your head with his heel, or your heart with his hands, you are to say: 'You have dishonored me; you have stripped my tree of life of its leaves; you have blighted the roses of my heart; let us fight! If I am the stronger, I shall kill you; if you are the stronger, you will kill me.'

"And they present their breasts to the traitor's ball or sword.

"Oh! it is not so with us, Verkovsky; but it was not enough that you should bind my hands, you would like to bind my conscience, too.

"Useless, wasted words!

"I have loaded my gun; my gun came from my father; my father had it from my grandfather. I have been told of many famous shots that it has sent home. True, never yet has it been fired in the dark, or in ambush. It has always breathed fire and spat death in battle, before the eyes of all, in the front rank; and it fought against noble warriors, worthy foes; it never had to avenge treachery or wrong. But now! Oh! tremble not, my hand! A charge of powder, a leaden ball, a flash, a report, an echo, and all is over.

"A charge of powder! what a little thing! Yet here it is in the hollow of my hand and barely does it cover it, yet it is enough to banish the soul from a man's body. Cursed be he that invented the gray powder that gives the hero's life to the coward's hand; that kills from afar the enemy off guard, that murders with a single look!

"So a single shot is to undo all my old ties and open my way to new ones. In the freshness of the mountains, on Sultanetta's bosom, my worn heart will regain its vigor. Like the swallow, I will make my nest in a foreign land and cast aside all past griefs, as one throws away an old garment tattered by brambles and thorns.

"But my conscience!

"Once it happened that I recognized in the enemies' ranks a man whom I had sworn to kill. I could have sent him a bullet without his knowing from where it came. I was ashamed. I turned my horse away and did not shoot. Yet I would pierce the heart on which I have rested as if it had been a brother's! He deceived me; but was it such a misfortune to believe in his friendship, however false?

"O that my tears could quench my rage, my thirst for vengeance,—that they could buy, could gain Sultanetta!

"But why does the dawn delay so long? Let it come! I will look upon the sun without blushing, and I will meet Verkovsky's eye without paling. My heart is pitiless. Treachery calls for treachery. I am resolved. Here is the day — it is the last.

"No. It was but a lightning flash."

And, to fortify himself with the courage which he felt he lacked, Ammalat Beg seized a bottle of wine that Sophyr Ali had brought him, and emptied it at one draught.

Then he fell back on his pillow; but it was of no avail; he could not sleep. A viper was devouring his heart.

Then he went to Sophyr Ali, who was asleep, and shook him roughly.

"Get up!" he cried; "it is light."

Sophyr Ali opened his eyes and regarded Ammalat with a yawn.

"Light! — on your cheeks; but it is the glow of wine that they reflect, and not of dawn."

"Get up, I tell you! The dead themselves must rise out of their graves to come to meet the one that I shall send them."

"What are you saying? Am I a dead man? You are going mad, by Allah! Ammalat Beg. Let the dead rise if it amuses them, let the forty imams come back with the dawn if it suits them; as for me, I am a live man that has not had enough sleep. Good-night!"

"You like to drink, Sophyr Ali. I am thirsty this morning; drink with me."

"Ah! that is another thing, and now your reason is returning. Pour out a glass full, pour a full horn. Allah! I am always ready to drink and to love."

"And to revenge yourself on an enemy, is it not so? Here's to the health of the devil, who turns friends into deadly enemies! Where I go, you follow, do you not, Sophyr Ali?"

"Ammalat, it is not only wine from the same bottle that we have drunk, but milk from the same mother. I will follow, should you build your nest on the top-most ledge of a Khunsack crag. However, a little advice — "

"No advice, Sophyr Ali; no reproaches, what is more. This is no time for either."

"You are right. Advice and reproaches would drown in wine like flies. It is no time for reproaches or advice, it is the time for sleep."

"For sleep, you say? There is no more sleep for me.

Have you examined the flint of my gun? Is it good?
Did you renew the priming? it is not damp?"

"What is the matter, Ammalat? There is some
mystery, some crime perhaps in your heart. Your eye
is feverish, your face is livid; your words smell of
blood."

"My deeds shall be more dreadful still, Sophyr Ali.
Sultanetta is beautiful, — my Sultanetta! Is this a
marriage song ringing in my ears? No, it is the roaring
of demons, the wailing of jackals. Howl, wolves! weep
demons! You are tired of waiting. Be quiet, you shall
not wait long. More wine, Sophyr Ali! more wine!—
and then, blood!"

Ammalat drained at a draught a second bottle, and fell
dead drunk on his bed, muttering a few unintelligible
words. Sophyr Ali undressed him, put him to bed, and
watched at his pillow the remainder of the night, casting
about in vain for an explanation of his words.

Finally, at break of day, he himself went to bed saying,—

"He was drunk."

XVI.

IN the morning, before taking up his march, the captain who was on duty reported at the colonel's quarters.

After announcing that everything was in proper order in the regiment, he looked about, and approaching Verkovsky uneasily, he inquired:—

"Colonel, can I speak with you?"

"Certainly," answered Verkovsky, absently.

"But it is on a serious matter, colonel."

"A serious matter?"

"Yes."

"Speak, captain."

"We are quite alone?"

In turn, Verkovsky looked about.

"We are quite alone," said he.

"Colonel, what I have to tell you is of great importance, of very great importance."

"I am listening."

"Yesterday, at Bouinaky, a soldier of our regiment overheard a conversation between Ammalat and his nurse. He is a Tartar of Kasan who understands Caucasian Tartar perfectly. Well, he heard Ammalat's nurse, old Fatma, telling your prisoner that you and the chamkal wished to send him to Siberia. Ammalat was furious. He declared that he had already been forewarned by Ackmeth Khan of such an intention, but that he would kill you with his own hand first. .

"Believing that he had misunderstood or that, if he had heard aright, you were in danger of death, the Tartar began yesterday to spy upon every movement of Ammalat's.

"In the evening Ammalat spoke with an unknown man, and, after greeting him, said,—

"'Tell the khan that to-morrow morning by sunrise all shall be over; let him be prepared; I shall see him soon.'"

"Is that all, captain?" asked Verkovsky.

"Don't you think that sufficient to disturb the men who love you, colonel? Listen to me: I have spent my life among the Tartars; he is a madman who puts faith in the best of them. The brother is not sure of his own head even at the moment when he rests it on his brother's shoulder."

"Jealousy is the cause of Ammalat's moodiness, captain. Cain left it as a heritage to mankind, and especially to those who dwell near Ararat. We have nothing to quarrel about, Ammalat and I. I have never done him aught but good, and I have no intention of doing him evil. Rest easy, then, captain. I have faith in your soldier's good intention, but not in his knowledge of the Tartar language. I am not so great a man that begs and khans seek to assassinate me, captain. I know Ammalat very well; he is violent, but he has a good heart."

"Don't deceive yourself, colonel; Ammalat is an Asiatic. Don't expect from him, therefore, either the virtues or the vices of a European. Here, it is not as with us; here, the word conceals the thought, the face masks the soul. A Tartar may seem an honest man on the surface; delve below it, and you will find vileness, fury, and ferocity."

"Experience may have given you the right to think thus, captain; but as for me, I have no reason to suspect Ammalat. What would he gain by killing me? I am his only hope. I was to have been dead by daylight; the sun is quite high above the horizon, and, as you see, I am still alive. I thank you nevertheless, captain; but do not suspect Ammalat. Now we must be on the march!"

The captain withdrew. The drums began to roll, and the regiment began its march.

The morning was clear and cool. The regiment looked like a long serpent with scales of steel, sometimes stretched at length at the bottom of a valley, sometimes crawling over the mountain.

Ammalat marched at the front, pale and sad. He hoped that the beating of the drum would drown the voice in his heart.

The colonel called him and said pleasantly, —

"I must scold you, Ammalat. You follow the teaching of Hafiz too strictly to the letter; wine is a good comrade, but a bad master. You have spent a bad night, Ammalat."

"Yes, a terrible night, colonel; Allah grant that I may never pass such another! I dreamed a great deal, — horrible dreams."

"Ammalat, Ammalat, we should not do what our religion forbids. Your conscience is no longer at peace."

"Happy is the man whose conscience has no enemy but wine!"

"What conscience do you mean, my friend? Every nation, every century has its own conscience: what yesterday was regarded as a crime, to-morrow will be glorified as a great deed."

"I presume, however," responded Ammalat, "that deceit, revenge, and murder were never regarded as virtues."

"I do not say that, although we live in a century in which success almost always carries its own absolution. The most conscientious men of this period do not hesitate to say and even to put in practice the proverb: 'The end justifies the means.'"

Ammalat cast a side glance at the colonel.

"Traitor!" he muttered to himself; "you talk indeed like a traitor."

Then, deeper down, within his inmost breast, within his heart, he added:—

"The hour is at hand!"

The colonel, unsuspicious, advanced beside the young man. At eight versts from Karakent they suddenly came in sight of the Caspian Sea.

Verkovsky became thoughtful.

"It is strange, Ammalat," said he, "I cannot look upon your sad sea, your wild country, full of diseases, and of men worse than the diseases, without a pang of the heart and a saddening of soul. I hate war with invisible enemies. I hate to serve with comrades who are seldom our friends. I serve my country with love, the emperor with loyalty; in order to perform my military duties, I deny myself all the joys of life; my mind is petrified from inaction, my heart interred in solitude. I have torn myself away from everything, even from my heart's beloved. What recompense have I received? A secondary rank. When will the hour arrive in which I may rush into the arms of my betrothed? How long will it be before, tired of service, I shall rest in my home on the banks of the Dnieper? At last I have my leave in my pocket. In five days I shall be at Georgievsk;

yet it is strange, but I approach her in vain; it always seems as if the Libyan desert, a sea of ice, an eternity as dark and infinite as that of the tomb, lay between us. Oh! my heart, my poor heart!"

Verkovsky became silent; he was weeping.

His horse, feeling his bridle abandoned, quickened his pace, and Ammalat and he outstripped the regiment.

He delivered himself into the hands of his murderer.

But, at sight of his tears, at the sound of his stifled sobs, pity stole into Ammalat's heart, as a ray of sunlight penetrates a gloomy cave.

He looked upon the grief of him who had so long been his friend, and he said to himself, —

" No, it is impossible for a man to dissemble to such an extent."

But, as if ashamed of his momentary weakness, Verkovsky raised his head, and trying to smile, he said, —

" Be ready, Ammalat, you are to go with me."

At these fatal words, every good impulse remaining in Ammalat's heart was crushed.

The thought of the agreement between the colonel and the chamkal presented itself to his mind, and the path of eternal exile unfolded before him.

" With you? " he said, his lips quivering with anger, " with you into Russia? If you are going there, why not? "

And he burst into a laugh so strange that it sounded like the grinding of teeth, and, whipping up his horse, he bounded ahead.

He must have time to get his gun ready.

Then he turned his horse, bore down upon the colonel and rode past him; then he began to circle about him . like an eagle with its prey.

At each round he became paler, more furious, more

22

threatening. It seemed to him that the breath of a
demon was hissing in his ear, and saying,—

"Kill! kill! kill!"

All this while, the colonel, suspecting nothing, looked
smilingly on at Ammalat's evolutions, thinking that,
after the fashion of the Asiatics, he wished him to admire
his adroitness in executing the whim.

He saw him bring his gun to his shoulder and thinking
that he was continuing the sport, the colonel lifted his
helmet from his head and shouted,—

"Into my fouraska! into my fouraska! I will throw
it up for you."

"No," said Ammalat Beg, "into your heart!"

And at ten paces from the colonel, he fired.

The colonel uttered not a sound, not a sigh, as he fell.

The ball had pierced his heart, as Ammalat had
intended.

Ammalat's horse, swept onward in his course, stopped
before the dead body, falling back on his haunches.

Ammalat leaped to the ground, and stood leaning on
his smoking gun, as if he would prove to himself that he
was insensible to that dead gaze, and cool in the presence
of the blood which streamed from the wound.

What was passing just then in the heart of the assassin? God alone knows.

Sophyr Ali came up and flung himself on his knees
beside the dead man.

He bent over the lips; the lips were still.

"He is dead!" cried Sophyr Ali, in dismay, as he
stared at Ammalat.

"Is he quite dead?" said the latter, as if he were
awakening from a heavy sleep. "In that case, so much
the better; for his death is my happiness."

"Your happiness!" cried Sophyr Ali; "yours, the

murderer of your benefactor! The day when you will
find happiness is the day on which the whole world shall
renounce God and worship the devil."

"Sophyr Ali," said Ammalat, roughly, "remember
that you are my servant, and not my judge."

And, springing upon his horse, he said,—

"Follow me!"

"May remorse alone follow you like a spectre, not I.
Do what you will, turn out as you may, from this day
we are nothing more to each other, and I renounce you
for my brother. Farewell, Cain!"

At this response from Sophyr Ali, Ammalat uttered a
groan, and, signing to his noukars to follow him, he
darted as swiftly as an arrow into the mountains. Ten
minutes later, the head of the Russian column halted
before its dead colonel.

XVII.

AMMALAT wandered three days in the mountains of Daghestan.

Although he was among the conquered villages, he felt secure, the mountaineers in spite of their submission keeping their sympathies for the enemies of the Russians.

But, beyond the reach of danger, he was not beyond the reach of remorse, and Sophyr Ali's curse clung to him with an iron grasp. Neither his heart nor his brain essayed to excuse his crime, now that it was committed. He had always before him that final moment of the murder when, in the midst of the smoke enveloping both assassin and victim, the colonel had fallen from his horse. It was an Asiatic who committed the first crime, who became the first traitor, and the tradition of everlasting remorse was born at the foot of Ararat.

Yet his task was not ended with the murder; it remained for him to perform a ghastlier deed than that.

"Do not show yourself in Khunsack without the head of Verkovsky," Ackmeth Khan had said; and, as if no degree of crime was to be spared him after his first, he must now secure the head.

Among the Orientals, an enemy is not regarded as really dead until he is decapitated. Vengeance is not complete unless his adversary's head is in the hands of the avenger.

Not daring to discover his intention to his noukars, upon whose courage on such an occasion he knew that he could not rely, he resolved to return alone to Derbend across the mountain.

And, indeed, none of his men would have hesitated to commit on the battlefield an act which every mountaineer regards as a matter of course in war; but none of them would have dared to enter a cemetery at night and violate a tomb.

However, this is what remained for Ammalat to do.

The night was dark when the young man emerged from the hollow cave a half-verst distant from the fortress of Marienkale, which serves as a citadel for Derbend. He tied his horse to a tree at the top of the hill from which Yermolof, yet a lieutenant, had stormed Derbend. A hundred paces from this hill lay the Russian cemetery.

But, in the total darkness, how was he to find the new grave of Verkovsky?

The sky was overcast and the clouds hovering over the earth seemed to rest on the mountains; the wind sweeping from the valleys seemed, like a night-bird, to beat the branches of the trees with its wings.

Ammalat shuddered as he entered this realm of the dead, whose funereal repose he had come to disturb.

He listened.

The sea roared as it broke upon its shore; around him re-echoed the howling of the wolves and jackals whose comrade he had become. Then, suddenly, every sound ceased, save that eternal, mournful soughing of the wind, which seemed like the wailing of the spirits of the dead.

How many times on just such a night had he waked with Verkovsky! What had become of that intelligent soul, who at such times had explained to him all nature's mysteries, in that unknown region whither he had hurled him?

At such times he used to listen to him, lying near him or

leaning on his arm. And now, after having snatched
life from the body, behold, a despoiler of tombs, he was
coming to snatch the head from the grave !

"Human terrors !" murmured Ammalat, wiping his
forehead that streamed with perspiration, "what are you
doing now in a heart where nothing human remains ?
Away ! away ! What ! I have taken a man's life and
now fear to take the head from the body, when that
head means a treasure for me ? Truly, I am mad ! Are
not the dead without feeling ? "

With a trembling hand Ammalat lighted some dry
sticks, and by their feeble and flickering light, he began
to search for the colonel's grave. Some newly turned
earth and a cross on which was to be read the name of
Verkovsky, indicated the last resting-place of him whom
he had so often called brother. He uprooted the cross
and began to open the grave.

The task was neither long nor difficult. In the
Orient, interments are made almost on a level with the
ground.

Ammalat's poniard very soon struck the lid of the
coffin.

By a last effort the lid was raised.

In the ruddy light of the burning branches he was
obliged to take a last look at the body.

The torture was terrible, supreme, unlike any torment
that human justice could have devised. While bending
over the body, Ammalat, more livid than the corpse
itself, seemed for an instant as if turned into stone.
What had he come there to do ? How and why was he
there ? Not a throb of his suspended heart, not a fibre
of his arrested brain could have made answer; the odor
of the dead enveloped him, a vapor of death dimmed
his sight.

"Yet it must be ended!" he murmured, trying to draw himself from his stupor by the sound of his own words.

But not vanity, nor revenge, nor love, nor any feeling whose frenzy had driven him to commit his first crime was sustaining him now in the accomplishment of his second. The second was more than a crime, it was sacrilege.

At last, he set his poniard against the neck which he must cut, cast his torch far behind him that he might conceal his infamous task from himself under the cover of darkness, and, after a few futile efforts, he felt with horror that he had achieved his end.

The head was severed from the body.

He took it, and, with an indefinable feeling of anguish and disgust, he threw it into a sack which he had brought for the purpose.

Until then, he had felt master of himself; but, in that moment, when he understood that the more cowardly of his two deeds was accomplished; when there hung from his arm that head which he thought to exchange for happiness; when he was forced to drag his feet from that soft and sliding earth, the earth of the tomb in which he was standing up to his knees; when, in shaking off the dust of the dead, his foot slipped on the pebbles and he fell back into the open grave, as if the corpse in its turn would not let him go, — ah! then all his presence of mind deserted him. It seemed to him that he was going mad.

The lighted sticks which he had flung behind him had set fire to the grass scorched by the burning sun of June. He had forgotten how the flame came to be there. For him it was that of hell. It seemed to him as if the spirits of darkness, laughing and crying, were leaping

about him.   He himself began to weep, began to laugh,
and then with a low moan in which were blended his
laughter and tears, he fled without looking behind him.

At last, on the hill he found his horse, mounted him,
spurred him on into the mountains unheeding of rocks
and precipices, taking every bush that caught him for the
staying hand of the corpse, and the cries of the jackals
and hyenas for the last death-rattle of his benefactor,
twice murdered by him.

He arrived at Khunsack on the evening of the second
day.

Trembling with impatience, he leaped down from his
horse, and untied from his saddle-bow the accursed sack.

He ascended the well-known flight of steps and passed
through the first rooms.

They were crowded with mountaineers in war costume.
Some walked about wearing breastplates of mail, others
were talking, lying side by side on their bourkas.

All spoke in low tones,— those, at least, who spoke,
for the greater number maintained a gloomy silence.

The frowning brows, the darkened faces indicated that
they were depressed by sad tidings at Khunsack.

Noukars ran hither and thither; all knew Ammalat
and yet none of them questioned him.   No one appeared
to notice him.

Near the door of Ackmeth Khan's room stood Soukay
Khan, his second son.   He was weeping bitterly.

"What does this mean?" demanded Ammalat, with
forebodings of ill.   "You, who are called the child
without tears, are now weeping?"

Soukay Khan, without answering a word, pointed to
the door of the room.

Ammalat entered.

There a terrible spectacle was presented.

In the centre of the room, on a mattress covered over with a rug, lay Ackmeth Khan, already disfigured by the touch of death. From time to time his breast heaved, but it was attended by painful effort.

He was just entering on that last agonizing struggle awaiting man at the entrance to the tomb.

His wife and daughter were on their knees before him, weeping. His eldest son, Montzale Khan, crouched motionless at his feet, his head buried in his hands.

At a little distance from the dying man several women and favorite noukars were weeping.

But, full of the terrible thought burning within him, Ammalat approached the khan, and, he alone standing in the midst of these stricken people, said,—

"Good day, khan! I bring you a present which might bring a dead man to life. Prepare the wedding; here is Sultanetta's wedding-gift."

And with these words he threw the colonel's head at the khan's feet.

Ammalat's voice had seemed to rouse the dying man. He raised himself to see the present which the young beg had brought him. Verkovsky's severed head was at his feet.

A shudder passed through his frame.

"May he eat out his own heart," said he, "who brings such a sight to the eyes of a dying man!"

Then, raising himself with a last effort, and lifting both hands to heaven, -the khan said,—

"Allah be my witness that I pardon all my enemies; but you, you, Ammalat, I curse you!"

And he fell back dead on his cushions.

The wife of Ackmeth Khan had stared with deep-seated terror at what had just passed. But, when she saw her husband dead, believing that the sight of Am-

malat and his fatal gift had hastened his death, with eyes
aflame she pointed to the dead man and cried,—

"Messenger of hell! look, that is your work. Without
you my husband would never have dreamed of setting
Avarie in revolt against the Russians; without you, he
would at this moment be well and at peace. But, for
you and through you, while going to rouse the begs, he
fell from the height of a rock; and you, wretch! you,
traitor! you, murderer! instead of coming to soften
his agony and ease his death, come like a wild beast
and throw amid the phantoms around the bed of a
dying man, that ghastly thing, that severed head! And
whose head? Your defender's, your friend's, your
benefactor's !"

"But it was the khan's will!" cried Ammalat, thunderstruck.

"Don't accuse the dead. Don't stain with useless
blood the body of one who cannot defend himself,"
returned the widow more and more exasperated,—"you,
who fear not to come and ask the daughter in marriage at
her father's death-bed, who expect to receive man's
reward while obtaining the curse of God. Sacrilege and
infamy! I vow by the tomb of my ancestors, by the
swords of my sons, by the honor of my daughter, that
you shall never be my son-in-law, nor my guest. Out of
my house, traitor!"

Ammalat uttered a cry.

"Go!" added the widow; "I have sons whom you
could strangle with an embrace; I have a daughter whom
you could poison with a look. Hide yourself in the caves
of our mountains; there teach the tigers to devour each
other. Go! and know one thing, my door shall never
be opened to an assassin."

Ammalat seemed stricken by a thunderbolt.

All that the low voice of conscience had already said was repeated aloud and with cruelty. He knew not where to look. On the floor was Verkovsky's head; on the bed was Ackmeth's body; before him, the widow — the curse!

Yet Sultanetta's eyes, drowned in tears, shone like two stars through a cloud.

He approached her saying, —

"Sultanetta, that I did it all for you, you know well, and I am losing you. If fate wills, it must be; but only tell me if you, too, hate me; if you, too, spurn me?"

Sultanetta lifted her welling eyes to the one she had so loved; but at the sight of Ammalat's face, pale and spotted with blood, she hid her eyes with one hand, and with the other pointing alternately to her father's body and the colonel's head, she said firmly, —

"Farewell, Ammalat. I pity you, but never will I be yours."

And, overcome by her struggle, she fell fainting beside the body of her father.

The native pride of Ammalat surged back to his heart with his blood.

"Ah! thus am I received here," said he, casting a look of contempt toward the two women; "thus are oaths fulfilled in the house of Ackmeth Khan! Ah! I am satisfied, and my eyes see clearly, at last! I was indeed mad to stake my happiness on the heart of a fickle girl, and I have been patient indeed in listening to the imprecations of an old woman. In dying, Ackmeth Khan took with him the honor and the hospitality of his house. Make way! I go."

Throwing a look of defiance at the khan's sons, the noukars and cavaliers who, attracted by the disturbance, were crowding into the room, he advanced toward them,

his hand on the hilt of his kandjiar, as if to invite them
to combat.

But all stood aside, avoiding rather than fearing him,
and not a word more was addressed to him, either in the
chamber of the dead or while passing through the other
rooms.

On the steps he found his noukars, and below, his
horse.

He sprang into the saddle without saying a word, left
the palace at a walk, went slowly through the streets of
Khunsack; then, from the height whence he had first
seen the khan's house, he gave it a last look.

His heart was full of bitterness, his eyes were charged
with blood; offended pride was grappling its hooks of
steel into the depths of his heart.

In lowering wrath, he cast a last look upon that house
where he had known and lost all the pleasures of the
world.

He tried to speak; he tried to pronounce the name of
Sultanetta; he tried to accuse; he tried to curse.

He could not utter a single word, a mountain of lead
seemed to have fallen upon him.

Finally, as a last expedient he tried to weep; it seemed
to him that this enormous weight oppressing him must
be of tears; it seemed to him that a tear, a single one,
would reconcile him with human kind and implore God's
pardon.

"One tear! one tear! only one tear!" he cried.

All was useless; his eyes remained dry, burning, arid.
Moreover, one must love and be loved in order to shed
tears, and Ammalat, like Satan, hated and was hated.

The days, the months, the years rolled by.

Where was Verkovsky's assassin? What had become
of him?

No one knew.

It was rumored indeed that he was among the Tchet-chens, where his kounack Nephtali had been unable to deny him hospitality. The curse of the dying Ackmeth Khan was said to have bereft him of everything: beauty, health, courage even.

But who could confirm it?

At last, little by little, Ammalat was forgotten; but the memory of his treachery is to-day still fresh and vivid among Russians and Tartars.

EPILOGUE.

In 1828, the fortress of Anapa was beleaguered by land
and sea, by the fleets and armies of Russia.

Every morning a new battery, sprung up in the night,
thundered nearer the town.

The Turkish garrison, backed by the mountaineers
forever at war with Russia, bravely held their ground.

On the south side of the town the Russians at last
succeeding in effecting a breach.

The wall was crumbling under their balls; but its
thickness made the work a slow and laborious task.

From time to time — especially during the intense
heat of the day — the reddened cannon and the wearied
gunners were accorded a respite of an hour or two.

During one of these resting spells, while the gunners
were sleeping, suddenly, from the top of the wall, a
horseman on a white horse was seen descending, sup-
ported by ropes passed under the animal's stomach.

Scarcely had he touched the ground, when the ropes
were withdrawn over the top of the wall, the horseman
cleared the fosse at a leap, and, setting his horse at a
gallop, passed like a streak of light between batteries and
soldiers.

A few shots pursued him, but without effect; he disappeared in the forest.

They had barely caught sight of him; no one dreamed
of following.

Very soon their minds were distracted by the renewed cannonading, and all forgot the horseman.

Before night the breach had become practicable; the Russians were preparing for the onset, when suddenly, from the side next the forest, they were attacked by mountaineers.

The terrible cry, "Allah il Allah!" was answered from the walls of Anapa.

But the Russians turned their guns on these unlooked-for assailants and soon scattered the mountaineers, who took to flight, leaving their dead and wounded on the battle-field, and howling, "Giaours! giaours!"

. But, from the beginning of this affair, and up to the moment when the battle-field was cleared, the Russians could see in front of them a Circassian mounted on a white horse held at a walk, and moving back and forth before the Russian batteries, unmindful alike of the balls and bullets that were raining around him.

The impassiveness, and, above all, the invulnerability of the mountaineer rendered the gunners furious. The balls, ripping the earth around him, dashed it under his horse's feet. The horse reared and plunged, but his rider kept the frightened creature to his course, soothing him with his hand, and apparently heedless of the danger enveloping him on every side.

"The horse for me and twenty-five roubles for you," said an officer of artillery to the artillery-man of his battery, "if you bring down that knave."

The artillery-man looked up.

"I have aimed at him three times already," said he, "and it must be that the devil himself is sitting that horse; but, captain," he continued, "you may load my gun with my own head for the next shot, if I miss him this time."

And, having pointed his cannon with especial care, he took the match from his comrade's hand and fired it himself.

For an instant, it was impossible to distinguish anything; but soon the smoke was dissipated and they saw the frightened horse dragging his master's body, whose foot was caught in the stirrup.

"Hit! dead!" cried the soldiers.

The young officer lifted his helmet, made the sign of the cross, and leaped over the battery to catch the horse, which was a fine animal, born, as well as they could judge, in Khorassan.

He was very soon caught. The animal kept moving in the same circle, dragging the mountaineer's body.

The ball had taken off an arm of the latter near the shoulder; but he was still breathing.

The young officer summoned four gunners and had the dying man carried to his own tent.

He himself went for the surgeon.

But, upon examining the frightful wound, the surgeon declared that the shoulder would have to be disjointed, and that the man would die under the operation.

It was better, then, to let him die quietly from his wound than to cause him to die sooner and more painfully.

The surgeon ordered a refreshing drink, the only relief that he could give the sufferer.

The officer sat alone in his tent beside his guest in the pangs of death, having no one near him but a Tartar interpreter, whom he could summon in case of returning consciousness, when the dying man, whom he easily recognized as a chief, might have some last request to make.

Towards one o'clock in the morning, the wounded man

seemed troubled, often sighing, as if some vision were taking part in his death-struggle.

The young officer rose, held the lantern close to the face of the injured man, who had not yet regained consciousness, and regarded him more attentively than he had yet done.

The expression of the man's countenance was sad; deep wrinkles furrowed his brow and disfigured a face that must have been beautiful before having been ploughed by the unruly passions of which it bore trace. It was easy to see, however, that its wan look proceeded rather from the sorrows of life than from the painful seizure of death.

His breathing became more and more labored.

With his remaining hand, he seemed to be striving to thrust back some vengeful apparition. At last, his speech found utterance, and, after a few unintelligible words, the officer and the interpreter succeeded in grasping these: —

"Blood! forever blood!" murmured the mutilated man looking at his remaining hand, the right hand. "Why have you covered me with his blood-stained garment? Am I not already wading in blood? Do not drag me in that direction, back to life. Life is hell! The grave is so quiet, and so cool! —" Again he fainted, and the words died on his lips.

The officer asked the interpreter for some water, dipped his hand in the glass, and with his fingers sprinkled the face of the dying one.

The latter quivered, opened his eyes, shook his head as if to avoid the enveloping shadow of death, and then, by the glimmering light of the lantern which the interpreter was holding, he perceived the captain.

From being vague, his gaze became fixed and wild.

23

He stared at the officer, tried to rise on the missing arm, fell back, and rose on the other.

His hair stood on end, the perspiration rolled from his brow, his pale face became livid, his countenance little by little assumed an expression of profoundest terror.

"Your name?" he said in a shaking voice, that no longer held anything of human semblance. "Who are you? Are you a messenger from the tomb? Tell me! speak! answer!"

"My name is Verkovsky," responded the young man, briefly.

These words, very simple in themselves, produced the effect of a kandjiar-thrust in the wounded man's heart. He shrieked, shuddered, and fell back on his pillow.

"This man was undoubtedly a great sinner," said the young officer, sadly, addressing himself to the interpreter.

"Or a great traitor," the latter added; "he must be, or he must have been,—for he is dead,—some Russian deserter. I have never heard a mountaineer speak our tongue with such purity. Let us look at his weapons; we shall there find, perhaps, some inscription. The armorers of Kouba, Andrev, and Koubatche often add to their own name the name of the one for whom the weapon is made."

And, drawing the kandjiar from the dead man's girdle, he began to examine the blade.

This inscription was engraved in gold on the burnished steel.

"*Be slow to offend, and quick to avenge.*"

The interpreter translated it for the young officer.

"Yes, that is a maxim of these brigands," said the latter. "My poor brother, the colonel, fell a victim of one of these wretches."

The young man brushed away a tear. Then, to the interpreter he continued: —

"Now examine the sheath."

The interpreter detached the sheath from the dead man's girdle, and found engraved thereon these words in the Tartar character: —

"I was made for Ammalat Beg."

Printed in the United States
123940LV00002B/224/A